Damselflies
An Ancient Mirrors Tale

Jayel Gibson

2777759

Damselflies: An Ancient Mirrors Tale
Published by Synergy Books
2100 Kramer Lane, Suite 300
Austin, Texas 78758

For more information about our books, please write to us, call 512.478.2028, or visit our website at www.bookpros.com.

ISBN-13: 978-1-933538-64-8
ISBN-10: 1-933538-64-3

Publisher's Cataloging-in-Publication available upon request.

Library of Congress Control Number: 2006930610

Cover art, maps and internal illustrations © 2005-2006
Michele-lee Phelan, Art of the Empath
Cranebrook, N. S.W., Australia
www.artoftheempath.com

This is a work of fiction. None of the characters or events portrayed in this book exist outside the author's imagination, and any resemblance to real people and incidents is purely coincidental.

Lake Calming

• Daplesfar

Castle
Halhmor

Castle
Wawne

WAWNE

HALHMOR

Ærathbearnæ

Grimmoire

Ælarggessæ

Tangled
Chasm

• Aendrith

Isle of Grave

Mungandr's Vortex

CHENEIS

Castle
Lamaas

Castle
Cheneis

LAMAAS

• Straeth

House of Hexus

Æselvanæ

EASTERN REALMS
OF THE DAMSELFLIES

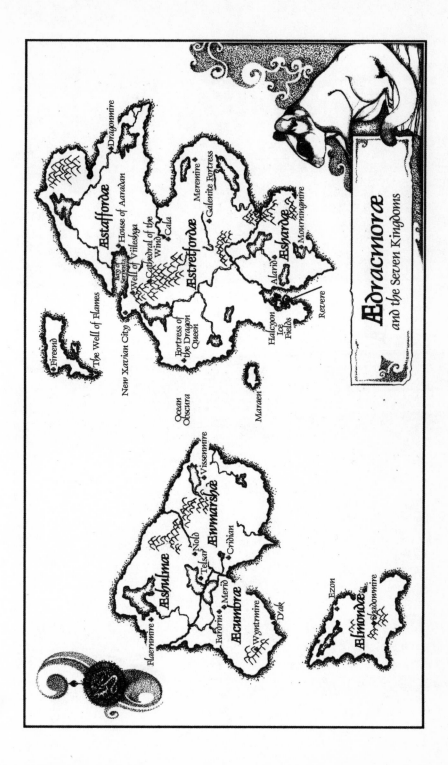

Ædracmore and the Seven Kingdoms

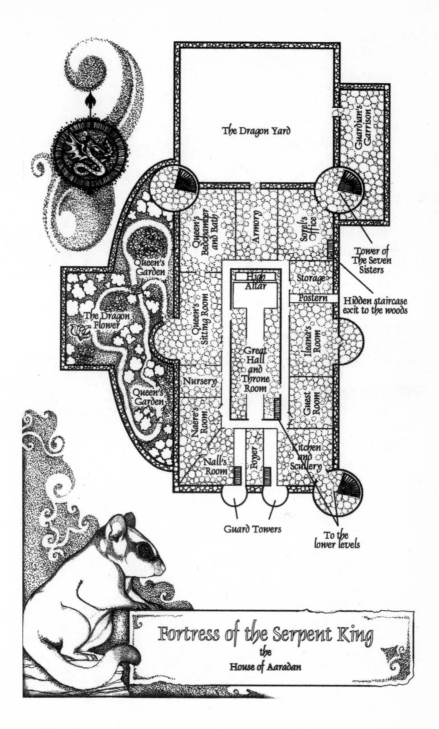

The Dragon Yard

Guardian's Garrison

Queen's Bedchamber and Bath

Armory

Sorpi's Office

Tower of The Seven Sisters

Queen's Garden

The Dragon Flower

Queen's Sitting Room

High Altar

Storage

Postern

Hidden staircase exit to the woods

Ileana's Room

Queen's Garden

Nursery

Great Hall and Throne Room

Guest Room

Naere's Room

Nall's Room

Foyer

Kitchen and Scullery

Guard Towers

To the lower levels

Fortress of the Serpent King

the

House of Aaradan

Dedication

In loving memory of Joni Anderson

And to:
Ken Gibson
Sarah Gibson
Peggy Brewer
GliderCentral
Jeff Shockey
Dan Bargess
Chris Overcash

For their friendship, support and encouragement

Acknowledgements

Any work of fantasy is a union of magic and madness that includes golden grains of potent sorcery from those who are sometimes totally unaware that their enchantment has rubbed off on the author. My gratitude to these and all my friends for their encouragement and touches of thaumaturgy:

Michele-lee Phelan, my artist and friend, for the inspiration of her artworks. They grace my books, website and walls and continue to fill my mind with magic.

The city of Port Orford, Oregon, my home, for her beauty, tranquility and people—truly a writer's paradise.

Gold Beach Books (the coffeehouse bookstore) in Gold Beach, Oregon, for the wonderful inspiration of the rare book room, a quiet table and lots of café brevés.

The South Coast Writers Conference for the encouragement they provide all writers and Southwestern Oregon Community College for their sponsorship of this annual event.

Josephine Ballantyne of Wordwing Editors, a true member of the Errant Comma Enclave. It is with tongue in cheek that I assure you any errors you may find belong to her.

Collaboration

Sean W. Anderson has collaborated with Ms. Gibson in the development of ideas and storyline, as well as created a number of characters used in the Ancient Mirrors novels. The characters Nall and Talin are based on role-play characters originally created by Mr. Anderson for online gaming.

Mr. Anderson lives with his family in southern California.

Illustration

Fantasy artist Michele-Lee Phelan is the official illustrator for the Ancient Mirrors series. Her artwork appears on the covers, as internal illustrations and website graphics for this series. Works are created using traditional and digital media. Ms. Phelan is featured as one of Epilogue's New Masters of Fantasy 2005.

The artist lives with her family in New South Wales, Australia.

Table of Contents

To enhance your travels through the realms of the Damselflies world maps are included in the front pages of this book and a full glossary can be found beginning on page 405.

PART I

LEGACY OF THE DAMSELFLY

Chapter 1: Hunters and Healers

The hunters dismounted their gryphons and cautiously approached the scorched remains. Intermittent flames flared as the last of the settlement's dry wood was consumed and cinders, caught in gusts from the light spring wind, scurried and hissed over the final drifts of snow.

"Harpies," Nilus dismissed, kicking at a smoldering body with disgust.

"Nay, I do not think so. They do not bear the talons of the harpies. See? The feet appear human," Ilerion said as he examined the charred remains, "and the harpies do not build bothies, only stick eyries."

Ilerion squatted next to another burned corpse, reached out and touched it, testing for heat. Finding it cool enough to handle, he reached under and turned it over to examine the vestiges of the amputated wings. The blackened flesh came away in his hands, and the delicate bones crumbled beneath his touch. Moving, he lifted another and discovered its wings had also been severed.

"Check the bodies beyond you," Ilerion called to Nilus. "It appears that the wings were severed from each body."

Nilus used the toe of his boot to lift the remains of several of the bodies, then shouted back, "Aye, I have not found a single one with wings attached."

As he wandered from corpse to corpse, Ilerion checked each one. None had escaped the blade of the butcher. It was impossible to tell if the wings had been amputated before or after death, but he hoped the butchery had only been on those already dead.

A high pitched keening shattered the silence of death and brought Ilerion to his feet with sword drawn, eyes searching for the source of the wailing. Atop a small knoll stood an apparition so covered in gore and ash that it was impossible to determine its identity. A second scream echoed through the smoke-filled glen as the body crumpled and fell backward to the earth.

Ilerion raced forward and dropped to his knees beside the fallen creature. It was a woman, naked and blood-smeared. Her features were distorted by swelling and dark bruises. Pulling the cloak from his shoulders, Ilerion covered her before placing his fingertips below her jaw, feeling for the pulse of life. It was slow and faint, but it was there.

"Out of mercy finish it off," Nilus said from behind him. "It will not live long, if indeed it lives at all."

"She lives," Ilerion said, gathering the woman into his arms and lifting her to his chest. "If we can reach the healer before the life fades away, there is hope that she may continue to live."

"Ilerion," Nilus's face darkened with concern, "it is not a woman, for there are great bloody wounds in its back where wings grew. It is…a beast. Ananta will chase us away if we bring her such a creature."

"Not a beast, Nilus," Ilerion said, his eyes warning against speaking further of beasts. "Without wings she is simply a badly beaten woman. The healer will help us." Squatting, Ilerion laid the unconscious woman across his knees to examine the gaping wounds high upon her shoulders. Pulling a shirt from his pack, he tore it into pieces and stuffed them into the holes to stanch the bleeding. He then lifted her and placed her gently over his shoulder as he whistled for his mount.

As he mounted Grundl, Ilerion heard the gryphon's question in his mind, *Whose life do we save today, Hunter?*

"I do not know her name," Ilerion answered.

Shaking his head at his master's foolish risk, Nilus leapt to his own mount and urged it skyward, banking toward the outskirts of Lamaas and the healer, Ananta.

❦

Ananta looked up at the gryphon's hoarse call. Wiping the sun-warmed soil from her hands, she shielded her eyes against the glare and searched for the caller. Two gryphons were landing beyond her fenced fields, their riders preparing to dismount.

"One comes," purred the blind cat at her feet. Ananta chuckled. "Nay, two come. Actually, four come: two gryphons and two men. Wait, there are five for one carries another. Keep trying, Cat!"

Washing her hands in the bucket of water next to her porch, Ananta watched the men approach from across the field. The first was tall and well muscled, the second short and stout. The first man did indeed carry another. One wounded in a tavern brawl most likely—a sword to the gut, perhaps.

"Healer, I need your help," Ilerion called as he drew closer. "A settlement in the mountains was razed, and this woman appears to be the only survivor. I can pay you."

"It is probably already dead," the second man called after them.

"Bring her," Ananta instructed, leading the way into her house.

She pointed to the empty table. "Place her there."

Ilerion gently laid the wounded woman down and once again placed his fingertips below her jaw seeking signs of life.

"Her life beat is very faint."

Tossing him a towel and some soap, Ananta said, "Go and wash away the blood. Bring fresh water in the pail when you return."

Without waiting to see if he complied, Ananta lifted the cloak from the woman and gasped when she saw her condition.

"Who did this to you?" Ananta whispered, taking a rag and beginning to clean away the blood and soot from the woman's face and body, exposing a seemingly endless series of scratches and bruises.

"Whoever it was believed you dead. It will not be wise to let them know that you are not." The healer spoke in conversational tones to the wounded woman as she examined the injuries sustained by rape.

Ananta pulled the woman toward her and inspected the wounds to her patient's back. The bleeding had clotted and slowed to ooze, but the wounds were deep and required stitching. Taking a curved needle and heavy thread from her healing kit, Ananta began the job of repairing the dagger's damage.

She heard the sound of the door opening behind her. "Do you even know what you have saved?"

"Naught but a woman." Ilerion's voice was sharp.

"And the other? Does he believe she is naught but a woman?"

Ananta glanced briefly over her shoulder.

"He will believe what I tell him to believe," Ilerion said, drawing a second glance from the healer.

"If he does not, I may as well cut her throat as stitch her up. Those who did this must never know she lives. There are only twenty left, you know, in that glen in Grimmoirë. They are a dying race, unable to keep the blood pure. They harmed no one."

"Now there is only one," Ilerion said, stepping forward to examine the stitch work. "I have never known hunters to enter Grimmoirë. It has always been considered the sacred realm of the enchanted."

"The wounds on her back will not heal cleanly or be beautiful, but the healing will allow her life if she chooses it. The scars she will carry in her mind will be far worse."

Ananta looked pointedly at Ilerion. "She was raped with unconscionable brutality and should not see a man when she first wakes."

"You will keep her here?" Ilerion asked, withdrawing his coin pouch.

"I will allow her to stay until she is strong enough to travel. It must never be known that she was here."

Ananta held up her hand as if to ward him off and declined the coins he offered, saying softly, "It is my gift to her, though she may not see it as such when she awakens. You may camp in the garden shed until the time that you can take her."

"I cannot stay and I cannot care for her. I am a hunter in the service of Lazaro. There is no room or time in my life to be saddled with a woman."

"Ah, even now the world darkens around her since it is quite probable that Lazaro is responsible for this. Because he is mad with the fear of ancient legends that speak of enchanted halflings, he systematically hunts, as you must know, all those who are not human. And now, since no one enforces the White Laws of Equality, it seems he grows bold enough to enter Grimmoirë to hunt them. While Lazaro calls them beasts, they are human enough to draw the attention of his men," Ananta snapped.

At the disbelief on Ilerion's face, Ananta laughed. "Just what is it that *you* hunt for him?"

"Men who carry the bounty on their heads for crimes against the crown," Ilerion answered.

"If you truly do not believe him capable of this treachery, then we are all doomed. Perhaps you should just cut the woman's throat. If you do not intend to care for her, she has no chance of survival at all. You are a hunter, and therefore you should know how to help her avoid them."

"I have heard rumors of such vile acts, but never before have I seen evidence of them."

Ananta pointed to the door. "You may sleep in the shed. I will give her as strong a healing elixir as possible so that you can be on your way more quickly. Come to first meal at daybreak, and I will introduce you as her savior. Warn your partner to watch his words and not to refer to her as 'it'."

Ilerion drew the door closed behind him and sat down on the steps, staring pensively into the distance.

"Whose life have we saved today?" The gryphon's question was beginning to plague Ilerion.

"A woman of great value," the hunter mumbled under his breath. "One it appears I am responsible for by the act of deliverance."

"Is it alive?" Nilus asked.

"It is a woman and, yes, she lives."

"What are you going to do with it? You cannot possibly keep it."

"Nilus, she is a woman, nothing more. Do you understand me?"

"Aye, you are going to pretend it is a woman and hope no one becomes the wiser. You do intend to keep it?" Nilus looked horrified.

Ilerion laughed. "Do not make me choose whether to keep the woman or you, Nilus. I fear the woman would win. She is far more beautiful."

"How could you tell she was beautiful? She wears too many scratches and bruises to say how she may look."

"Nilus, any woman is more beautiful than you," Ilerion assured his short, round friend. "And from this moment forward she is only a woman."

"Do you suppose it…she…can speak the language of Man?" Nilus asked.

"I do not know," Ilerion answered, noting this addition to the growing list of questions. He stood to stretch his tense and weary muscles. "Come, Nilus, and let us rest. The healer has offered us refuge within her shed."

They gathered their rucksacks from the backs of the gryphons, removed the tack and released their mounts to return to the eyrie.

"I will call for you, Grundl, when we are ready to travel," Ilerion said as he ruffled the gryphon's feathers.

"She is not a woman, Hunter," the gryphon replied as it rose from the ground. "She is a Damselfly."

Looking after the gryphon, Ilerion whispered, "Aye, I know. But no longer can she be if she is to survive, for now she must learn to be a woman."

Relentless screams of terror and despair woke the hunters from their sleep. Ilerion threw off his blankets and raced for the house, his long sword in a death grip, convinced the women inside were being murdered.

Ilerion crashed headlong into the door, but merely bruised his shoulder. The door remained bolted but the jolt from his furious dive drove him backward down the steps.

"Go away," called Ananta from behind the door. "We are fine. It is only a nightmare, and you may as well get used to the sound of them."

"Is she awake?" Ilerion asked.

"Nay, the worst is still to come, Hunter. She does not yet know just how much she has lost."

Ananta opened the door a crack and peered out at Ilerion.

"When you come to first meal, try to remember to wear trousers." Ananta shook her head.

Ilerion looked down to find he was wearing nothing but his woolens.

"I thought…"

"We were in danger? It is good to know a brave man rests in the shed."

At first light Ilerion and Nilus washed and dressed and then, in an uneasy silence, headed for the house each wondering what they would find at breakfast.

Ilerion tapped lightly and was surprised to find the door opened at his touch. The table was laid with three place settings, bread and jam, and a pot of steaming tea. Ananta was nowhere to be seen, nor was her patient.

The healer's voice called from behind the closed door of the bedroom, "Sit and have tea. I shall join you shortly."

The hunters sat and drank the warming tea and looked about at the orderliness of Ananta's kitchen. Heavy iron pots were hung above a large chopping block. Shelves were neatly stacked with dishes, and utensils hung from holders fastened to the walls. There were curtains on the window, and the dirt floor had been swept clean and covered with a layer of fresh-smelling hay.

"She is awake," Ananta said without preamble, as she entered the room and took her seat at the table.

"She has not spoken and simply stares at the ceiling, weeping, but her wounds show no indication of infection and her life signs are strong. She has taken broth and some tea; neither stayed in her stomach more than a few minutes."

Ananta held out her cup and waited patiently for Ilerion to realize he should pour her tea. Adding honey, she sipped it with a sigh of gratitude.

"The night was long. She screams in terror in her sleep and weeps when she wakes. She did not fight me when she woke, and that concerns me, but she lives. With each day that passes she will grow stronger. She needs to see you and to learn not to fear you before you take her with you."

"I cannot take her with me," Ilerion reminded Ananta.

"You must. She cannot remain here. It is only a matter of time before some ruffian is wounded at the tavern and comes here for healing. You would not leave her to his drunken mercy would you? After the trouble you went through to bring her here?" Ananta glared at him.

"We are hunters," Nilus said, as if that explained everything.

"Aye, so I have been told. I cannot think of any better to protect her."

A low moan brought Ananta to her feet. Beckoning Ilerion to follow, she entered the room and sat on the edge of the bed. She took the young woman's hand in hers.

"He saved you, girl, brought you here more corpse than alive. A good man, a brave man, not like the others," her voice soothed. "He will keep you safe and teach you how to fight."

Ilerion stared at the woman in the bed. She did not appear to be far past childhood, thin and fair of skin. The bruises stood out boldly against her bloodless skin but the swelling had lessened with Ananta's treatment.

The woman's eyes were those of a frightened bird, darting from Ananta to the hunter and back again, her pupils black and widely dilated against their golden brown irises. Her hair had been rinsed clean of blood, and then brushed. Like armor against his gaze, it fell over her small breasts. She reached up with her left hand to touch the back of her shoulder, her eyes never leaving Ilerion's face.

"She wants her wings," Ananta said. "She has asked for them over and over."

"I thought you said she did not speak." Ilerion shot her a look of confusion.

"What do you think she wants, then? A weapon? Were any of them armed? Of course, they were not," she continued. "She wants her wings."

"There is no hope of that. They are gone. Burned to ash," he said, looking at the woman on the bed.

Her eyes fell from his face and he watched as tears slid from beneath her lashes.

"She understands our words?" Ilerion asked Ananta.

"Aye, she seems to. And she will probably speak when she is good and ready."

The woman's eyes opened and she stared at Ilerion.

"Why?" Her small voice trembled.

"I do not know," he answered, deliberately keeping his voice low and calm, speaking in the Grimmoirën language of her question. "They were gone before I arrived. Do you know who they were?"

She shook her head slowly, "They came in the night and… killed us."

He stepped closer. She drew back against the wall, pulling the covers over her body.

In an attempt to look less threatening, Ilerion sat down on the chair at the side of the bed.

"I will not harm you," he said, returning to the words of human speech.

"That is what they said, 'Come, we will not harm you,' but it was not true. They set fire to the bothies where we slept. Those of us who had escaped the fire met their swords…and worse. Why did you not let me die?" she asked, as tears welled in her eyes.

"Because you lived," he frowned, "and you must continue to live in order to bring these men to justice."

Shaking her head, she choked on a sob, "Look at me. I am nothing."

"You are a woman and I will help you," Ilerion said. "You will heal and we will find the men who did this and see that they pay for their crime."

"Even when they turn out to be your Lord Lazaro?" asked Ananta.

"Aye, even then. Rest and heal. I will wait for you," Ilerion promised the woman.

As he stood to leave he asked, "What should we call you?"

"Arcinaë of Grimmoirë."

"I am called Ilerion." He bowed, avoiding her eyes, for the sound of her name brought with it thoughts of his past and threatened a speedy descent into despair.

As Ilerion returned to the table, Nilus looked at him in disbelief. "You have pledged us to her?"

"Aye, it seems I have at least pledged myself. She has no one. How could she protect herself against them?"

"Them? We do not know who 'them' is," Nilus answered.

"It does not matter. It is right," Ilerion said with a stony glare.

"You should eat, Hunter. The task you have accepted will require strength as well as wisdom." Ananta held out the bread and jam. "Perhaps you could slay a boar or stag while you remain as my guests."

"Aye, perhaps we can," Ilerion agreed. "How long will we be your guests?"

"She is weak and the muscles of her shoulders could take long to heal without magick. There is a wizard called Fenris hiding in Lamaas. I will go for provisions on the morrow and bring him on my return. I think he can help her."

Ilerion placed his hand on Ananta's arm. "Can the wizard be trusted?"

"Aye, he will not betray us. As a Feie, he is also at risk from Lazaro's hunters."

Beneath the table, the blind cat purred, "One comes."

Ananta jumped up and began grabbing things off of the table, gathering them into a bag.

"Hurry, help me. They must not know you are here."

Together they cleared the table and Ilerion carried the bag filled with evidence of their visit into the bedroom where Arcinaë slept. Nilus slipped in behind him and closed the door.

Looking down on the woman for the first time, Nilus said, "You are right, even beaten she is far more beautiful than I."

"The shed! Did you close the door?" Ilerion whispered.

"Aye, and hid our belongings beneath the hay."

At the pounding on the door and Ananta's call to those beyond, Arcinaë's eyes flew open and she drew in a breath to scream.

"Shhhhh, there is danger," Ilerion hushed, holding out his hand toward her.

She stifled her scream and gripped his wrist with both hands. "Give me a weapon."

He pulled his dagger from his belt and he held it out to her. She accepted it, turning it back and forth, as if it were foreign to her hand, before slipping it beneath the covers.

"I will not be taken again," she said.

Ananta stepped outside with a smile pasted on her face, assessing the threat as she made small talk with the hunter who stood on her porch. Three more hunters, mounted on horseback, were stationed in the yard.

"Do you require healing?" Ananta asked, peering at those in the yard.

"Nay, we seek sign of a wounded woman."

"I have treated no women, only the fools who duel in the taverns of Lamaas. Who shall I tell if I do see this woman?"

"Send word to the castle of Lord Lazaro," the hunter said.

"You can be sure that I shall. What does the woman look like?"

"Tall, heavy, dressed as a man. She is sought for the murder of Lord Brytwaer," Lazaro's hunter explained.

"Until she is in irons, I shall be very careful to whom I open the door," Ananta said with a shiver of revulsion that passed for fear.

"It is best that you use caution," the hunter said, retreating to his waiting mount.

Ananta watched until the dust of their leave-taking had settled. Returning inside, she leaned against the door, waiting for the trembling in her knees to pass.

A moment later she tapped at the bedroom door and looked at the three hidden there.

"It seems there is another hunted by Lazaro's men," Ananta sighed. "How is it that such a vile man is allowed such power over the innocent? Why does no one rise against him?"

"Most find life too precious to risk against such overwhelming odds," Ilerion replied.

Moving quickly to the bed, Ananta withdrew the dagger from Arcinaë's hand.

"Do not give her a weapon." The healer shot Ilerion an angry look as she handed the dagger back to him and returned to the kitchen.

Ilerion followed her. "Why should she not be armed against a threat?"

Shaking her head at his ignorance, Ananta answered quietly so that Arcinaë would not overhear. "She will not use it to defend herself against them. She will merely take her own life rather than suffer at the hands of others. At this time her fear is a form of madness. She cannot conceive of being strong enough to fight against men. You will have to teach her that she can.

"It will be like watching her walk the edge of a blade. You must be careful that she does not fall into madness on one side or take her own life on the other. She will never be free until all of them are dead." Ananta shrugged. "You are a hunter. Hunt them. All of them."

"It is not so simple. I do not know who I am looking for. She says she does not know them," Ilerion said.

"She knows every face as if it were drawn on the inside of her eyelids. She told me they made her father watch them rape her as punishment for his attempt to hide her. Now you are all she has, Hunter."

"How many do we hunt?" Ilerion's eyes met Ananta's.

"Seven. And the one who sent them."

"Lazaro. You seem certain of this." Nilus' voice startled them.

"Aye, I am certain," Ananta said with conviction. "Begin with the seven. They will lead you to Lazaro."

⁂

Screams of desperation brought Ananta to the shed where the hunters sat, unable to sleep.

"She asks for you, but I must give you warning. She sees you as her savior, a god, invincible against her foes. Right now she believes that if you are present she is safe. Do not betray her trust, Hunter. Promise me you will not. I have not saved her life to see her killed by treachery or a man's pride."

"I swear it," Ilerion said, glancing at Nilus.

"Aye, I swear it too, even though I am only a short, round, bald man. Still I swear to protect her as best I can," Nilus muttered.

Laughing, Ilerion said, "Do not be deceived by the little man's self-pity, for he is a formidable short, round, bald man."

As Ilerion entered Arcinaë's room, the first thing he noticed was the evidence of her extreme exhaustion. Dark circles below red-rimmed eyes now defined the extreme pallor of her skin, adding yet another hue to that of her bruises.

"Have you eaten or slept?" he asked.

"Nay, I cannot," she answered.

"You must do both if you are to grow strong enough to lift a sword against your enemies. If I bring you tea, will you try it?"

"I cannot seem to keep it down," she said, color rushing to her cheeks.

"If it comes up, I will take full responsibility for it. But you must try to eat."

He returned with a tray holding willow bark tea, broth and bread. Holding the cup with her, Ilerion watched as Arcinaë drank the tea.

"The tea will help settle your stomach before we force the broth on it, and a bit of bread will help to soak up the liquids and make you feel better. You cannot sleep if you are hungry," he said, holding out a morsel of bread.

He watched her break off a tiny piece and put it in her mouth. Slowly

14

she chewed, her skin turning a sickly shade of green as she did so.

"Breathe," Ilerion said, "through your nose. It will keep you from feeling sick."

She took a deep breath through her nose and her color warmed slightly.

Taking another piece of bread, she asked, "How is it you know so much about stomach ailments? Are you a healer as well as a hunter?"

"Nay, but I have had sufficient ale in my lifetime to know about the stomach ailments that follow it."

She placed the bread back on the tray and picked up the steaming broth, sipping it daintily.

"I was to be married in the spring," she said, suddenly talkative. "Now I suppose I shall never be married. Are you married?"

"Nay, I do not have the time for marriage. Wives have a right to expect husbands to remain home and keep food on the table. I do not even have a home."

"Are you never lonely?" Arcinaë asked, finishing the broth and putting the cup on the tray.

"Perhaps. I do not think about it," Ilerion said.

"I will always be lonely, always…" Her voice trailed off as she was overtaken by an involuntary yawn.

Ilerion lifted the tray from the bed and headed for the door, but her voice stopped him.

"You bear the mark of nobility? Are you a lord?"

"Nay, no longer." He placed the tray on the table and returned to sit in the chair next to her bed. "How is it you recognize the mark of nobility?"

"I bear it also." She lifted the hair from her neck, revealing the small brand he knew would have been placed there at her birth.

"You seem surprised. It is not only humans who recognize life's stations." Arcinaë smoothed her hand over her hair. "I know that you call me a woman, but I am not human and their butchery does not make it so."

"I know that you are not, and I do not refer to you as a woman with any disrespect intended, but it must be so if you are to survive. Do you understand?" Ilerion asked.

"Aye, Ananta has explained. She says you can make me strong, a warrior—strong enough to kill a man. Can you? Is it in your power to do so?"

"Aye, I can teach you. But it will be difficult and the power will be yours, not mine."

"I have never held a weapon, except the dagger you gave me. Never. Damselfly do not fight. There was never a need…before."

With another yawn, Arcinaë moved the pillow from behind her shoulders and placed it on the bed, wincing as she did so at the pain the movement caused her wounds. She lay down on her stomach and turned her face away from Ilerion.

He heard her whisper as she drifted off to sleep, "I know that you drugged the tea, for it was too bitter. Next time use more honey."

Chapter 2: Wizardry

Ananta left for Lamaas at daybreak, leaving her patient in the care of the hunters.

"Bandages must be changed if we are to avoid infection, and she will not welcome your touch, Hunter. This salve will ease her pain. Try to get her to eat. I understand you were quite successful in the night," she instructed Ilerion.

"Only tea laced with a bit of heavy ale to help her sleep and a little broth and bread," he admitted.

"It is your talk that helps the healing. She told me she found your voice soothing, so talk to her. She does not eat flesh, so do not offer it."

Ananta called back to him as she climbed into her cart, smacking the reins sharply against the horse's rump, "I should return before nightfall—if the wizard is not too well hidden."

⋆⊰⊱⋆

Ananta pulled her hood forward to hide her face and entered the small, dusty candle shop where the wizard had last been seen.

"I seek Fenris the Feie," she told the shopkeeper as she showed the golden coin of enchantment the Feie had given her.

Nodding, the shopkeeper opened the door behind the counter and gestured for Ananta to enter. A small man was seated at a table. He looked up and then quickly got to his feet in recognition of his guest.

"Ananta the healer," he chirped in his singsong voice.

"Fenris the Feie," Ananta acknowledged in return.

"A social call?" Fenris asked.

"Nay, I need your wisdom and magick as I have never needed it before. I hide a Damselfly at the farm. She is badly beaten, brutalized by men, and her wings have been crudely amputated. I have sewn the wounds and done all that I can to heal what I can see, but I fear there are more serious injuries within her body; her belly grows darker."

"And how did a Damselfly end up at the farm?" Fenris asked, his tone indicating suspicion.

"Hunters brought her," Ananta admitted, watching as the Feie's ruddy complexion paled.

"Ananta, it is a ruse, a trap to capture me when you call for my service. Can you not see it?"

"Nay, these men are different. They have sworn to protect her. One is Lord Ilerion. Other hunters came seeking the murderess of Lord Brytwaer. They did not mention a missing Damselfly. They believe her dead and we shall keep it that way, Fenris. It is her only hope."

"Ilerion is a lord no longer. And it is rumored he once killed a Damselfly. Lord Brytwaer is not murdered. He has gone off to his mistress in Cheneis. His hateful wife reported him murdered and blamed a half-witted scullery maid in the hope of ridding herself of at least one of his mistresses. Lord Lazaro does not seek the truth, but merely takes Lady Brytwaer at her word. None is safe from that man's taste for cruelty. Soon he will call you 'witch' and hunt you as well," Fenris said.

"Fenris, help me. I cannot let her die. She is the last," Ananta implored. "And Ilerion did not kill the Damselfly."

"How do you know?" Fenris asked. "Did the hunters tell you so?"

"Nay, Arcinaë of Grimmoirë speaks of his honor."

"Arcinaë? The Damselfly you hide is Arcinaë? Why did you not say so, wench? Let me gather my cloak and bag. Did you bring a cart suitable for hiding a small wizard?" the Feie's words tumbled forth.

"Aye, it is filled with straw deep enough to foil a hayfork," Ananta said with a sigh of relief.

"Do the hunters know who she is?"

"They know her name. I do not believe they know of her importance," the healer answered.

"Do not trust them with this knowledge," urged the wizard, "until I have a chance to test their mettle and honor."

Helping Fenris gather his belongings, Ananta ushered him out the back of the shop and ensconced him beneath the deep hay of her cart. With a quick lash of the whip, she urged the horse away from the city.

❦

Ilerion stood in the doorway of the bedroom holding clean bandages and healing salve.

"The dressings must be changed and Ananta is off seeking a wizard to help with your healing. Will you allow me to do it?"

"Nay, the other. Nilus. He may do it." Arcinaë said.

"Nilus's hands are as calloused and rough as a cooper's," Ilerion laughed.

"If he will not do it, I shall wait for Ananta to return with her wizard," Arcinaë said stubbornly.

"Oh, he will do it. I will see to it," Ilerion said, and shouted, "Nilus! The lady needs your help!"

Heavy footfalls hit the porch and Nilus stood in the doorway, breathing heavily.

"Were you screamin' for me?" he asked Ilerion.

"Aye, the patient needs her dressings changed. Use the salve on her deeper wounds and bind those on her shoulders. Do not fumble the task for she has requested you specifically." Ilerion handed Nilus the bandages and salve. "Call if you have need of my services, milady."

"Close the door," Arcinaë said, slipping the nightdress over her head.

Nilus sat down next to the bed and looked at the heavy bandages on the woman's shoulders. She turned her head away to avoid looking at him.

"Try not to hurt me. I have been hurt enough," she whispered.

"I shall be as gentle as if you were my daughter," Nilus assured her.

"And do you have a daughter?"

"Nay, but if I did I would be gentle with her, for I am not as bumbling as Ilerion would have you believe." He peeled away the old bandages, recoiling at the sight of the suppurating injuries she had sustained.

19

He placed the healing salve in the palm of his hand to warm it before carefully spreading it across the wounds where wings had once been.

"You are kind," Arcinaë said as Nilus replaced her bandages with soft clean gauze, binding them carefully across her chest as she sat before him.

"Do not let that be known. I am legendary for my ruthlessness," Nilus said with a frown.

"I do not believe it so."

"Aye, it is. I would have left you to die," Nilus told her.

"Only out of kindness. I know you saw what was done to me and thought it would be better if I died. I do not fault you. It is true. Death would have been far easier. But now I must live to repay the evil that was done. That is what Ilerion and Ananta tell me. What do you say, Nilus?" Arcinaë asked.

"I say you should fool them all and accept the challenge. Take back your life. Ilerion is a great swordsman and teacher. Let him help you."

"And you, Nilus. What will you teach me?"

"I can teach you how to drink a great deal of ale without becoming drunk. I can teach you sleight of hand, for I was once a thief. Beyond that I know nothing."

She raised her arms, allowing him to slip a clean nightdress over her head.

"Thank you," she said.

"You are welcome, milady," Nilus said, gathering the soiled bandages and retreating to the kitchen.

"She will die," Nilus said with a sigh. "I have seen her wounds and they are a great deal graver than Ananta has admitted. Black blood pools within the woman's belly. I have seen it many times in dying men. She will not live, Ilerion."

"She will not die," Ananta said from the doorway. Beside her stood a diminutive man with muddy brown eyes, flaming red hair and whiskers.

"I am Fenris the Feie. Come to heal the Damselfly," the little man said briskly, striding toward the bedroom without further ado.

"Arcinaë," they heard him say, but could not hear her response for he swiftly closed the door.

"Why did you not tell me how seriously she was hurt?" Ilerion asked Ananta. "I could have released the pooled blood. I have done it on the battlefield."

"Nay, you could not. She is not a woman. She is a Damselfly. Enchanted, as is the Feie. He can treat her. We cannot," the healer sighed. "I knew he would come to heal her. There was nothing else to do."

"I dressed the wounds," Nilus said, receiving an astonished look from Ananta. "She chose me herself. A fine lady she is."

"Can he give her back her wings?" Ilerion asked.

"Nay, not even the Feie can do that," Ananta said.

"Fenris? How is it you have come?" Arcinaë slipped into the language of the Grimmoirëns, tears filling her eyes at the sight of her friend.

"Hush," he said. "I have come to finish your healing. Lie back and let me see your belly. There is great pain there?"

"Aye!" She hissed through gritted teeth as he poked, pushed and pulled at her belly.

The wizard opened his bag and took out several jars of herbal ointment, quickly mixing them in a stone bowl.

He lifted her gown and shook his head at the black blood pooled beneath the swollen tissue of her abdomen. He began to rub the salve into her skin, pressing deeply, causing her to moan in pain. Mumbling the spells that would ease the pain and draw the blood, he covered her belly with sheets of soft spider gauze and watched as they blackened with the killing blood.

After three applications of salve and a profusion of magickal medicine spells, he was pleased to see the darkness fading to a pale blue.

"You will live," Fenris pronounced, "for whatever purpose you are intended."

"I trust them, Fenris," Arcinaë said, seeing the dark thoughts of distrust within the wizard's mind. "Ilerion speaks the language of enchantment. He cared enough to learn."

"You cannot trust them. They are hunters, Arcinaë. They are in the employ of the demon that sent the men who left you for dead."

"Test them. You will find them honorable. I am certain of it."

"We cannot risk you, Arcinaë," the Feie reminded her.

"If that is so, then allow me their protection and training," Arcinaë said. "I would already be dead if not for the hunters. Yesterday I wished to die. Today I wish to live at least long enough to avenge my father's death."

Placing her hand on Fenris's shoulder, she continued, "There is nothing left for me but revenge."

"Lady Arcinaë, you know nothing of war, yet you seek to wage it against men. Men who…"

"Aye, against the men who killed my father and my betrothed, men who left me nothing. I will learn to wage war, Fenris. I will learn. And when it is finished I will die at peace."

"You cannot simply lie down and die. You have responsibilities," Fenris blustered.

"Nay, I do not. They have been lifted from me by an act of treachery," she said.

"Not true," said Ilerion from the doorway. "Responsibilities are never lifted from nobility. Am I right, wizard?"

"Aye, you are."

"But sometimes they are put on hold by some dire circumstance, such as yours, Arcinaë. Then we must have revenge before responsibility.

"I will help you. I will teach you to defend yourself against all manner of men, honorable and ignoble, friend and traitor. I will make you strong enough to make your own peace, to seek your own revenge."

"She knows nothing of battle," Fenris cautioned. "Her kind has never lifted a weapon against another. She believes that kindness is a rule by which all races live. She has never raised her voice in anger, never hated another."

"Nay, I know now that kindness is not a rule by which Men live," she whispered, closing her eyes against the raw memories of savagery. "I will learn to live by the rules of men, and they will die by their rule of brutality and wickedness. The hunter will teach me."

"I cannot teach you hatred. You must feel it. Ananta said that when you first awoke, you did not fight against her. Why?" Ilerion asked.

"I was afraid."

"Fear is not good enough. It will not save you. Cold hatred will give you strength, but it will also blacken your soul beyond redemption. Be certain it is what you want. Rest and heal. I will wait for you," Ilerion said as he bowed and returned to the kitchen.

"I think it is going to require more than your sleight of hand and drunkenness, Nilus. She is as tender as a lily, as fragile as fine crystal. What if she cannot learn to be a warrior, to raise a sword against another?" Ilerion sat down at the table and held his head in his hands.

"Then you will kill them for her and save her the stain on her soul," Ananta said, sitting a bowl of steaming gruel before him. "There is no meat because you have brought none."

"On the morrow I shall hunt for you, Healer," Ilerion said as he stood and carried the soup into the bedroom.

Dragging the table to the bedside, he handed the spoon to Arcinaë. "Eat and sleep. Those are your first instructions. We shall see if you can follow them."

"Will you stay?" she asked. "Talk to me?"

"Nay, I must eat in the kitchen."

"Why?"

"To talk with Ananta and Nilus," he answered.

"About what?"

"You ask too many questions. Eat and sleep. Talk to the wizard. I will see you again tomorrow," Ilerion said.

⁂

When his patient finally slept, Fenris joined them over tea.

"You have taken on a great responsibility," he said, still eyeing Nilus and Ilerion with suspicion. "Why do you wish to help her fight her demons?"

"The men who did this should be punished. Do you not think so?" Ilerion asked the Feie.

"Aye, I think they should be hung, drawn and quartered. But I am just an old Feie, not a man."

"Being a man does not mean I condone their crime. Not all of us are evil, Fenris. Some of us are even honorable."

"Honorable. Aye, that is what she told me. 'Test them, you will find them honorable—suitable to protect me,' she said. Will I?"

"Administer your test. If you do not find me honorable, I will leave her with you." Ilerion scowled.

Fenris brought a crystal sphere to the table, placing it before Ilerion.

"Place your hands on it, and I shall see what you are," the wizard said.

Ilerion placed a hand on either side of the sphere, allowing Fenris to see within his soul.

"These same men killed your wife?"

"Nay, merely others like them. Led by another madman, but her suffering was the same and I was not there to save her. I have not had the courage to die by my own hand."

"Nay, but you have had the courage to live. And what of your revenge?" asked Fenris.

"I no longer seek it."

"And your redemption?"

"I will not deny it. I could not save my wife, but I could save Arcinaë. I do not believe that it absolves me of any offense I have committed, but I could not allow her to die alone in a field filled with the stench of burning flesh."

"But Arcinaë is not a woman. As your friend said, she is merely a beast," Fenris said, looking sharply at Nilus.

"Neither was my wife a woman," Ilerion said. "If you will forgive my leaving, I must prepare for tomorrow's hunt."

"Why did you make him remember?" Nilus fumed. "It was over long ago; he had forgotten."

"Nay, he merely pretends to forget. And you, Nilus? Are you honorable?—I think you are," the Feie asked then answered himself. "You found him and stayed his hand when he would have taken his own life. You helped him bury his wife and have served him since. And yet you called the Damselfly a beast."

"I did not want him to watch Arcinaë die," Nilus admitted. "It was the same. I saw it in his eyes."

"There is great honor in friendship," the wizard said, moving off to lie down near the hearth.

"You lied," Nilus said, throwing himself to the ground near Ilerion.

"Aye, and he knows I lied."

"Why did you lie if he was going to know anyway?"

"I did not want to risk Arcinaë overhearing it," Ilerion said. "If I had finished it, killed Lazaro, she would still have her wings, her father, her betrothed, and her self-respect."

"There is no way to know that."

"You are too kind, Nilus, always too kind. Tomorrow we must bring down a stag for Ananta," Ilerion reminded.

"Sunrise?"

"Aye, while they graze. A large one to match our debt," Ilerion said and closed his eyes against further conversation.

Chapter 3: The Art of Revenge

Twenty days hence Nilus and Ilerion arrived at the house to find Arcinaë sitting in a chair on the porch.

"How did you get to the chair?" Ilerion's voice was sharp with disapproval.

"I walked—holding on to the tables and chairs, and the door frame."

"And the wizard told you that you could walk?"

"Aye, I did," Fenris called from the kitchen. "Now, if you will offer your arm, she can walk inside without so much effort."

"Milady." Ilerion offered his arm.

"You will have to help me stand," Arcinaë said, as she tried to rise on trembling legs.

"Are you sure she should be up and about?" Nilus fumed.

"Aye," the wizard shouted. "Stop mollycoddling her!"

After their meal, Arcinaë asked to sit outside again.

Ilerion grabbed the chair from the porch and moved it to the grass below.

"If you are well enough to sit in a chair, you are well enough to learn to defend yourself," he stated.

"I cannot even stand alone. How can I defend myself?" Arcinaë asked.

"There may come a time when you are attacked while seated. You may as well learn how defend yourself from that position. But first you must harden your mind and your heart, for they are far too tender to allow you to kill a man, even a guilty man. To learn how to kill is one thing, but the actual act of taking another life is very different. Do not ever look into the eyes of the one you intend to kill, for if you do you will hesitate and your enemy will strike you dead."

"Have you ever killed a man?"

"Aye, many. But the one whose eyes I met still lives," Ilerion answered.

"The man who killed your wife?"

"No, the son of the man who ordered her killed. The man who ordered her death was old and dying. I sought only to kill the son so that the father would suffer the loss of one he loved, as I had. But I could not kill his son. I looked into the boy's eyes and thought him innocent."

"You told me you did not have time for marriage, but you were married," Arcinaë said.

"Aye, but I was not there for her. I should have been there to stop them," Ilerion said.

"You cannot always be there, and even if you are, you cannot always overcome a greater strength. It was not your fault any more than my pain was my father's fault. What was your wife's name?"

"Cylacia. Cylacia of Grimmoirë." The name still brought forth the image of her fair enchanted beauty, the memory of her honeyed laughter and wings alive with the shimmering colors of polished lightning glass.

"Cylacia," Arcinaë repeated, her voice a soft prayer. "She died seven years ago. My father told me that her husband lost everything because he sought revenge. He spoke against it. He said revenge did not bring the husband peace or Cylacia back."

"Your father was right. I have no peace and she will never come back. Houses can be rebuilt, titles reclaimed, but a life taken is lost forever. Enough talk. Let us see if you can defend yourself from the chair," Ilerion said, brisk and businesslike.

"Ananta, do you have a staff?" he called to the house.

"A staff?" Ananta asked, stepping out onto the porch.

"Aye, a walking staff for Arcinaë to use."

28

"Nay, I do not have a walking staff."

"Then I shall cut one from the chale tree, but greenwood will hurt far worse when she strikes me than dry wood."

Ilerion cut a branch from the tree, trimming it until it was a comfortable length for Arcinaë when she stood. The staff was slightly crooked and had a knobby end that curved into her hand nicely. He handed it to her and began instructions in its use.

"As I pass, I want you to trip me. As soon as I fall, strike me sharply on the head."

"I cannot."

"Why not?"

"You could be hurt."

"You are not strong enough to hurt me."

"Aye, it is true," Nilus called from the porch. "You are far more likely to crack the stick than damage Ilerion's hard head!"

"Perhaps I should demonstrate using Nilus as the ruffian who comes to offend the damsel," Ilerion offered as he took the staff from Arcinaë's hand and dropped cross-legged to the ground beside her chair.

"Nilus, walk past and let your gaze fall upon the seated beauty."

"It is my pleasure to assist the fair lady with her practice," Nilus said, bowing. As he came abreast of them, Ilerion drove the staff forward between the short man's legs causing him to fall face forward. Then, with a resounding thud, he swiftly brought the staff across Nilus's back.

Nilus rolled over and leapt to his feet, bowing before Arcinaë to show that he was unharmed. Taking the staff from Ilerion, he growled, "And now the short shall smite the tall."

Glaring, Ilerion strode past them. Nilus slammed the staff into the back of the taller man's knees, dropping him to the ground before swinging the stick down sharply against Ilerion's head.

Arcinaë gasped in alarm, "Stop!"

Moaning, Ilerion climbed slowly to his feet.

"As you see, I am not dead and Nilus's strike is far harder than yours will be."

"I cannot do this!" Her exclamation came as a sob.

"Then you are not strong enough to sit outside where Lazaro's hunters may encounter you on their next visit. They would see your weakness and consider you a tender morsel to help satisfy their appetites," Ilerion stated harshly. "Come, I shall escort you to the house."

⚜

For the next cycle of the moon, Nilus and Ilerion worked Ananta's fields, felling trees and pulling stumps in readiness for plowing. They took their meals in the shed, deliberately avoiding Arcinaë.

"She will come when she is ready," Ilerion muttered beneath his breath.

"She may never be ready." Nilus shook his head. "She is no warrior. There is not a glimmer of a fighter within her."

"Then you will place a glimmer there, for you have promised to teach me. I will do as you ask, strike you when you want," Arcinaë said, arriving without warning, and in a tone that indicated she did not intend to be dissuaded.

Turning around and seeing the staff clutched in her hand, Ilerion demanded, "Strike me!"

Arcinaë raised her arm and brought the staff down, landing it softly on his shoulder.

"Strike me again, harder!"

Again she lifted the staff, her arm trembling from the weight, and allowed it to tap against his chest.

Ilerion grabbed the staff from her hand and threw it to the ground.

"Slap me," Ilerion's voice was cruel, "or I will slap you!"

Arcinaë stepped back at his threat but not far enough to avoid his hand. The sound of his palm striking her face was loud in the silence of the morning, the mark of its impact red against her pale flesh.

"*Ilerion!*" Nilus grabbed his friend's arm only to have his hand flung away.

"Slap me or I will strike you again." Ilerion's cold tone and angry eyes fed Arcinaë's growing fear.

As he lifted his hand a second time, her eyes widened and she flew at him, slapping and kicking, balling her fists and pounding against his chest, her frenzied screams bringing Ananta and Fenris racing from the house.

Ilerion grasped Arcinaë's elbows as her knees buckled and she collapsed sobbing against him. "Aye, there is a glimmer there," he whispered as his mouth relaxed into a small half smile.

"She is well enough to travel," Fenris said, "and it is not safe for her to remain here. Where will you take her?"

"Through Cheneis and across the border into Baene; there is a long abandoned castle there. The furnishings are gone, destroyed or stolen, and it is partially burned out, but the wine cellars and servants' quarters will offer sufficient shelter that we might be warm and dry." Ilerion paused, thinking his plan through. "None will search for us there. Lazaro will merely think two more of his hunters have been killed or wandered off in search of better pay. It is common among those in his service."

"Can you truly keep her safe?" the wizard asked.

"As safe as it is possible for two men to keep a woman. I can only promise that we will not leave her alone," Ilerion said, remembering his failure to protect Cylacia.

The Feie cocked an eye at Ilerion while he considered his next words. Deciding there was naught to lose he took a deep breath and began, "She is called to lead the enchanted folk. Not just the Damselflies, but all of Grimmoirë. She believes she has lost everything, and perhaps she has, but there is a tale among our folk of a race of elemental beings known as the Sylph. It is said the Sylph have a power to heal that is greater than that of any others."

"And you believe they can restore her wings?" Ilerion's look was skeptical.

"It is not known, for since the fall of Arcaedya—long before the memories of Man—none have seen the Sylph," the Feie admitted. "Though there is a story telling of a map to their sect painted on the wings of buttermoths. Another legend says the Sylph traveled through an ancient mirror to Réverē on Ædracmoræ. We would pay you handsomely, in gold, if you were to take on the task of seeking them out."

"I do not require payment, Wizard," Ilerion stated, hearing Nilus' groan of disappointment. "When her revenge is complete, we can talk of her redemption and responsibilities. I will help her seek these healers if she wishes it."

Fenris held out a small dark bottle. "For sleep without night terrors," he said, handing it to Nilus.

"Her screams will offend no one where we go, and it is not wise to cover the truth of pain beneath the shadow of nightshade and magick. She will go mad from her fear if she never faces it. As she grows stronger, she will fight her battles first within her sleep and then by the light of day," Ilerion stated.

"Oh, and now you are a healer?" the wizard snapped.

"Nay, but I have been healed," the hunter answered without anger, "and it was not by drunkenness or magick." With a glance toward the Damselfly, he added, "She cannot be trained to fight in nightclothes or a dress. Tomorrow we will go to Lamaas and buy her a hunter's leathers."

⊰⊱

"These must be small, for a lad who weighs not more than eight stone and is less than seven spans tall," Ilerion said to the Lamaas tailor, looking through the piles of soft tanned hides. "They should be soft and supple, suitable for long hours of training. They must not chafe the skin."

"You should have brought the lad with you," the shopkeeper scolded. "You know how difficult it is to fit one I cannot see."

"But you will do it admirably, I am sure."

With a sigh, the tailor laid out three pair of leathers, all as soft as the fur of a downy flier. They were small and narrow in the waist, almost as if made for a woman.

"And woolens? Does he require woolens, a shirt? A cloak?" the tailor asked.

"Aye, the young squire requires all of those, socks as well and a nightshirt. Two of everything, for it will be some time before we return," Ilerion said, fingering the heavy wool cloaks and thinking of the chill in the wine cellars.

The door flew open and Nilus entered holding up a pair of finely crafted boots. "Fit for royalty," he winked, "and the smallest they had."

"Is the squire someone I know?" asked the tailor.

"Nay, he hails from Cheneis," Ilerion lied.

"And he seeks knighthood?"

"Aye, the young always do," the hunter nodded solemnly.

"Nilus and I intend to make him a fine warrior, worthy of an appointment by the crown. Do we not, Nilus?"

"Indeed we do," Ilerion's partner answered with a grin.

Arcinaë ran her fingers over the soft leather that now covered her legs. It fitted as if it were a second skin over the heavy woolens Ilerion had provided. A leather shirt with heavy shoulder armor gave her the look of someone heavier and broader shouldered. It also served to flatten her breasts and make her look more like a boy. The boots were a bit loose in the calf, but a second pair of socks had taken care of the problem.

"I do not look like a woman," she said to Ananta, as the healer deftly braided Arcinaë's hair into a single strand.

"Aye, but there is no hiding that you are female. You face is fine and your bones give you away, but you will look like a woman hunter rather than a Damselfly," Ananta said, tying off the braid and letting it fall.

"If you swing that braid hard enough, it will be a weapon on its own," the healer chuckled, as she held out the heavy cloak for Arcinaë.

"Are there truly women hunters?" Arcinaë asked, slipping into the cloak and tossing the braid forward over her shoulder in a very feminine gesture before lifting the hood.

"Aye, they are generally foul and as cruel as the men."

"Why are Ilerion and Nilus not cruel? Why have they chosen to be hunters?"

Ananta sat down on the bed and pulled Arcinaë down beside her. "Some men are so brave and so principled that they do not fear showing kindness. They do not need to hurt others to prove their strength. Lord Ilerion and Nilus are such men."

"He says that he is no longer a lord."

"Aye, but it is by his own choice. For seven long years he has lived as a pauper. He feels that his failure to save Cylacia requires that he suffer eternally. It is why he has chosen to hunt the worst of all men and live as a man without a hearth. He destroyed his own castle and by his madness drove away those in his service. He feels some release by helping you, and that is why you can trust him.

"What you seek to do will not be easy. Every day you will suffer the aches of your growth. You will struggle for the strength that he will demand, and he will not comfort you. But, if it is at all possible to create a warrior from a Damselfly, he will do it," Ananta declared. "Now let us show them the new hunter."

Ananta pushed Arcinaë out the door ahead of her and watched with pleasure as the hunters examined their new charge. Their scrutiny left Arcinaë uncomfortable, fidgeting in her nervousness.

"What?" she finally asked.

"If you could only wield a sword, you would indeed be a hunter," Ilerion told her. "You certainly look like a hunter, though you are a bit on the puny side," he added.

"We shall fix that," Nilus promised, "for I shall do the cooking and you will eat it. I will have you fattened up in no time!"

"Do not make her so fat she cannot fit into those leathers, for we will be far from a tailor."

"I do not wish to be fat or I will not be able to fl—" Arcinaë stopped, her eyes filled with the pain of loss. "I am sorry, I forgot for a moment I could not fly."

"Oh, you will fly, milady, and though it will not be on the luminous wings you lost, it will still give you flight that those bound to the earth will never know. The gryphons will carry you. Grundl seems to know quite a bit about you already."

"Grundl? Mate to Nesika of the Isle of Grave?"

"Aye, that one. He and Nesika should arrive soon. Nesika has demanded she be allowed to carry you, and it is not wise to argue with her," Ilerion said.

"I served on the Winged Council with Nesika and Grundl. They brought me spun gold for my hair, but it was taken by the men who came. Everything of value was taken."

"Then we shall give you more," shouted a gravelly voice in the language of Arcinaë's birth, "for the eyrie of the gryphon is known for its wealth."

A rustle of feathered wings and the clicks of the gryphons' speech were followed by heavy landings in the rich earth of the field. In the hop-step gait of their mismatched legs, four gryphons presented themselves before the waiting hunters.

"You know Grundl and Nesika, the others are Baeob and Olcus."

"I told you she was Damselfly," Grundl reminded Ilerion, his beak clicking rapidly in excitement.

"But you did not tell me which Damselfly," Ilerion accused.

"Well, no. It is best that humans be made to discover some things for themselves," the gryphon replied. "One day this one will be sovereign of Grimmoirë."

"First she must become a warrior and avenge the death of her people, and then we shall see about her responsibilities."

"This is her wish?" Grundl queried with a frown.

"Aye, and mine," Ilerion confessed. "She cannot rule beasts as querulous as gryphons while she is distracted by sorrow."

"Nesika," Grundl called to his mate, "Ilerion has called us querulous beasts again!"

"Then perhaps you should drop him into Felldan's Fen on the way to Baene," Nesika sniffed, feigning offense and adding a series of small clicks for emphasis.

"Do not lose the hunter, for I need his help," Arcinaë said.

"I suppose if Arcinaë requires him, then we shall be forced to bear his humiliating remarks," Nesika replied with a laugh that sounded like a raspy cough.

Ananta and Fenris brought jars of healing salve and the herbs for a tea that would ease Arcinaë's aches as she trained with the hunters. Pulling Ilerion aside, Ananta again cautioned him against the Damselfly's attachment.

"Unlike Cylacia, Arcinaë cannot simply walk away from Grimmoirë and its future."

Ilerion felt a fist squeeze his heart and responded curtly, "Your fear is unfounded, for I have no intention of seeking or allowing her affection. I have seen the destruction the adoration of a human brings to a Damselfly, and I am not likely to forget. We go to the castle in Baene where reminders of my failure will be ever present. In fact, it is far more likely that she will grow to hate me."

"I did not mean—" Ananta began.

"Aye, you did. And you are right to caution a man who has been known to err so grievously. In a world of humans so filled with fear and superstition, I should have known there was no place for Cylacia and me. But I thought that within my own kingdom where the White Laws of Equality were upheld, that we would be safe from the hatred of outsiders. I never stopped to consider betrayal from within my castle walls.

"I will guide Arcinaë and free her of weakness. I will drive her as I would a squire seeking knighthood, and she will become strong and fearless. When she is ready, I will lead her into battle against those responsible for her losses. While I no longer claim my title, I remain a man of gallantry and will therefore always defend the weak and innocent and seek to destroy evil in all its monstrous forms. And if, as you believe, this evil is led by Lord Lazaro, I will see him dead by her hand or by mine. It is all that I can promise. In the end I can only hope to die with honor and valor."

As Ilerion bowed courteously, Fenris tapped Ananta's elbow. "He is a bit full of himself but still, being so tightly bound by such rules of conduct will not allow him a second failure."

After last goodbyes, each rider mounted his gryphon. With Olcus carrying their provisions in the lead position, they set off for Cheneis and thence across the border into Baene. Looking back in fond farewell, Arcinaë caught a glimpse of Ananta as she hastily hid Fenris under the load of hay in her cart.

❧❦❧

As they made their way toward the safety of the distant castle in Baene, Arcinaë felt the involuntary struggle of useless muscles trying to stretch her missing wings. Her eyes filled with sudden tears that blurred her view of the landscape below.

Sensing her rider's anguish, Nesika spoke in soft mental tones, *Do not despair; lore says you will once again fly. Do you not hold store in the legends of enchantment?*

In an attempt to control her tears, Arcinaë shared her hopelessness with the gryphon, "Not even the Feie can grant new wings. It would be dangerous for me to hope for something so unlikely. It is better that I learn to fight, as others do who cannot flee to the skies."

"Until you can fly again, I shall carry you," Nesika pledged.

Chapter 4: Testing Times at Baene

They arrived at the abandoned castle under cover of darkness and bone-chilling rain, and immediately set about unloading their supplies. Three trips from the gryphons to the cellar left Arcinaë exhausted and her skin covered with the sheen of cold sweat. Nilus forbade her to make a fourth trip and settled her in an empty servant's room no larger than the smallest dungeon cell.

Ilerion observed the compassion of his companion with a grim smile. He knew there would be no sparing of Arcinaë's pain if she were to grow strong.

❦

Arcinaë's terrified screams reverberated around the cold, stone walls of the fortress. Turning to the dark bottle given him by the wizard, Nilus began to creep towards her room, but Ilerion's voice stopped him. "It will not serve to help her and will only leave her foggy-headed in the morn. I shall go sit with her and make sure she does not harm herself."

Ilerion slipped silently into the darkness and entered Arcinaë's room, lighting a single candle that he might watch over her as she suffered the anguish of reliving her violation. Her hands were locked together as if in prayer although he knew that in her dream they were locked together from being bound. Her head tossed right and left, and she drew up her knees as she relived her beating, but never once did she strike out against the captors in her night terrors, not even when they rolled her over and took the dagger to her wings. When finally she calmed, too exhausted for even the nightmares to take hold, Ilerion covered her with the heavy cloak and made a silent promise, "I will see you fight against them, Arcinaë of Grimmoirë. I will see you fight and win."

"How bad was it?" Nilus asked from the darkness.

"It could not have been worse," Ilerion whispered in return.

❦

As the shroud of the morning mist lifted, it became apparent that the castle had been torn apart by war. The heavy portcullis had been broken and burnt, and the stone walls were scorched as if by dragons' breath or the catapulting of burning stones. Within the castle interior no chair remained unbroken, no tapestry untorn.

The charred remains of a funeral bier rested on the floor of the lord's chambers. It was here that he had intended to set his wife's tortured soul free, burying the soft ash of her remains beneath the willow near the stream and leaving it unmarked in fear of defilement— even after death.

Arcinaë wandered slowly about the ruins that had become her home.

"So much anger," she whispered.

"Aye, something you do not have." Ilerion's voice was loud in the silence. "I, on the other hand, never lacked fury. It flooded my soul upon my return home to discover Cylacia's dead body lying on the silken sheets of our marital bed. The chamber maids were weeping. They said my soldiers had been taken, arrested for defending an unnatural union between a man and a beast. In the madness of my rage, I drove the servants out and destroyed everything that could be broken or burned. Then I buried my wife."

Arcinaë stepped toward him, her offer of comfort obvious.

Warding her off with his hand, Ilerion said, "There is no comfort for it. Only the five years of my revenge brought any satisfaction. The death of those responsible allows me to sleep without dreams. Would you like to sleep without reliving your violation every night, Arcinaë?"

Without waiting for her answer, he turned and left the room, calling over his shoulder, "Come, we begin."

Ilerion led Arcinaë to the kitchen where Nilus had scrubbed every surface and was stirring something in the large pot that hung suspended from a hook above the fire.

"Sit," Ilerion said, indicating a barrel. "Had I known I would have need of a chair, I would have spared one."

Nilus handed Arcinaë a bowl filled with gray sludge and a large wooden spoon. Seeing her look of disgust, he said, "Gruel thickened with grain. It will have you stout in no time. It would be better if you ate meat, but I am told you do not."

"Nay, I do not eat the flesh of others." She spooned a bit of the gray mass and giving a shudder of anticipation, placed it on her tongue.

"It is sweet," she said with surprise.

"Aye, sweetened with honey and berries, both guaranteed to fatten a goose," Nilus said.

"Now I am considered a goose?"

"Nay, merely a frail, motherless fawn found in the woods—one that needs a bit of looking after. Tonight we shall have a draught of heavy ale and begin your drinking instruction," he said, holding up a bottle of stout ale. "From the demon's own cellars!"

"Eat," Nilus encouraged, handing her a cup of tea, "for it will taste far worse if you let it grow cold."

As they ate, Ilerion described Arcinaë's first day of training.

"Today we will stretch your muscles, for tomorrow you and I will fell a tree. We will walk until you can walk no more. Tomorrow we will run. Tonight we will soak you in a tub of hot water to ease the aches of today's pain and, if you like, Nilus will rub you down with liniment in the areas you cannot reach yourself. We will begin working with the staff and the dagger, followed by the bow, sword, horse and lance. In one year we will find a challenger and see what you can do."

"In one year?" She asked with a look of hopelessness on her face.

"Aye, it takes a young squire, one who has watched knights wield weapons since he was born, eight years of practice before he can apply for knighthood, but since I intend to drive you far harder and you are already an adult, we will test you in one year."

A solitary tear escaped and rolled down Arcinaë's cheek.

"Do not cry, for it only wastes the water you will need to train," Ilerion said, standing. "Come."

"But I have not finished my tea," Arcinaë said.

"Tomorrow drink faster. Nilus will have more tea for you at nightfall."

❖

Arcinaë stared at the heavy log resting on the floor before her. It was attached by a heavy rope that had been run through a pulley and tied off to a beam, one that had not completely burned through during Ilerion's days of rage.

Ilerion untied the rope and showed her how she was supposed to lift the log from the floor by dragging the rope back through the pulley.

"It is heavier than I," she said.

"Indeed it is," Ilerion admitted, pulling the rope toward her.

"I cannot lift it."

"Not alone, but with my help you can. Take the rope in both hands, there, in front of mine."

She reached ahead of his hands and grabbed the rope, feeling the pull as he allowed her to take some of the log's weight.

"Now we just hold it," he stated from behind her.

"For how long?" she asked.

"Until you scream for mercy."

"I will not scream for mercy," she denied.

"Good, then we shall hold it forever."

Within minutes, Arcinaë felt a burning ache in the muscles of her shoulders. Gradually it encompassed her back and legs until finally the pain became nearly unbearable along the muscles of her forearms. But still she did not ask to let go. She closed her eyes and bit her lips until she felt blood flow.

Ilerion felt the trembling in the rope and knew her pain must be agonizing. Unused muscles were being called on to do a man's job. Rather than relieving her of any weight, he allowed a bit more to fall to her hands. He heard her cry out and watched as she sank to the floor still holding the rope.

"Enough," he said, lifting her to her feet. "And now we walk."

She stumbled out before him, shaking with the effort to simply stay on her feet. Down the road and across the field they walked, her steps growing slower and slower until finally she simply stood before him.

"Walk," he commanded.

"I cannot walk," Arcinaë gasped.

"Then you will sleep here and grow cold and wet. Wild beasts may eat you in the night."

"Then they will have to eat me, for I do not care. I can walk no further."

"There is a hot bath and tea laced with ale waiting at the castle," Ilerion whispered in her ear before striding away. "Nilus will miss you if you do not return."

With great effort she raised her head and looked after him. "You would truly leave me here, after you promised to protect me?"

"Aye, I would. You are of no use to anyone, including yourself, if you cannot even stagger back to supper."

Looking around she whimpered, "I cannot even see the castle."

"It is just over the rise," he said, walking back to stand beside her.

Slowly she took a step in the direction of the castle. He shadowed her until she finally fell, and then he lifted her and carried her back to the warm kitchen.

Ilerion saw Nilus's look of alarm. "She is merely weary. Food and the tub will refresh her, and liniment will ease the aches if she will allow your ministration. Check her wounds to be sure they remain closed, for she would not cry for mercy as she held the log."

Her back against the wall so that she would not topple forward to the floor, Ilerion gently placed Arcinaë on the overturned barrel that served as a chair.

"You did well," he said.

Her eyes opened very slowly as the warmth seeped into her body. Nilus stood before her with a bowl of hot soup, heavy with grain and vegetables.

"Can you hold the spoon and bowl, or shall I hold them for you?" he asked.

Looking around, Arcinaë asked, "Where is he?"

"Gone. He will return before daybreak though. He always does.

He grows grim here. Her soul haunts him, and I imagine he will spend the night beside her grave. That puts you in my care, so eat. Then I am to soak you in the tub and rub liniment on the aches you cannot reach yourself."

"Revenge did not end it. Still he is haunted and heartbroken. Does it never end? Will we bear the pain forever?" she asked, tasting the soup and surprised to find that she was hungry.

"Well, I am only a short, stout, bald man, but I believe that it can heal. Revenge helps by clearing the mind, freeing it to move on. The problem is Ilerion has not moved on. For him it is not finished; he still owes Cylacia one life."

"The man who ordered her death?" asked Arcinaë.

"Or his son," Nilus whispered.

❧❦❧

Ilerion sat beside Cylacia's small burial mound, brushing away dried leaves.

"She is strong, I think. There is anger hidden deep within her, though she fears its release. I grow tired, Cylacia, and wish to rest with you. But I must see this one safe and finish with Lazaro. Then I will come."

Ilerion lay down with his hand on the soft mounded earth and dreamed of his wife. Her voice was soft and her words, meant only for him, were tender. He felt the involuntary flutter of her wings as their passion grew. The cool water of the hidden falls caressed their hot skin and a soft breeze dried them. Evil no longer came to claim the Cylacia of his dreams.

When he awoke, he felt the touch of her lashes against his cheek and smiled when he saw it was only a small buttermoth that had landed there. Lifting it to his hand, he examined its brightly colored wings.

"Is it possible you carry the map of the Sylph?" he asked the silent moth.

❧❦❧

When he could no longer bear Arcinaë's nightly screams, Nilus moved into one of the towers. His words were angry as he argued with Ilerion. "She never rests. Her days are filled with the cruelty of your incessant training regimen, and her nights are filled with terror and pain. Dark circles mar her eyes and she cannot—"

"I do not care. I will not see her drugged or drunken to silence her screams. She grows stronger. Slowly she gains skill with the staff, and soon she will lift a sword. Then I will show her how to kill a man," Ilerion interrupted.

"She is not skilled at anything. You only fool yourself and her," Nilus shouted, as he stormed up the stairs.

"He does not believe I grow stronger?" Arcinaë's voice was small.

"He believes me a brute and insensitive to your needs. What do you believe?" Ilerion asked, raising his eyebrows.

"I believe you are trying to save your own soul by restoring mine," she answered.

"And you are probably right. Do you wish to take the elixir that will kill the night terrors or drink heavy ale until you are too drunk to care whether they come or not?"

"Nay, I wish to feel the pain and see their faces every night until I am strong enough to kill every one of those men."

"The one who ground your face into the ash and took your wings, do you know his face?" Ilerion asked.

"Aye, he was the last," she whispered, averting her gaze. "And then he killed my father."

"We shall seek him first, when you are ready," Ilerion said.

"Why does Nilus think you fool me?"

"Nilus does not believe striking a bag of straw proves that you can kill a man," he answered as he walked away.

Her eyes followed his retreating back, and she whispered, "Then perhaps I shall strike you."

⁂

Ilerion sat on the ground reading a book. Arcinaë stood an arm's length away, holding the staff in the palms of her outstretched hands. While he never seemed to look at her, each time her arms would drop even the slightest bit, Ilerion would reach up with a stick and tap the staff. "Up. Keep it up."

As her arms grew tired, the stick struck the staff more and more often, and Arcinaë became annoyed. She watched him out of the corner of her eye and felt her arms failing again. She saw the stick rise and suddenly swung on him, striking him sharply on the shoulder with the staff.

"Stop it! I grow tired and I do not wish to hold the staff any longer," she snapped, realizing she held the staff aloft as if to strike him again.

"I am sorry. I do not know what came over me…I just…"

"Have had enough?" Nilus asked from the doorway.

"Aye," Ilerion agreed, "I believe she has had enough. Shall we run?"

With a grin, she shot out the door past Nilus and raced down the road.

Nilus looked after her. "Perhaps I was wrong. Perhaps she does become stronger."

"Indeed she does," Ilerion said, rubbing his shoulder as he headed out after his student.

Anger and Blood

"**N**o! I will not allow it!" Arcinaë's angry words shattered the silence. Ilerion leapt to his feet and rushed to her room, expecting to see an intruder, but no one was there except Arcinaë. She stood in the center of the room, breathing heavily, her hands gripping an imaginary staff, her face contorted with anger.

"What is it you will not allow, Arcinaë?" Ilerion urged.

Her eyes rose to his face, as her empty hands dropped to her sides.

"I will not allow them to defile me again."

He saw her chin quiver and reminded, "Do not weep, Arcinaë. It is good your terror shifts toward anger. Tomorrow we will use the dagger, for the staff will not stop them when they come for you."

"Will they come for me?" she asked, her eyes glazing with fear.

"Aye, the moment they know you live. This is why you must remain hidden, Arcinaë of Grimmoirë, until the ashes of each of them have drifted on the seven winds. Before we leave this place to hunt them, it would be best for you to take another name, a name you can use to hide yourself until you mete out your revenge."

She called after him as he turned to leave her, "A woman's name?"

"Aye, a woman's name."

"But I do not want a woman's name! I am Arcinaë of Grimmoirë! I am a Damselfly!"

"Aye, Arcinaë, indeed you are, and I did not expect you would actually comply. But it would have made it far easier to hide your presence from Lazaro."

Seeing the book he still held in his hand, she asked, as much to change the subject as out of any real curiosity, "What is it you read?"

"'The Code of the Gallant'—the law by which I live my life."

She ran a hand through her hair. "It is the law of all men?"

"Aye, all men are taught this law."

"Teach me this code that I might know how many laws of men were broken."

"We will speak of it, though I believe that you already carry it in your heart. Sleep, Arcinaë of Grimmoirë, for tomorrow you will fell a tree," Ilerion said as he closed the door.

⁂

Together, Ilerion and Arcinaë felled a tree. The work had become more balanced as Arcinaë grew stronger. She no longer used the axe of a child but raised that of a squire to notch the trunk.

"Tell me of the code," she called. "If indeed all of its laws have been broken, why does the crown not stop them?"

"Because the crown is weak," Ilerion replied. "Is the notch complete?"

"Aye," Arcinaë said, stepping back from the tree and peeking around it at him.

"Do you wish to fell the tree today?" he asked.

"Do you think I can?"

"We will not know if you do not try," Ilerion said, handing her his heavier axe.

As she took it from him, the blade dipped toward the ground before she grasped it more tightly and brought it up to her shoulder. She examined the line, opposite and slightly above her notch, that he had made in the trunk.

"I do not believe I can do it with three blows as you do."

He remained silent, watching as she measured her stance and prepared to strike a blow.

The axe struck the tree, sending great chips of bark flying. Again she drew back and the axe hit the trunk, and again. She turned, seeking his approval, and saw that he was seated on the grass reading his book. With a smile, Arcinaë felled the tree.

At the sound of the cracking trunk, Ilerion looked up. "Well done. Now let us use the dagger."

The grass-filled bag she used for practice with the staff was gone, and in its place hung a leather figure of a man.

Curious, Arcinaë asked, "What is this?"

"This is a man. It is easy to strike the bag of grass, for it feels like nothing more than a bag of grass. The leather of this effigy will prepare you for the cutting of skin and muscle," Ilerion explained.

Drawing the same dagger he had offered her in defense of the hunters at Ananta's, he whirled and drove it into the belly of the leather man.

Arcinaë gasped as blood flowed from the wound.

Flipping the dagger over, Ilerion offered her the hilt.

The shadow of refusal passed quickly across her eyes before she took the blade in her hand.

"Why does it bleed?" she asked.

"Because it is a man," he answered.

"He lies," Nilus called out. "It is filled with the bladders of boars. Bladders I filled with blood and sewed into this leather 'hunter' at his request."

"I do not lie, Arcinaë. When you cut a man, he will bleed. When you kill a man, he will bleed a great deal. You must see the flow of blood as you practice. If you do not, you will freeze when first you see it, and your opponent will strike you dead."

She stepped toward the leather hunter and poked it gently with the tip of the dagger, feeling the leather give. Drawing the dagger back, she thrust it forward more forcefully, making a small cut in the skin. Again she drew it back, but Ilerion gripped her wrist and took the dagger, flipping it over so that her hand held the hilt toward her thumb.

"When the blade comes from your thumb, you have no power. Now, drive it into his chest."

Raising her arm above her head, Arcinaë drove the blade into the chest of the leather hunter. Blood splattered, covering her arm and hand and dotting her face. She gasped, dropped the dagger and backed away, trying to wipe away the blood.

"Nay, do not fear the blood of your enemy, for it is evidence of your success. Fear only your own blood, for it can mean the loss of your life." Holding out the dagger, Ilerion said, "Again."

By the end of her lesson, the hide-covered man hung in shreds. Arcinaë was covered with nearly as much blood as she had been on the day Ilerion had found her so near death, but she no longer cringed each time the blade struck, and she made no attempt to wipe the leather hunter's gore from her face.

"Very good, Arcinaë." Ilerion patted her shoulder. "I will leave you in Nilus's care for a few days while I re-provision. You can work on your sleight of hand."

❧❦

Nilus watched as Arcinaë deftly palmed the stone he had placed before her. Had he not been a thief, he would not have noticed the sweep of her gesture as anything more than part of her conversation. She brushed back an errant strand of hair and with the practiced, perfectly fluid ease of the skilled thief, slipped the stone—without hesitation—inside her shirt.

"Why has Ilerion not returned?" Arcinaë asked.

"He re-provisions and seeks information. It may simply have taken longer than he anticipated," Nilus answered, sensing her concern at Ilerion's overdue return to the castle. Placing a ring at the edge of the table, he continued, "If you can capture the ring without drawing my attention, it is yours."

Deliberately walking away from the table, Arcinaë frowned. "He could be in trouble."

"Ilerion? It is unlikely. He is extremely cautious, and I have seen him dispatch six armed men without assistance."

"And he can teach me to do this? Dispatch six men unassisted?"

"Nay, Arcinaë. Ilerion is trained as a warrior. He was granted knighthood at twenty-one summers and was the lord of this castle for three years before…it fell to treachery.

"You stand less than six spans and weigh a mere eight stone. You will never have the power of a man. Do not let him lead you to believe that you will. This is not to say you will not be able to avenge yourself against the men you seek, but you must do it when

48

each is alone and unsuspecting," Nilus said.

"Do you believe he lies to me?" Arcinaë asked, as she leaned against the table and took the ring, placing it on a finger of the hand she held behind her back.

"He lies to himself. He wishes you to be what you are not and can never be—a Damselfly warrior."

"But I do learn. He has not struck me once with the staff during sparring in over two months. I no longer fear the blood of others. He has promised to bring a sword for me when he returns. I do learn, Nilus, I do."

"And at best, Arcinaë, you might win against the challenge of a boy. It would be far better if we returned you to Grimmoirë and allowed the enchanted to protect you," Nilus said with a sigh.

"You forget, Nilus, I am no longer worthy of living in Grimmoirë. There is naught left of the fair, enchanted Damselfly."

The sudden shrill whinnying of excited horses reached them, and they rushed to the tower windows to discover the source. Mounted on a heavy stallion that called repeatedly as it pounded toward the castle, Ilerion was racing along the road toward them flanked on either side by additional mounts, two tacked and ready for riders, and a third weighted heavily with provisions.

"Caval," Nilus muttered. "If he brings Caval, we are in trouble, for it means it is not safe to call the gryphons. Grab your things and meet us at the gate," he instructed, pushing Arcinaë ahead of him.

Dropping reins and leaving a swift command to stand steady, Ilerion left the horses and stormed down into the kitchen, his boots thundering on the stone steps.

"Grab what you can and come!" he shouted. "Ananta is dead at the hands of hunters and they seek Arcinaë in the city. Women are being stripped in the streets as they search for her scars."

Arcinaë froze.

"Not now, Arcinaë. Now you must flee. We shall mourn death and cry foul when we are safe within the Mountains of Algor. Come." Ilerion grabbed her wrist and pulled her up the stairs behind him. "Bring her bag," he called back to Nilus.

Outside, Ilerion lifted Arcinaë to a waiting mount, instructing quickly, "They are no different than managing a gryphon, save for the jarring of your spine as their feet strike the earth. Stay low and do not fall."

"Nilus!" he shouted, urgently, leaping to the back of the great stallion called Caval.

Nilus raced from the castle, heavily laden with sacks filled with supplies. Throwing them on the already burdened packhorse, he swiftly secured them and jumped to the saddle of the fourth horse.

Bellowing, Caval rose to his hind legs before leaping forward and leading them away toward the distant snow-covered wastelands. Ahead the dark clouds amassed—a precursor to the numbing cold and snows of deep winter.

Within her terror-stricken mind, Arcinaë imagined Ananta's tortured screams and envisioned the blood of her death.

Chapter 5: Beneath Algor

As the altitude increased so, too, did the difficulty of the terrain through which they traveled. The extreme body heat generated by the exertion of the horses in the icy world of Algor manifested in great clouds of condensation that hung about their heads and necks. To the east, the ground fell away in an angry wound left by the slippage of a glacier. To the west, a thin finger of ice extended over an otherwise open precipice. In the empty stillness of the pass, the massively deep respiration of the horses was amplified as they climbed along an increasingly narrow and treacherous path towards the summit.

"Ilerion!" Nilus called ahead as he slid to the ground, just managing to catch Arcinaë as she toppled from her mount. "She can ride no further."

"She must. We cannot stop until we reach the Algorian settlement. They will shelter us and provide the warmth of a fire and a meal. The pass will close behind us before Lazaro's men reach it," Ilerion shouted.

Sliding from Caval's back, Ilerion pulled a heavy fur cape from a pack and wrapped Arcinaë in the warmth of its soft pelt. Tossing a second cape to Nilus and pulling on his own, he climbed back into the saddle, settling Arcinaë's unconscious form before him. Sensing the warhorse's displeasure, he murmured, "She weighs a good deal less than nine stone, Caval, and you have less than three leagues to carry her."

The heavy snowfall blotted out the surrounding landscape, leaving the travelers in an ever-contracting world of whiteness. Ilerion stopped, smelling the acrid smolder of fires hidden deep beneath the ice caverns of Algor. Small chimney holes allowed the smoke to rise and disperse in the air above the caverns. The Algorians were nomadic, living beneath the ice throughout the frozen winter and above ground in tundra-sod hovels during the spring and summer. They protected their settlements fiercely and did not welcome those who were unknown.

"How will we find the entrance?" Nilus whispered at Ilerion's side.

"It will be among the hummocks, hidden by a great sphere of ice —a tel. Even the Algorians cannot find the entrance without the tel."

"How is it you come among us in the depth of darkness, Hunter?" a gravelly voice asked from beyond the range of their vision.

"We hide a woman from Lord Lazaro. It is said in the legends that it is here the last Damselfly shelters during her winter of woe," Ilerion called back.

"That is no more than a doomsday tale from the legends of Baene," the Algorian said as he stepped into view and extended his hand to Ilerion.

"Nay, Yce. A piece of the legend lies within my arms. I am sure of it," the hunter replied. He freed an arm from Arcinaë, allowing him to grip the hand extended in friendship.

"Bring your legendary woman," Yce said, reaching back to grip Nilus's hand in welcome. "Tresa brews fire tea and a fat waterbear roasts on the spit. Wearing its winter fat, it was not swift enough to outrun my bolt.

"You will remain until the melt?" Yce asked Ilerion.

"Aye, if you will have us. The woman still heals from Lazaro's brutality, and wintering safely will allow us time to train. She seeks revenge against those who killed her father," Ilerion explained.

"Arcinaë of Grimmoirë? Do not look so surprised. We hear the words of the warmlanders—they are carried on the western winds," Yce chastened. "You believe that only the crown hears all, but it is not true, Ilerion. The magick of the wind brings our knowledge."

"Who else do you hide, Yce?" Ilerion asked, positive the news had not been carried on the western winds.

"Not one you will care to see. But I must warn you that your personal disputes may not be settled here." Yce threw back his head and laughed. "Come, your face shows your suspicious nature, Ilerion. Place your woman by the fire."

Ilerion laid the still unconscious Arcinaë on a pallet of furs and stood to embrace Tresa, mate of Yce.

"You only grow warmer, Lord Ilerion," the Algorian chieftain's mate said by way of compliment. "Warmth is the greatest treasure and it is good you share yours with us. This is the Damselfly?"

"Aye, beaten, butchered and left for dead. I fear not much remains of her. She has returned to madness over the death of Ananta the healer."

"Shall I teach her how to make a man kneel?" Tresa asked, her eyes sparkling.

"As long as I am not the sacrificial victim, it could do no harm. She has gained strength and I have begun instruction with the staff and dagger, but she still has no confidence."

"Lord Ilerion?" called a deep voice filled with disbelief.

"Edric? Edric of Baene?" Ilerion answered, laughing. "Yce said there was someone here I would not be pleased to see, but I never imagined it to be you. It has been long, my friend." Ilerion clasped the tall, heavy soldier to him in a warm embrace.

"No wars have called us. I see that you have brought that fine steed. I challenge you to a duel if you will grant him as the prize. I can always use a good warhorse. Why is it you hide among the Algorians? I thought you collected bounty for Lazaro," Edric said.

"I fear that soon Lazaro's bounties will include Nilus and me. We spend the winter training a woman. She is not safe beyond the frozen wastes. Yce has already cautioned me against challenges while we are here. He still recalls the last joust beneath the ice," Ilerion said with a chuckle. "It would do you no good to win Caval, for he would merely refuse to carry you. And you, Edric?—from whom do you hide?"

"I ran afoul of Lazaro's hunters. Found them torturing field sprites. Catching them and bagging them, then burning them for sport. The White Laws no longer stand, Ilerion. Not for Lazaro. And the crown does not care."

"I stand for the law, Edric, and at the thaw I intend to mete out a bit of justice on behalf of the innocent. I would welcome your sword."

"You have it, Ilerion. Always you have had it."

"Come, there is tea," Tresa called from the fireside.

Tresa poured a cup of fire-tea and handed it to Ilerion. "She wakes, though she does not see." She pointed to the bundle of furs where Arcinaë rested, her eyes open but glazed and unfocused.

Taking the tea, Ilerion knelt next to Arcinaë and lifted her to a sitting position. She offered no resistance, nor did she acknowledge him.

"I am sorry for the loss of Ananta. I should have foreseen their treachery."

"Nay," Arcinaë spoke sharply, now looking with awareness into Ilerion's eyes, "it is no fault of yours, but the evil of those who seek me. I must try harder to learn and you must try harder to teach me. Nilus says you alone can defeat six armed men. If you can teach me to defeat one, I will be ready to hunt them."

"Drink this." Ilerion raised the spicy tea to her lips. "It is made of the fire fern. Hot both to the tongue and to the mind. You will sleep and awake refreshed. Nilus and I will unpack the supplies and make arrangements for our rooms. The woman over there," he said, pointing to Tresa, "will watch over you as you rest. She is called Tresa."

"What is this place?" Arcinaë asked, sipping the fiery tea.

"We are beneath the ice of the Mountains of Algor among a tribe of men who still serve the laws of which we have spoken. Yce, the chieftain, is an old and trusted friend. Rest, Arcinaë. Rest and regain your strength. We will remain here until the thaw. We will both try harder to make you strong."

Tresa watched Arcinaë's eyes follow Ilerion until she could no longer see him.

"He is a noble man. One of great courage," Tresa said.

"He saved my life, though many times I have wished he had not," Arcinaë answered. "How is it you know him?"

"He was once lost and we showed him the way. He has never forgotten."

Arcinaë felt her eyes grow heavy and whispered, "The tea?"

"Will repair your soul. Ilerion does not believe that the wind speaks, but it does. I shall help you listen to its words."

"What foolishness do you speak, Tresa?" Yce asked at her side.

"I will help this woman with the power of the wind. It is not foolishness, husband. It will take a strong woman to lead her. Ilerion can teach her weapons, but he cannot give her back her sense of self. Only a strong woman can do that, and I am a strong woman."

Kissing his wife's soft mouth, Yce agreed, "Yes, you are a strong woman, Tresa."

Arcinaë awoke to the sound of deep male voices laughing. Her heart began to race and her limbs trembled.

"You are safe," Tresa said, brushing Arcinaë's hair away from her face. "They plan to hunt the waterbear; their laughter is to show they have no fear."

"I find their laughter frightening," Arcinaë admitted.

"You may someday come to find it a comforting sound, as I have. Ilerion has called you part of a legend. Are you familiar with the tale of the halflings?"

Arcinaë looked bewildered, "I am Arcin—"

"Aye, but perhaps you are also to be a part of the legend. In the lore of humans, there is the tale of halfling women born of enchantment and Man. These are women who will rise to lead the race of Man, saving the enlightened world from destruction by a dark enemy of overwhelming strength. Perhaps there is some small part of the legend in you, Arcinaë."

Words of the Wind

Tresa stood before Ilerion, a small crossbow in her hand. "She must see death. I shall take her with the women to hunt the wombe. They are small and hold no threat and remain still in the snow for long periods of time, making them easy targets."

Seeing the doubt in Ilerion's eyes she continued, "You are a great warrior and can teach the skill of the sword, but you cannot give back what was taken from her. Only a woman can show her the way. The western winds will soothe her shattered soul. The words of the wind are powerful, Ilerion." She held up her hand to stop his words of contradiction. "I know that you have never heard them, but that does not mean they do not speak to others."

With a deep sigh, Ilerion said, "Perhaps it will be good for her to spend time with women."

"Not just spend time with them, Hunter, become one with them. I shall listen for words of the Sylph on the winds," Tresa added.

"How do you know of the Sylph? The winds told you?" Ilerion asked, his frown showing his uneasiness.

"How else could I have known?" Tresa walked away without waiting for his reply.

⚜

Under Tresa's watchful gaze, Arcinaë fumbled with the bowstring.

"Do not rush. Speed will come with practice."

Sighing in frustration, Arcinaë finally got the bowstring stretched taut across the bow, the bolt lying ready in its chamber. The small target sat a dragon length before her, about the size of a man's head.

"What is that supposed to represent?" she asked Tresa.

"It will be a wombe when you hunt with us. It is a small, flightless, fur-covered bird that sacrifices itself in the winter so that my people will not starve."

"Sacrifices itself? You mean you kill it and eat it?" Arcinaë gulped as she sought to control her rising bile.

"We accept their sacrifice. It would be disrespectful to refuse them," Tresa said.

"What makes you think they want you to kill them?"

"The wind brought their words. In the warmth of the summer, no human can catch the wombe because they are so very swift and joyous. But in the winter, when life becomes difficult and their own food becomes scarce, they welcome the hunter's bolt in preference to the long painful death of starvation. You will see, Arcinaë," Tresa explained.

"I do not eat the flesh of others."

"You need not eat them. Simply send the bolt to accept their sacrifice. Now, send the bolt into the wombe, Arcinaë."

Arcinaë raised the crossbow, seeking the target above it, but Tresa's sudden touch caused her to look up.

"You have the gift of far sight?"

"Aye, all enchanted folk do."

"It is a strong advantage against the men you seek."

With a grim smile, Arcinaë returned her eyes to the target and let the bolt fly. It struck the wombe-shaped figure squarely in the ring that marked the heart.

"I need an advantage," Arcinaë whispered.

The chatter of the women was lively as they gathered for the hunt, and Arcinaë listened as they spoke of children and husbands, cooking, dancing and weddings and discussed the men's waterbear hunt and the wombe.

Noticing that she was having difficulty with the laces of her densely furred cloak, a tiny, aged woman approached Arcinaë.

"Around," the woman stated, gesturing for Arcinaë to remove the cloak. "While the fur is beautiful, it is not to be shown. Place the furred side against your body to keep you warm, then the laces will make sense."

Seeing Arcinaë's look of embarrassment, the woman laughed. "How can one who has come from the warmlands be expected to know? I am Koiy, mother of Tresa."

"It seems I know nothing," Arcinaë apologized.

"Tresa says you are wise and kind and will one day lead Grimmoirë and mother the halflings. I believe you know much more than nothing."

"I was taught to be kind, but I am no longer fit to rule and I doubt I shall live long enough to grow wise. I love no man and no man loves me. It is unlikely that I shall bear young."

"Why do you say this? That you are no longer fit to rule or find love. Because men tortured you? Took you against your will? Cut and burned your wings? None of these matter. It does not make you any less a Damselfly or a sovereign. You are uncertain and filled with self-pity like Ilerion. It is these emotions that make both of you unfit to lead." Koiy's voice held disappointment.

Arcinaë felt the heat of color rise to her cheeks. "You do not know," she whispered, feeling her heart constrict at the memories.

"Nay, perhaps I do not. I never had wings. But all the rest is what comes to women with war. Fathers and husbands die, and women are beaten and violated because they are weak, but we do not give up. If we did the world would be barren. Listen to the words of the wind, Arcinaë. Let them guide you."

"I do not hear words in the wind," Arcinaë said, her voice choking as hot tears flooded her eyes and burnt her cheeks in the cold air.

"You soon will. Just listen," Koiy promised as she walked away.

Leading Arcinaë up the pass, Tresa told her, "Our tribe was once decimated by hunters, much the same as yours. They came while the men were away. Only a dozen women survived the slaughter. My mother was one of them. It is the strength of those women that made it possible for the Algorians to grow strong again. Do not give up, Arcinaë of Grimmoirë. Now, come. Let us accept the gift of the wombe."

Outside Tresa pushed Arcinaë down among the hummocks. "This is your place. When the wombe come to you, mercifully accept their lives."

"I do not think that I can kill them," Arcinaë said.

"Then they will suffer greatly through a long cruel death," Tresa shrugged. "This is your place."

Arcinaë lay down on the frozen ground as she saw the others do and lifted the crossbow before her, balancing it on the low hummock. There were no wombe to be seen. In fact, there was nothing visible save the women, the whiteness that blanketed the world around them, and the small snowflakes, lifted by the wind, that floated against the darkness.

As she rested on the snow, Arcinaë felt herself grow sleepy in the dark silence and the warmth of her furs. Closing her eyes, she listened to the wind, thinking of Koiy's words. "Uncertainty and self-pity make you unfit to lead." She had spoken of Ilerion as well as Arcinaë. Ilerion was not weak. He could defeat six armed men without aid. Six men! Arcinaë's eyes closed and she tried to imagine him fighting six men. It was not his image she saw but her own. She stood with a sword in one hand and a dagger in the other. Men surrounded her, laughing and taunting as they tried to touch her. She spun in circles, trying to keep them all in sight, but in the end she was dragged to the ground, disarmed, and the violation came again and again. She wept softly, feeling more the pain of defeat than the pain of her defilement. "I will kill you all," she murmured.

Opening her eyes, she saw the small, furred bird crouched before her. Its bright black eyes bored into hers, the wings hung loose and it looked very cold. "Mercifully accept their lives," she heard Tresa's voice.

She allowed her eyes to seek its heart and nocked the bolt in her crossbow. "I accept your gift," she whispered, releasing the bolt and watching it strike the wombe's heart.

By the end of the hunt Arcinaë had accepted the lives of seven wombe. She gathered their small bodies and placed them inside her cloak to keep them safe. She looked for the other women and saw them far ahead, moving back toward the entrance to the cavern. Striking out after them, she heard a low voice call to her. There was no sense of its gender, and the voice carried a thin, slight whistle.

"Arcinaë of Grimmoirë, do not fail."

"Where are you?" Arcinaë asked as she looked about her for the speaker.

"I am everywhere, for I am the wind," the voice answered. "I will be a salve to your soul and clear the way before you that you might accomplish your task. The wombe thank you for your mercy." A sudden tendril of air caressed Arcinaë's cheek before the wind pulled away.

"Arcinaë!" Ilerion's voice cracked in the stillness.

"Aye," she called, hurrying forward to meet him. "I have been merciful and accepted the lives of the small wombe, saving them from the long cruel death of starvation." Drawing the wombe from her cloak, she handed them to him. "And the wind has spoken my name."

She entered the cavern ahead of him, her back straight and her head held high. "Tresa has tainted you with her madness," he muttered, "but if madness and the words of the wind can make you strong, they are acceptable."

⬩⊱❀⊰⬩

"She killed the wombe," Ilerion said.

"She has taken life and discovered it is not always evil. Justice will be hers, Ilerion; it is only a matter of time," Tresa explained. "She will grow strong in spirit as the wind speaks and the winter passes. Prepare her sword arm in the time that you are allowed. Did you know that she has the gift of far sight?"

"Aye, but I have never seen her use it."

"She used it to sight the distance to the practice wombe and to hit her mark on the hunt. Each kill was struck in the heart, mercifully done indeed," Tresa said with approval.

The Sword

Ilerion demanded that Arcinaë should practice daily with the staff and dagger. They ran the frozen ridgelines and low-lying mountains just beyond the cavern. Each fortnight they ran up the pass to check the snow levels and look for evidence of Lazaro's hunters.

Finally, he told her she was ready for the sword.

"I brought a woman's sword from the city. It is old and tarnished, but will serve for your practice. Yce has his sword maker readying another; it will be finished by the time you are competent to use it.

Pulling the sword from its scabbard, he pressed Arcinaë's hand around its hilt. "While the staff and the dagger have other uses, the sword is for naught but to kill a man."

Her fingers tightened around the hilt, and she looked at him with directness. "Show me how to kill a man."

Ilerion stepped behind her, placing his arms around her, and grasped her arms at the wrist. "Two-handed is best for those without great strength, and a thrust to the gut will almost always ensure the death of your victim, though it may not be as immediate as a strike to the heart or the throat."

He pushed the sword out, away from her body, as if driving it into someone in front of her.

"We will begin with offensive strikes. Short, tight thrusts intended only to kill. Later we will work on defense."

His eyes never left her. His voice was constant, his correction sharp and forthright.

"We have no time for courtesy or softness. The time of your revenge approaches swiftly. When the snow melts, the hunters will come in hopes of catching us here before the Algorians move to the far fields where they spend the summer. We must be gone before they arrive."

"And Yce and Tresa? Will they be safe? Or will they die like Ananta?" Arcinaë asked.

"The Algorians are skilled fighters and can defend themselves against the hunters if need be, but it will be best if all are gone from this place before the summer thaw." His words were brusque.

"Keep the blade up. A lowered sword is an invitation to death. Forehand to the throat, backhand to the throat, thrust to the chest, thrust to the gut." The practice lasted hours until Arcinaë could no longer lift the sword. Then Ilerion made her watch him as, in turn, he battered Nilus, Yce and the one called Edric. When they would no longer agree to stand against him, the lesson was over and Arcinaë was allowed her rest.

⁂

Ilerion stood watching as Arcinaë slept. Her face was calm and peaceful. No night terrors had touched her this night.

"You grow fond of her." Tresa's voice was light.

"Nay, I grow more weary, but I cannot leave her. Soon I will join Cylacia; I have promised it." He closed his eyes, breathing deeply and thinking of his wife.

"You are a fool," Tresa whispered. "The winds speak that Cylacia's soul seeks its freedom but that you hold her, refusing to let her go. If all who lost a mate abandoned life as you have done, there would be only plants and beasts inhabiting Ælarggessæ. The death of one should not mean the death of the other, Ilerion. You live. Do not give up your life for a dead woman."

His eyes grew soft as he looked at the wife of his friend. "Too many have kept me here—Nilus, revenge against those responsible for my wife's death, men with bounties on their heads, and now a wingless Damselfly. I should have gone to Cylacia long ago. There is no life here." He touched his heart. "Without her, there is just the empty shell of an angry man."

Tresa added, "The winds say that you should seek the Sylph in

62

Révéré on Ædracmoræ. There is safety for her in Révéré and healing. The map to the mirror is on the wings of the buttermoth you hold."

"And I suppose the wind told you I hold the buttermoth?" he asked, lifting an eyebrow.

"Aye, you should really listen to the wind, Ilerion. It has much to teach you," she answered.

⁂

As the winter deepened, Arcinaë's practice intensified. The hours became longer and Ilerion's temper became shorter.

The force of his sword striking Arcinaë's was fierce, driving her back as she attempted to keep her sword before her as a shield. Again, Ilerion struck her, and again—driving her to her knees. With a forceful backhand, he drove the sword from her hands, causing her to fall backward to the cold earth of the arena. He placed his sword against her chest between her breasts.

"They will not kill you, Arcinaë, not right away. But it is not death that you fear, is it? It is life at the hands of madmen." He withdrew his sword and held out his hand, but she refused it, rolling away and slowly rising.

"Yes, I fear life, just as you do," she shouted, grabbing the sword from the ground and turning back toward him. "Why did you not allow me death? Why, when you know what will happen? Do you think I want a life like yours? No hearth, no love, nothing! At least you have people of your kind."

"So do you." He allowed the truth to fall between them.

"Nay, we were the last. Twenty, no more." She stared at him balefully.

"Trew, son of Astomi of Grimmoirë, remains hidden in Cheneis under the protection of Lord Iydaen."

"You knew? And you did not tell me?" She sank to the ground, growing pale at the possibility of another living Damselfly.

"I did not know until today," he said, placing his sword in its scabbard and lifting hers from the ground. "The wind told Tresa. Do you believe the wind, Arcinaë? If you do, perhaps you will not have to live a loveless, homeless life like mine."

He left her weeping on the ground.

"Why are you so cruel?" Arcinaë asked Ilerion when she met him for the next day's practice.

"I am not," he denied.

"Is it because you do not like what I am, or because I remind you of your wife?"

"You do not remind me of Cylacia. You are nothing like her," he snapped.

"I no longer need your help," Arcinaë murmured. "Edric of Baene has offered to instruct me with the sword if you will allow me the use of it."

Ilerion swung on her. "Why did he offer to help you?"

"Because he knows that you have become too cruel. May I use the sword?"

He tossed the sword to her, surprised when she caught it by the hilt and swung it quickly from forehand to backhand, as if testing it.

As he stormed back toward his quarters, he found Tresa leaning against his door.

"She is so much like Cylacia you cannot bear it."

"All the more reason I should avoid the entanglement. Do you forget that Cylacia is dead because of me? Because I took her from Grimmoirë and left her alone where the hunters could take her? I will take Arcinaë to Cheneis at the first thaw and then reunite her with her kind. Then it will be in Lord Iydaen's hands to keep them safe."

"Your frustration causes you to become spiteful and bad-tempered, Ilerion. Go to her and tell her you will teach her without your tantrums. If you do not, I will tell her that you fancy her." Tresa glared at him.

"You are impossible, woman! How does Yce stand your interfering nature?" Ilerion snarled.

"My beauty and ability to soothe his savagery more than make up for my faults." She grinned. "Now go apologize. Edric is loyal, but he is not nearly the swordsman you are."

Fuming, Ilerion headed back toward the arena, wondering just what he would say to Arcinaë. He had been cruel, deliberately so, and Tresa's words stung.

"Are you going to apologize?" Nilus asked, falling into step with Ilerion.

"Aye, I have been threatened by Tresa. She will make me look a fool if I do not resume my instruction without further 'tantrums' or spitefulness."

"You were a bit unkind. Arcinaë cried long into the night. Why must you be so unreasonable? You like her, I know you do," Nilus said.

"I cannot like her. It is not possible." Ilerion shook his head violently.

"Then what do you believe the problem to be?" Nilus asked.

"I fear for her. She will never be a warrior, and they will capture her and torment her…I fear for her."

"Then see that it does not happen. We are hunters; let us hunt them. We can leave her in the care of Lord Iydaen of Cheneis. Since you have told her another of her kind is there, she most likely will wish to meet him straightaway," Nilus encouraged.

Seeing the glowering face of his friend, he let out a loud laugh. "You are jealous. Of the male Damselfly, of a man you have never even met. It is far worse than I thought, Ilerion, far worse." Nilus laughed again.

"He is not a man and I am not jealous. I will take her to Cheneis as soon as it is sufficiently thawed to do so. I do not wish to speak of this again. Is that clear?"

Ilerion looked up to see Arcinaë sparring with Edric. Her form was perfect, just as she had been taught. Edric was gentle, careful not to overwhelm her with his strokes, allowing her to feel confident as an opponent.

"I really am a hateful bastard," Ilerion sighed, stepping into the arena and shouting at Edric.

"Get out! You cosset my student and make her weak. Arcinaë, get your sword up." Seeing Edric's grin, Ilerion snarled even more viciously, "And do not come back here undermining her training, or I shall be forced to deal more harshly with you."

Edric and Nilus departed, leaving Arcinaë standing alone with her sword drawn ready to defend against Ilerion's anger.

"You cannot hurt me," she said, lifting her chin and staring at him. "I will not let your words hurt me again."

He lowered his eyes and looked away in shame.

"I am sorry. You were right. You remind me very much of my wife, and I fear for you. It has left me rather…uneasy. I do not like the feeling and I have taken it out on you. I am truly sorry, Arcinaë. I would like to resume your training without further incidents."

"Further incidents?"

"Aye, further episodes of ungentlemanly behavior. I promise I shall keep my anger in control."

"I do not understand your anger," Arcinaë said. "I thought you were becoming my friend, as well as my teacher. Was I wrong?" Her eyes glistened with hurt.

"Nay, you are not wrong." He held out his large calloused hand and accepted her small soft one. "You are not wrong."

"Now, lift the sword and defend against me." Seeing her doubt, he added, "I will let you win."

The following morning as Ilerion watched, Arcinaë worked the staff. She whirled and struck the leather hunter across the throat, then quickly across the groin as she had been instructed. The next stroke was across the small of the back. Had the leather hunter been a man, he would have been down.

"Now the dagger," Ilerion called, pleased at how quickly she made the transition from the staff to the dagger. With the dagger, she repeated the strokes of the staff, leaving trails of boar's blood flowing over the hard-packed earth of the arena.

"Nilus, draw your sword and prepare to defend yourself against her," Ilerion shouted to his friend. "Arcinaë, come here."

She sheathed the dagger and stepped before him, waiting for his instructions.

He lifted a long, narrow cloth bag from the ground at his feet and opened the drawstring. From it he drew a sword. The blade was golden and bore the mark of a dragon's talon. The hilt was slender, made for a woman's hands, and tightly covered with flat woven braid. The guard was designed of heavy filigree, replicating the lacy wing pattern of the Damselfly. Holding it within the palms of his outstretched hands, he offered it to her. "For you."

Arcinaë looked up at him, not touching the sword. "Am I competent enough to accept it?"

"Aye, now go show Nilus how competent you are."

Accepting the sword, she curled her hands around its hilt, turning it and feeling its balance. It was heavier than the older sword she had practiced with for so long, and she knew it would strike more powerfully because of it. It also provided an additional hand's length, giving her the ability to reach her opponent from further away.

"It is beautiful," she whispered.

"It is meant to kill a man. The dead will not care anything for its beauty," Ilerion reminded.

With a nod, Arcinaë turned to face Nilus.

He beckoned her forward, teasing her with the tip of his sword. As Ilerion had taught, she avoided his eyes and, instead, watched the muscles of his mouth and forearm, awaiting the tenseness that would indicate his intent to strike.

Nilus brought a strong forehand against her, and she nimbly blocked it with a high backhand, whirling away and returning with a series of forehand strokes that locked Nilus's blade and caused the cold metal to slide to the hilt. Pushing off, Nilus swung low in an attempt to catch her off balance, but Arcinaë's blade was waiting, sweeping under his and forcing it away. Her strong thrust missed by inches, and she saw his eyebrows raise in surprise.

"You would cut me?" Nilus shouted.

"Aye, it is what I have been taught to do."

"Then I shall be more careful," he said, shaking his head.

She swept the blade across, causing him to duck away to avoid it. He came back with an upward thrust, blocked and swept away by her ready backhand.

She watched Nilus back away, taking time to catch his breath. "Remember, I am a short, stout man and tire easily," he called, snapping forward and locking his blade against her challenge.

"Do you concede?" she asked through gritted teeth.

"Nay, I am a warrior, you will have to kill me," he responded with a grin.

"Very well," she answered.

She slammed into him, forcing him back in surprise and dropping him to one knee, as her fierce overhand stroke drove his sword up in defense of himself.

"Edric," she heard Ilerion call behind her, "help Nilus."

Arcinaë felt her heart hammering against her ribs as she backed away in order to keep them both in front of her. As she had seen in her vision, she drew her dagger from the sheath at her waist. Not six men, but two. She would not allow them to knock her to the ground.

Ilerion watched in solemn silence. He could feel her fear and knew she no longer considered this practice. As her sword thrust out toward Edric, her dagger blade swept out less than a thumb's width from Nilus's gut. Edric circled around her, causing Arcinaë to swing about to face him, her dagger held behind her slashing at the unseen threat posed by Nilus. Suddenly her boot struck out, catching Edric behind his knee and sending him to the ground. She stomped on his sword hand, kicking the blade away, as he screamed and released it. Ilerion saw the dagger flip in her hand, ready to throw, and rushed her from behind, grabbing her arm and causing the dagger to land in the earth at Edric's feet. Looking down, Ilerion found her sword at his heart.

A slow grin spread over his face and he asked, "Do you seek to stain your new blade with my blood?"

"Nay, I seek the blood of others," she said, allowing the blade to drop.

"The eastern passage thaws. We will leave at first light for Cheneis," Ilerion called, backing away and bowing to Arcinaë.

"Nay!" she called after him, "We go to Lamaas."

Returning, he took her hand. "Trew awaits you at Cheneis. Do you not wish to at least meet him before you die?"

He saw her eyes cloud and knew she thought of her losses.

"You are no less Damselfly, Arcinaë."

She swallowed hard and nodded. "Cheneis, and then Lamaas."

⁂

"You have no intention of taking her to Lamaas, do you?" Nilus asked, as they readied their packs.

"Nay, none at all. I will keep Arcinaë safe, even if she has to be bound in the dungeons of Lord Iydaen's castle," Ilerion admitted.

"She will see it as deceit and believe you a man of no honor."

"It cannot be helped. It is better that she finds me deficient than that I find her dead," Ilerion said, becoming silent at Arcinaë's arrival.

Caval rumbled his deep pleasure as Arcinaë scratched the stallion's withers and soothed him with her voice.

"You have won his heart," Ilerion said.

"He has the heart of a hero. Integrity, verity, temperance and stability are held within his great heart, but he hides them beneath a cloud of grimness. He misses the mare," Arcinaë said, avoiding Ilerion's eyes.

"Aye, his mare rests with the farrier Dompet near the castle in Baene. He shall return to her when I no longer require his service."

Sighing, Arcinaë lifted her pack and mounted the small gray gelding that had carried her from Baene to Algor. "It is easier for the geldings," she stated.

"Aye, but I do not believe Caval would choose to give up his maleness just to relieve occasional frustration," Nilus called from behind the packhorse.

"Nay, I do not believe he would," Ilerion agreed, staring hard at Arcinaë and wondering if she had been talking to Tresa.

Edric laughed heartily from his position in the rafters above them. Tossing down a bale of hay, he called, "Though they share the same complaint, Caval is even-tempered compared to his master."

"Secure the bale and follow! We will be headed east toward the river passage."

Leaping to Caval, Ilerion led Arcinaë out of Algor toward the safety of Cheneis. Behind them the Algorians abandoned the cavern and headed for the safety of the high grasslands to the north.

Chapter 6: Cheneis

The warmth of the spring thaw caused the river levels to rise, bringing the constant sound of dripping water and cracking ice. The five horses trotted briskly, the iron cleats of their shoes giving them a secure footing on the increasingly muddy trails. Camps were cold and damp, for Ilerion insisted that no hint of firelight be visible, nor any whiff of smoke drift on the winds. By returning along the more arduous and lengthy eastern route, they would remain ahead of Lazaro's hunters who, most likely, would track the Algorians as they moved northward, expecting Ilerion and his companions to remain in the safety of the larger, more battle-ready group. Yce would create a slide on the trail, blocking the way of their enemies into the summer hunting grounds and sending them back to Lazaro with word of their failure.

Drenched from the heavy spring rains that still carried the chill of winter, Ilerion and his companions left the frozen north and entered the kingdom of Cheneis. Their woolen cloaks were sodden and they were cold, wet and miserable. At a settlement twelve leagues from Cheneis castle, Ilerion took pity on them and arranged rooms at the inn.

"Nilus will share your room," he told Arcinaë, as he removed Caval's tack and rubbed down the stallion's water-logged coat. "He will join you as soon as the horses are bedded down."

"I am hungry for a warming meal."

"Aye, and I will have him fetch you something from the tavern and bring it to your room. You cannot be seen here, Arcinaë," he reminded, seeing her glance toward the well-lit pub. "Use the back stairs to reach your room."

"And tea. A hot meal and tea," she said, heading for the inn.

"Follow her," Ilerion instructed Edric. "Nilus and I will see to the horses and bring supper to the rooms."

In the dim light of the tavern, Nilus and Ilerion made their way to the bar, ordering meat, bread and jam, ale and tea.

A familiar but unwelcome voice spoke from behind them. "I was told you had headed north in the company of a fugitive. And yet I find you here, sitting in a tavern."

Ilerion swung around to meet the eyes of Lazaro's hunter, Leuc.

"What brings you here, Leuc?" Ilerion asked, sipping his ale as he searched the crowd for others.

"I seek a fugitive. A beast, one called a Damselfly. Disgusting creatures—this one is wanted for murder, the murder of a healer called Ananta. I have heard the beast travels in the company of two men, you and Nilus. Lazaro thought perhaps you had forgotten the lesson you were taught about keeping beasts as companions."

Ilerion felt his fists clench but forced himself to relax. "Obviously you are wrong. Nilus and I still track the woman accused of murdering Lord Brytwaer. We merely stopped here for a hot meal and some ale to soothe the aches of the day."

"Why would a Damselfly who can simply fly away seek the protection of men?" Nilus asked.

"This one's wings were cut as punishment for an earlier offense. It butchered the healer rather messily. The bounty is five hundred in gold if you bring it in dead. There is no bounty on it alive," Leuc said.

"Just what was the earlier offense?"

"It lived," Leuc said with a laugh.

"Male or female?" asked Ilerion.

"Female, a rather tasty female," Leuc replied, "for a beast."

"You have seen it?"

"Aye, Ilerion, I have seen it up close," Leuc sneered.

Gathering the meal set before them by the bar wench, Ilerion explained their need for haste.

"We hope to be in Cheneis by noon tomorrow. I heard the woman bountied for the murder of Lord Brytwaer was seen there only yesterday."

"I shall let Lord Lazaro know that I have seen you."

"He will follow, and he will not be alone," Nilus muttered.

"Aye, and I will kill him and any in his company. Take the meal and go to her room. Do not tell her. I will meet you there when it is done."

Ilerion waited until Nilus entered Arcinaë's room before slipping down the shadowed stairway to the back of the inn. Drawing his dagger and sword, he crouched and waited for the men he knew would come.

To keep himself alert, Illerion thought of Cylacia's death and Arcinaë's beaten and brutalized body. He heard the soft scrape of boot leather on stone long before the hunters drew close. Rising slowly to avoid making any sound that might alert them to his presence, he stood in the darkness listening as the telltale sounds of their approach neared. As the first hunter stepped within reach, Ilerion slammed his elbow into the man's throat, silencing him with a crushed windpipe. The second received a sword to the gut, as Ilerion swept his boot around to break the knee of the third. The fourth was Leuc who paused, then suddenly turned to flee. Ilerion heard his soft exhalation with satisfaction as he drove the blade of his dagger into the small of the man's back. Returning to each hunter, Ilerion checked for life signs, finding them in only the third man and Leuc.

Squatting next to the man with the broken knee, Ilerion placed his dagger beneath his chin and asked, "Were you with him in Grimmoirë?" He pointed to Leuc.

"Nay, I do not hunt defenseless beasts or women. Leuc and six others went to Grimmoirë. Lazaro wanted the Damselflies dead, all of them. One escaped; he seeks her now. It is said you have her and keep her safe."

Ignoring the man's last remark, Ilerion warned, "You only live today because you are innocent of Leuc's crimes. If you track me or hunt the Damselfly, I will see you dead."

Hearing Leuc moan, Ilerion went to his side. A great pool of blood lay beneath the fallen hunter, growing larger as he attempted to rise.

"You have a death wound, Leuc, there is no healing for it," Ilerion said.

Blood bubbled from Leuc's lips as he spoke. "I butchered the sow, Ilerion. Cut the disgusting wings from her back as her father watched. Then I gutted him. I should have gutted her, too, but I wanted one last…"

Leuc's head flew back as Ilerion grabbed his hair and drew the dagger across his throat to silence his filthy words. "You should have stayed in Lamaas," Ilerion whispered, wiping the blade of his dagger across Leuc's shirt. Then he went to get Arcinaë.

"I need you to…," Ilerion began, "I need you to tell me if this is the man who took your wings."

Arcinaë's eyes widened at the sight of all the blood. Three men lay dead, but only one caused her face to pale. She dropped to her knees, gagging and vomiting up the night's meager supper. "He…he…"

"Aye, he told me that he did, but I wanted to be sure," Ilerion said, scooping her up and wiping her mouth with his hand.

He carried her to her room and left her in Nilus's care, whispering as he went out the door, "Give her the wizard's potion. Let her sleep this night without terror."

As Nilus poured water into the basin, he kept up a running conversation for Arcinaë.

"See, I told you he was good. That may have only been four men, but all of them were hunters. You will feel much better when you have bathed your face and neck with cool water, and I have tea for you as well."

Nilus looked back over his shoulder and saw her face crumple as she was once again overcome with sorrow.

"Here," he said, handing her the cool cloth, but she merely held it and wept.

Overwhelmed, Nilus went to the wall and pounded against it, shouting, "Ilerion! Get your wicked heart over here."

The door flew open. Ilerion stood with his sword drawn, eyes afire with intent to kill. Seeing no threat, he sheathed the sword and looked questioningly at Nilus.

"Here is the bottle, and there is the woman. You care for her." Nilus shoved the bottle into Ilerion's hands and stormed out of the room, slamming the door after him.

Ilerion gently pried the damp cloth from Arcinaë's fingers and began to bathe her face, lifting her heavy braid to lay it against the back of her neck.

"Do not cry. He is dead and cannot do you any harm," Ilerion said. He lifted Arcinaë's chin, forcing her to look at him. "He was an evil man, Arcinaë, a very evil man. Not repentant, even at the moment of his death. Do not weep for him."

"I do not weep for him." Her voice was muffled and her body shuddered with a deep sigh. "Why do they hate me so? I have never harmed any of them."

"They do not hate you. They fear the ancient legends that tell of powerful halflings born of a Damselfly's enchantment and man, and they are weak men who feed on the terror and pain of others. By taking the lives of those who cannot defend themselves, they feel stronger. You were defenseless against them, Arcinaë. Now you are not. You will no longer lie down weeping and allow evil men to have their way. You will fight back!"

"How can you know that?" she asked.

"I saw you fight Edric and Nilus. You would have killed them both, rather than allow them to take your weapons and knock you to the ground. You have become strong," Ilerion said truthfully. "Far stronger than I expected."

"You will abandon me in Cheneis," she said, looking up at him. "I know that you will. I heard you say it."

"I do not wish to abandon you. I wish only to see you safe. If Lord Iydaen and the Damselfly Trew can protect you, you should remain with them. Nilus, Edric and I will hunt the hunters who were at Grimmoirë."

"Trew cannot protect me. He does not fight," she whispered.

"You know him?"

"Of course, I know him. He sought my hand, but my father would not allow it. He found him weak, even for a Damselfly. Trew must have known the hunters were coming—that is why he fled Grimmoirë."

"Still, he is the only one of your kind left. You must do what you can to live, Arcinaë."

"There is no hope of survival for the Damselfly, if there are only two. There was no hope when there were twenty. Is what has happened not bad enough? Must I accept a mate I do not love or respect? One who will not really want me?" Her eyes brimmed again. "You will not accept another mate and you have hundreds from whom to choose."

"What of your betrothed, the one who died? Did you love him?" Ilerion asked.

"No, but my father had chosen him and I respected his family. He was kind and strong; he upheld the laws of my people. I suppose I would have come to love him, if there had been the chance," Arcinaë sighed. "I know nothing of love."

"You will know it when it comes, Arcinaë. It crashes in like a giant wave upon the shore and whips your life to ribbons like a brutal wind. Its heat will sear your heart and burn the breath from you lungs. You cannot escape it," Ilerion whispered, remembering.

"This is what it was for you? What you felt for Cylacia?"

"Aye, love does not end, which is why the pain of loss is so great. Now, drink your tea and sleep. We will leave at daybreak for Cheneis."

"Promise you will not leave me there." She placed her hand on his heart. "Promise it."

"I promise I will not leave you if I feel you are in danger," he answered, gently lifting her hand from his chest and placing it in her lap. "Sleep, Arcinaë. I will watch over you."

As her eyes closed, Arcinaë dreamed of the crashing sea and searing heat that would be love.

⬥⬥⬥

Nipping at the rump of Arcinaë's gelding, Caval sent the gray racing ahead at full gallop to escape the stallion's powerful teeth.

"Not terribly chivalrous, my friend," Ilerion whispered to his mount, as he felt the great horse change leads and surge forward, neck outstretched in the hope of a second pinch.

Looking over her shoulder, Arcinaë frowned and urged the small gray forward at a dead run. Sweeping in and out among the trees, the smaller horse's agility gave him the edge. At the tree line, Arcinaë drew her mount in sharply, causing Ilerion to bring his stallion to a skidding halt to avoid crashing into her.

"The castle." She pointed at the gleaming white structure silhouetted against the dark horizon.

"Aye, home of Lord Iydaen of Cheneis. A good man to know," Ilerion said, leading the way forward across the open field.

At the sound of the first herald, Lord Iydaen came racing to meet them.

"He has gone! In the night—left without a word. I have never seen anyone so fearful," Iydaen called, pausing to examine Arcinaë closely.

"You are the Damselfly female?" he asked.

"Aye, Arcinaë of Grimmoirë," she said, tossing back the hood of her cloak that he might see her features better.

Reaching up to help her dismount, Iydaen continued, though with a little less urgency, "One of my soldiers brought him to me—Trew, son of Astomi of Grimmoirë. He was badly beaten, his wings torn and dragging. I called the healer, and the boy seemed to be doing well. Too well it seems, since he has gone without a word. My men search for him near the river in hopes of finding him before Lazaro's hunters cross his path again."

"Stay here," Ilerion shouted to Arcinaë. "We will find him and return him to you." Without waiting for her argument, he spun Caval and raced away, followed by Nilus and Edric.

Slapping away Lord Iydaen's restraining hand, Arcinaë grabbed the reins of the gray and leapt to the saddle, swinging the horse around and charging off in pursuit of the men. As she cleared the rise, Ilerion reached down from Caval and snatched her from the back of her horse, swinging her around in front of him.

"Have you suddenly discovered a talisman to keep you protected against your enemies? Or has your death wish returned?" His voice was laced with a scintilla of sarcasm. "It could just as easily have been Lazaro or his hunters who dragged you from your horse. Then where would you be?"

He felt the pressure of her dagger and looked down to see it against his gut. "You are my talisman," she answered, withdrawing the dagger. "And you are not Lazaro or his hunters, so I will seek Trew with you. It is my right," she added, swinging over to the back of the gelding.

"Nilus and Edric wait at the river," Ilerion said in a voice made deliberately harsh to conceal his concern.

The body lay chest-down in the mud. The pale face was turned to the side, eyes wide with the shock of death. Remnants of tattered wings drifted in the slowly ebbing current.

"It is as you suspected, Ilerion. His neck is not broken. I have found no evidence of injury. I would say he drowned," Nilus said, moving to stand and stare at Arcinaë. "You should not be here."

Ignoring him, Arcinaë slipped from her mount and knelt beside Trew's body. "Why did you not wait?"

Looking up at Ilerion, she said, "He would never have entered the water. Damselflies cannot swim. Someone from your 'safe' castle must have frightened him into running. He was either murdered or took his own life to avoid further pain. There is no safe place, Ilerion, not for him and not for me."

"Aye, there is. Réverē on Ædracmoræ. I have been told that unlike Grimmoirë, it is shielded from men. Only the enchanted may pass into its safety. You will go there."

"And what of my revenge?" she asked.

"There is no revenge for you, Arcinaë. At the first glimpse of revenge, you were on your knees in your own vomit. Let me deal with those who have wronged you. Let me bear the darkness on my soul." He pulled her to him, crushing her against his chest and whispered, "Do not make me find your body in the river. I beg you, do not. That is the stain I cannot bear, Arcinaë."

She pushed against him, nearly falling at his sudden release.

"I will not be cloistered in some foreign land, hidden among strangers and forgotten—a salve for your conscience. If you do not help me, I will hunt these men myself."

"We waste time." Nilus held Trew's body. "Whatever it is we are going to do, it should be soon. If Arcinaë is right and there is a threat within Cheneis, it will not be long before it seeks us out."

"What burial does he require?" Ilerion asked, glaring at Arcinaë.

"A pyre to release his soul," she snapped, glaring back at him.

"Bring him. It cannot be done here," Ilerion said, mounting Caval and swinging away from them. "We will take him to Grimmoirë on the way to Lamaas."

"Fear prevents its expression," Edric whispered at Arcinaë's shoulder, holding her mount's reins, "but he cares deeply for you."

Her smile was brittle and brief as she snatched the reins, throwing herself to the gelding's back to gallop after Ilerion.

"Nay, he sees me merely as a burden."

The Agreement

Five days' hard ride in tense silence brought them to the border of Grimmoirë. The land ahead was enveloped in dense fog and heavy rain, the Mountains of the Three Sisters appearing in the distance like floating islands amidst the swirling mist.

As surly as his mount, Ilerion drove them forward. Camps were cold and made more dismal under the mantle of his increasingly foul humor. He refused to speak to Arcinaë and only muttered curt orders to Nilus and Edric when necessary. Trew's body had begun to putrefy, and the stench was unbearable, lending more unpleasantness to the bleakness of their journey.

As they stopped to make camp at the base of the mountains, Ilerion leapt from Caval and dragged Arcinaë roughly from her mount. Seeing Nilus's look of warning, Ilerion snapped, "I need to talk to her and she needs to listen."

Nilus held up his hands in submission, watching Ilerion pull Arcinaë after him and toward the shelter of the trees. "This should be good," he assured Edric. "It is best we build a fire and ready a hot meal and medicinal tea, for one of them is likely to be bloodied, and I am no longer certain it will be Arcinaë."

"Do you trust me to keep you safe?" Ilerion's voice was sharp.

"I always have," Arcinaë answered, her eyes turned up to him.

"It is a slender thread on which to hang your life," he said, his voice choked with emotion and rubbing his face as if he wished to erase it. "What if I cannot keep you safe? What if you are taken?"

"Then I will be taken, but at least I will have tried. Do you not see, Ilerion? There is nothing else. Trew is nothing but rotting flesh, not even fit for what is left of me. When we numbered twenty, my father had hope for the Damselfly through the path of diluted blood. But I am only one, and the race of Man is wicked. There can be no hope."

"What is this path of diluted blood?" Ilerion frowned.

"It no longer matters. I want only to see my people avenged. Then like you, I can die at peace. Another sovereign will be chosen—if there is need of one. Soon Grimmoirë will be an empty place. Already there is no sign of the enchanted. No Feie or faery, no dragon or gryphon. Not even the raucous harpies screech in the air above us. Men do not understand what the world will be like when we are gone, when there is no longer any trace of magick on Ælarggessæ."

"What is the path of diluted blood?" Ilerion asked again, ignoring her speech.

"My father thought," she said, averting her eyes, "that we could marry with humans. Bear children with them, diluting the blood of the Damselfly, but creating a new race of Halflings. He thought the new children would carry the best of both races, the gentle magick of the Damselfly and the stubborn strength of Men. He did not realize how much men hated us."

"This is why Cylacia was allowed to marry me," Ilerion stated.

"Aye, she was the first."

"She did not marry me because she loved me."

"That is not so, Ilerion. She was the first *because* she loved you. I saw her the day you were wed. It was my thirteenth summer, and I wanted nothing more than to be like her. She could not keep her feet on the ground, for the flutter of her wings was loud in the chamber where they prepared her for your union. She loved you fiercely, Ilerion. Do not ever doubt it." Arcinaë's voice was soft with the memory of Cylacia's joy.

"Five men," Ilerion said. "I will help you hunt and kill the five remaining men if you will promise to go to Réverē on Ædracmoræ when it is done. Will you promise this?"

"And you promise that you will not try to rid yourself of me until it is finished?" she asked.

"Aye, I give you my oath."

"Then I give you mine, Ilerion. I will go to Réverē when the last of them is dead." She held out her hand as she had seen men do to seal a pledge.

Taking her hand, he held it, his fingers feeling the pulse in her wrist as she felt his.

Returning to the glade, they found that Edric and Nilus had erected a bier and placed Trew's body on it. Arcinaë went to mourn her last remaining kinsman.

"It seemed a fitting place, the place where Man and Damselfly vowed the oath of revenge," Nilus said.

"Do you always eavesdrop, Nilus?" Ilerion scowled.

"I did not eavesdrop. Your voice carried, and Edric wanted a hot meal so what is a little more smoke?"

"Not very reverent," Ilerion gave him a warning look.

"Our camp lays half a league to the west, a small cavern there. Edric prepares the meal. I will leave you alone with Arcinaë to see Trew to his final reward," Nilus murmured. "And if you believe she will leave you, you are a fool indeed."

"She has given her oath. I do not believe she will break it. There was no evidence of deception in the beat of her heart," Ilerion replied quietly to be sure Arcinaë did not overhear. "We will join you when his soul is gone," he added.

Ilerion went to Arcinaë and handed her a torch, watching solemnly as she lit it and touched it to the dried grass beneath the funeral bier.

"May the stars hold your soul," she whispered, as the oily black smoke drifted toward the sky.

She looked up at Ilerion, knowing he recalled another bier and another soul. One he had called back, a soul that would be held beneath a small earthen mound until he set it free. She wanted to take his hand, but dared not touch him in his grief.

Chapter 7: Vengeance

They crossed into the kingdom of Wawne in search of information about the massacre at Grimmoirë. Populated with bands of malcontents and drifters united in their contempt for, and ill-will towards Lazaro and his hunters, it seemed a relatively safe place to begin.

With the heat of midsummer, Arcinaë had begun to look more human. She no longer carried the pale translucent skin of the Damselfly, for it now lay hidden beneath a deep tan. Still, Ilerion refused to take her with him when he and Nilus left camp and headed for the taverns in the city of Kleal.

"We cannot risk it. Stay with Edric. He will look after you in our absence. We should not be gone long. I will not abandon you, Arcinaë. Have I not promised it?" He waited for her nod.

Mounting Caval, he shouted to Edric, "Keep her safe. Do not leave her unattended. Not even for a moment."

Edric gave a brief wave of his hand to show that he had heard and continued hobbling the horses. When he could no longer hear the sound of Ilerion and Nilus's retreating mounts, he called to Arcinaë.

"Let us hunt a stag. It will give them something warm to fill their bellies with when they return." Seeing her grimace, he laughed. "You do not have to eat it, just come along and use your far sight to get me near."

"I still do not like it," she admitted, "but I will help you. I would not like Ilerion and Nilus to go hungry."

The stag Edric killed was large and heavy. One to be proud of he told Arcinaë, as he toted it back to their small camp at the edge of a small glen.

"I shall clean it, if you will go fetch some water while I do. It will spare you the sight of his bleeding," Edric said, pulling the bolt from the heart of the stag.

Shuddering and laughing at her own foolishness, Arcinaë replied, "I shall get water. I do not know why I never seem to grow used to the sight of butchering."

"Because you are a Damselfly, kind and gentle through and through," Edric answered with a smile. "None can ever take that from you, Arcinaë. Not ever."

She reached up and wiped a bit of blood from his cheek, giving a wink as she grabbed the pail and headed for the stream.

Kneeling at the small creek, Arcinaë took a moment to cool her cheeks with the fresh running water. Then, humming a melody from her childhood, she filled the pail and headed back to camp.

"Edric, I—" Arcinaë froze. She stared uncomprehendingly at the horrific scene before her.

Edric hung by his feet next to the stag he had been cleaning. Like the stag, he had been gutted, his entrails still steaming on the ground below his head.

Arcinaë dropped the pail and moved forward, shaking her head as if to dispel the nightmarish vision in front of her.

"Edric?" she whispered.

Rough hands grabbed her, pulling the dagger from her waist and the sword from her back. Spinning her around, the hunter laughed, "Well, if it isn't the precious daughter of the Damselfly!"

She stared at him, her mind still numbed by the image of Edric's butchered body.

"Name's Gaztin. I don't believe we were properly introduced last time." He pushed her hard, driving her to the ground.

"Make yourself comfortable; the others will be back soon. Then we can all celebrate your return. You'll like it, just like you did the last time. Celebrating with hunters—and get that braid out of your hair! We like you better when your hair is wild and free."

She gaped at the man in disbelief. He intended to take her against her will and he cared how she wore her hair? Her fingers touched a flat stone beside her, curling around it and pulling it toward her.

"I said get that braid out of your hair, you sow!" Gaztin shouted, leaning down to grab her hair.

With a scream of rage, she slammed the stone into the side of his head. He fell to his knees, clutching the bleeding wound. Over and over she struck him until she could no longer lift the weight of the stone.

Gagging at the sight of his bloodied head, Arcinaë dropped the stone and fell to the ground, retching violently. Curling into a ball, she lay on her side weeping as she clutched herself in a forlorn attempt to ease her grief.

At the sound of distant voices growing louder, she caught sight of her sword and dagger lying where the hunter had tossed them. Pulling herself together, she snatched them up and raced away from the direction of the approaching hunters.

Deep within the woods, Arcinaë collapsed at the base of a great tree, wrapping her arms around herself and shaking uncontrollably. She covered her mouth in an attempt to silence her sobs but found she could not draw sufficient breath. Pressing her face into the earth she sobbed noisily, her mind replaying the horror of Edric's butchered body, Gaztin's vile remarks, and her fury. She saw herself strike him, and felt his blood, sticky on her hands and arms. Rocking back and forth, Arcinaë made herself as small as possible and prayed the hunters would not find her.

She had killed a man.

She had *killed a man*!

At last, exhaustion and grief claimed her in an uneasy sleep.

A shout awoke her, sending her crawling quickly away.

"Noooooo!" she wailed, as hands lifted her. She reached for her dagger but it was missing. Closing her eyes tightly, she screamed again.

"Arcinaë, shhhhh, it is me," Ilerion whispered softly against her hair. "Are you hurt?"

Great sobs convulsed her body and she clung to him so tightly he could barely breathe. Sinking to the ground, he pulled her closer and shouted for Nilus.

"Nilus! I have found her!"

The sound of Nilus's heavy body crashing through the undergrowth announced his arrival. He dropped beside Ilerion, draping his cloak over Arcinaë.

"Is she harmed?"

"I do not think so. She is still clothed—they would not have dressed her."

"I killed him," Arcinaë sobbed.

"Who did you kill, Arcinaë. We found only Edric, and I do not believe you killed him," Ilerion said, brushing hair away from her face.

"The hunter. Gaztin. He said his name was Gaztin. He wanted me to let my hair loose before he…they…" She collapsed against Ilerion, gripping his shirt and weeping.

"I am going to lift you now. Then I am going to take you to the inn at Kleal. Do you understand me, Arcinaë?" Ilerion asked, attempting to rise from his awkward position. Shaking his head at his inability to do so, he started again. "I am going to give you to Nilus while I get to my feet. Do you understand, Arcinaë?"

The attempt to have Nilus take Arcinaë was futile, for she would not let go of Ilerion.

"Can you stand? For a moment? You can keep your arms around me while I rise."

Arcinaë became aware of his intention and allowed him to stand her before him, hanging on to his clothes as if she were afraid of falling. When Ilerion finally managed to rise, he lifted her again and carried her quickly to Caval. He mounted awkwardly, and the stallion turned to look at him before nuzzling Arcinaë's dangling legs.

"I have lost my dagger," she murmured against Ilerion's chest.

"Nay, I took it from you for fear you would kill me when I touched you. I have your sword as well. It was on the ground beside you."

❧❦

After making arrangements for two rooms on the ground floor and taking a pitcher of water from one, Nilus doused the torches in the hall,

86

signaling Ilerion when the passage was dark and clear of guests.

Ilerion tried to put Arcinaë on the bed, but she refused to release him, so he simply sat on it with his back against the wall, holding her in his arms. Her weeping had subsided to a series of small sobs, and he was finally able to offer her some warm tea laced with heavy ale and a great deal of honey.

Relaxed by the ale, her hands finally fell away. Ilerion gently laid her down, exhaling a deep sigh of relief as he drew the covers over her.

"I thought she was lost, Nilus. Gone. Taken. How she escaped after what was done to Edric I cannot imagine."

"I know," Nilus said as he placed a hand on Ilerion's shoulder. "You should tell her you care for her before it is too late."

"That is not possible. You know that is not possible. Do not speak of it again, Nilus."

"Ilerion, you are a fool. What do you intend to do? Just send her to Réverē and never see her again? Why?"

"Why? Because she will be with her own kind, and safe."

"She does not have a kind. We just held the funeral for the last of them… Well—you did!" Nilus reminded him, drawing a sour look in response.

"You know what I meant."

"Aye, I know what you mean and you are a fool. I have never seen a man more full of boar scat. There is no more to be said for it."

"I cannot keep her safe."

"But you could make her happy."

Nilus stood and opened the door between the rooms. "Sit here and watch her. Tell me again tomorrow you are going to send her away," he said as he walked into the next room and closed the door.

Sitting at the table, Ilerion laced his fingers together and tapped them lightly against his mouth. "I cannot love you, Arcinaë," he whispered to her sleeping form, "for I cannot keep you safe," all the while feeling within his heart the pounding of giant waves. Eventually he laid his head on the table and slept.

When he awoke, the sun blinded Ilerion with its brilliance. Shielding his eyes, he realized that although still on the bed, Arcinaë was propped up on one elbow and watching him.

"I killed a man."

"I know."

"I beat him to death with a stone. For what he had done to me and what he said he would do to me again. It had nothing to do with what he had done to the others."

"If you had not killed him, you would be dead or in Lazaro's dungeons with the other women who are used to satisfy the vile pleasures of his hunters. Do not regret Gaztin's death, Arcinaë. What he did to you, he did to others, and many did not live to seek revenge. You are their champion, Arcinaë, even though they are not here to tell you so."

A tap at the door brought Nilus with morning buns and jam. Ilerion stood, stretching the aching muscles of his back, and received a disgruntled look from Nilus.

"I had hoped she would make you see reason," Nilus hissed under his breath.

"Then your plan worked, for she did. I shall take her to Réverē as planned," Ilerion murmured softly, gazing at Arcinaë as she splashed water from the basin over her face.

An Oath of Protection

Anxious to be away from Lamaas, the hunter Evalio stood before Lord Lazaro. With the assistance of Ilerion and Nilus, the Damselfly remained alive, and Evalio intended to gain great favor for himself by returning their heads to Lazaro.

"There is no room for failure, Evalio. Those who have joined us must not see us as weak," Lazaro said. "I will begin to look a fool if my hunters cannot even capture and kill one defenseless Damselfly. Take the men you need to do the job—just get it done. Ilerion and Nilus have already killed Gaztin and Leuc. I want Ilerion alive. The others can be killed in the field and their heads brought to me. Bring Ilerion to me, and I will personally deal with his betrayal."

"Yes, my lord. Word comes that they have crossed into Halhmor to seek sanctuary with Lord Tondhere," Evalio said.

"Lord Tondhere is weak. He will not risk my wrath to protect a beast."

With a wave of his hand, Lazaro dismissed his hunter.

"Cethe, Colne!" Evalio called as he entered the hunters' barracks.

"Aye?" Colne asked, looking up from the blade he had sharpened.

"Lord Lazaro instructs me to capture the Damselfly. There is no need to involve any who were not present in Grimmoirë, for the one we seek travels only with Ilerion and Nilus—a hunter bound to the old codes and a fat man."

"You would do well not to underestimate Ilerion, Evalio," Cethe advised. "He lives with darkness by choice and those codes you disparage so glibly are the codes of nobility and gallantry. Ilerion is a formidable opponent. I have seen him take down six men under the rules of the tournament."

With a loud guffaw, Evalio spat back, "Within the rules of the tournament? He will find there are no rules when I come for him. Do you join me or not?"

"Aye, we seek Lord Lazaro's favor as you do, Evalio. Just do not get us killed by your lack of respect for Ilerion's skill," Colne answered.

"We shall take him as he sleeps. A blow to the head or a draught of tampered ale, for Lazaro wants him alive. The Damselfly can die slowly for the trouble she has caused. Tack up. We ride within the hour."

Looking thoughtful, Cethe's eyes followed Evalio. "It will be best if we have our own plan. Death follows the rash, young Evalio."

A curt nod from Colne indicated his agreement as he rose to ready his mount.

❧

In the keep of Castle Halhmor, Lord Tondhere gave Ilerion warning. "Lazaro sends Evalio for the Damselfly. Evalio is a lad who is not known for courtesy or caution, and it is his recklessness that will bring him death by your sword, Ilerion."

"It is Evalio's acceptance of Lazaro's wicked orders that brings my wrath, Tondhere, and naught else. Along with five others, led by Leuc of Lamaas, he razed the Damselfly settlement, butchering every last one. How can we not rise against such evil?"

Around the great table sat the leaders of three kingdoms: Elduuf of Twode, Reduald of Durover and Tondhere of Halhmor.

"Grimmoirë falls. Little by little it is stripped of the enchanted. Soon there will be nothing of magick left in all of Ælarggessæ. No dragon's flight, field sprite or gryphon; no Feie wizard, faery or Damselfly will grace this world. There will be no touch of enchantment in the hidden vales of childhood. We cannot allow Grimmoirë to fall simply because a few evil men fear what they do not understand. Will not one of you lead against Lazaro's sinful purge? Will you not accept the challenge, Reduald?" Ilerion asked them once again—exhorting the men to respond—"Or you, Elduuf?"

"Nay, we are not valiant, Ilerion, and Lazaro no longer wars against the enchanted alone. The kingdoms of Breden and Wawne have joined him in his desecration of Grimmoirë. Only Cheneis remains neutral. Unlike you, Ilerion, we are not great warriors. Our kingdoms hold farmers and merchants, not soldiers. Our leadership has always been secondary to yours, Ilerion, and the men of our garrisons would follow you into the great abyss if you asked it of them. Why do you not lead? We will stand with you if you choose to show the way. Unite us against Lazaro's strength," Reduald said, joined by a chorus of "ayes" from the others seated around him. "Let us be as we were in the old days, those days of the Code when we were united in battle against that which was injurious to Ælarggessæ."

Ilerion's laugh was bitter. "There is no Castle Baene, Reduald. It is gone, dust in the wind. Its soldiers scattered, serving as hunters in the service of Lazaro rather than see their families tortured and their lands burned. I cannot find blame with them. I would have done it to save my wife had Lazaro offered it."

"Ilerion, you are the kingdom of Baene; the condition of your castle has naught to do with it." Arcinaë's voice was soft behind them. "Have you forgotten that Edric died in your service?"

Ilerion spun around to face her. "I have not forgotten the name of any who has died in my service or because of my desire," he snapped.

"I will go to Révere. If you will give me your word that you will lead these men to save Grimmoirë, I will go now."

Ilerion stood and went to Arcinaë, holding out his hand to her. Slowly she accepted it, watching as his fingers came to rest on the life beat pulsing in her wrist.

"I do not seek to deceive you," she whispered, her heartbeat slow and steady.

Reaching out with his other hand, he held hers within his two. "I will finish it, Arcinaë, and seek each man who had a hand in the destruction of the Damselflies. I have given you my oath."

To the men at the table, Arcinaë spoke in the tone of a sovereign,

"The wind has spoken. In the days of our greatfather's fathers, the race of Men gave a sacred promise, a promise to grant Grimmoirë sovereignty and safety from the rule of Ælarggessæ. The promise has been broken, shattered by the evil of one man. The Damselflies are gone. Never again will their flight grace the soft breezes of Grimmoirë. But others wait. They are there, still hopeful and hidden within their eyries and caverns, waiting for the race of Man to intervene on their behalf. Always we have blessed your world with wisdom and magick, granted your wishes and kept your gold hidden. In return, you have protected us with your strength and honor through your vows. Together we gave the world balance, but alone neither Man nor Enchanted can stand. I have freed Lord Ilerion of his bond, lifted his vow of protection. He will lead your armies, thereby defeating our enemy and restoring Ælarggessæ's rich tradition of Man and magick."

"Then it is decided and the lines drawn? We will join forces and sweep down upon Lazaro and his supporters from the western borders of Lamaas, slipping through the Tangled Chasm, which still remains unguarded?" Elduuf asked.

"Your strategy stands, Elduuf, but I must see Arcinaë to Réverë on Ædracmoræ," Ilerion replied. "In my absence, draw your men together—only those willing to serve under the banner of the fallen kingdom of Baene. We will meet in the abandoned fortress at the northern end of the Chasm on my return. Send someone to collect the warhorses I have hidden with Dompet the Farrier. Have them shod with heavy iron."

"The legends speak of another sacred land beyond an ancient mirror, but no man has ever gone there. How do you intend to find it, Ilerion?" Lord Tondhere asked, his brow furrowed with doubt.

"It is a place we do not often tell humans about. A secret place, shielded against the treachery of wicked men," Arcinaë said. "The mirror that leads to Réverë is hidden in a cavern high in the mountains of Grimmoirë and protected by the Dragons of Fire. Ilerion already carries the map and, if he wishes, we can leave now."

"How did you know?" Ilerion asked. "Never mind." He held up his hand. "I know—the wind told you!"

"Nay, Tresa told me when we wintered with the Algorians,"

Arcinaë answered. "She also spoke of the Sylph and a woman called Cwen who may know where to find them."

"Then let us be off, for the sooner you are safely cloistered in Révéré the sooner we can stop Lazaro."

The leaders of the four kingdoms exchanged hand clasps of friendship and then proclaimed an oath of protection for Grimmoirë.

Separation

They left Castle Halhmor at dusk. The scent of the sea grew fainter as they urged their horses across the kingdom of Halhmor. Early autumn showers sent them searching for cover for the night, and the great hollowed trunk of an ancient braid tree was able to provide the protection they sought.

While boiling tea over a tiny flame, Nilus entertained the others with his sleight of hand, laughing when Arcinaë appeared nearly as accomplished as he.

"I have taught you too well, Damsel," he admitted, sweeping the golden orbs beneath his coat and handing Arcinaë and Ilerion cups of steaming tea laced with ale to "warm them."

"Perhaps in the new world I shall become a thief," Arcinaë said.

"Nay, you will become a councilor or high ambassador for the enchanted folk of Réverē," Nilus assured her.

"Do you believe I shall ever be able to return to Grimmoirë?" Arcinaë asked Ilerion.

"Aye, we will rid the world of Lazaro and those who serve him. Grimmoirë will be safe. Those who hunt you will pay for their wickedness with death. Then you can return home without fear," Ilerion promised. "I will send for you when it is safe."

⊰※⊱

Within the hollow tree Ilerion and the Damselfly lay side by side, their heads close together as they examined the map on the buttermoth's wing. Arcinaë tried to identify the locations marked.

"Here are the Mountains of the Three Sisters," Arcinaë said as she pointed to three peaks along the edge of the wing, "and this is where we will camp, beneath the Lake of Rhymes. It seems we must follow the paths to the other side of the water, exiting here, before making our way upwards to the second of the Three Sisters." She touched a brilliant yellow, red and orange flame shape. "This mark is the symbol for the Dragons of Fire. It is there we will find the mirror we seek."

"I shall miss you."

"What?" Arcinaë looked at him, suddenly aware that Ilerion was very close and very still.

"I shall miss you, Arcinaë of Grimmoirë," he whispered.

"And I, you. Who will help me with the sword?"

He laughed and drew back a bit. "The reason I am sending you to Réverë is so that you will not have to use the sword or dagger or staff. You are nobility, Arcinaë, destined to be a sovereign."

"I do not wish to be a sovereign. Not alone. I do not wish to be alone, Ilerion," she answered as she fought back tears. "And I will never give up the sword, never."

"More tea?" Nilus asked, the suddenness of his appearance causing them to jump.

Later, as Arcinaë drifted between wakefulness and sleep, she heard the deep sounds of their male laughter and smiled at the realization that it brought her comfort. Ilerion brought her comfort.

❧❦

By the end of the third day, the smoke-filled air of Grimmoirë was affecting their breathing, and they tied cloth about the lower half of their faces to keep the drifting ash from their lungs.

The bodies of tiny sprites and the slightly larger faeries littered the road. Some had been burned while others, stripped of their wings, were crushed beneath the boots of those who had been intent on destruction.

"Where are the dragons and the gryphons? Surely with their help, the enchanted could overcome this threat," Nilus asked.

"As the magick fades, the dragons and the gryphons retreat, awaiting the next calling by the enchanted. The dragons rest below the earth, and the gryphons have retreated to the Isle of Grave, drawing the mist around them so that they cannot be seen by men," Arcinaë said. "The Feie have gone. There is no glimmer of their magick. Was Fenris killed with Ananta?"

"Nay, I do not believe so. Rumor says he has gone to Réveré in search of support among the enchanted," Ilerion answered. "Look for him there. The world of Ædracmoræ is said to hold heavy magick and is ruled by a strong crown, Yávië of Aaradan, the Dragon Queen."

Pointing ahead, Arcinaë called, "The Lake of Rhymes lies beyond the village of the Kerleucans."

"You are loud," a cranky voice called from among the trees. "You will draw the hunters with your shouts. Go 'way. Get out!"

"Kerleucan?" Arcinaë called more softly.

"Aye, and what's it to you? A bunch of humans come to finish what the hunters began?"

"Nay, I am no human. And we do not come to harm you. I am Arcinaë of Grimmoirë, Damselfly, daughter of Aewicaen," she said, slipping from her mount and squatting to make herself shorter.

A small fur-covered man no more than seven hands tall stepped from the shadows, his arm extended toward the men who remained on horseback. "I shall smite you if you move," the Kerleucan growled, his long snowy beard quivering with fury. "Truly, you are Arcinaë?" his eyes shifted briefly to the kneeling woman. "Why do you travel upon the earth?"

"My wings were taken by the hunters nigh on two years ago. I travel with Lord Ilerion and his servant Nilus, for they have vowed to keep me safe and lead an army against Lazaro's hunters in order to protect what remains of Grimmoirë. Are you many?"

"Aye, most have fled to the kin on Réveré. Our village is a smoldering ruin, but the Kerleucan are sharp and spry and most fled without capture. The Feie and the wee folk who were not slaughtered have already gone. I wait for the return of my kinsman, and then we too shall pass through the mirror to safety. It is what you should do, milady."

Ilerion's voice brought a sudden brightness to the little man's finger tips and an array of sparkling light shot toward the man seated on the horse.

"Nay!" Arcinaë said sharply.

Startled, the Kerleucan recalled the magick that would have temporarily turned the man into an ass.

"I seek only to ask a question," Ilerion repeated.

"I do not speak with humans," the Kerleucan snapped, backing toward the safety of the trees. "And I advise you the same, Lady Arcinaë. Take yourself to Révere. Grimmoirë darkens with the loss of magick." With a flick of his bushy white tail, the Kerleucan disappeared into the woods.

"I must find the Feie," Arcinaë murmured, thinking aloud. "They are the only ones who can cast the magick of restoration. Even if you defeat Lord Lazaro, Grimmoirë will remain dark and without enchantment if it is not restored."

She raised her hand to grasp Ilerion's, drawing him near as he slid from his mount.

"I shall go on in the company of the Kerleucans. The lake is near and the Dragons of Fire will protect us. You must raise your army quickly, Ilerion. If I am ever to return home, you must defeat Lazaro and the kingdoms that stand with him. Go! You waste time guarding the last Damselfly." She pushed him away, swinging toward the woods that had swallowed the Kerleucan.

"Arcinaë…" Ilerion grabbed her arm and pulled her to him, kissing her quickly. "For providence and a touch of enchantment. No man should enter battle without the magick of the Damsel's kiss."

She stood with her fingers touching her lips, as if to hold the kiss in place, watching Ilerion and Nilus race away, followed by the riderless gray gelding. "I shall miss you, Ilerion of Baene," she whispered, running quickly into the trees where she had last seen the Kerleucan.

❦

"Is that written in the Code of Gallantry, Ilerion? That no man should enter battle without the Damsel's kiss?" Nilus asked, a grin tugging at the corners of his mouth. "For if it is, I do not recall it."

"Do you not believe that a man about to lead the army of a fallen house against an army of treacherous murders led by a powerful lord should have a touch of magick?"

"A touch of magick cannot hurt, and I believe, my friend, that you have needed that particular touch of magick since first you found Arcinaë. But you never listen to me, for I am just a short—"

"Stout, bald man," Ilerion finished for his friend.

Through the Mirror

"Come!" the Kerleucan hissed, grabbing Arcinaë's hand and pulling her along. "My kinsman waits at the Lake of Rhymes. What were you doing with the husband of Cylacia?"

"He saved me when the hunters left me to die amid my butchered kinsmen. I am the only surviving Damselfly."

"Nay, you are the surviving sovereign. Your predecessor is dead. When we reach Révere, you must call a council meeting for those of us who remain. Tell us what we will do now that our home has fallen beneath the feet of the humans."

"Kerleucan, I cannot. I am not prepared to rule, nor am I fit."

"You had best get prepared, for you are the sovereign." The Kerleucan was peevish. "It is not your choice. You bear the mark. You are the sovereign. I am Kintol. You may use my name. Now come—you move too slowly!"

They forced their way through dense underbrush at the edge of the Lake of Rhymes. It was filled with floating ash and bodies, a reminder that soon there would be nothing left of the beauty and enchantment that had been Grimmoirë.

Ducking under the low entrance of the underground labyrinth, they came face to face with the angry finger of another Kerleucan.

"Kintol! I nearly turned that woman into a wolverine. What are you doing with a human?"

"She is no human, Wad. She is the sovereign of Grimmoirë, and we are going to take her to Réverē before something else awful happens to her. She had her wings taken by the hunters nearly two years ago! She's been held by humans ever since."

"Kintol, the humans did not hold me. I traveled with them for safety. They protected me and taught me to use weapons," Arcinaë corrected.

"You mean you can use weapons?" Wad asked in amazement, his bushy brown tail wagging with excitement. "A sovereign of strength and beauty, just like in the legends, the human tale of the halfling woman—the legend of the halfling who raises an army of men and unites the worlds after defeating a Heteroclite ruler."

"It is what Lord Ilerion spoke of, the tale of a woman from their lore," Arcinaë recalled with a sigh. "I know nothing of any Heteroclites. I am not a warrior who can lead the people. I cannot even protect myself, though I did kill a man."

"You killed a man!" Kintol squealed. "No enchanted has ever killed a man. We have turned them into beasts, made them itch, given them boils and put them in deep sleeps, but not even the dragons have ever killed a man! It is against the laws of Ælarggessæ."

"Not when they try to kill you first! As sovereign, I shall change the law," Arcinaë said with passion.

"I told you she was the sovereign." Kintol winked at Wad. Lifting a torch from the wall, he lit it and handed it to Arcinaë before dropping to all fours and leading the way below the Lake of Rhymes toward the ancient mirror that would allow them access to Réverē.

As they ran through the long, narrow passages, Arcinaë was constantly aware of the dripping water from the lake above. She reminded the Kerleucans that should the water suddenly rush in, she could not swim.

"You need not worry my sovereign. If the lake rushes in, the ability to swim would not save you. It is too far to swim beneath the water without a breath of air," Wad explained.

"That is not very reassuring, Wad," Arcinaë said.

The Kerleucan looked up at her with one eye closed. "It was not meant to be. 'Tis merely an observation."

Her companions seemed quite amused by Arcinaë's discomfort,

and it was with a feeling of great relief that she made her exit on the far side of the lake.

"There!" Kintol shouted, pointing ahead. "The Three Sisters. The Hall of Mirrors lies beneath the second."

⁂

Her body bent and hands resting upon her knees, Arcinaë breathed in great gulps of air. The run up the steep slope leading to the Mountains of the Three Sisters had exhausted her.

"Ahead lies the entrance to the Hall of Mirrors. A fire dragon awaits our passing before shielding the mirror from the eyes of men. Come, my sovereign. Today you enter the safety of Réverē," Kintol said, taking Arcinaë's hand and pulling her along.

They entered a large cavern that appeared to be filled with mirrors of polished brass from which a thousand reflections of themselves gazed back at Arcinaë and the two Kerleucans.

"How will we know which is the mirror to Réverē?" Arcinaë asked in confusion.

The Kerleucans laughed raucously as the mirrors rattled and their multiple images shifted.

Arcinaë drew her sword, backing away from the movement and pushing the laughing Kerleucans behind her.

"Sovereign," a deep voice rumbled, filling the cavern with dust from its vibration, "I have awaited you." A large head rose to reveal eyes of flashing blue-white light. Gradually the form of a fire dragon could be discerned among the many mirrored scales. "You are the last?" the dragon asked, pushing its long sinuous neck past Arcinaë to address the Kerleucans.

"Aye," Wad responded. "We collected the sovereign and came straightaway. Grimmoirë holds no life. Even the trees and grasses wither and fade."

Pulling back, the dragon rested his head on the ground before Arcinaë, his flaming eyes locked on her face. "Sovereign, you are ready to darken Grimmoirë and hide the mirror?"

"I do not know what you are asking, Dragon," Arcinaë said, feeling suddenly alone and lost.

"You are the sovereign and as such you rule the Dragons of

Fire, guardians of the mirrors between the worlds. It is only by your command that we can summon or conceal the mirrors. Do you wish to pass into Réverē and hide the mirrors from the eyes of humans?" the dragon explained, waiting patiently for the sovereign's decision.

"How many mirrors are there, Dragon?" Arcinaë asked.

"There are seven, my sovereign. Each will be cloaked until your call to return. At that time, the seven dragon protectors will once again release the mirrors." Slowly the dragon unfolded its body, revealing the great mirror it protected. The mirror was massive, easily large enough to allow even an adult gryphon to pass. Its polished surface gleamed, alternating shimmering reflections of the cavern in which it stood and the hall beneath Réverē. Within Réverē could be seen Fenris the Feie as he awaited the arrival of his sovereign.

"Fenris," Arcinaë whispered, her eyes clouding with emotion.

With a deep breath, she straightened her shoulders and raised her chin. "Aye, Dragon, we are ready. Allow us passage and seal the mirrors."

Wad and Kintol swept past her, leaping through the mirror. With a final nod to the fire dragon, Arcinaë followed.

Chapter 8: Armies and Councils

The dark and forbidding northern entrance to the Tangled Chasm loomed ahead. A seemingly endless labyrinth of winding passages, it connected the kingdom of Cheneis to the kingdom of Lamaas and was unguarded in the belief that no army could ever navigate its endless switchbacks and blind, dead-end canyons. It was within the seclusion of the Chasm's eternal shadows, gorges, rifts and canyons that Ilerion had once trained a great army, a united army that had been led against the demon of another day.

As they approached, the herald sounded and a rider suddenly emerged from the mouth of darkness. Ilerion felt Caval surge beneath him, ready to meet the charge.

"Nay, Caval, not today, but the time of the charge comes," Ilerion said, soothing his mount.

"Lord Ilerion." The soldier nodded with respect. "We await you at the fortress. The garrison has been provisioned and your warhorses collected and shod. The men have been training under Lord Reduald in your absence."

"And what are your numbers?" Ilerion asked.

"We are only seven hundred, my lord, but more men join us daily."

Nilus grinned as he watched Ilerion revert to the role of general.

"What number are lancers, archers and swordsmen?"

"There are over one hundred lancers, though there are only eighty warhorses, including those of yours collected from the farrier

Dompet. Two hundred men are fine archers, and all are skilled with the sword. Over six hundred are from the garrisons at Twode, Durover or Halhmor. At least fifty are from Baene, my lord," the soldier acknowledged.

"From Baene?"

"Aye, my lord, your men return to your service. Word of retribution against those who attacked your castle and killed your wife continues to spread throughout your kingdom."

"Take me to Reduald," Ilerion ordered.

Ædracmoræ and Révere

Fenris grabbed Arcinaë as she stepped through the mirror. "I thought it was certain that we would lose you, too. Lazaro's soldiers swept into Grimmoirë and murdered everyone they found, including the sovereign."

"We are the last," Arcinaë said, indicating the two Kerleucans who had accompanied her through the mirror. "These are Kintol and Wad. They brought me through from Grimmoirë."

"And the hunter from Baene? Where is he? He promised he would keep you safe!" Fenris stated in his customary fussy manner.

"He builds an army to fight against Lazaro. Ilerion and three other leaders stand against this evil. They are our only hope of justice. And you, Fenris, you and the other Feie can restore Grimmoirë when it is safe to do so. Without you there is no possibility of our return."

"The Winged Council will hear your request seven days hence. Choose your words wisely, Arcinaë, for Révere is held within a net of fear over what has happened to Grimmoirë. It will not be easy to garner their support," the Feie warned.

"Then I shall rest and prepare. Is there a pool for divining?"

"Aye, I will take you, Arcinaë." Fenris took her arm.

❧❧❧

Arcinaë knelt at the divining pool, her eyes focused on an image of Ilerion mounted on Caval before an army of hundreds of soldiers.

"I understand you are the Damselfly who uses weapons," a feminine voice said from behind her.

Swiftly wiping the image from the pool, Arcinaë leapt to her feet, swinging toward the speaker with dagger and sword drawn to defend herself.

The voice belonged to a woman dressed in the leathers of a warrior. Her waist-length auburn hair gave off sparks of crimson highlights under the daystar's brilliant light, but it was her eyes that drew Arcinaë's attention, for they were as golden as the star itself.

"I am Arcinaë of Grimmoirë," Arcinaë acknowledged. "And you are?"

"Cwen of Aaradan," the woman stated, "and this is Talin." She gestured to the tall, well-muscled hunter behind her.

The man nodded without speaking.

"You can sheath your weapons, Arcinaë. We do not intend you harm," Cwen said, eyeing the dagger and sword Arcinaë held before her.

"I lost my innocence and my wings believing humans who spoke those words. I have been taught to be wary," Arcinaë replied, without replacing her weapons in their scabbards. "What is it you want?"

Cwen dropped to the grass in a cross-legged position, staring at Talin until he did the same.

"We need your help and you need ours. You seek the help of Révérē's enchanted. They are not likely to offer it," Cwen stated bluntly.

"I assure you," Arcinaë stated, working hard to keep from sounding defensive, "I am no novice dealing with the Winged Council."

"Perhaps not, but the citizens of Révérē have been thrown into a state of fear by what has occurred at Grimmoirë. One man has single-handedly managed to raise an army against the enchanted and, according to your own words, has brought Grimmoirë to darkness, killing or driving out every last remnant of magick."

"A man—" Arcinaë began.

"Lord Ilerion of Baene raises an army to defend you," Cwen interrupted. "Fenris the Feie has spoken of it, but it does not change the fact that Grimmoirë has already fallen. Without Révérē's Winged Council, Grimmoirë is gone, already lost beyond your ability to restore it.

"Talin and I can help you, Arcinaë. My aunt is the Queen of Ædracmoræ. The Dragon Queen of legend. Her voice carries great power with the council. I will take you to her and help you sway her to Grimmoirë's request," Cwen said, eyeing the still armed Damselfly.

"And what is it you require in return?" Arcinaë asked, her eyes narrowing with suspicion.

"A quest for the gryphonstone. It is hidden on the Isle of Grave."

"You want me to take you, two armed humans, through the mirror into Grimmoirë?" Arcinaë paled. "To the Isle of Grave, a place deliberately hidden against treachery from your kind?"

"Aye," Cwen said, "we cannot cross if you do not summon the mirror and lead us safely past the fire dragon guardian. And we could never locate the eyrie of the gryphons without you as our guide. We do not wish Grimmoirë harm. In fact we wish to see your kingdom restored and your world at peace, but we must collect the gryphonstone in order to restore our own world to balance. We can help one another, Arcinaë."

"I cannot. It is treason. I am Grimmoirë's sovereign. I cannot betray that trust."

"Then you will never go home. You will never see Grimmoirë reborn or your wings restored. The Winged Council will refuse your request and offer only asylum within Réverë's borders. Perhaps that will be good enough for the Grimmoirëns." Cwen shrugged. "The choice is yours, Arcinaë, and you have not taken the vows of sovereign."

"Wings cannot be restored, it is not possible. Not even a Feie wizard has such power," Arcinaë whispered. "Making promises you cannot keep will not sway me to your cause."

"The Sylph can give the gift of flight." Talin's deep voice startled Arcinaë, causing her to draw back a step.

"You may have been taught to be wary," he continued, "but you are no warrior. You have neither the mind nor the heart for it. If you did, you would have struck Cwen down when she first spoke. I felt your fear. Even here, within the safety of Réverë, you are afraid."

"Those who are known as the Sylph are only legend. The woman did not draw her sword and offered no threat. If she had I would have killed her," Arcinaë said, attempting to sound warrior-like.

The bolt from Cwen's crossbow struck the earth at Arcinaë's feet, causing her to fall back and cry out.

"The woman's name is Cwen," Talin stated, "and if she wanted you to be harmed, then you would already be dead. And, as we have seen the Sylph, we can tell you they are far more than legend."

"How did you do that?" Arcinaë stared at Cwen. "I did not even see your hand touch the bow, and you remain seated! Will you teach me?"

A smile played at the corners of Cwen's mouth. "Does this mean you will help us reach the gryphons?"

"Only after we have secured Révère's promise to restore Grimmoirë's magick...and I have wings," Arcinaë added, staring at Talin with disdain, confident she would never be called to honor her part of the bargain.

"You are very small," he remarked with the lift of an eyebrow, "very small for one so bold."

Arcinaë sheathed her weapons and pointed at Talin. "I do not like you," she said with a deep frown. "I believe you are brutish and ignoble like the hunters."

Cwen laughed. "That appears fair, since I do not believe he likes you either. But we have accepted a charge to protect you, so you are safe from the blade of his axe—at least for the moment!

"I shall summon Brengven the Feie to create a rift that will take us to the Fortress at Æstaffordæ. There we will consult Yávië the Dragon Queen about the restoration of Grimmoirë."

The House of Aaradan

Brengven the Feie arrived, fussing as he always did in the presence of humans. "Why do you not call someone else? I am tired of you acting as if I am simply here to serve you, Cwen."

Averting her head to hide her grin, Cwen replied, "It is very important that we speak with Yávië before Arcinaë is required to address the council."

"Hmph! Do you think that the queen of humans can convince the Winged Council to charge into such a dangerous place as Grimmoirë to tidy up the aftermath of a war? I do not think so! But, considering that you are such a hard-headed girl, I am sure you will waste the council's time with it anyway!"

"Brengven, I do believe Yávië will help the council to see that it is to their advantage to help the Grimmoirëns, and I do not think that she will take up too much of their time."

"Bah! Do what you will. Anyway, it will never get past the final meeting of the Council of Elders even if the Winged Council should foolishly decide to present it. Never will you convince the Feie to risk themselves for a wingless Damselfly, a few Kerleucans and some singed sprites. I guarantee it!" the Feie snapped with a haughty shake of his head.

"And if they do? Would you like to wager on it, Brengven?" Cwen asked the little man who could not resist a wager.

"What will I get if I win?" Brengven sniffed, looking out from beneath his bushy red brows.

"I shall never ask you to call another rift for me," Cwen answered. "And if I win? What do you offer?"

"You will not win. But I shall offer to call your rifts without complaint should madness strike the council."

"And all the gold in your shoe?" Cwen added.

Brengven pulled off his shoe and dumped his coins. "And two lule and three laud," he agreed, counting out the golden coins.

"A deal!" Cwen said, spitting into her palm and extending it to the Feie. Doing the same, he accepted the wager with a firm handshake.

"Now, where was it you wanted to go?" Brengven asked, as if he had forgotten.

"To the House of Aaradan, Brengven," Cwen reminded.

"Aye, to see the Dragon Queen." The little man chuckled. "This will be the last rift I ever call for you, girl!" The Feie chuckled again and, with a flourish, rent the fabric of the world to reveal a shimmering split before them. With a wave of his hand, he shouted, "Go! Go that I might be done with you!"

Grabbing Arcinaë's hand and laughing at her startled expression, Cwen pulled her through the rift.

"What a rude Feie he is," Arcinaë exclaimed as she stepped through the opening behind Cwen.

"I heard that!" followed the sound of Brengven's voice from behind Talin.

"He is rude and horribly cantankerous, but he is a true friend," Cwen admitted. "He has helped us before, and he will help us again. I am positive I shall win that bet."

There before them was the magnificent vista of the House of Aaradan, the fortress that was the residence of Yávië the Dragon Queen, and the ancestral home of her husband, Sōrél.

"What a grand palace," Arcinaë said in awe, recalling the burned-out ruins of Ilerion's castle.

"Aye, for many generations it was hidden from all by the magick of the wizard Grumblton, perfectly preserved and ready for the new Dragon Queen on her arrival," Cwen told her. "Her coronation was held here."

At the portcullis, Cwen asked the Guardian stationed there where they might find her Aunt Yávië.

"In the dragon yard," he replied. "Your father is with her."

"An added treat," Cwen muttered under her breath to Arcinaë. "If you do not like Talin, you are sure to hate my father."

⁂

Cwen, Talin and Arcinaë stood staring, mouths agape. In the middle of the dragon yard stood the Queen of Ædracmoræ and the Seven Kingdoms.

Yávië was holding tightly to the right forefoot of an immense war dragon. Her warrior's leathers were slick with blood, and her waist-length raven hair was in tangles around her face. As the dragon continued backing away, the queen was dragged along the ground, adding a layer of dust to the blood. She was screaming at the top of her lungs, "If you do not stand still, Faera, I cannot remove the stick. Now, stand still!"

The dragon bellowed and shook her great head, continuing to back away.

"If I must, I will call Grumblton and have him put you in a wizard's sleep!" Yávië shouted.

Suddenly the dragon noticed the new arrivals and, in the brief moment of her distraction, the queen grabbed the offending twig and yanked it from the pad of the dragon's toe. More bellowing ensued but not for long.

"Now for a bit of healing salve and you will be as good as new." Yávië glanced over her shoulder and called to Cwen, "Your timing was perfect. For a moment, I thought I was going to require Grumbl's help."

"Talin," Yávië acknowledged, her eyes locking on the small, unknown woman with the long dark braid and golden brown eyes. "You must be the Damselfly. My wizard, Grumbl—Grumblton—said you would arrive shortly.

"Nall!" the queen shouted.

"Aye, Yávië?" came a voice from the far side of the dragon yard.

"I have need of you."

The man who approached across the yard was even taller and better muscled than Talin. He was no human, for he bore a radiant amber

III

aura that spoke of his station as Guardian of Ædracmoræ. His hair was cut close, a rich chestnut in color, and his amber eyes were deep, without the dark centers that belonged to most races.

He glanced at Yávië, shaking his head. "I could have helped and you would have been cleaner."

"Perhaps, but you were busy with the acolytes and I did not wish to interrupt," Yávië replied. "This is the Damselfly."

"I am Arcinaë of Grimmoirë," Arcinaë admitted, staring up at the Guardian. "I have heard of Guardians, but I have never seen one."

"They are not much different than anyone else," Cwen sighed, "except for glowing in the dark, having exceptional strength and practically living forever—beyond that, they are virtually human.

"Father," Cwen stepped forward and gave the Guardian a hug, "this is indeed Arcinaë of Grimmoirë, a Damselfly who uses weapons."

"And you have come to train with the Guardians?" Nall asked, examining the small Damselfly and her weapons.

"Nay, I seek the Queen's help. I must convince the Winged Council to allow me to present Grimmoirë's request for help to the Council of Elders in Réverē. No one seems to believe there is much hope."

Yávië wiped a bit of dragon's blood from her face. "It would be best if you remained with us until you are more skilled with your weapons. Grumblton tells me you are a woman of legend, somehow tied to the threat of the Heteroclites foretold in Ælarggessæ's lore. What do you think, Arcinaë of Grimmoirë? Are you more than just a Damselfly?"

"I am not a woman at all, nor a halfling as the tale tells. I am only a Damselfly." Arcinaë drew in a great shuddering breath. "Will you not help the enchanted of Grimmoirë?"

Yávië's eyes shifted to Nall. "Perhaps you would like to take Talin and Cwen to see Näeré? Arcinaë and I have much to discuss."

Without waiting for his response, Yávië led Arcinaë off toward the fortress.

Arcinaë gazed out over the queen's gardens. Their lushness reminded her of Grimmoirë's verdant beauty before Lazaro's treachery. She inhaled deeply, drawing in the delicate fragrance of the blossoms while waiting for Yávië to, as she put it, "wash off the dragon's blood and become a bit more presentable."

On Yávië's return, she guided Arcinaë to a secluded table and chairs.

"Tell me," she commanded.

Arcinaë's face became ashen and Yávië watched her swallow bile at the sudden, forced recollection of the defilement and death of the Damselflies at the hands of the humans.

"They came in the night—Lazaro's hunters—we had no chance. They burned us out of our bothies. All of the males, except my father, were immediately butchered, their wings ripped from their bodies. My father was forced to watch the rape and murder of the women and girls. I was saved for last, a final gruesome memory before his death.

"When I awoke and heard the men's voices, I cried out for them to kill me, but they did not. They took me to the healer, and so I live."

Looking up through her tears, Arcinaë repeated, "And so I live. Alone. The last Damselfly."

Yávië tilted her chair and propped her boot-encased feet on the edge of the table. Crossing her arms, she stared at Arcinaë with interest.

"I will help you," Yávië said. "But, you must agree to help yourself," she continued as she slipped her sword from over her shoulder and placed it before Arcinaë.

"I do not understand," Arcinaë frowned.

"Grimmoirë was weak, which is why it was so easily destroyed by Lazaro and his men. The enchanted of Ælarggessæ made no effort to defend it or themselves. You must grow strong and fight if you are to lead your people and keep them safe."

"I do not intend to lead the enchanted any longer than is required for them to choose a new sovereign. I am a representative of none but myself and have insufficient training to rule. I should not have become sovereign for at least another ten summers," Arcinaë said emphatically.

"Do you know the name Grumblton?" Yávië asked.

"Aye, he is the wizard who sees both history and future of the seven worlds. The keeper of all knowledge."

"He is. He has spoken that you are far more than a frail Damselfly. He says that you will mother a new race, bear one who will rise to be a great leader against the dark Heteroclites who will one day bring war to our worlds. Do you doubt his prophecy?" Yávië's violet eyes were shadowed with the comprehension of the wizard's words.

"I…perhaps if my people had not been slaughtered, perhaps then I would have risen to greatness. Now I am nothing. I have no one. I have no place among the enchanted and the humans hunt me as if I were a stag."

"Grumblton's divining is rarely dependent on individual events. You are far from alone. A man of honor raises an army in your defense. The enchanted of Grimmoirë revere your name and call you sacred. You have been brought before the Dragon Queen and will speak before the Council of Elders. Do you not believe these events to be connected?"

"Ilerion promises to avenge my people by striking down those who killed us. No more, no less," Arcinaë responded, looking away.

"It is far more!" Yávië's hand slammed onto the table top, rattling the sword that lay there, her voice sharp with impatience. "He raises an army to end a madman's wickedness against the enchanted. He is a man who may well rise to lead Ælarggessæ or die in its defense. Which would you have him do, Arcinaë?"

Shrinking from the queen's sudden anger, Arcinaë whispered, "I would not have him die."

"Then do not wallow in self-pity. What is done is done. Become the one you are meant to be. If you choose to do this I will help you. If not, you are free to go." The sound of the door opening sent Yávië leaping to her feet, snatching her sword from the table and readying it for battle against those who would dare come for her guest.

A small angry man holding a blazing wizard's staff out before him entered the room, slamming the door behind him.

"Fool! I told you I was coming," Grumblton muttered, pushing Yávië's sword to the side and striking her sharply with his staff before striding purposefully toward Arcinaë.

"Do not let the queen be your guiding hand or you will fail miserably, Arcinaë of Grimmoirë," the wizard sniffed, glancing back at Yávië with a frown. "Yávië has never learned diplomacy and draws blood daily without reason. But she has Guardians who will teach you what you need to know, sovereign of Grimmoirë."

Lifting her hand in defense of the wizard's confusing words, Arcinaë said, "I cannot remain here. I am needed in Réverë."

"Nay, you must remain here, Arcinaë of Grimmoirë. The wind calls your name"

"I am too tired and too lost to understand. Your words are a riddle to me, wizard," Arcinaë murmured, as she felt herself slipping into sleep.

"Aye, but on the morrow when you wake, you will see your path with brilliant clarity," Grumblton said, weaving Arcinaë's sleep with dreams of her future.

"Tell Nall to take her to Näeré. She should wake there without the muddle of confusion that binds her heart with fear." Grumblton glared at Yávië. "You will go to the Winged Council on her behalf, convince the harpy, and she will sway the others."

Deception and Death

At Castle Lamaas the hunters approached Lazaro. In their midst was a woman who staggered slightly as if she was drunk. Her face, lips and breasts were blackened and swollen from the bruising, violating hands of his men. A hunter gave the woman a brutal push, causing her to cry out as her back struck the floor—it was clear they had known exactly what they were doing with the lash.

"Tell me what I want to know and I will end your pain, Healer." The sound of Lazaro's voice made her cringe.

Extending an arm, he backhanded her, adding yet another bruise to a once comely face. "Once more, what is your name, Healer?" he asked, raising his hand to strike her again if she refused to answer.

"Ananta," she gasped, her breath coming sharply with the pain of her wounds.

Lazaro roared—his laughter coarse and cruel. "I have set a bounty on your murderer, Ananta," he said. "A vicious Damselfly butchered you in your home over a year ago. Are you not grateful that I seek to avenge your death?"

Not waiting for her answer, he again asked the questions he had asked each day of her long captivity. "Where will I find them, Ananta? Where are the beast and her keeper?"

Silently, Ananta drew herself into a ball, hoping that this time the beating would kill her.

As the hunters roughly jerked her to her feet and Lazaro stepped forward to administer her punishment, Ananta whispered through her bloodied lips, "Why do you hate them so? It is something more than just the legends."

With the swiftness of a snake, he grabbed her cheeks and pinched them painfully.

"The beast refused me! The Damselfly Cylacia refused me, *me*!—as if she had the rights of a human! I offered her the gift of life. She had only to accept me but said that she would rather die and flew away. My father saw to it that she died as she requested. When I kill the last of the beasts and there is no threat left in the legend of the halflings, you will discover just how horrible death can be, Healer." Releasing her face, he slammed his fist into her belly, watching with satisfaction as she retched and sagged beneath the power of his hand.

Using her last conscious breath, Ananta whispered, "Lord Ilerion will kill you."

She did not feel the second blow.

⇢⊙⇠

Lazaro led three hundred hunters into Cheneis, arriving in the depths of darkest night at the castle of Lord Iydaen. The hunters rapidly dispatched the few guards patrolling the grounds and, murdering soldiers and servants on their way, swiftly dragged the sleeping Iydaen from his bed to toss him on the ground before Lord Lazaro.

"I come as a friend," Lazaro offered. "I am told you hold a beast. A male Damselfly called Trew."

"He is dead," Iydaen answered as he drew his nightshirt around him against the chill.

"Then I will accept his body as a token of your belief in the cleansing of Ælarggessæ. It will serve as a warning to others, staked upon your rampart."

"The body is gone, burned," Iydaen shrugged.

A brutal laugh erupted from Lazaro's chest. "I was told as much. Taken by another beast and her keepers, is this true, Iydaen?"

Iydaen's eyes grew wide with fear as he watched Lazaro's men push Lady Iydaen to the ground before them.

"I beg you, do not harm my wife." Iydaen's voice was pleading.

"She has done nothing, Lazaro. Nothing. She did not even know they were here."

"She accepted your vow of protection. A mistake, Lord Iydaen," Lazaro hissed.

"Burn her!" he commanded, his eyes glittering as the hunters bound Lady Iydaen's hands and tied her to an almost denuded chale tree, its remaining leaves parched and brittle from the season's dry winds.

"Please!" Iydaen implored.

Lazaro raised his hand, stopping the action of his men. "You would prefer she live?" he asked Iydaen. "The choice is yours."

"Yes, let her live!" Iydaen screamed, wiping his streaming nose.

"Very well," Lazaro nodded to his hunters, watching as they dragged the terrified woman to the ground and stripped away her clothes.

"No!" Iydaen shouted hoarsely, dropping to his knees and clinging to Lazaro's coat. "Do not let them do this, Lazaro, I beg you by all that is holy."

"Kill all who serve this fool!" Lazaro shouted. Pushing Iydaen away with his foot, Lazaro drew his blade and slit the man from bowel to sternum. As Iydaen struggled to hold his escaping intestines, Lazaro turned the lord to face his wailing wife. "You should have let her burn, Iydaen."

"Bring her!" Lazaro called to his hunters, leaping to his horse and wheeling away toward Lamaas and a meeting with the lords of Wawne and Breden.

❧❧

"They are gone," Lord Oeric of Wawne said, wiping the blood from the edge of the axe between thumb and forefinger and flinging it away. "Grimmoirë lies in darkness, empty of all magick. We have searched every settlement and cavern—not so much as a harpy remains. The deed is done, Lazaro. Ælarggessæ is free of the enchanted beasts, and there is no threat from the Damselfly's blood."

"Cheneis is in chaos over the loss of Lord and Lady Iydaen," Lord Saebar of Breden added. "You go unchallenged in Cheneis, Lazaro."

Lord Lazaro raised his eyes to meet those of his allies. "Then we shall bring down the kingdoms who do not bow before us. Halhmor and Durover can be brought to their knees by our strength. We shall rule the world of Ælarggessæ."

"Do you forget our king?" Lord Saebar asked, bringing loud laughter from Lazaro.

"The king is a fool who hides his head beneath the skirts of his courtesans. He will be no more difficult to deal with than Lord Iydaen was. Weakness abounds, my friends, and we shall sweep it away with the strength of our armies."

"And what then, Lazaro? Do you intend to take the crown?" Oeric asked, without looking at Lazaro.

"There will be no crown. We will divide the kingdoms among ourselves, ruling as we wish within our own realms. Do you not find that an attractive offer, Oeric?" Lazaro placed his hand on the hilt of his sword, ready to rid the world of one more threat if need be.

Laying his axe on the table, Oeric extended his open hand to Lazaro, clearly relieved when it was accepted.

"And you, Saebar? Does this meet with your approval?" Lazaro asked, eyeing the ruler of Breden expectantly.

"Aye, indeed, as long as you leave me a few fair young women, I shall be content," Saebar replied with a laugh.

"It is agreed then. We shall prepare to challenge Halhmor and Durover on their home grounds. Even if they resist, victory will be ours before another year's harvest."

"And Baene?"

Saebar and Lazaro both laughed at Oeric's question.

"Baene will simply be divided three ways. It has no ruler. Its soldiers fled in embarrassment at the exposure of Ilerion's relationship with the beast. They either joined me as hunters or became farmers or merchants. Ilerion has gone to ground, flown with his beast in tow. He will not return to Ælarggessæ for fear of losing her," Lazaro said with distaste. "His unnatural desire to lie with the beasts leaves him powerless to defend his kingdom. He has been reduced to nothing more than a beast himself.

"Bring us ale," Lazaro snapped to his newest serving wench, grinning wickedly, as she curtsied and hurried off to fulfill his request. Disobedience brought pain and already she had learned her lessons well.

Entering the kitchen, the serving wench, Twica, gathered the mugs and filled a pitcher with heavy ale. Setting it on the tray before Ydeta, she whispered very softly, "'Tis time. I must seek Ilerion and give him news of Lazaro's plans. Take this to his lordship and remain obedient until we come for you."

Hugging her sister tightly, Ydeta gave a frightened smile. "His lordship can do no more harm than he has already done. All that is left is death, and I should not mind that too much."

"If he asks of me, tell him I fell ill and was taken to the healer in Cheneis. He will not question you, for he does not really care."

With a last embrace for her older sister, Twica fled the kitchen of Lazaro's castle and raced to the stable where a saddled ass awaited her.

"They train an army in the Tangled Chasm," the old farrier said, handing Twica a white cloth. "Wave this high as you near, for they will be well guarded, though a young and beautiful maiden riding a stout ass will probably not be seen as much of a threat. Tell Ilerion I send my best. Now go, girl!" The old farrier gave the small beast a slap on the rump and watched as it trotted awkwardly off into the darkness.

"I hope Ilerion carries the magick of the enchanted," the old man said with a sigh.

⋇

"A rider comes!" shouted the young soldier standing guard at the entrance to the canyons. "A woman on an ass."

Ilerion raced forward on Caval, staring into the dying sun that silhouetted the figure of the approaching rider. "Keep an arrow nocked," he called to the soldier and swung his mount around to meet the woman. Caval charged forward, his teeth clamping on the bit in an effort to take control from his rider.

"Do not make me curb you, old friend," Ilerion warned, receiving an angry shake of the head from the warhorse.

The woman lifted a long white cloth, allowing it to trail behind her on the wind. A sign of peace, or treachery, Ilerion sighed and wished he knew which.

"I am sent by Dompet, the farrier," a child's voice called out. "He shoes the horses at Lazaro's barn and has sent me to warn you. Lazaro seeks to take the kingdoms of Halhmor, Durover and Baene and rule them as his own."

"And how is it Dompet came by this information while working in the stable?" Ilerion questioned.

"Nay, he did not get the information. I did. I am Twica of Baene, daughter of your warder, Garell of Baene."

"And how did you get the information Twica, daughter of Garell? You are but a child," Ilerion asked.

"I am not a child to Lord Lazaro. I was taken from my father's house and placed in the lord's service when last the moon showed her face."

Ilerion saw her look away and swore once again that he would kill Lazaro for his debauchery.

"What can you tell me of Lazaro's plans?"

"He said that the three kingdoms, Lamaas, Breden and Wawne, would attack the kingdoms of Twode, Halhmor and Durover. Lord Lazaro said Baene had no ruler. He said you were weak and they would simply divide Baene among them. You are not weak, are you, Lord Ilerion?"

"Nay, I am not weak. We merely remain hidden to keep Lazaro from realizing our strength. Together with Lord Elduuf, Lord Tondhere and Lord Reduald I lead an army of a thousand men. With the knowledge you have brought us, we will prepare to meet Lazaro when he arrives within the kingdom of Durover.

"You no longer serve Lazaro, Twica. From this day forth, you serve Baene. Come, I shall tell the cook you are in her charge," Ilerion said, holding out his hand and lifting the young girl to the back of his mount. With the flat of his sword, he sent the ass back the way it had come.

Chapter 9: Metal and Magick

Nall got to his feet but then dropped back to the chair at hearing the soft tones of his wife's silent words.

Do not frighten her, Näeré said.

With a lopsided grin, Nall's words teased in the unspoken communication of the Guardians. *I cannot teach weapons to a woman who fears the sight of me standing.*

Näeré flipped a small sparkle of the magick she was working toward Nall, causing him to duck and laugh out loud.

"You speak to one another without words, like the Feie."

Arcinaë's quiet voice startled them from their companionable nonsense. She stood barefoot, wearing the night cloak that Näeré had left on the foot of the bed.

"Aye." Näeré's voice was soft and melodic, intended to soothe and reassure the young Damselfly.

"And you are a sorceress?" Arcinaë directed her question at Näeré, keeping her eyes fixed on Nall.

"I am."

"And he," Arcinaë pointed to Nall, "is a Eunean?"

Nall's eyebrows rose. "Aye, I am, but how would you know that?"

"Your eyes. The Euneans were once a race of enchanted, but most lost the eyes in the diluting of the blood. Their union with humans was not a successful one, and it ended in the death of the race at the fall of Arcaedya." Arcinaë shrugged as if it were common knowledge.

"Both my parents were Eunean. I am also the last of a race." He smiled sadly at the nearly forgotten recollection.

"And you, Sorceress? You are a human?" Arcinaë asked.

"Nay, I am a halfling. My mother is a Sojourner, my father a human. As Guardians, we are given gifts that humans do not hold. I shall teach you magick, and Nall will teach you skill with your weapons."

"And you must forget that I am enchanted? Treating me as Ilerion said I must be treated? Treating me as a human?"

"We will never forget that you are enchanted, Arcinaë, for your life light hums with its force, but we will help you as you prepare to fulfill the legend of your daughters to-be, and counsel with the Sylph."

Looking confused, Arcinaë asked, "I have no halfling daughters, I am not wed, nor do I intend to be, and where is this city of the Sylph?"

Cwen's lilting voice called from the doorway, "I know nothing about any halfling daughters, but I do know that Keslbaen is the home of the Sylph. When the twin moons are cast dark by the shadow of Ædracmoræ's face, the doorway to Keslbaen will open once again, and Talin and I shall take you there. Until then, you will train with us and grow stronger, and I will teach you how to kill with the crossbow without a whisper of your intent."

Kissing her mother's cheek and nodding to her father, Cwen grabbed two morning buns, tossing one to Arcinaë. "Get dressed and we shall begin."

"You are the daughter of the Sojourner halfling and the Eunean?"

"Aye, it is where I get these golden eyes and the glimmer of the magick I do not use," Cwen admitted with a wink at Näeré.

"If you have the gift of magick, why do you not use it?" Arcinaë asked with a curious tilt of her head.

Cwen's solemn look was grim with truth. "Because I do not require magick to kill evil men. I prefer to hear the weapon strike their flesh. To see the blood flow from their wounds," adding lightly—"though it vexes my father greatly that I have become no more than a common ruffian."

Nall's laugh was deep. "Do not let my daughter fool you, Arcinaë. There is nothing common about her. She seeks to enter the order of the thaumaturge at the cloister of Belasis when her commitment to restore the House of Lochlaen is fulfilled. She has more than a little interest in magick."

"The restoration of the House of Lochlaen? That is why you sought my help?" Arcinaë asked Cwen.

"Aye, I have pledged to help a wizard called Lohgaen. You will meet him when the time comes to seek the gryphonstone. Come, the hour grows late. We have much to do, Arcinaë of Grimmoirë," adding with a chuckle, "and Talin grows impatient…," as she flung open the door to reveal him standing there, hand poised to knock.

"I tire of waiting." Talin frowned, bringing more laughter from Cwen and the others.

Cwen sparred with Arcinaë, nodding her approval at the Damselfly's form.

"The one who taught you, taught you well," she called breathlessly, as her sword rose to meet Arcinaë's backhand swing.

"But he said he could not teach me hate, nor a passion for killing," Arcinaë responded, frowning in her effort to keep Cwen at bay.

Suddenly Cwen stepped back.

"You do not want a passion for killing, Arcinaë, for you come from a world bound by a strict code of honor. If you break it, you are no better than those who hunt you. Do not let anger lead your sword; instead always use it to protect yourself or others."

Arcinaë shook her head. "I want the passion to see those who killed the Damselflies pay for it. I want to see the one who sent the hunters die by my own hand. Ilerion will seek them out, but the one who ordered the death of all Grimmoirëns will not be caught. I have seen it in the divining pool. I must be strong enough to end his life."

Cwen shrugged. "You are small and will never be strong enough to best a man with a sword. You must win by trickery and cleverness rather than muscle."

"How is it that you have the strength to best a man?" Arcinaë asked, examining Cwen's slender figure.

"I use the crossbow and travel with men who are strong. The bow allows the advantage of distance. You have the gift of far sight and an accurate aim. This is good and will keep the bolt's flight true. When the day comes for you to face this man, you will be ready."

"You waste time with your idle chatter," Nall's voice called from the edge of the practice field. "I cannot assess Arcinaë's form if you stand around with swords hanging loosely at your sides."

"He teases?" Arcinaë asked, uncertain.

"Aye, it is what he does best!" Cwen laughed, raising her sword and beckoning Arcinaë forward.

"She needs a second sword. The dagger is too short to use for defense," Nall mumbled as he came forward.

"It will not matter, Nall. She is far too small and fragile to wield the swords against her human enemies. She needs magick. Keep her strong with practice, and I will teach her to use the power that lies hidden at her center. It will not be long before she must go with Cwen to Keslbaen," said Näeré. With a quick kiss, she left Nall watching the women practice and headed for the house to prepare lessons for her enchanted student.

Calling back over her shoulder, Näeré suggested, "Set Talin against her. She fears his strength, and he is not very good with a sword."

Talin harrumphed from his seat on the other side of Nall. "I may not be skilled with the sword, but that woman is so small I could simply step on her. There is no hope for this, Nall. Look at her! Cwen is small, and Arcinaë does not even reach her shoulder."

"Aye, but she defends well against Cwen, even though Cwen holds back. The Damselfly's form is sound. She needs only an edge to become a threat. And we will give her an edge." Nall looked meaningfully at Talin.

"You cannot possibly expect me to allow her to best me?" Talin spluttered. "Nall?"

"You did it for Cwen," Nall reminded him in a hushed voice lest his daughter hear.

"Aye, but she was my friend. The Damselfly does not even like me."

"I cannot imagine why. Your surly personality should have won her heart at your first meeting." Nall laughed. "Cwen likes her. Do it for Cwen."

Talin jumped from the wall, carefully removing the double-bladed battleaxe from its place against his back and handing it to Nall.

Drawing his short sword, Talin walked off to let the tiny Damselfly beat him in a sparring match.

And make her believe she has won fairly, Nall's voice whispered inside Talin's head.

Arcinaë's heart thundered in her chest as she backed away from Talin.

"It is merely a sparring match," Talin reminded. "I shall simply knock you to the ground, and it will be over."

He watched the shadow of fear cloak her eyes and gave her his most dastardly grin. "And I shall enjoy doing it."

She swung her sword viciously and unexpectedly, catching Talin off guard as he scrambled to lift his own to repel her strike. With an eyebrow raised in surprise, he muttered, "Now I shall enjoy it doubly!"

Arcinaë drew Ilerion's instruction from her memory. Taking a deep breath, she met Talin's hits defensively, striving only to stay upright against the tall man's superior strength.

Catching an opening, she swept her sword low and was pleased when Talin had to leap away to avoid it. Knowing that her strength lay in her backhand, she brought her sword crashing against his shorter one before pushing off from him and rolling away. Arcinaë leapt to her feet and thrust solidly, sending her sword neatly between his ribs and arm and drawing a line of blood near his elbow.

"You cut me!" Talin shouted with surprise, frowning and charging forward.

Arcinaë spun sideways as Ilerion had taught, allowing Talin's sword to sweep within inches of her body. As his momentum carried him past, she slammed the flat side of her sword against his back, sending him sprawling face down to the ground. Leaping forward, she straddled him, her sword ready to plunge into his back.

"Do not move, hunter," she hissed.

"Well done!" Nall shouted, running forward uncertain of her intentions. Gently drawing the sword from her hands, he pulled her away, allowing Talin to roll over and get to his feet.

You owe me a great debt, Talin's voice laughed into Nall's mind, *because I let her draw blood.*

Cwen approached Talin, her eyes narrowing in suspicion as she stared up at him.

"Nay, Cwen," he answered her unspoken question, "it was never necessary to let you win."

"Shhh," she hissed. "Arcinaë will hear you. Well, you did it admirably. It looked like she bested you fairly," Cwen said with a wicked grin, grabbing his arm to examine the small wound. "The angry shout at the sight of your own blood was particularly convincing." With a healing touch, she sealed the cut, stopping the bleeding. "You will have to get a healing salve from Näeré."

Seeing the pale look on Arcinaë's face, Cwen placed her hand on the Damselfly's shoulder, "What is it?"

"Why do I fear him? It was not real. He would not harm me— would he?"

"Nay, he sought only to make you angry so that you would fight with more strength. You fear him because he is so much larger than you. Were he not my friend, I would fear him too," Cwen admitted.

"The rest of your day will be spent with Näeré, away from the brutality of the swords. She will teach you spell casting and how to magickally enhance your weapons. She will teach you healing, if you like. My mother is a very accomplished sorceress."

As Arcinaë turned to go, Cwen called after her, "Talin will say he let you win to salve his male pride, but I do not believe it is so."

Talin pushed Cwen from behind, sending her stumbling forward and collapsing in laughter. A sudden flicker of movement at the far edge of the field sobered her and she quickly got to her feet, brushing the grass from her hair.

"It is Lohgaen. I will return shortly."

Setting off at a gentle run, Cwen went to meet the wizard.

Lohgaen's voice and his soft, calm words pierced her mind even before she saw him. *She is the one?*

"Aye," Cwen said, discerning Lohgaen's dark form among the lighter shadows. "She is Arcinaë of Grimmoirë and, following the meeting of the Council of Elders in Réverë, she will take you to the Isle of Grave."

The wizard was tall with hair the color of smoke that curled about his shoulders. His strength was hidden beneath the blackness of his cloak, but there were signs of it in the piercing dark eyes that were were fixed upon Cwen as she spoke.

"Lohgaen, it is best if she not see you until the time for us to meet at the mirror. She will be more comfortable if she takes only one armed human through into Grimmoirë."

"I cannot afford to be interested in her comfort, Cwen. I must have the artifact from the Isle of Grave if we are to restore the House of Lochlaen. Do not make the task harder by becoming emotionally involved with the Damselfly. She is merely a tool," Lohgaen reminded.

"But she has suffered so, Lohgaen. She nearly died at the hands of men. She is the last of her kind. Allow her some dignity by treating her with respect. Is it not the right thing to do?"

Lohgaen's eyes softened as Cwen's words touched him. Soon he would have to tell her that her lover, Caen, lived. Lohgaen knew that he would lose her company when he did. Honesty had never been high among the wizard's list of qualities. He also knew that although he had stolen Cwen's memories of Caen, the hurt still rested against her heart, leaving an ache that could be neither placated nor assuaged.

Placing his hand on her shoulder, he searched her golden eyes and asked, "You are well, Cwen?"

"Aye, I am well. Your kindness and sleeping spells have allowed it, though sometimes I hear a man's call, as if he is searching for me. His voice is deep and soft and does not threaten." She shrugged it off, smiling up at Lohgaen. "Perhaps one day I will find such a man."

"Summon me when you have need of me." Lohgaen released his grip on Cwen's shoulder, watching as she ran effortlessly back toward the training fields.

"Why did you not call Talin?" the thaumaturge Synyon's silken voice purred at the wizard Lohgaen's elbow.

"Because you distress him with you beguiling nature—you render him useless, Synyon," Lohgaen glared.

"You know it is simply my way. He is handsome and strong… and willing." She chuckled at Lohgaen's furrowed brow and obvious discomfort. "It is not my fault you have chosen celibacy, my friend."

The thaumaturge continued softly, "I heard he was in Bael, the one she hears in her dreams, Caen. You do remember Caen, don't you, Lohgaen?"

"Do not bait me, Synyon. I told you, I will return her memory when the artifact has been reclaimed."

"I do not believe you, Lohgaen. So I shall do it for you, if you find yourself falling short of the task. She will have him, Lohgaen. It is cruel to keep him from her." Synyon placed her hand against Lohgaen's heart, feeling its slow steady beat, knowing he had slowed it deliberately so she would not feel the thunder of his deceit.

"You do not fool me, my friend. I have known you too long. I am sorry her heart is so encumbered, but I will not allow you to hold her through dishonesty." Dropping her hand, she slipped away through the forest, leaving the dark wizard alone with his torment.

Visions

"It will not work with the humans. Well…you will be able to hear their thoughts, but they cannot hear yours," Näeré explained, keeping one eye on the crystal Arcinaë held so carefully between her hands, not letting it touch her fingers.

Arcinaë was delighted with the art of magick. She excelled at the casting of simple spells, quickly learning the incantations and gestures necessary to cast a veil, deflect an arrow and hold an object without touching it. She pored over the tomes, memorizing pages of text written in the language of the enchanted.

The wizard Grumblton was surprised by her aptitude for the arcane.

"For naught but a Damselfly, she is as sharp as a blade," the old wizard muttered to Näeré as he observed her student. "Maybe she really is the one who will bear the halflings."

Staring at Grumblton with disbelief, Näeré asked, "You told Yávië that Arcinaë was the vessel for the halflings. Are you saying you are not sure?"

"Well, there is always a bit of doubt in the divining of a prophecy. I was not sure I had all the details. But, aye, she is the one. It shows in her now."

Suddenly the crystal dropped to the floor. Arcinaë stood perfectly still, staring into the distance.

"What is it girl? What do you see?" Grumblton asked, placing a hand on Näeré's arm to keep her from touching Arcinaë.

"A battle. The battle for Ælarggessæ begins at the castle of Lord Tondhere in the kingdom of Halhmor." Arcinaë blinked away the images of war. "How is it that I can see what is happening in Ælarggessæ?" she asked the little wizard.

"You are changing, growing. The moons will soon fall beneath the shadow of Ædracmoræ, and Cwen will take you to the Sylph. They know the answers. I do not," Grumblton answered.

Arcinaë turned away from Grumblton and Näeré, her eyes fixing on the shimmering vision she had of the Castle Tondhere under heavy attack by Lazaro and his vicious hunters. She shut her eyes against the images of the castle's fall, opening them only to see Lazaro himself lead the breaching of Castle Elduuf.

⚜

For sixteen days the sound of stones striking the castle walls had been incessant and unrelenting. It was as though a giant were pounding to get in. Over and over the mangonels were loaded for the release of the stones to crash against the masonry and breach the walls.

Lazaro's miners dug furiously to tunnel beneath the gatehouse tower wall and provide access to Castle Tondhere.

Tondhere's remaining soldiers—the thirty who had volunteered to stay behind when most of their garrison joined Ilerion's army within the Tangled Chasm—released a volley of arrows through the bow loops, their only task to keep Lazaro believing the castle was occupied.

"Lazaro heads away with three riders," shouted their captain, Danfor. "There will be an extra ration to the man who can tell me who rides with him."

"Evalio, Norgeau, and Colne," shouted Geiter, an archer in the tower, "three of the men being hunted by Lord Ilerion for the murder of the Grimmoirëns."

"Excellent eyes, lad!" Danfor called back. "How good a rider are you?"

"I am a fine rider, sir," the young soldier answered.

"Out with you, then. Through the tunnel into Hawksblood Woods. A horse waits there. Ride to Lord Ilerion and let him know that Lazaro has left our walls in search of new mischief. Tell Lord Tondhere his plan holds. They believe him to be within his castle, mounting its grand defense. Be swift and do not get caught."

As Geiter exited the postern on the opposite side of the castle and crept into the woods in search of the waiting horse, Lazaro's miners broke through into the castle bailey. Swarming up the stairs, they met Tondhere's loyal guards in a fierce and bloody battle. As the last of Tondhere's soldiers fell, Lazaro's hunters realized they had seized an empty castle.

"Most likely Tondhere has taken his troops and fled before us," Lord Saebar of Breden assumed, "gone to beg refuge with Reduald or Elduuf. Stake the bodies of his men high along the parapet and fly Lazaro's banner."

His voice filled with the excitement of impending success, Lazaro shouted, "Bring it down!"

Heavy ropes hung from the iron grapnels that had been thrown to the top of the portcullis, each being pulled rhythmically by ten of Lazaro's men. The shock of their combined weight sent the portcullis shuddering with each backward tug.

There were shouts of triumph from the hunters as the iron bolts broke from the heavy mortar at the side wall and the massive gate was dragged from the opening. Lazaro's troops rushed inside to be met by the defending soldiers of Lord Elduuf of Twode.

⊰❀⊱

"The castles in the kingdoms of Halhmor and Twode have fallen," Arcinaë said in a quiet voice, utterly devoid of emotion. "Lazaro's banner flies above both." She turned to Grumblton, her eyes filling with tears and whispered, "I must look into your divining pool," as he nodded and quickly led the Damselfly off toward the House of Aaradan.

As she gazed into Grumblton's reflecting pool, Arcinaë spoke the name of the one she sought, "Ilerion." The waters of the pool bubbled from its depths bringing the face of the one she must see. Sighing with relief, Arcinaë leaned forward, her braid floating on the surface of the pool.

What is it you do, Ilerion? You do not save the castles of our allies, why are they allowed to fall? she wondered silently, her lips only a finger's width from Ilerion's image in the magick waters.

How is it I hear your voice, but do not see your face? Ilerion's image answered in puzzlement. A smile softened the hard lines around his mouth as a thought came to mind, *Is it the bewitchment of the kiss?*

Arcinaë drew back, touching her lips lightly with her fingertips, recalling his kiss—a kiss for the touch of enchantment.

Turning, she stared at Näeré. "How is it that a human hears my thoughts? You said it was not possible."

"Perhaps I was wrong," the sorceress Näeré replied. "Perhaps this human you speak of is held by your magick?"

"And perhaps he is held by more than magick," Grumblton muttered with a shake of his head. He hoped the queen would be successful with her plea to the Winged Council.

The Winged Council

The harpy's head tilted with curiosity at the words of the Dragon Queen.

"If what you say is true and the fragile Damselfly grows strong, why does she not speak before us on behalf of the Grimmoirëns?"

"A fair question, So-elle," Yávië acknowledged. "Arcinaë of Grimmoirë seeks the Sylph. Even now she prepares for the journey with the help of Cwen of Aaradan."

The hum of many whispers filled the council chambers. All present knew that not since before the memories of man had any sought the Sylph and that an enchanted had not asked for their help since the fall of Arcaedya.

Yávië scanned the faces of the council members, seeking allies. Grumblton had said the harpy was the voice of power, and this harpy was definitely interested in the fate of Grimmoirë. Nearly as old as the dragons, the harpy So-elle could recall the fall of the enchanted kingdom of Arcaedya at the hands of evil—the evil that had risen from within the realm of enchantment itself. So-elle remembered the journey of Arcaedya's sovereign, Lyrë, to the city of the Sylph.

"Does no one recall the fall of Arcaedya and the lessons learned there?" Yávië asked, seeing the nods of those old enough to remember.

"Aye," So-elle admitted. "Many are too young to recall, but all in Réverë have been taught the lesson of watchfulness. The Grimmoirëns placed their trust in Men. Men were to have held watch over the Grimmoirëns, but they did not."

"This is true, Councilor, though Men do rise to wage war against the evil on Ælarggessæ in hopes of bringing back the magick. Only the Feie can return the light of enchantment. The Damselfly asks only that you petition the Council of Elders to hear her request. She does not ask the Winged Council to speak for her, nor does she ask that you support her plea for the help of the Feie."

"The Feie are timid and unreasonable," the harpy hissed with distaste. "The decision should not be left to them. We shall vote."

Yávië nodded and withdrew to the antechamber, hoping that the harpy's dislike for the Feie would win Arcinaë her moment before the Council of Elders.

"It is my recommendation," So-elle advised, "that the Winged Council grants the request of our sister, the Damselfly. I vote that the Council of Elders be petitioned on her behalf. How vote you, Fáedre, Matriarch of the Deathstoneflyte?"

"I vote against the Feie and for the Damselfly," the enormous war dragon snarled.

"And you, Kasia, Matriarch of the Stone Sprites, guardian of the tels?"

"Aye, I vote also for the wingless Damselfly," Kasia answered.

"Torpa, what is your vote?" the harpy asked the elegant leader of the Wyndwryn, dark kindred of the fair Damselflies of Grimmoirë.

"She asks naught but a moment to speak. I agree we should give her that. The Council of Elders will never force the Feie to bring back the light of Grimmoirë, but Arcinaë should be allowed to ask."

"Azrea, Matriarch of the Emeraldflyte, what say you?" The harpy eyed the great green dragon of the Verdant Forest.

"Aye," Azrea's voice boomed, "let her speak."

"Faera, Matriarch of the Kilstoneflyte, how vote you?"

"Let the Damselfly speak to the Elders. It can do no harm," the black and red war dragon responded.

"Field Sprite?" So-elle sought the tiny matriarch.

"I too say let her speak," Wehta answered.

"Azaeria, Matriarch of the Suunflyte, what is it you say?" asked the harpy.

"Aye, all should have the right to petition the Elders, even a single Damselfly," the wind dragon said.

"Ilvaria, ruler of the ice dragons, what is your vote?" asked So-elle.

"Aye," Ilvaria nodded her agreement.

"And Cesta of the Wood Sprites, how say you?"

"Let her speak," the little matriarch answered with a bob of her head.

"Summon Yávië, the Dragon Queen," So-elle indicated, watching as the Wyndwryn rose with a flutter of her wings and called Yávië back into the council chamber.

"We will petition the Council of Elders to hear the plea of Arcinaë of Grimmoirë when next the twin moons are full. So says the Winged Council," the harpy declared, her hard green eyes glittering. "I do not know if we vote for the Damselfly or against the Feie, but the result is the same."

Yávië nodded her thanks and exited the Winged Council chambers, knocking Brengven the Feie to the ground as she opened the door.

"Eavesdropping, Brengven?" she asked, helping the little Feie to his feet.

"Nay, I was wiping the dust from the door," Brengven huffed. "And the door is so thick I could not hear a word. What did the council say? Keep her at the fortress? Give her a scrap of woods here in Révérē?"

"Neither, my Feie friend. They agreed to petition the Council of Elders on the Damselfly's behalf. Arcinaë will be allowed to ask the Elders for the help of the Feie."

"It will never be allowed. The Elders will never force us to enter such a dangerous and fearful place, one filled with evil men and who knows what else. Never, I tell you, *never*!" Brengven sputtered.

"Afraid you will lose the bet with Cwen?" Yávië asked, laughing at the Feie's furious expression.

"That girl will never win. I promise it. You wait and see."

"Indeed I shall. Now be a good Feie and summon a rift to the House of Aaradan for me," Yávië said, raising an eyebrow at Brengven's momentary hesitation. "I am not the daughter of Nall. You would be wise to remember that, Brengven."

With a sniff, Brengven complied, shouting after the queen as she stepped through the rift, "Tell Cwen I will win and Arcinaë of Grimmoirë will never see the Feie of Réverē stand on Grimmoirën soil."

"Tell her yourself," Yávië shouted back.

Chapter 10: The Sylph

The twin moons of Eun and Euné neared alignment between Ædracmoræ and the Topaz Star. Cwen pointed to the sky. "Within the hour, we must stand in the deepened shadow of the moons' path and ascend the steps to the city of the Sylph. The gates of Keslbaen open only when the darkest shadows caress the Euclasestone seal."

"How do you know this, Cwen?" Arcinaë asked.

"We saw it happen," Talin answered with a shrug. "From the trees—there." He pointed to the heavy trees along the edge of the Verdant Forest.

"We had accompanied Nall and Näeré to New Xavian City and were chasing a sleepy stag, pretending it was a deadly deathshade. We were very young. As we reached the edge of the woods, the stag bounded into the clearing and was struck by the deeper darkness of the shadowed moons. We climbed the trees and watched the path of shadow move across the meadow. When it reached a certain point, we saw the glittering blackness of the polished stairway leading into the city. The doors opened as the shadow struck the seal."

"And you saw the Sylph?"

"Only one, the one who is said to slip away—"

"And share the secrets of the Sylph," Arcinaë took up the story. "I know the legends. They also say the Sylph's generosity is as shadowed as the entrance to their city." Pensively, she added, "Naught is ever given freely but purchased with something held dear."

"What do you hold dear, Arcinaë," Cwen whispered, "that has not already been taken?"

"Ilerion," Arcinaë admitted to herself, watching with dread as the moons fell deeper into shadow. "I hold the life of Ilerion very dear."

"It begins," Talin said, rising from a crouch. "Shall we see where the path will lead us?"

Arcinaë's soft words brought startled looks from Cwen and Talin. "Into discord and death…"

"A bit of discord is acceptable, death is not," Talin snapped.

Arcinaë's eyes met his, "The death will come, hunter."

"Who, Arcinaë? Who will die?" Cwen grabbed Arcinaë's arm.

Jerking her arm away, Arcinaë stared up at Cwen. "I do not know! Only that death will follow us when we leave this place. It will cling to us as a cloak, taking one of us. I do not know who. I did not see the one who fell," she sighed. She did, however, recognize the voice of the one who had called out. It had been Lord Ilerion of Baene.

"Come away, Arcinaë. This cannot be so important that you would risk the life of another." Cwen reached for Arcinaë's hand. "Do not risk Ilerion's life."

Arcinaë jerked away and raced for the shimmering stairway now appearing before them, following as it led upward toward Keslbaen, City of the Sylph. "If it is Ilerion, I will find a way to save him," she shouted over her shoulder, "for I am enchanted."

"And if it is not? Will you still find a way to save the one you threaten?" Talin called after her.

Spinning around to face him, Arcinaë pointed her finger at him. "I am not the threat, hunter! It is another, someone in our future."

Cwen stepped between them. "The darkness approaches the seal. We do not have time for your bickering. It was only a vision—a feeling. You did not see someone actually die, did you, Arcinaë?"

Glaring at Talin, Arcinaë shook her head. "Nay, I did not see the death."

"Go, the shadow touches the gates!" Cwen pushed Arcinaë up the remaining stairs, glancing back to see Talin following slowly.

When they stood before the doors, Cwen reached out and touched the seal. It flowed as if liquid, shifting from deep emerald to darkest sapphire blue and every hue between, in long ripples of subtly graduated color. Rising around them, the darkness deepened as the last light was driven from the face of each of the twin moons. As the shadow reached the edge of the seal, it was accompanied by the deep resonance of stone grinding against stone. From the center of the rapidly widening gap between the heavy doors, a sudden, brilliant, cerulean light began to emanate.

A high, thin whistling sound pierced the silence a second before the arrival of the Sylph. The elemental entity formed and hovered in front of the three beings waiting to enter Keslbaen. Drawing the air towards her center, her form shifted to reveal an opalescent beauty that drifted from a brilliant white through nacreous grays to the deep indigo of night. Her eyes sparkled with the prismatic incandescence of the stars, subtly changing with each flutter of her lids. Smoky tendrils floated about her face, tantalizing and enigmatic.

"Talin…" Her voice was little more than a whisper of air as her cool, ethereal fingers stroked his face. Then, as quickly as she had come, she swept away down the stairs and into the depths of the night.

Talin rubbed his face, still feeling the chill of the Sylph's touch. He heard Arcinaë's words again: "I am not the threat, hunter. It is another, someone in our future."

Arcinaë watched him, a tear falling for the death one of them would meet. As their eyes locked, she whispered, "I cannot stop it." Then she turned and walked into Keslbaen.

Cwen looked from Arcinaë's retreating back to Talin's face. "What does she mean?"

"I do not know, Cwen, but I already regret having ever met her."

Gesturing for Cwen to proceed, he followed her into the blinding light.

Keslbaen, City of the Sylph was not so much a city as a palace of crystal, crystal as clear as lightning glass. Shards of Gaianite lay scattered about—as if flung by the hand of a child who had tired of his playthings—and emanated flashes of the same bright cerulean blue light they had seen earlier. Six of the Sylph glided around Arcinaë, examining her from every angle.

"She must not have wasted any time asking for wings," Talin muttered.

"Talin, whatever it is, I will make it right. It is my fault we are here," Cwen whispered. "I will not let what we have done harm us or those we know."

Talin reached up and ruffled Cwen's hair. "Do not dwell on it. It was only a vision, remember? I do not hold a strong belief in the Damselfly's visions… Now if it were Grumblton, well, that would be different."

"She is sovereign," said the wispy voice of the Sylph nearest them. "Who brings her here?"

"I do," Cwen answered, holding up her hand to ward off Talin's protest. "I am Cwen of Aaradan."

"And how did you know how to find us?" asked another.

"I saw the doors open and your sister escape when I was a young child. I have never forgotten it."

"From the trees? When last the door opened?" the Sylph prompted.

"Aye, from the edge of the Verdant Forest."

"And this one? He saw also?"

"Aye, I was with her," Talin said, stepping nearer to Cwen.

"Sharaga does not escape. She seeks the one who—" A sharp sibilant whisper, almost a hiss, from another of the Sylph brought her words to a halt and a rapid pulsation within her form. "My sister's tongue is loose," said the second Sylph who now addressed them, the nebulous features of her face forming a fleeting smile. "Why is it that you seek the Sylph?" she asked, her dazzling eyes finding Arcinaë.

"It is said you have great power, greater than any enchanted. I seek help restoring Grimmoirë of Ælarggessæ. Legend says you once helped the enchanted of Ædracmoræ—that you helped them when Arcaedya collapsed." Arcinaë spoke softly, drawing surprised looks from Talin and Cwen.

"The sovereign—" A raised hand silenced the speaker as swiftly as it had the earlier interruption.

"It is true. The sovereign Lyrë sought a new home for those dispossessed by the evil loosed within Arcaedya. Réverē was given to her by the Sylph. Cloaked and sealed against future attacks. Is this what you seek, Arcinaë of Grimmoirë? Nothing more?" the Sylph asked, as she reached out toward Arcinaë's shoulder, allowing the cool airiness of her touch to extend beneath the leather shirt to the scars that marred Arcinaë's back.

Biting her lip as if to keep herself from speaking, Arcinaë shook her head.

"Can you restore her wings?" Cwen's voice shattered the silence.

"She does not ask for wings," the Sylph answered, swirling to face Cwen's interruption. "Do you ask it for her?"

"No!" Talin shouted, grabbing Cwen's shoulder and dragging her back. "Do not ask anything on her behalf."

"Why do you fear us, Talin?"

He froze for an instant and then pointed to Arcinaë. "She had a vision, a vision that told of the death of someone. And the other one…touched me." His hand rose to his cheek at the recollection.

"And you are fearful of visions and touches?"

Hearing it spoken aloud by another made it seem foolish, and Talin shook his head angrily. "I do not know."

"What Arcinaë saw had nothing to do with the Sylph. She only thought it so because you approached Keslbaen at the time of the vision. And Sharaga's touch has saved your life. We harm no one. We bring only wisdom and strength to those who seek us. Do you believe my words, Talin?" murmured the shimmering Sylph.

"I do not know," Talin said again, frowning to cover his discomfort.

"Do you not believe I should grant the Sovereign of Grimmoirë wings?"

"You can grant her wings?" Talin asked his disbelief so evident as to bring forth a ripple of laughter from the sisters.

"We could grant *you* wings Talin, if that were your desire."

"I do not want wings, but she does. If you can grant them, do it. It is what she came for." Talin looked knowingly at Arcinaë, feeling satisfaction as she blushed and looked away.

"Go." The Sylph pointed toward the gates. "Go. Arcinaë will remain with us. I will return her to Révaré in time for her meeting with the Council of Elders."

Without a backward glance, Talin pulled Cwen after him.

"Wait! Talin, we cannot leave her here alone," Cwen shouted, pushing Talin away. She raced back toward the stairway only to find it fading like an evanescent dream as the shadow of Ædracmoræ passed beyond the faces of the two moons.

Arcinaë looked longingly after Cwen and Talin, fearing that having entered Keslbaen, the city of the Sylph, she would never leave it.

"You may go whenever you wish," the six Sylph spoke as one. "Your path is steep and filled with more pain than the paths of most, but you are the vessel of legend and by your suffering strength is built."

"Damselfly, I am Wysdym. I shall speak for all of us. You ask that Grimmoirë be sealed as was done for Révaré, yet Talin's belief is that it is wings you truly wish."

Arcinaë hung her head and wept, glad that Talin and Cwen did not see. "Grimmoirë must be safe. I will convince the Council of Elders to send the Feie to restore the light, but if you do not shield our kingdom, I know that it will fall again. There will always be evil men."

"And also good men," Wysdym added, her eyes burning into Arcinaë's heart. "Why is it you do not speak of Ilerion's quest to restore order to your world?"

"I do not wish him to die."

"And you believe that speaking his name to us will bring about his death?"

"Legend tells that the Sylph require something dear in exchange for their gifts. I do not wish to give Ilerion's life," Arcinaë sobbed.

The tinkle of Sylphen laughter caused her to look up.

Wysdym's eyes glittered with amusement as she spoke. "You must have been listening to the Feie. The Feie are known to tell wild tales about those things they do not understand, and they understand very little."

Reaching out, Wysdym allowed the soft, cooling air current from her fingertips to again flow across Arcinaë's back.

"It will not be easy or painless. The gift of wings requires a spell of transformation and comes with a high price. As a being of enchantment, barring death by violence or sacrifice, your life is endless. The gift of wings will bring mortality, leaving you with a life not much longer than that of a human. Wings are a very costly gift."

"If the cost of wings is my own life, what then will be the cost of the safety of Grimmoirë?"

With a sweep of her hand, Wysdym brought a vision before Arcinaë. To see again the vision of hunters slaughtering the Damselflies drove Arcinaë to her knees, causing her to wail in sorrow and despair as if it had all happened only moments ago. Still she could not look away. She saw herself tossed to the ground, her life ebbing—left to die. She watched herself rise to her feet, legs shaking, and scream at the men who searched her settlement. She watched as Ilerion lifted her gently and carried her away, thus saving a life that should have ended.

"Why do you show me this? Why?" Arcinaë wept.

"The price of the Grimmoirën seal has already been paid with the blood of the Damselflies. I shall cast the cloak and seal over Grimmoirë at its restoration, just as I did for Réverē when the blood of the Euneans bought its safety. But there is still the question of your wings."

"What of Ilerion?" Arcinaë whispered, again ignoring the question of her wings.

"His fate is tied to yours, and to the Damselfly's soul that he holds."

Arcinaë paled. "Please do not take his life."

Wysdym's eyes searched Arcinaë's. "Ilerion's life is held in your hands, Arcinaë, not in the hands of the Sylph. He must free Cylacia's soul before it is taken by the evil. If he does not, he will die by his own hand—a surrender born of loss and failure."

"His loss and my failure?" Arcinaë asked, but her question was met with silence from the Sylph. "How will I know what to do?"

"Divine your truth." Wysdym's soft voice caressed Arcinaë's hair, causing little tendrils to waft around the Damselfly's face.

As Arcinaë raised her hand to brush her hair from her eyes, a vision of her path formed before her. Her eyes widened and she sought the faces of the Sylph, watching as they shimmered and pulsed with the knowledge of the vision they now shared with her. Wysdym's words were more insistent this time. "There is still the question of your wings."

Arcinaë's chin rose with determination—her voice was true and carried no hint of doubt. "I accept the gift of wings."

"Remove your shirt."

Arcinaë untied the slender laces and drew the shirt up over her head, dropping it to the floor. She covered her breasts with crossed arms, shivering in the chill of Keslbaen. As the words of transformation began, Arcinaë's eyes remained locked on Wysdym's lips. Even so, she was unprepared when the Sylph struck. The elemental forces inherent within her Sylphen body were driven through Arcinaë's chest with the powerful charge of a warhorse.

Arcinaë's screams of agony shattered the crystal palace, bringing its walls down in innumerable cascades of small sparkling shards. Wysdym's exit though her body had left two tiny golden circles smudged high on Arcinaë's shoulders, one on either side of her backbone. The pain intensified, striking like the sword of a hunter up the length of Arcinaë's spine, from the small of her back to the base of her skull. Arcinaë believed she would be torn apart by the power unleashed in the creation of her wings, but long unused muscles flexed, stretched and grew strong in preparation for their new burden. In a crescendo of anguish, Arcinaë's final scream of terror traveled across the palace, the vibrations from her voice bringing a further cascade of splintered crystals raining down. Into the center of each golden circle, a crystal spear struck, driving her face forward to the ground.

Arms around her knees, Arcinaë cradled herself, aware only of the pain of her transformation. Dazzling white lights played across her field of vision—the light of suffering—as her blood was drawn into the wings that were emerging from the crystal spears. As fragile as the skeletal leaves of autumn yet as supple as the new growth of spring, luminous and pale, swirling with iridescent color, four translucent wings unfolded. Veined with gold, pulsing with life, the wings unfurled, extending until they reached their full length, each longer than Arcinaë was tall. She rocked, sobbing with exhaustion, pain and fear.

With a wave of her hands, Wysdym gathered the shards that littered the floor and sent them swirling back to their proper places. Pulsing rapidly, the Sylph heated the air that formed her body, cloaking the tremulous, weeping Damselfly in warmth.

"By your choice, the wheel of life turns, the vessel awaits its filling, and the world's history races toward the time of the halflings, toward the war with the Heteroclites. The immortality of the enchanted is taken from you, Arcinaë of Grimmoirë. In its place, you have been given the gift of wings, strength of sword and the power of persuasion. Sleep, Arcinaë of Grimmoirë. Dream."

Ilerion's Choice

Far beyond the city of Keslbaen, the Sylph Sharaga observed the castle of Twode below, alive with torchlight and the wails of the dying. Survivors of Lord Lazaro's attack were being hanged along the battlement, their tortured screams ending abruptly as each fell to meet the knot of the noose. Sharaga pulsed in agitation, wanting to intervene—to crush this man's wickedness within the folds of her elemental power—but it was not to be. Her task lay with the man hidden in the trees, a man who would do something extremely foolhardy if she did not stop him.

Ilerion and Nilus lay in darkness, watching as Lazaro's evil ended the lives of those who had remained to defend Elduuf's castle.

"Bastard does not even free the souls of the dead!" Nilus cursed, as Lazaro's hunters continued to hang victims atop the parapet.

"We shall free them when he has been dealt with, Nilus. Until then, they must wait." Ilerion's knuckles whitened across his clenched fists.

The wind shifted, and they shivered in its sudden chill.

"Ilerion of Baene." A whispered voice little more than a breath embraced them.

Rolling on to his back, blade drawn, Ilerion stared up at the ethereal beauty of the Sylph Sharaga.

"Stay your weapons, for you cannot harm me. I bear warnings

and the gifts of the Sylph. I have also come for the soul of the Damselfly."

"She is safe, sent to Révere, where not even one such as you can harm her," Ilerion said.

Sharaga's color shifted from the depths of indigo to blazing white. "The other, the one whose soul lies trapped in darkness beneath the earth of the river bank, warns that Evalio of Lamaas is sent to murder your king while you lie here in the grass planning to die by the wicked lord's sword. She begs that you allow me to take her soul before it is too late."

"Cylacia," Ilerion whispered, his brow furrowed in confusion. "I freed her soul upon the funeral pyre. I do not hold her."

"By your actions, you have bound the souls of two, not allowing either the freedom of death or the fullness of life." Sharaga's pulsing anger heated the air around them, causing it to rise and flurry, blowing leaves and dust across the hunters. "Choose, Ilerion, for you must not bind them both."

"I do not understand." Ilerion shook his head. "I have no desire to hold Cylacia's soul from its rest, and Arcinaë…" Her name brought her image before him, so small and fragile, so gentle and kind and… fearless. His heart pounded, his hands shook and he found himself drenched in chilling sweat. "And Arcinaë belongs with the enchanted," he finally choked out.

"And you, Ilerion? Where do you belong?" Sharaga prodded gently.

"Nowhere—I belong nowhere."

"He belongs with Arcinaë." Nilus' voice cut through Ilerion and diverted Sharaga's attention. Her eyes searched those of the short man.

"Indeed? And why do you know this when he does not?"

"Because he is a fool and I am not. I have seen him look at her when he believes no one sees. He fears his feelings for Arcinaë somehow lessen his love for Cylacia. Like I said, he is a fool."

"Come. I shall bind time and let you sort this out with the Damselfly," Sharaga called, casting a spell to hold Ælarggessæ still and silent.

Ilerion stared at Nilus, looking for signs of life but saw none.

"What have you done?" he shouted furiously at the Sylph.

"He merely waits, as do the others." She gestured, indicating the frozen scene below them at Elduuf's castle.

"If you have this kind of power, why do you not stop Lazaro's treachery?" Ilerion snapped.

"That, Lord Ilerion, is your task. Come," Sharaga said again, drifting toward the rift she had created.

Ilerion did not see the palace or the Sylphen sisters. He saw only Arcinaë, as she sat on the ground, huddled within a heavy cloak of darkness. Quickly striding to her side, he knelt and lifted her to him, holding her against his chest and softly whispering her name, unaware that the darkness of the seeming cloak covering Arcinaë had shifted, subtly reformed itself and quietly stolen away.

"Free her." His voice was sharp as he looked up, seeking Sharaga.

"She has freely chosen, Ilerion. Now you must choose. Will you walk the path she has chosen, or will you follow the dead?"

Ignoring Sharaga's question, Ilerion repeated, "Free her, free Arcinaë of her sleep."

"Very well, you have chosen life. With your choice come the gifts of the Sylph: strength and the power of peace are granted to you, Lord Ilerion of Baene. Use these gifts wisely to raise the halflings. The soul of Cylacia rises to meet those who await her among the stars." With a slight bow of her head, Sharaga and her sisters faded, leaving Ilerion alone with Arcinaë, alone in a familiar room at the inn of Kleal.

He sat on the floor with his back against the bed. Arcinaë rested in his arms, her breath warm beneath his chin. What he had thought to be part of her cloak was now a set of iridescent wings, threaded with gold, pulsing with the blood of life.

Arcinaë moaned softly and shifted against him, drawing his gaze to her pale breasts as her arms reached up around his neck. Her eyes opened. They were bright and fearless, filled with love and trust. Ilerion's mouth sought hers with urgency and a passion he had believed lost to him. Drawing back to seek acceptance in her eyes, his breath came in ragged gasps and his heart hammered against his ribs.

A moment before, he had wanted nothing more than to pull her down beneath him, but now, as she stared at him so intently, he hesitated and lifted her to her feet instead.

"I do not know how we have come to be here, Arcinaë, or why, but I must tell you what I feel for you."

"You feel the thunder of the waves upon the shore and the heat that sears your heart and burns the breath from your lungs. I feel it too, Ilerion, and I am not afraid."

He drank in the beauty of her face and allowed his eyes to move to the softness of her slightly parted lips and to the hollow at the base of her throat, where he saw the steady beat of her heart. His hand trembled as it rose to touch her, and his eyes closed as he felt the heat of her skin.

When his eyes opened, he stood once again on the hill above Elduuf's castle, Caval's reins held loosely in his hand. Lazaro and his men were gone, only the dead remained as evidence of the madman's passing. Taking a deep breath, Ilerion felt a vicious ache within.

He mounted, then turned Caval, and looked into Nilus's concerned face.

"I am well. We must seek Evalio at the palace of the king,"

Ilerion took another deep breath and urged the stallion forward, past his friend.

"Where did you go?" Nilus asked as Ilerion passed.

"To Arcinaë," Ilerion answered. "I went to Arcinaë."

Nodding, Nilus followed Lord Ilerion toward the palace of King Úlanovë.

⊷⧖⧴

"Why must you take him from me?" Arcinaë asked wistfully, her skin still tingling from Ilerion's touch.

"There is much work to do if Ælarggessæ is to be saved and Grimmoirë restored. The time for your passion will come, Arcinaë of Grimmoirë, and it will be sweeter because of the time you have lost here," Sharaga answered. "Let us go. I must return you to Wysdym and you must prepare to meet the Council of Elders."

Chapter 11: Seven Names

Outside the palace of King Úlanovë, Ilerion's fist slammed into Evalio's jaw, silencing the man's laughter and dropping him like a heart struck stag. Nilus's blade swiftly incapacitated the hunter to the left of Evalio, leaving him gasping and clutching his gut. The third man drew his sword and faced Ilerion's wrath.

"Bind Evalio!" Ilerion shouted to Nilus, as he moved forward to meet the one now threatening him.

"Norgeau," Ilerion's voice was an angry hiss, "I remember when you were a man of honor."

"That was before my lord turned to the comfort of a beast, Ilerion. I remember you when you were a man."

A violent backhand threw Norgeau to his knees. "Man or beast I am a far better swordsman than you." Ilerion smiled wickedly. "Fight me and die today, or take a message to Lazaro and live until next we meet."

"And Evalio?" Norgeau asked, circling away from Ilerion's sword.

"Evalio is already dead for his crimes against the Damselflies. I have heard he hunts me, and today he is unfortunate enough to have found me. We have business, Evalio and I. King Úlanovë has never done ill though it may also be said he has never done good, either. Who placed the indoli in the palace well, Norgeau? Was that you? Or Magyr?"

Seeing the look of shock and horror on Norgeau's face, Ilerion lowered his sword. "Nay, I did not think so—neither of you has the stomach for this type of crime. Lazaro ordered the king's murder, but Evalio chose the coward's way. Poison all, rather than risk any of his own blood.

"Go. Tell Lord Lazaro his life runs short. That I will meet him on the battlefield at Durover, and there I will deliver the Damselflies' revenge. The blood of his hunters will flow freely, and I will see Ælarggessæ purged of the very name Lazaro.

"Make sure he leaves," Ilerion told Nilus, before kneeling beside the still unconscious Evalio. Checking the bonds to ensure their strength, Ilerion lifted the body of the limp hunter over his shoulder and carried him to Caval. Throwing his burden over the horse's back, Ilerion mounted behind it and headed back toward the king's palace.

The grounds were littered with the bodies of humans and beasts. All had been poisoned by the well. Ilerion knew that each had died in agony, the potency of the indoli-tainted water acting swiftly, causing a few minutes of unimaginable pain and then death. The stench of the self-soiled bodies rose about them, rousing Evalio from his unconsciousness.

Tossing water from his flask into Evalio's face, Ilerion watched with satisfaction as the hunter drew back in fear that he too had been subjected to the poison's power.

"Nothing so swift for you Evalio, indoli would be far too kind an end for evil like yours." Grabbing the man by the shirt collar, he dragged him up the steps and into Úlanovë's palace.

"Where is the king?" Ilerion asked, dropping the bound hunter to the floor.

Evalio glared up at his captor and spat toward Ilerion's boots, crying out as Nilus kicked him from behind. "It would be wise to show a bit of respect to Lord Ilerion. His fuse is a bit short and I cannot guarantee your safety if you continue to torment him with vile looks and stringy spittle. Now answer him! Where is the king?"

"I do not know." Evalio glowered.

"You do not know the whereabouts of the man you were sent to kill?"

"Where he lies is unimportant as long as he lies dead."

"How do you know he is dead? Perhaps he was not thirsty and did not drink, or perhaps he chose wine instead of water," Ilerion said, drawing his dagger from its sheath at his belt and smiling as Evalio's eyes widened. "I do not intend to kill you."

"The king is dead. I know he is dead because I had three heavily salted stags delivered to the palace at midday to guarantee his majesty's thirst."

"And at Grimmoirë? Who ordered the butchery of the Damselflies? You or Leuc?" Ilerion's eyes narrowed as he awaited the answer.

"Leuc commanded the detail, led the revelry, though I believe the men's appetites were larger than he expected. There were not enough females so they had to be shared. Lazaro himself ordered the cutting of the wings. It seems he has never forgiven the one who refused him and flew away," Evalio laughed.

Ilerion's arm shot forward, slicing the leather that bound Evalio's wrists. Gesturing ahead, he said softly, "Let us find our king."

Evalio hesitated, eyes searching for the closest weapon. Nilus pricked the hunter's side and pointed ahead with the sword. "To the dining hall. It was always Úlanovë's favorite room."

The long table displayed the remains of a feast—roast stag and boar, bread and jam, pitchers of ale and water—and bodies. The king and his favorite courtesans were lying facedown in their vomit-filled plates.

Squatting beside the king, Ilerion lifted the dead man's hand and pulled the signet from his finger. "The king has no heirs so I assume Lazaro intended this ring for himself." He tossed the ring toward Evalio and laughed when the hunter missed the catch and fumbled to retrieve the royal signet from the slick muck on the floor.

"Sit and enjoy the meal," Ilerion said, pulling out an empty chair.

"I do not eat with the dead," Evalio snarled. "If you are going to kill me, do it. If you do not have the stomach for it, I will leave."

"Give him your sword," Ilerion called to Nilus.

"Ilerion, we need the names."

"Ah yes, the names of the murderers. Who were the others at Grimmoirë, Evalio? Leuc, one called Gaztin and you. Who else?" Ilerion asked pouring a glass of water from a pitcher on the table. "You look thirsty, Evalio? Are you thirsty?"

"Nay, and if I were, I would choose ale."

"Give him your sword, Nilus," Ilerion said again.

Nilus suddenly grabbed Evalio from behind, dragging him to the floor, choking off his breath. "If you do not tell me who killed the Damselflies, I will pour the water down your throat myself!" he hissed into the hunter's ear. "Tell me, and Ilerion will kill you in a fair fight as suits his honorable nature. Stay silent again, and I will cut off—"

"Nilus." Ilerion shook his head. "We will not torture Evalio as he tortured those around us and the defenseless Damselflies. We will allow him a fair fight for his freedom when we have what we require."

Tightening his hold on Evalio's throat, Nilus whispered, "Tell me. He cannot help you, for I can cut you before he takes a step." Evalio let out a high pitched squeal as he felt the knife's blade pierce the leather at his crotch.

"She was just an innocent girl," Nilus said. "Not much more than a child. I saw her injuries, you piece of filth. Now tell me what I want to know, and I will let you die like a man at the hands of Lord Ilerion. If you do not, you will die screaming as I flay you—provided you can scream around what I intend to cram down your throat!"

"Nilus, he turns blue. He cannot answer if he cannot breathe." Ilerion took a step toward his friend. "Let him go, Nilus."

"You did not see." Nilus looked up at Ilerion with tears in his eyes. "You did not see what they did to her."

Ilerion reached down and took the knife from Nilus's hand. "I held her broken body in Grimmoirë, I heard her screams every night, Nilus. We do not torture others. We are not madmen or monsters."

Evalio grabbed Nilus's arm and pushed it from his throat, rising to his feet and staring at both Ilerion and Nilus as if they were a species as yet undiscovered. "You weep for a beast?"

Ilerion's hand shot out, grabbing Evalio by the throat. "I am all that stands between you and a man who feels like a father to the woman you butchered." He released Evalio's throat and pushed him to the ground, laughing as the hunter scrambled away from the body he fell across. "You fear the dead? I weary of protecting you. Tell Nilus the names."

Evalio's eyes shifted from Ilerion to Nilus, who now stood with his sword drawn, red-rimmed eyes ablaze.

Ilerion grabbed Nilus's sword and tossed it to Evalio. Grabbing the sword, Evalio shook his head at Ilerion's foolishness, a cruel smile touching his lips.

"Cethe, Lymaen, Colne, Obour, Gaztin, Leuc and me. That is who went to Grimmoirë and killed the beasts, used them, butchered them and burned them. It was no different than using a serving wench or butchering a sow. They were not even human, Ilerion. When did you forget you were a man?"

"I have never forgotten I am a man, Evalio, but it seems you have," Ilerion said.

"I will kill you, my lord, and then I will kill the fat man," Evalio sneered.

With a roar, Nilus charged Evalio, slamming into him and knocking him backward across the urine- and vomit-slicked floor. His fingers clawed at Evalio's windpipe, crushing it and ripping it from his throat, sending a pulsing stream of blood across the room. A faint gurgle escaped the dead man's lips as his hands fell to his sides and his fingers released the sword of Nilus.

"Steaming pile of putrid flesh," Nilus spat, kicking the dead man.

Ilerion looked at Nilus with a tight smile.

"What?" Nilus asked with a frown, wiping the blood from his hands onto the back of his leathers before reclaiming his sword and the signet of the king. "We got the list of names."

"Aye, we got the list of names. By midday two day's hence, Lazaro will be warned of our intent, and Reduald will have already taken five hundred men into the castle at Durover. There is naught left to do but for us to sweep in behind and crush the madman in the vise. The plan is sound."

"And what then, Ilerion? When Lazaro is defeated, what will you do?"

"According to Sharaga, the Sylph, I have chosen life, so I suppose I will be forced to live it, to raise Castle Baene from the ruins and begin anew. And you, Nilus?"

"I shall serve the new king," Nilus said without hesitation, holding up the signet ring. "I shall keep this safe until such time that he requests it."

Laughing, Ilerion slapped his friend on the back. "That will require a challenge for the crown since the old fool left no heirs."

"Or a vote of the council," Nilus muttered.

"The Council of Ælarggessæ has not been called to meet since the crown was challenged by the kingdom of Carribeg. And that was even before my father's time. It is not likely that a new king will be chosen peacefully by the vote of a council. When the fear of Lazaro's army is withdrawn, the lords will discover they are more interested in the crown than they believed. Reduald would make a good king. He is solid, a man of honor and reason. I would support him."

"And Rádek of Baene led an army against Carribeg, preserving the crown and being granted Carribeg's land holdings. Is that not so?"

"Aye, it doubled the holdings of Baene and is why the king's palace lies within its borders. It was considered the safest place." Glancing around at the death, Ilerion gave a shake of his head. "But today it was not. Let us free the souls of these dead and be away to meet Elduuf and Tondhere."

Ilerion and Nilus watched as the sun rose and the first light of a new day flooded the mound of still smoldering bodies. Only Evalio's dark soul remained trapped in its body, awaiting consumption and scattering by the scavengers that would later be drawn by its rotting stench in the mid-afternoon heat.

As Ilerion mounted Caval, he paused to whisper the ancient blessing that would guide the souls of the dead to their final place among the stars of Ælarggessæ's heavens.

Nilus's sudden shout, "For the crown and Arcinaë," brought a smile. Ilerion swung his horse around, sending the stallion pounding past Nilus and toward Lazaro's rendezvous with death at Durover.

Chapter 12: Council of Elders

Willowort the Ancient was holding Arcinaë's soft leather shirt and cutting away the arms and collar, adjusting it to fit a Damselfly with wings. Arcinaë sat cross-legged on the floor before her. As she worked, Willow watched Arcinaë test her new wings, slowly opening and closing them. The girl had not flown yet and for some reason seemed reluctant to do so.

Willow smiled as Arcinaë glanced over her shoulder, catching her image in the polished bronze of the mirror. The wings were beautiful though unlike those of a Damselfly, for the edges had a ragged appearance, resembling those of a buttermoth. Laced with the golden veining that carried her blood, the rich colors of her wings shifted and shimmered as if from the internal ebb and flow of viscous oil upon water.

With a "hmmph," Willow gestured for Arcinaë to rise and handed her the finished shirt.

"'Twill be a perfect fit and not interfere with your flight." The Ancient nodded to herself. "If you ever decides to fly." Pointing at Arcinaë, Willow added, "They have treated you as a human for so long you have comes to believe them."

Arcinaë fitted the altered shirt around her slender body and tightened and tied the laces under her right arm. Examining herself closely in the mirror, she allowed a small smile to touch her lips. With a gentle flutter, she lifted from the floor to hover before Willow. The little Ancient clapped her hands and whooped, "You really can fly! You looks so beautiful!" Suddenly embarrassed, Willow stopped, clamping her tiny hand over her mouth.

Arcinaë laughed and leaned down to hug the Ancient. "Willow, thank you. Do you think beauty will sway the council?"

With forehead furrowed, Willow looked at Arcinaë. "Nay, the council is filled with elders full of fear. The Feie have been bustling about, telling tales of woe and terrors. Beauty will not calm the council's worries. Only the truth of your needs will do that."

"And the threat of the Sylph," Willow added, mumbling under her breath.

A knock at the bothie door brought the wizard Grumblton with news that the council awaited Arcinaë, Sovereign of Grimmoirë.

With a heavy sigh, Arcinaë lifted her sword and settled it over her shoulder. Pulling her cloak around to cover her shoulders and wings, she replaced her dagger in the scabbard at her waist. With a last look in the mirror and a final brush of her hair, she nodded that she was ready and followed Willow and Grumblton toward the council chambers.

Willowort and Grumblton took their seats, and Arcinaë approached the dais from which she would petition the Council of Elders. A thousand words swirled inside her mind, threatening her composure and making her long for Ilerion to be at her side. In recent years, his presence had come to give her strength, and she yearned for his spirit, its purity and honor. This council, these elders, could not be allowed to vote against her. If they did, Ælarggessæ would fall to darkness.

Lyrë the Enchantress, current Sovereign of Réverë, stood to address the Council of Elders.

"We have been asked by the Winged Council to hear the petition of Arcinaë, daughter of Aewicaen. Ghyvol the Feie has also asked to speak on behalf of the Feie Council. The plight of Grimmoirë's enchanted is well known to all, and we have made them welcome among us as they await their sovereign's plea and this council's decision. It has been long since this council has been asked to consider a request of such gravity, and we shall weigh the costs carefully."

Arcinaë stood before them, thinking that she should have worn a gown rather than leathers and weapons. She lifted her chin in an attempt to look more like a sovereign, and examined the council members before her. Though wishing she had more experience in diplomacy, she took the time to assess each member individually as her father had taught. Finally, with a shake of her head, she began.

"Grimmoirë lies in darkness, the dragons gone to ground and the gryphons covered by the mists of time. The enchanted folk are dead or seeking refuge among those of Réverē. No spark of magick floats in the air on Ælarggessæ, no faery flies, no harpy rents the air with her scream. The only remnant of magick on Ælarggessæ is the last kiss of the last Damselfly. Without magick, all of Ælarggessæ will soon be dark. The souls of honorable men will be lost to wickedness; the lust for power will cause even the noble to rise up against one another, warring until the last man falls, his mind overcome with jealousy and rage because no enchanted is there to soothe it.

"I have seen the good in men, the honor and purity of spirit. Surely the compassionate hearts of the enchanted cannot allow all of Ælarggessæ to fall into darkness by a refusal to command the rekindling Grimmoirë?

"Nesika, long have you known the humans of Ælarggessæ. They kept you safe from harm by freeing you and your kin to return to the Isle of Grave. As a child, I wore the gold of your eyrie in my hair.

"Paeric, my cousin, would you keep me and my subjects from our homes for all of our days? Would you truly do that by refusing to demand that the fearful Feie rekindle our light?" Arcinaë watched with a heavy heart as Paeric looked away, his fearfulness plain to see.

"Sovereign Lyrē, I beg it of you and of you, So-elle. I know that you remember the fall of Arcaedya with great disquietude. Do not let Grimmoirë remain dark because of your fears and the fears of the Feie. I beseech you, do not." Arcinaë choked back tears and her eyes sought those of Ghyvol the Feie as he stood to speak.

"The Feie beg the council to see that there is no hope for Grimmoirë. Even their sovereign says the land already lies dark and lifeless. Allow their sovereign to call her gryphons and dragons into Réverē. The enchanted are safe here. The humans who vowed to keep Grimmoirë safe have failed. It is, in fact, the wickedness of the humans that is responsible for the death of the enchanted. Surely the council must see that to send the Feie into Grimmoirë is far too dangerous to consider."

Sovereign Lyrë's voice was soft as she said, "You must understand, Arcinaë of Grimmoirë, that it is not possible for this council to act in such a way that any enchanted may be threatened. Moreover, the fate of Ælarggessæ's humans is not the responsibility of this council. As long as Grimmoirë remains dark and her mirrors sealed, there is no threat to Réverē. To summon the mirrors and open the way between our kingdoms brings threat not only to the Feie but to all of us."

"A human saved my life and kept me safe. Do not tell me there is more honor in the code of a man than in the Council of the Elders," Arcinaë said fiercely, tears of anger welling. "There is no danger to the Feie! The Sylph have promised to seal Grimmoirë against any further threat."

"The Sylph are not represented here," Lyrë pointed out.

"Aye, they are," Willowort said, looking with a tender smile at the weeping Damselfly. She made a small beckoning gesture toward the far corner of the chamber.

The atmosphere thickened and the light dimmed. A sudden cooling current of air swept over the assembly. The room grew cold. Feathers ruffled, fur lifted and hair stood on end as the ethereal form of Wysdym emerged. Addressing the council, the strength of her whispered words was enhanced by their soothing tones, falling upon her listeners like the soft rustle of leaves.

"It is shameful that those we have helped do not see fit to help others. What if I had refused you, Sovereign Lyrë? At the fall of Arcaedya, what if the Sylph had said no? Would you sit here so comfortably protected in Réverē? Nay, you would lie dead, butchered at the hands of your own kind."

Wysdym's voice caressed the council, the pulsing elements within her form shifting to deep indigo, thence nacre and returning to brilliant, blinding white as she continued. "A pact has been entered into between the Sylph and the Damselfly wherein the Syph agree to seal the sacred ground of Grimmoirë and protect the Feie as they rekindle its light. Will this not satisfy this council and the Feie as well?"

"This council seeks only to protect the enchanted and Réverē. If the Sylph are willing to accompany the Feie and guarantee their safety as well as the protection of Grimmoirë and Réverē, this council will not oppose the rekindling. Feie Ghyvol, will the Feie accept these conditions without a direct command of the council?"

"Perhaps. Though Brengven has assured the Feie Council that only death awaits us in Grimmoirë, if the Sylph will vow their protection it is possible that the others can be convinced we shall remain safe," Ghyvol said.

"Paeric, summon Brengven the Feie," Lyrë's soft voice commanded.

Paeric the Wyndwryn hurried off to seek the Feie, returning momentarily with Brengven in tow, the little Feie's toes barely touching the ground as his agitated escort flew into the room.

"He was leaning against the door in hopes of hearing the council's deliberations!"

Brengven fell to the floor, covering his eyes and quaking in fear at the sight of the Sylph and the angry faces of the council members.

Wysdym hovered over Brengven. "Little man, bring the others and tell them if they do not heed my call, I shall rescind my gifts. I am very displeased with you, Brengven the Feie."

Brengven looked up through squinted eyes. "You would take your gifts from the Feie?" he asked in disbelief.

"And sweep you into the black abyss!" said the Sylph, pulsing with irritation.

Shuddering, Brengven tried one last appeal. "It is death to go to Grimmoirë! The evil there is no less than that we would face in the abyss. Men will kill us in Grimmoirë!" he squealed.

"Stop shivering and hear my words," the Sovereign Lyrë said. "While the Feie rekindle Grimmoirë's light, the Sylph will see it safe, as they saw Réverē safe so long ago. Even as we meet, a man of honor seeks to end the tyranny of the wicked on Ælarggessæ. If he is successful and Lord Lazaro is defeated, Grimmoirë will be restored. We will not lead you into the war of the humans, little Feie. Now bring your kin that they may hear the will of your Council of Elders."

Brengven scrambled out on all fours and immediately began desperately calling in a shrill voice for his kin to join the gathering.

On a whispered glissando of air that pervaded every recess of the chamber, Wysdym allowed her star-filled gaze to return to the Council of Elders and then tabled the motion to be voted upon. "It is your wish to have the Feie rekindle the light of Grimmoirë and the Sylph to cast the seal of secrecy above the sacred ground, is it not?"

The council's chorus of voices called, "Aye."

Sovereign Lyrë then issued the proclamation: "It is this council's command that the Feie rekindle the light of Grimmoirë under the protection of the Sylph,"

"And, Arcinaë, this meets with your approval?" the Sylph asked, cloaking Arcinaë once again in the warmth of soft currents of air.

"Aye." Arcinaë's distracted response was barely audible, for her mind was already with Ilerion at the battlefield that lay before the castle of Durover.

Chapter 13: Battle of Durover

Ilerion stood with his hands clasped before him as seven hundred soldiers lay hidden within the woods to his rear, awaiting the herald of the horns from the castle in the valley below. Inside the castle, Reduald warred against Lazaro's threat. The sound of stones flung from the mangonels and the insistent crash of the battering rams against the gates accompanied the shouted orders, hissing arrows and screams of dying men. Already the braziers blazed, ready to light the fire arrows. Soon Ilerion's men would join those of Reduald, for the first screech of splintering wood had been heard only moments earlier, a signal that the gates would not hold much longer.

The crash of the battering ram breaking through the heavy grillework of the portcullis was accompanied by roars of success from Lazaro's hunters.

The gates flew inward, providing the hunters amassed before it with an entrance to Reduald's castle. From the parapet the horns trumpeted and the sound of Ilerion's echoed across the battlefield in reply.

As Lazaro's hunters flooded into Castle Durover, Ilerion's troops emerged from their mantle of invisibility within the forest and, like a mighty wave upon the shore, flowed over the embankment and onto the battlefield.

Lazaro's hunters wheeled around at the sound of the battle cries from the latest contingent of soldiers, dividing their attention between the army surging forth from the castle under Reduald's orders and the seven hundred soldiers led by Ilerion's charge.

As the approaching first line of archers dropped to allow the second volley of flaming arrows, Lazaro spotted Ilerion and turned his mount to meet his enemy.

Lancers flooded downward between the archers, crashing into Lazaro's swordsmen with a fury that drove them back, their heavy shields then crushing them against those hunters still facing Reduald's attack from the castle.

Nilus waded into the fray, sword viciously slashing any hunter in his path, knowing that victory would come at the cost of many men, some who had once been friends.

Dividing his men as Lazaro had ordered, Oeric of Wawne swept in on Ilerion's troops from opposite ends of the battlefield, drawing their attention away from Lazaro's hunters in order to meet the new threat.

From the wall, Reduald's archers released a new volley of death arrows upon the hunters below, forcing them to retreat from the castle walls. The battle raged amid the fallen bodies, the sickly smell of blood heavy upon the air.

Atop the embankment that had earlier held Ilerion's archers and lancers, Elduuf of Twode led the mounted charge, bringing a new attack raining down on Lazaro and his allies. The thundering sound of the massive warhorses resounded as lances locked against their saddles, the mounted men crushing those on the ground beneath pounding hooves and skewering bodies along the length of their iron-tipped lances.

Seeing Lazaro approach, Ilerion pushed Caval forward at a hammering gallop. As he drew abreast of the madman, Ilerion's lance struck Lazaro's shoulder armor, driving him from the back of his horse and onto the blood-soaked ground.

Movement to Ilerion's left brought Caval around, instinctively allowing his rider to meet the new challenge. Tossing his lance away, Ilerion pulled his sword to meet the broad axe swung by an approaching rider. As the blade met the hunter's wrist—severing it and dropping both hand and axe to the ground—Ilerion recognized the man as Lymaen, one of those responsible for the attack on Arcinaë's village. With a snarl, he dragged Caval around and drove his sword into Lymaen's chest.

"For the Damselflies!" Ilerion hissed through clenched jaws.

Within the castle, Reduald's men drove the hunters back, paving the stones with their bodies. As the last of Lazaro's men fell within the castle walls, Reduald sounded the victory horn, alerting his allies that the castle was clear.

⚜

Willowort the Ancient watched as Arcinaë hurried away from the Council of Elders.

"Follow her!" Willow urged the gryphon, observing as Nesika dipped her head in acknowledgment and swept away in pursuit of the Damselfly.

Arcinaë summoned the Dragons of Fire, her voice powerful within their minds, drawing them upward and freeing the mirror that would allow her to re-enter Grimmoirë.

She threw off her cloak and checked her weapons, grabbing the crossbow from the table and the quiver of bolts from its hook near the door.

Racing toward Réverë's chamber of mirrors, Arcinaë felt the muscles in her shoulders flex, lifting her from the path and speeding her along with strong sweeps of her wings. Without hesitation, she slipped through the mirror, without pause to acknowledge the great dragon that served her.

With arms tight against her sides, she let her wings carry her through the dark underground passages beneath the Lake of Rhymes, no thoughts of drowning entering her mind. She burst out into the darkness of a dead Grimmoirë and headed toward the distant light of Ælarggessæ.

"Sovereign!" a hoarse voice cried behind her.

Closing her mind against the intrusion of those who followed, Arcinaë increased her speed and moved higher, leaving the heavy ash-laden air of her home.

Behind her came the sounds of weighty wing beats and stirring feathers. A clatter of scales and the deep bellows of dragons brought Arcinaë's head around. Behind her, the sky was filled with a small army of gryphons and dragons, all calling sharply as they raced toward their sovereign.

"Nesika," Arcinaë whispered, before swinging back toward Durover and Ilerion's army.

Ahead, beyond the deep woods, Arcinaë saw Durover Castle surrounded by an immense hoard of fighting men. The din of war assailed her senses: the clash of steel on steel, the deep bellows and terrified protests of warhorses, the harsh cries of angry men, the high-pitched screams and low moans of the wounded and dying.

Using her far sight, she scanned the armies below for Ilerion and Nilus, almost missing Nilus in his blood-covered state, recognizing him only by his short stature and stout body.

"Arcinaë?" Nesika, the gryphon, clicked at the Damselfly's side. "What is your command?"

Arcinaë's blank stare brought a round of loud beak clacking from the gryphon matriarch. "You are the sovereign. What is your command? The dragons and gryphons will obey."

"I want it to end—the brutality and death. I just want it to end." Arcinaë looked back at the destruction below. "How can you tell good from evil when they all fight so furiously?"

"Feel the black wickedness in the souls of the evil," Nesika replied. "It surrounds them with darkness, as the glow of righteousness cloaks the pure of heart. Do you not see it, Sovereign?"

"Aye," Arcinaë nodded.

"You fear for Lord Ilerion? Call him to withdraw his men and we shall bring death to the madmen who war against Ælarggessæ."

Arcinaë looked into the wise eyes of the gryphon who had been her friend for so long. Nodding her consent, the Damselfly resumed her search for Ilerion. Fear drove her furiously beating heart when she saw his splendid warhorse, Caval, slick with blood and foam. Caval's rider sat tall, sword raised, face contorted in anger as they sped forward toward a hunter on horseback. As the sword pierced the man's chest, Arcinaë heard Ilerion's words clearly: "For the Damselfly!" Even though she did not recognize the hunter, she knew without a doubt he had been present in her village.

Caval reared, charging forward after a fleeing rider, up the field, away from the main battle.

Ilerion! Arcinaë called into her savior's mind. *Withdraw your men. Nesika leads the enchanted against Lazaro's hunters!*

Ilerion brought Caval to a sudden, sliding halt. His eyes searched for Arcinaë and found the winged army hovering above the forest beyond. He waved a hand in acknowledgment and lifted the battle horn to his lips, sounding a piercing call for retreat. From the castle and the blood-soaked grass before it came the answering calls of Reduald and Elduuf's horns. Without hesitation, Ilerion's soldiers battled their way upward, away from the castle, toward the safety of the woods.

Touching Nesika's warm feathery shoulder, Arcinaë gave the enchanted her command, "Drive this evil from Ælarggessæ. Leave no dark heart beating."

At Nesika's shrill call and sharp clicks of direction, the dragons and gryphons committed themselves to the new sovereign's order. Wings swept back and necks extended, they charged downward toward the enemy hunters.

"For Grimmoirë!" Arcinaë shouted, as she flew toward Ilerion. She hit the ground running, as he leapt from Caval's back and raced to meet her. Sweeping her off her feet, he held her tightly, breathing in the scent of her hair, before pushing her away and shaking her.

"You should not be here! You promised you would go to Réverē," he said, his frown a forlorn attempt to appear angry.

"I did not promise I would stay. See, Ilerion—the enchanted fight for Grimmoirë and Ælarggessæ! No longer will we be meek, allowing evil men to slay us without tasting our revenge."

As Ilerion's soldiers surrounded them, he and Arcinaë looked down into the valley below, watching as the dragons swept across the battlefield, belching fire and grasping in their great talons those who attempted to escape, crushing and ripping away wickedness. On the ground, the hop-step walk of the gryphons was visible among the men and horses, as sharp beaks slashed sword arms and dagger-like claws punctured skulls. Around Arcinaë and Ilerion, men began to shout victoriously, many racing back down the hill to join the enchanted in sweeping madness from Ælarggessæ.

A hand on her shoulder caused Arcinaë to turn and look into the eyes of Nilus. His bald head was covered with bloody handprints, his face streaked with the gore of those who had fallen beneath his sword. His voice was hoarse as he chastised her. "You were supposed to stay in Réveré until we summoned your return."

Ilerion laughed and slapped Nilus on the back. "She did not promise to stay in Réveré."

A rustling of feathers brought a bloodied Nesika, her eyes scowling in pretended annoyance. "You should have called us, my lord. No man should enter battle without the magick of enchantment."

Drawing Arcinaë near, Ilerion teased, "I had the magick of the Damselfly's kiss, a far better enchantment than that of the querulous gryphons."

"For once, I can find no argument, Ilerion," Nesika clicked. "You were wise to steal a kiss."

"I did not say I stole it," Ilerion said with a slow smile.

"Nay, but the eyes of the Damselfly do," Nesika called as she rose skyward.

"The dragons will consume the souls of the wicked," Grundl hissed as he approached. "Reduald asks that you join him in the castle, and your soldiers begin the recovery of the fallen heroes."

Turning his head, he peered at Arcinaë through one eye. "Ilerion has made you strong, and the blood of your ancestors has made you wise, Sovereign. It is far better to fight than to hide in the mist." With a nod, the gryphon lifted from the ground, joining the others as they followed Nesika back toward the Isle of Grave.

"Come, milady. We must search the bodies of the dead to be certain that those responsible for the attack on the Damselflies are no longer a threat," Ilerion said. Seeing the shadow of fear cross her eyes, he whispered, "Those who live have fled. Nilus and I shall see them relieved of their lives soon enough. You will not be left in danger, Arcinaë. I swear it."

"I know. It is just that there are so many dead," Arcinaë said, her eyes filling with tears.

"Aye, both heroes and madmen died today. We will honor those who fought for Ælarggessæ's freedom and allow the dragons to devour the souls of the wicked, but first we must seek the bodies of those responsible for the destruction of your settlement and the death of your people. As the days move us forward, our armies will make Ælarggessæ strong again. A new king will rise to lead men, and you will reign as sovereign of Grimmoirë for all of your days."

Arcinaë's eyes slid away from him as she bit her lip in uncertainty.

"What is it?" Ilerion gently pulled her face around to meet his gaze.

"I have sought the Sylph, entered a pact with them for the rekindling of Grimmoirë and the sealing of the sacred lands." Arcinaë paused, once again looking away.

Very gently, Ilerion stroked the leading edge of Arcinaë's nearest wing. "It is not only Grimmoirë that is restored."

"Nay, I also accepted the Sylph's gift of wings."

"And you wish that you had not?" Ilerion probed.

Arcinaë shook her head. "I would have given almost anything to have my wings restored. I have given away my immortality in exchange for the gift of flight, and I do not regret it. But, Grimmoirë needs a…more permanent sovereign. I cannot lead Grimmoirë."

With a deep sigh, Arcinaë rested her hand against Ilerion's heart. "Let us not speak of this. Let us search the bodies and see to the funeral pyres of our dead heroes." She held out her hand and watched Ilerion's larger one close around it.

Nilus shouted up at them, "Colne lies dead, as does the one called Lymaen!"

"Aye," Ilerion shouted back, "I killed them!"

"And I purged Cethe of his black heart!" Nilus said proudly as they neared. "For the Damselfly."

Reduald approached from the castle, gripping the hands of Nilus and Ilerion before crushing Arcinaë to him as if she were a long lost child. "The enchanted have sent the wicked fleeing, at least those they could not catch. Elduuf and Tondhere await us in the tower. A victory feast is being prepared. Then we shall attend to the sad task of seeing these brave souls to their resting place among the stars."

"We seek the hunter called Obour, preferably his dead body," Ilerion said. "He is the last of those responsible for the butchering of the Damselflies."

"The news is not good. He was seen escaping with the body of

Lazaro. It is not known whether Lazaro was dead or alive," Reduald stated.

"It does not matter," Ilerion responded, seeing Arcinaë shiver with the chill of fear. "Our soldiers will hunt them down on the morrow. They will not hide for long, for there is no safe haven for them on Ælarggessæ. Let us break bread with the living and honor the dead, then Nilus and I shall see you safely home to Grimmoirë."

The victors dined to the shouts of Ælarggessæ's glory and the toasts to heroes, living and dead. They spent the long hours until daybreak lighting the funeral biers. Within the oily black smoke the souls of the fallen heroes ascended to the heavens, Arcinaë's murmured blessings accompanying each soldier on his way.

As the daystar rose, it was agreed that the remaining lords would meet in council at the herald of the new moon to set the challenge for the crown. Reduald ordered the release of the flood waters to cleanse the battlefield. The few greatly engorged dragons still present lifted off the ground and turned away toward Grimmoirë as Ilerion, Nilus and Arcinaë mounted their horses and slowly followed.

Restoration

Ilerion led them across the rolling hills of Durover and into the densely forested mountains of western Cheneis. In the city of Grēine, they sought the comfort of a tavern and the warmth of a meal.

"Draughts of ale," Nilus called to the bar wench.

"You have been unusually quiet, Arcinaë," Ilerion said. He was rewarded by Arcinaë's gentle smile and her hand upon his forearm.

"There is much on my mind," she answered. "The rekindling of Grimmoirë's light and the sealing of the sacred grounds by the Sylph are enormously important, yet I find myself more concerned with the crowning of Ælarggessæ's new king. How will he be chosen?"

Nilus held up his mug, signaling for another, and said, "The Council of Lords will decide, but Ilerion believes there will be a challenge and bloodshed."

Closing her eyes at the thought, Arcinaë asked, "Why is it you do not believe the council of men will choose a ruler peacefully?"

"It is the way of men, Arcinaë. Power and passion bring the blood to boil and make men willing to risk their lives to possess them. I do not believe there will be a peaceful agreement." Ilerion shrugged. Seeing her look of concern he added, "I do not wish the crown, Arcinaë. I shall recommend Reduald as King of Ælarggessæ. If there is a challenge, it will be his."

Come with me to Grimmoirë. Come watch the Feie bring back the light of enchantment. Stay with me, Ilerion, Arcinaë whispered silently.

Cupping her face in his hand, he spoke aloud, "And then you will come with me to Baene?"

"Aye, I shall go with you to Baene when my tasks are complete."

"And Nilus? Will you return with us to Baene?" Ilerion asked.

"I shall go on to Baene while you see Arcinaë to Grimmoirë. She should not be made to sit on a barrel or sleep on a pallet on the floor in the servants' quarters as she did before. If you are taking a lady to Castle Baene, it will require a bit of work. I shall see to it during your absence." Lifting his mug of ale, Nilus proposed a toast: "To Lady Arcinaë and the halls of Castle Baene."

"Aye," Ilerion agreed, "to Milady and to Grimmoirë and Castle Baene."

Arcinaë blushed and raised her mug. "And to you, Ilerion and Nilus, and to Grimmoirë and Castle Baene."

Filled with a warm meal and flushed from the ale, they made their way to their rooms.

Ilerion closed the door to Arcinaë's room and turned to the one next door that he would share with Nilus. He met his friend's disappointed look with a chuckle. "I know what you are about to say, Nilus—so do not say it."

Nilus shook his head and muttered something unintelligible before following Ilerion into their room.

The following morning Nilus left Arcinaë and Ilerion and began the long journey to Castle Baene. "I shall hire only the best weavers, wood carvers and stone masons," he shouted back, "and pay them with your gold, Ilerion!"

Laughing, Ilerion waved after him, then swung around to lift Arcinaë to her gelding. "He has always spent my gold freely. It was because of it that we first met," Ilerion said. "Though that time he did not ask."

"He is a good friend and an honorable man." Arcinaë looked after Nilus.

"He thinks me a fool," Ilerion said, looking after his friend with a frown.

"And are you a fool?" Arcinaë asked, giving Ilerion a sidelong glance.

"Nay, at least no longer. Your Sylph Sharaga says that I have chosen life over death. I believe that makes me somewhat wiser than a fool."

The day's ride brought them into the narrow valley running along the Tangled Chasm where it passed through Cheneis and into Grimmoirë. There, while Arcinaë unpacked tea and the remaining bannock and jam, Ilerion built a fire and erected a small shelter. Neither of them saw the man watching in the distance, nor did they see him slip away.

❦

"They camp in the trees across the valley. It is Ilerion and a winged woman. From my hiding place I watched them settle into their camp for the night. I do not know where the woman came from, but she looks like the others. They are not expecting trouble or they would not have built a fire." Obour was breathless with excitement as he told Lazaro of his discovery.

Lord Lazaro hissed through his broken jaw, clutching an arm tightly to his side to avoid the pain of its movement from his dislocated shoulder, "Kill Ilerion and bring the Damselfly!"

"Yes, my lord," Obour said with a smile of satisfaction at receiving a direct order from Lazaro. There would be plenty of time for Obour with the winged woman while the lord healed. He would take her deep within the canyons where no one would hear her screams.

❦

"I shall fetch the water," Arcinaë volunteered.

"Wait and I will come with you."

"Ilerion, it is within shouting distance, and there is no threat here. We are nearly to Grimmoirë's border," Arcinaë teased. "And all of the wicked are either dead or in hiding, hunted by your soldiers."

"Aye," he agreed reluctantly, an uncomfortable feeling centering in his gut. "Aye, I am being foolish. Fetch the water and we shall have our tea."

Ilerion watched as she picked up the bucket and walked off toward the stream, swinging the pail and humming, and then he slipped into the dense underbrush to scout the camp's perimeter.

Arcinaë filled the bucket and examined her face in the clear water. Pulling her braid around, she removed the leather from its end and shook out the plaiting, running her fingers through her hair to loosen it and set it free. Picking up the pail, she headed back the way she had come, but her path was blocked.

Standing in front of her was a very large man, the stench of whose breath made her feel nauseous and dizzy.

"Obour, little buttermoth, my name is Obour. Lord Lazaro has sent me to collect you." The man's voice was raspy, a voice she knew, one that made her knees weak and her hands shake so badly that the water-filled pail dropped to the ground.

She screamed Ilerion's name and, with a flurry of wing beats, lifted from the ground, away from the man's threat. A sudden jerk drew her backward as his hand clasped tightly around her ankle.

"*Free her!*" Ilerion's voice was the crack of thunder after a lightning strike. Ilerion loosed a bolt, hitting Obour mid-thigh, causing him to release Arcinaë as he grabbed his own leg instead. Ilerion strode forward and struck him with a backhand that knocked him to the ground.

Arcinaë landed lightly and came to stand beside Ilerion. "I remember his voice," she whispered, "and the stench of his breath."

"He will know if Lazaro lives. It is important that we know this, Arcinaë. Go to the camp and pack our things. I will follow."

Nocking a second bolt, Ilerion looked after Arcinaë to make sure she did as asked. When he turned back, Obour was on his feet, eyes afraid but sword drawn.

"I would not like to cause you unnecessary pain. It is not my way. But, I must know if Lazaro is dead or alive. The depth of your pain is therefore in your hands," Ilerion said.

When Obour simply stared, Ilerion released the bolt, sending it through the big man's left shoulder, watching as the sword fell from his grasp and he sank to the ground again.

"Is he alive or dead, Obour?" Ilerion asked, nocking a third bolt in the crossbow.

Glaring up at Ilerion, Obour snarled, "Lazaro is dead, as you soon will be!" He threw the blade he clutched in his right hand, catching Ilerion high in the shoulder. The impact of the blade caused the release of Ilerion's bolt. It struck Obour in the throat, sending him into a spasm of gasping and retching as his life bled out on the ground around him.

Pulling the slender blade from his shoulder, Ilerion tossed it to the ground beside the hunter and made his way back to camp.

Seeing the blood-soaked shoulder, Arcinaë paled. "You bleed!"

"Aye, but Obour bleeds worse. I will need a bit of bandaging, but it will heal without a healer's touch," Ilerion responded, sinking to the ground with his back against a tree. "If you will bring me a strip of cloth and a bit of bloodmoss, I will be as good as new."

Searching Ilerion's pack, Arcinaë brought the moss and cloth, slapping his hands away when he tried to take them from her.

"I will do it," she snapped. "Do you know that I fear nothing more than I fear losing you!" Her eyes flooded and she sagged to the ground beside him. "Do not put yourself in harm's way, Ilerion. Do not ever put yourself in harm's way."

Blinking away her tears, she pulled his shirt away and looked at the ugly puncture the dagger had left. She packed it with bloodmoss to stop the bleeding and bound it tightly with strips of cloth. Finished, she drew back a little, staring openly at the muscles of his naked chest. She placed her open palm over his heart and looked up into his eyes. Slowly he opened his arms, reaching around her and pulling her close as her wings fell over them, loosely, like a soft, warm cloak.

"I do not wish to hurt you."

Her words caused him to laugh softly. "I would be willing to suffer great pain for the magick of your kiss, Arcinaë of Grimmoirë."

As their kiss deepened, he felt the tremulous, involuntary flutter of her wings.

"Lord Ilerion." The unmistakable, whispery rustle of the Sylph Sharaga startled them. Arcinaë drew away, blushing deeply.

Tilting his head, Ilerion asked, "Is it my destiny to have the Damselfly taken from me every time I seek her warmth?"

"If it is warmth you seek, I suggest a cloak or a shirt," Sharaga replied, shimmering with humor. "Come! The Damselfly is needed for the sealing of Grimmoirë."

Seeing Ilerion's bandaged shoulder, the Sylph reached out and gently stroked the wound with a healing drift of her fingers. The airiness of her form shifted, and her face was illuminated with a smile. "Bring her, Lord Ilerion of Baene."

Sweeping Arcinaë up into his arms, he carried her quickly to her mount. Kissing her, Ilerion whispered, "Someday, Arcinaë, perhaps there will be time for us." Then, leaping to the back of Caval, he swung around and, with the reins from Arcinaë's gelding in his hand, raced off after the disappearing Sylph.

Chapter 14: Grimmoirë

The dark skies of Grimmoirë were alive with the susurrous sounds of the Sylph. Each of the seven sisters held a tall, elegant brass brazier that would hold the eternal flame of protection. Four would be placed along the border shared with Lamaas, and one at the tip of each finger of Grimmoirën land where it touched Wawne, Halhmor and Cheneis. With this protection, the sacred enchanted earth would be sealed from viewing and entry by humans unless they were accompanied by a Grimmoirën. A hidden rift would be held within the sky overhead for the use of the winged enchanted.

Wysdym hovered before Ilerion and Arcinaë. "By the power of the ancient words of the enchanted, you shall call the Sylph to seal Grimmoirë with the eternal flames of protection. Do you know these words, Arcinaë of Grimmoirë?"

"Aye, I know the words."

"And Ilerion of Baene, are you willing to serve the Damselfly and see her safe as she calls upon the dark winds of the Sylphen Sisters?"

"I will do whatever needs to be done to ensure her safety and see Grimmoirë restored for the enchanted," Ilerion replied.

"So be it." Wysdym nodded, rising to join her sisters.

Below them, on the earth of Grimmoirë's center, Arcinaë began the ritual that would end with the invocation of the spirits of the Sisters of the Seven Winds, the Sylph of Keslbaen. With a silent plea to her ancestors for strength, and careful to remain within the sacred symbol beneath her feet, Arcinaë extended her arms outward. As she began to turn slowly to her right, her voice carried skyward the ancient words in the melodic language of the enchanted.

"Spirits of the Seven Sisters,
Spirits of the Seven Winds,
Keepers of the powers,
Transporters of knowledge, wisdom, truth,
Guardian Sisters of the earth, sea and sky,
Hear this pleading of the enchanted.
Grant them audience before the seven winds
That they may be heard
And their needs be seen.

"Those who fear the Seven Sisters—seek to harm us;
Humans who thou dost loathe—abhor us.
In the path of the Seven Sisters we wish to walk,
And with the wind of thy voices we wish to talk.
Clothe Grimmoirë with the strength of thy strengths,
Fortify Grimmoirë with thine solid foundations
That in thy wisdom and truth, by thy strength
And through the purity of the Seven Winds
Will Grimmoirë's safety be assured.

"Sisters of the Seven Winds hear this sovereign's cry,
And let this thus be so."♥

As Arcinaë's final words were whirled away on the winds, a wild howling began, as shrill as the deathshade's wail and as fierce as the breath of the dragon.

Ilerion moved to Arcinaë's side, holding her tightly, allowing her wings to cover them against the blinding dirt and ash swept up by the fury of the wind.

Each of the seven Sylph sisters sped to her appointed task, planting the braziers firmly within Grimmoirë's soil and lighting them with fiery breath. Sharaga swiftly returned toward the zenith of the sky above Grimmoirë. With a great sweep of her arms, she set the seal to unite the space above the sacred land with each of its eternal and earthbound flaming braziers.

Dropping lightly to the earth before Arcinaë and Ilerion, the seven sisters once again spoke as a single voice. "As invoked by the wisdom of this sovereign, paid for by the blood and pain of the Damselflies, Grimmoirë lies secure in the safety of the sacred seal and shall remain so for all eternity."

Enveloping Ilerion and Arcinaë in the blanket of her warmth, Wysdym's whispered words were like a soft sigh. "From a silken cocoon shall spring the redeemer of the hidden world. By your perfect joining shall a halfling rise to seek the key and serve the man who would be king. As we seal Grimmoirë, so is your union sealed upon the sacred ground."

Sharaga's form shimmered before Ilerion, blinding him with its brilliance. She stroked his face with a waft of air from her fingertips. "The warmth you seek will soon be yours, Ilerion of Baene." The starlight within her eyes glittered with mischief as she shifted away, leaving only a drift of soft laughter in her wake.

"My sister teases for she spends far too much time free among men," Wysdym said. "Your union is blessed by the Sylph, and your steps will be guided by the seven winds, as will be the steps of your daughters. I shall send the Feie to rekindle the light of Grimmoirë as ordered by the Council of Elders."

The air grew still and silent as the Sylph left Grimmoirë. Ilerion stood holding Arcinaë's small hand, afraid to speak for fear of weeping. He reached out to lift a strand of hair from her eyes and found its silken softness bringing him to his knees before her, clutching her to him, his tears falling freely. Tears of sorrow for the years he had lost and tears of joy for the promise of the future. "How is it possible such a gift has been given to me?" he murmured, holding her close.

"Ilerion, the gift is not yours, it is mine. I could not live without your strength," Arcinaë said, slipping to the ground before him. Wetting the tips of her fingers with his tears, she touched them to her heart. "Together we live, Lord Ilerion of Baene. Apart we were nothing more than two broken hearts, two dying souls."

Rising, she took his hand and brought him to his feet. "Come, let us meet the Feie and see Grimmoirë's light so that we can go home to Baene."

"The castle may not be ready—"

Arcinaë silenced him with her lips, her sudden tears mingling with his.

"Nilus is right. You are a fool," she said with a catch in her voice. "Do you not see that I would live with you among the fallen stones or in a cave beneath the ground? I do not need a kingdom or a castle. I need only your heart."

Shrill voices shattered their solitude as the seven Feie scuttled into the new security of Grimmoirë. Seeing Ilerion and Arcinaë, Fenris hurried forward, hugging them fiercely and frowning at the evidence of their tears.

"Why are you so sad?" he fussed. "Grimmoirë bears the sacred seal of the Seven Sisters, does it not? You should be happy!"

Arcinaë laughed. "We cry from happiness, Fenris."

"Never heard of such nonsense! We bring the orb to rekindle the light of enchantment. Are you going to cry then, too?" the fiery-haired Feie asked, his bushy red beard waving as he shook his head.

"I might," Arcinaë admitted, bending down to hug the Feie wizard tightly.

"Very well. Where is the seal?" Fenris asked, suddenly brusque and business-like.

Together they moved to the center of Grimmoirë and watched as the Feie settled in a circle around the dark orb. They had placed it upon the same seal where Arcinaë had stood to invoke the protection of the Sylph, and around the orb lay a ring of seven braziers. Beyond them stood the Council of the Feie, a representative from each of the seven enchanted kingdoms. Led by Ghyvol of Réverē, they began the chant that would bring fire to the orb.

"Spirits of the light draw near and hear our cry.
Evil rose and brought the darkness.
We beseech ye spirits of the flame
Hear this sacred kingdom's name,
Wash the ash of Grimmoirë's darkness clean,
Light the light that brings back bright.
These things we beg, spirits of fire, spirits of flame
That thus the light may come to pass."♣

As the final word was uttered, flames leapt forward from the braziers and pierced the orb's surface. The sudden brilliance of the daystar surged forth, spreading out across the kingdom, driving the darkness away before it. Its blazing radiance cleansed the earth of death and ash and left the tender shoots of grasses behind. As the light shot up the trunks of trees, bark curled and burned away, revealing the untainted wood that lay beneath. A carpet of flowers was unfurled across the new fields, and the magickal sparkle of life returned as Grimmoirë's enchanted streamed home from Réverē.

"Sovereign!" the Grimmoirëns called in joyful support as they passed Arcinaë, but Ilerion caught the shadow of sorrow that fell across her face on hearing their happy voices.

"We could remain here awhile, until you sort things out, Arcinaë."

"Nay, I will speak to Grimmoirë's council now. We need not stay longer." Arcinaë spoke with finality.

Calling Fenris to her, she asked that he gather the council in the Glen of Wisdom and watched him hurry off to do her bidding.

"I shall miss him," she turned bright questioning eyes on Ilerion, "unless your kingdom requires a wizard. Fenris is quite skilled."

"Arcinaë, if it will make you happy, my kingdom will definitely require a small Feie wizard."

There was much jocularity and teasing among old friends as members of the council assembled, most of whom Arcinaë had known since childhood. As she approached they rose as one, cheering and applauding the young sovereign who wore leathers and weapons and had brought light and safety to Grimmoirë.

Ilerion paused as they reached the glen, squeezing Arcinaë's hand and releasing it. Suddenly Arcinaë found it difficult to breathe, and tears welled yet again as she raised her hand to call for silence.

"Your wings are beeeooooouuutiful!" shouted the Kerleucan representative, sending a ripple of laughter through the assembly.

"Please, I do not belong here," Arcinaë began, as tears spilled over and made their way down her cheeks.

Fenris made his way to her side and stared up at her. "This is not crying for happiness. What makes you so sad? You have done what no other could have done for Grimmoirë. Never has a sovereign been so strong and fierce."

"I cannot be your sovereign. I have traded my enchantment for my wings. Grimmoirë needs the strength and stability of a sovereign who will reign long, growing wiser as the years pass, a sovereign who belongs here with her race. I no longer have a race or the gift of time."

Nesika's voice clacked as she approached Arcinaë, "You are the sovereign. You have led us into battle against our enemies, given a fierceness the enchanted of Grimmoirë have never had. We have watched you grow wise through your suffering and seen you make laws to serve the enchanted. You cannot walk away from Grimmoirë, my Sovereign."

"Aye, I must. Have I not earned the right to choose? Do I not deserve to spend what remains of my life in happiness?" Arcinaë asked, seeing many of her council members nod. "Nesika, would you not choose Grundl above all others?"

Nesika drew back her head and eyed Arcinaë closely. "It is Lord Ilerion you choose?"

"Aye, I want very much to go to Baene. I cannot be Grimmoirë's sovereign and Ilerion's mate. It is not possible. What would you have me choose, the joy of my heart or the responsibility of the sovereignty?"

"And who will rule Grimmoirë?" Nesika asked.

"You will be sovereign, Nesika. I ask it of you. You are strong and fearless and led the gryphons and dragons into battle against our enemies. You are not afraid to change Grimmoirë's laws, not afraid to lead the enchanted. You are the perfect choice for sovereign. Council of Grimmoirë, will you accept Nesika as the new sovereign?"

There was an outbreak of whispering among the council members, followed by a loud chorus of "ayes."

"I have not accepted," Nesika clicked, frowning as only a gryphon can.

"Do not be so querulous." Ilerion's voice carried across the glen. "At last we find the perfect post for such a petulant, irritable, bad-tempered, downright cantankerous beast and you want to refuse it?"

Arcinaë covered her mouth to hide a smile but only succeeded in coughing and spluttering as she attempted to muffle her laughter.

"You find him amusing?" Nesika glared in pretended offense.

"I find him far more than amusing, Nesika. Please say that you will accept the position of Sovereign of Grimmoirë, and I will promise to remove him."

"Do not take him so far that I cannot seek his counsel should I need it—or yours for that matter. Aye, Arcinaë of Grimmoirë, I shall relieve you of the burden of sovereignty, allowing you to attempt to control the human." The deep rasping sounds of the gryphon's chuckle joined with the Damselfly's musical laughter.

Arcinaë bowed and announced, "Nesika, Sovereign of Grimmoirë," to shouts of acceptance and pleasure among the council and the enchanted ones who surrounded them.

"Fenris," Arcinaë pulled the Feie close, "come with us to Baene. Ilerion's kingdom does not have the wisdom of a wizard, and you know you will not remain in Grimmoirë. You never have."

The Feie wizard frowned and looked up from beneath his bushy brows toward Ilerion. "He is a bit full of himself…"

"Please! It would add much to my happiness," Arcinaë pleaded. "I am sure you can find rooms far from Ilerion and a workroom as well."

"And I can teach the halflings magick?" he asked.

"How is it you know of the halflings?"

With a twitch of his lips, he winked. "The wind told me."

"Aye, Fenris, you will teach them magick." Arcinaë grabbed the Feie and swung him around, lifting off the ground in her excitement.

"Put me down!" Fenris fussed. "And do not fly with me again—it is not wise for those who are short and wingless to rise from the ground."

Alighting gently, Arcinaë released Fenris and ran to meet Ilerion.

"Do you not think Nesika will be a brilliant sovereign?" she asked, hugging Ilerion to her.

"Aye, you are wise for one so young," he said, his eyes glistening with pride. "There is no greater ally than a wife with great wisdom, Arcinaë of Grimmoirë."

"Do you wish to marry me?" Arcinaë asked shyly.

"I wish to marry you and bind your heart to mine for all time. Grow old with me, Arcinaë. Be the lady of my manor and the mother of my children, be my friend and my lover. Grant me the magick of your kiss every morning when I wake and every night before I sleep. I do not seek power. I seek only the passion of your heart. Will you share vows with me, Arcinaë?"

Arcinaë frowned and bit at her lower lip as was her habit when uncertain. Tilting her head and sighing deeply, she closed one eye and looked carefully at Ilerion through the other.

"Is that a no?" Ilerion asked.

She shook her head, suddenly solemn with the realization of the truth. "Time is no longer enchanted for me, and I will grow old. I may not always be beautiful."

"I shall always see your beauty, for I see you with my heart. I too shall grow old. Know this, Arcinaë, that I would suffer any agony and fight any foe to gain your favor. I love you above all others and hold you dearer than all the gold in my coffers," Ilerion answered, dropping to one knee before Arcinaë and taking her hand between his. "Arcinaë of Grimmoirë, will you share the vows with me?"

Arcinaë's voice grew husky. "Above all others?"

"Aye, above all others."

Ilerion watched a single tear slip from beneath Arcinaë's lashes, saw the shudder as she drew her breath. Pulling her down before him, he lifted his hands to her shoulders and held her eyes with his. "Aye, above *all* others, and I do not believe Cylacia would wish it any other way."

Arcinaë's tears flowed freely as she leaned her head against Ilerion's chest and whispered, "Aye, I shall share the vows with you and bind my heart to yours."

A cough brought Ilerion's attention to Fenris.

"She weeps yet again," the Feie wizard observed. "Is she sad or is she happy?"

Tilting Arcinaë's face so Fenris could see, Ilerion grinned as she laughed through her tears, sniffing and wiping her nose with the back of her hand.

"I am happy, Fenris, and I wish a wedding before I leave Grimmoirë, for I cannot be wed without the blessings of the enchanted."

Holding out his left hand, Fenris drew the joined circles of forever upon his palm and murmured the words of the binding rings, nodding his approval as they appeared, gleaming and golden within his hand. Placing his other hand above the rings, he spoke the magick of the names and then revealed them to Ilerion and Arcinaë so they could see the burning words within the bands of gold.

"I shall call the enchantresses to prepare the bride," Fenris muttered gruffly. "And it shall be my honor to bring her before you and allow you to claim her hand," he added, patting himself on the chest as he headed off to find the enchantresses.

"Oh! And you, Ilerion? Who shall prepare you?"

"Tovag," Arcinaë said without hesitation. "It is what my father would have wanted."

"Tovag? Tovag is a Minotaur! A *Blue* 'Taur," Fenris blustered. "A great bull-headed 'Taur!"

"Aye, Ilerion has sworn his willingness to suffer any agony and fight any foe to win my favor. I do not believe he will be intimidated by a Blue 'Taur.

"Should I be intimidated by a Blue 'Taur?" Ilerion asked.

Arcinaë allowed a mischievous smile to touch her lips, as she rolled her eyes skyward. "Only if you should ever cause me sorrow."

Choking back a nervous chuckle, Fenris sped off to summon Tovag, the Blue 'Taur.

Union

Tovag shook his massive head. The coarse black hairs bristled around his neck and down his back to the base of his spine. Midnight blue tattoos rippled along the pale blue iron-like muscles of his chest and arms as he moved. "It cannot be done," he stated unequivocally, his voice harsh and his black eyes boring into Ilerion's. "Arcinaë is the last noblewoman of her species. She cannot be bound to a human! Find a Wyndwryn to wed her. Even a 'Taur would be better than a Man!"

"Hear me," Ilerion shouted. "Arcinaë has lost everything, given up everything to save the enchanted and bring Grimmoirë back to light and safety. She no longer has the gift of time and will grow old as humans do. Does she not deserve this happiness, Tovag? Would you keep it from her because you do not like me?"

"I more than 'do not like you,' human! I know who you are. A warrior, a fighter, lord over many humans, a man who will not be there if evil men come for her," Tovag snarled, raking his horns against the wall in aggravation.

Ilerion sank to the ground before the angry 'Taur, holding his face in his hands for a moment before looking up and asking, "Do you believe I would ever leave her alone after what happened to Cylacia?"

Tovag squatted before Ilerion, the muscles of his calves and massive thighs bulging. "Are you saying you would not?"

"Stop!" Arcinaë raced toward them, flowers falling from her partially braided hair, the gauzy fabric of her gown flowing and swirling around her as she half ran, half flew across the grass. Her fists struck the 'Taur in the chest, bouncing off without effect. "Leave him alone!" she screamed. "I would not have asked for you if I had known you would be so unreasonable! Go! Go away! I do not want you here!" she yelled, beating her fists against Tovag's back and head.

Still as a stone, Tovag the 'Taur remained unmoved by her beating or her words.

Tears streamed down her face, and Arcinaë finally dropped to the ground in a heap, sobbing hysterically. Only then did Tovag move. He knelt beside Arcinaë and gently lifted her to his chest before standing and walking back to the bothie where the enchantresses waited, watching anxiously.

"Dry her eyes and give her the gifts she will need for her wedding night. A human prepares to accept her hand," he said as he placed Arcinaë on a chair.

"You will allow it?" Arcinaë asked tearfully.

"If this man can bring out such fury in a docile Damselfly, there is much more to him than what I see. I will prepare him to honor you," Tovag answered, stooping to make his exit.

"Tovag?"

Arcinaë's voice caused him to stop and look back as he crouched uncomfortably in the doorway. "Aye, milady?"

"Do not mark his face. I like his face the way it is."

The corner of the 'Taur's upper lip rose as if in a snarl, exposing large well-sharpened teeth, but Arcinaë knew it was a smile of understanding. With a slight nod, he headed back toward the man who would wed the Damselfly.

Davnë, the enchantress, remained with Arcinaë while the others prepared the Glen of Secrets for the wedding.

Arcinaë stood before the large brass mirror, gazing at her reflection. Her wedding gown had been created from diaphanous spider cloth, loomed and sewn by the spirits of the woods, the dryads. It refracted the shifting colors of her wings and danced in a swirling pattern about her bare feet as she moved. The fragrance of lavender and lilac emanated from her body, and her hair and skin glistened with the droplets of purification.

"You are indeed very beautiful, Arcinaë of Grimmoirë. Your husband will be weakened by your beauty, find himself unable to breathe, burning with fever—even be a bit frightened by your allure. Do you understand the gifts you have been given?" asked Davnë.

"Aye," Arcinaë said, playing over the words of the enchantresses in her mind, words of magick, words of passion to bind a man, to make him weak with desire for the woman of his vows.

"Do not fear him, for he is gentle and he will not rush you, Arcinaë."

"But what if I—"

Davnë interrupted with soft words of encouragement. "You are a Damselfly, already enchanted, shrouded in the mysticism of the enchantresses. Do not doubt your magick, Arcinaë. You have already won his heart, he adores you and this will merely bind him.

"Come, they call us to the glen." Davnë stood and held out her hand to Arcinaë, drawing the Damselfly near in a final embrace, enfolding her in the beguiling grace of the enchantresses.

❧❦

"Unlike Cylacia, Arcinaë is a noblewoman. Since her father cannot choose for her, she has chosen for herself. I suppose it is her right. She will require a gift. Do not touch her until it is accepted and she touches you," Tovag instructed, as the long sharp tip of the artificial claw that Tovag wore on the first finger of his right hand placed another bit of deep purple dye beneath the human's skin. "You will bear her mark of ownership always. It is forbidden that another female touch you. Is this understood, human?"

"Aye. What gift should I give?" Ilerion asked, cringing as the sharp claw again pierced his skin.

"You did not bring a gift?" Tovag's gravelly voice echoed off the stone walls.

"I did not know we would be wed today."

"Wait here. I will seek the Feie. Perhaps the wizard can invoke an appropriate jewel." Opening the bothie door, Tovag bellowed Fenris's name several times before ducking back inside and resuming the marking of Arcinaë's intended mate. "He will come, and then we will discuss the gift again."

Wiping away the excess dye with a soft cloth dipped in healing salve, the 'Taur examined his work. "You should be proud, human. To bear the mark of the Damselfly is a great honor, even among the enchanted. For an unenlightened human to bear such a mark is without equal. There can be no greater honor, human, save her touch."

Ilerion stood and moved to stand before the mirror, examining the dark tattoo that covered the left half of his chest. The lines curved and turned, evoking the spirit of the Damselfly from every angle. An involuntary shiver ran along Ilerion's spine. Tonight he would at last belong to Arcinaë, and she would belong to him. He touched the slightly swollen lines, tracing them with his fingers. "I am very proud to bear the mark of Arcinaë," he said as Tovag opened the door to Fenris.

"You bellowed?" the wizard crabbed. "We were blessing the glen and making sure everyone was invited. It would not serve to offend anyone, lest they leave a curse instead of a blessing. Well? What? What is it, Tovag?"

"He has no gift." Tovag shrugged his great shoulders, giving Ilerion a sideways glance of disapproval.

"Oh…" Fenris gave Ilerion a squinty look. "So why do you need me?"

"Make him one. He cannot approach her if he does not bear a gift."

"Aye, I suppose you are right. It is the way of Damselflies. She will not accept you if you do not bear a gift. What gift do you wish?" Fenris asked expectantly.

"I wish to give her the gift that she desires."

Fenris tilted his head and examined Ilerion closely. "You do truly care for her above all others. I shall invoke a jewel of life. As long as she wears it, your mind will touch hers and grant her peace."

Once again the little wizard held out his hand and drew upon its palm with his forefinger, this time a circle bound at the top by a triangle. With a stirring motion and an invocation, Fenris called forth a dragon's tear, clear as crystal and red as blood. It was clasped within a golden dragon's claw and hung upon a braided gold and silver chain.

Tovag nodded his approval. Lifting the gift by its chain, he handed it to Ilerion. "Do not lose it, human."

Shaking his head, Ilerion reached for the soft silken shirt the enchantresses had brought for him after his purification, drawing it over his head and lacing it over the mark of the Damselfly. The boar's hide leathers were soft and black and fitted over the clean, lightweight woolens as if tailored just for him. The boots were of heavily tanned stag hide, dyed black to match the leathers. As he brushed his hair, he noticed it still held the droplets of the purifying waters. Finally, he slipped the chain holding his gift for Arcinaë over his head and tucked it inside his shirt.

A tap at the door brought the enchantress, Davnë.

"Arcinaë awaits you in the glen, Fenris," she said to the Feie while boldly assessing Ilerion.

As the wizard hurried off, the enchantress looked at Tovag and gestured toward the door. "I will speak to Ilerion alone."

With a nod, the 'Taur ducked out the door, closing it firmly behind him.

"She is frightened she will not please you," Davnë stated, watching Ilerion's eyes closely. Seeing only deep concern, she allowed a slow smile. "But she will. You know her fears, her weaknesses and her sorrows and yet you seek to bind her. You are a good man, Ilerion, a strong man. She deserves this happiness. See that you do not disappoint." As Davnë brought her hand up to touch him, Ilerion drew back out of her reach causing the enchantress to smile again. "I see it is not your wish to betray her, so you must be an honorable man as well. Tovag will bring you to the glen."

She swept out the door, leaving in her wake small sparkles of light that drifted over Arcinaë's betrothed.

⊰※⊱

Ilerion stood beneath the arbor of flowering vines and felt the magick of enchantment in every breath he drew. The air was warm and moist, filled with the scent of the surrounding woodlands. He stood next to Tovag, who had changed into a scarlet cloth tied around his strong hips with a slender braided leather band. His chest remained bare, save for a strap of woven gold that held his great axe nestled against his broad back. Even in this peaceful setting, Tovag remained alert for threat against the Damselfly.

"You have known her always?" Ilerion asked.

"Aye, I watched her play. I saw her the day she first flew, and I honored her father with my promise to prepare her husband to serve her properly." Tovag's eyes narrowed. "You will serve her properly, will you not?"

"If I err, it will not be by intention," Ilerion replied.

As the long horns sounded the herald, Ilerion and Tovag turned to see Arcinaë approaching with Fenris. The Feie wizard held her hand and kept pulling her down as her wings fluttered, lifting her feet from the ground. Her gown shimmered, ebbing and flowing around her, repeating the changing colors of her slowly moving wings. Her eyes locked with Ilerion's, never wavering as she drew closer, until at last she was near enough to take his hand.

You look beautiful, she shared silently, causing him to smile and speak.

"You were supposed to let me say that."

"And am I beautiful, Ilerion?"

"More beautiful than all the night stars, none sparkle nearly as brightly."

Standing alongside them, Fenris cleared his throat. The enchanted gathering whispered softly together as they awaited the arrival of the sovereign who would officiate at the ceremony.

From the shadow of the trees, Cwen of Aaradan backed away. She had come to remind Arcinaë of their pact and to claim her for the quest, but the wizard Lohgaen's search for the missing gryphonstone would have to wait a fortnight, for the Damselfly's vows were far more important.

The rustling of feathered wings brought Nesika and Grundl, who nuzzled each other before Nesika stepped away to lead the vows that would bind Ilerion and Arcinaë.

Watching Nesika approach, Arcinaë withdrew her hand from Ilerion's and nervously smoothed her gown.

The gryphon moved slowly to avoid the awkward hop-steps of her normal gait and appeared both sovereign and matriarchal as she positioned herself before the human and the Damselfly. As she opened the ceremony her usually raspy voice was soft, its clicks and clacks less strident.

"We have come together to celebrate the joining of Ilerion of Baene and Arcinaë of Grimmoirë. The law of life is love unto all beings. Together in love, these two beings grow strong. Arcinaë has no father to give her hand, and so I shall ask only if the she gives herself freely."

You are perfect. Arcinaë's silent, smiling intonations filtered into Nesika's mind, causing the gryphon's feathers to rustle in pleasure at the compliment.

"Arcinaë of Grimmoirë, is it true that you come here of your own free will and agreement?"

"Aye, it is true," Arcinaë answered, glancing at Ilerion from beneath lowered lashes.

"With whom do you come and who gives you his blessings?"

"She comes with me, Fenris the Feie," the wizard responded, "with the blessings of all of the enchanted."

"You may join hands with your betrothed. Hear my words. Above are the stars, below are the stones. As time shall pass remember that like the stars should your love be ever burning, like the stones should it be ever strong. Let the strength of your hearts bind you together. Let the power of your desire keep you ever close to one another. Be free in giving your affection and warmth. Do not fear and let not the ways of the unenlightened give you unease, for the magick of enchantment is with you always."

Turning her head, Nesika fixed her eye on Ilerion.

"I have not the right to bind you to Arcinaë. Only you have this right. If it is your wish, say so and place your ring in her hand."

Turning to Fenris and taking the ring that bore Arcinaë's name, Ilerion pressed it into the palm of Arcinaë's hand as he said, "It is my wish."

"Arcinaë, if it is your wish for Ilerion to be bound to you, place this ring on the third finger of his left hand."

With trembling fingers, Arcinaë drew the golden circle Fenris had created over the knuckle of Ilerion's ring finger and watched it glow as it rested there.

Focusing her look on Arcinaë, Nesika said, "Arcinaë, neither do I have the right to bind you to Ilerion. Only you have this right. If it is your wish, say so and place your ring in his hand."

Fenris offered Ilerion's ring to Arcinaë, squeezing her fingers gently as she took it from him.

Arcinaë placed the ring that bore his name in the palm of Ilerion's hand and closed his fingers around it as she whispered, "It is my wish."

"Ilerion, if it is your wish for Arcinaë to be bound to you, place this ring on the third finger of her left hand."

Lifting Arcinaë's hand, Ilerion slipped the ring on her finger.

"Ilerion of Baene, speak the words that bind," Nesika directed.

In a strong clear voice, he pledged his heart. "I, Ilerion of Baene, in the names of my ancestors, by the life that courses within my blood and the love that is held within my heart, take thee, Arcinaë of Grimmoirë, to my hand to be my chosen one. To desire thee and be desired by thee, to possess thee and be possessed by thee, without shame, for none can exist in the purity of my love for you. I promise I will love thee always, now and forever."

Nodding to Arcinaë, Nesika instructed, "Arcinaë of Grimmoirë, speak the words that bind."

Ilerion smiled as Arcinaë bit her bottom lip and reaching out, gently touched her lip with his fingers, winking at Tovag's fierce frown.

In her gentle voice, the Damselfly pledged her heart. "I, Arcinaë of Grimmoirë, in the names of my ancestors, by the life that courses within my blood and the love that lies within my heart, take thee, Ilerion of Baene, to my hand to be my chosen one. To desire thee and be desired by thee, to possess thee and be possessed by thee, without shame, for none can exist in the purity of my love for you. I promise I will love thee always, now and forever."

With her great claw, Nesika lifted the chalice that held the potent binding wine and handed it to Ilerion. "May you drink your fill of the wine that binds."

Taking the chalice, Ilerion held it to Arcinaë's lips as she sipped the wine of binding, allowing her to take it and then lift it to his lips as he drank.

"May your love endure, its flame rekindled nightly," Nesika concluded, looking out over the gathering of the enchanted.

"I give to you, Lord Ilerion and Lady Arcinaë of Baene," Nesika clicked joyously, her wings flapping in a very unrestrained and unsovereign-like manner.

The Kerleucans played the pipes and lutes, and Ilerion drew Arcinaë against him and kissed her.

"Do not forget the gift, human." Tovag's large hand on his shoulder and his hoarse whisper made Ilerion laugh.

"What did Tovag say that makes you laugh?" Arcinaë asked, her eyes following the 'Taur as he moved toward the serving table.

Smiling, Ilerion said, "He reminded me not to give you cause for sorrow."

⟡

Beneath the pulsing of Grimmoirë's newly safeguarded sky the firmament darkened into a deep blue-violet, tiny pinpoints of starlight flickering through the shimmering protection of the shield.

"Always there will be safety here," Arcinaë murmured, as she leaned back against Ilerion's shoulder. "I could not have given a greater gift in my brief time as sovereign."

"Nay, you could not," Ilerion agreed, kissing the top of her head.

"Come," she turned suddenly, pulling him after her with both hands, "I grow weary and a room has been prepared for us within the sovereign's palace. There will be no one there. Nesika and Grundl have returned to the eyrie, and the enchantresses shall guard us against any foolish mischief by Grimmoirë's faery folk."

Laughing, she lifted her skirts about her and raced off through the trees, leaving in her wake the lovely lilting sound of her voice and the trailing, luminous glow of her gown.

"Arcinaë," Ilerion called as he followed in her translucent slipstream at a brisk walk.

Amidst the dark shadows of the trees, the soft shining light led him forward but he seemed no closer. He called to her again, "Arcinaë?"

"Here," the Damselfly's silken voice whispered near the pool hidden deep within the woods. Slipping from the edge of darkness, Arcinaë hovered just above the soft carpet of moss, holding out her hand to Ilerion and smiling as he took it and pulled her toward him.

Catching the sparkle in her eyes, he asked, "Do you ply an innocent man with magick, milady?"

"Nay, Ilerion, it is no magick. Though I have been given the gifts of the enchantresses, I do not wish this night to be a lie. Because you are a human, it is feared that you will not remain bound to me. That perhaps you will tire of me and move on to another, as is often the way of men. With the enchantresses' magick, you would be held beyond your ability to ever leave me, but it is not what I wish. I want the bond to come from here"—she placed her hand over his heart, feeling the immediate surge of his response as she touched him.

"Already I am bound to you. Your very touch burns me and steals my breath." He placed his hand over hers. "Do you feel the pounding of the waves, Arcinaë?"

Without giving an answer, she led him quickly down a stone pathway to the hidden entrance of the sovereign's palace. Once inside they slipped along a dimly illuminated corridor, across the great hall with its massive fireplace and throne and up the wide staircase to the bedchamber of the sovereign.

Arcinaë pushed open the door and entered, turning back to face Ilerion as she reached the center of the room. "Will you light a candle?" she asked, a slight quiver catching her silken voice.

Ilerion moved to the blazing fireplace and lit a small twig. Cupping it with his hand, he crossed the room to the table near the window and lit three tapered candles. Their faint light cast a warm glow, enriched with flickering shadows.

Lifting the chain that held the dragon's tear over his head, Ilerion went to Arcinaë and offered it to her from the palm of hand. The brilliant red crystal in its golden setting was afire, and its long braided chain of gold and silver glinted in the candlelit chamber.

"What is this?" Arcinaë asked, clearly surprised by the gift.

"It is a dragon's tear."

"Nay, I do not mean what is it, I mean why do you offer me a gift when you are not a Damselfly?" Her voice was husky with emotion.

"I offer it because you are a Damselfly, and it is your way, is it not? To be offered a gift by the male who woos you? You will find it is a fine gift, one that will keep me close to you, bring you comfort and give you peace, for you will always know my thoughts."

"Ilerion." The word came soft as a prayer as Arcinaë lifted the dragon's tear from his hand, careful not to touch him during the acceptance of the gift, as was the custom of her people.

She placed the chain over her head, settling the blood-red stone against her skin, gazing upon the brilliance of its fire as it reflected the light from the candles.

Looking up, she saw Ilerion waiting, his hands hanging loosely at his sides and eyes alight with love for her. She recalled the words of the enchantress, "He is gentle and he will not rush you."

Unhurriedly, Arcinaë reached down and drew the laces from the bodice of her dress, allowing it to fall with a whisper to the cool stone floor. She smiled as Ilerion's eyes rose slowly from the dress to her face. As his eyes met hers, she stepped forward to touch his cheek.

His breathing had become hoarse and he trembled with emotion, but still he did not reach for her. The flutter of her fingers was soft against his skin as she loosened the laces from his silken shirt and pulled it free from his leathers. Ilerion raised his arms as Arcinaë lifted the shirt, helping her to pull it off over his head and dropping it beside him on the floor.

Her touch was cool and soothing, as she traced the mark of the Damselfly across his chest, suddenly rising to her tiptoes to kiss his lips. The touch of her skin against his was scorching. She pulled away from him and he chilled instantly. "Come with me," she said, taking his hand and leading him towards the tall bed. Stepping gracefully up the steps of the low footstool, she lay down on her side facing him, waiting for him to join her.

Slipping from the remainder of his clothes, Ilerion joined Arcinaë, covering her with his warmth, kissing her eyes, her face and her throat.

"Wait," she whispered urgently, causing him to draw back slightly, searching her eyes for rejection.

"My wings." She smiled.

Lifting his weight from her, Ilerion allowed Arcinaë to shift her folded wings and stretch them out across the bed. He lightly traced the leading edge of one wing where it rose above Arcinaë's shoulder, watching as her eyes closed and she sighed with pleasure.

"Have I told you—"

But the Damselfly's kiss silenced him, stealing all thought from his fevered mind.

Deep into the night, Ilerion awoke chilled and drew the coverlet over them, smiling at Arcinaë's tousled hair and lips full and pink from his kisses. She murmured his name within her dream as he touched the dragon's tear where it rested deep crimson against the creamy swell of her breasts and whispered, "Always you will know my thoughts."

"Aye, I do." Her eyes were bright with love as she lifted her arms to accept him.

❦

Wearing only his woolens and a foolish grin against the morning's cool air, Ilerion sat cross-legged in the center of the bed watching Arcinaë dress.

Feeling suddenly shy in the light of day, she stood tying the leather laces of her shirt, being very careful not to look at him.

She moved to the dressing table and lifted the brush to her hair, grimacing as it pulled through the tangles.

Hearing the soft padding of Ilerion's bare feet, she looked up into the mirror to meet his eyes, blushing slightly, still unused to the passion of his gaze. He took the brush from her hand and gently brushed her hair until it was at last tangle-free and glistening.

"Have I told you, Lady Arcinaë, that I find you a flawless jewel among a sea of stones?"

She blushed deeply and turned to rest her cheek against the warmth of his bare chest. "Nay, but you have shown me."

"Today I shall take you home to Baene," he whispered against the softness of her hair.

Baene

Since the return of Arcinaë and Ilerion from Grimmoirë, the reconstruction of Castle Baene had continued unabated. Scaffolding seemed to stand at every wall. With the din from hammering and shouts of craftsmen and workers beleaguering them from dawn until dusk, they had gotten into the habit of slipping away early in the morning and not returning until the day's work was completed.

Ilerion delighted in the opportunity to show Arcinaë the kingdom of Baene, and they traveled far and wide, from the elegant coastal city of Maelau to the giant braid trees of the Darkwoods along the border near Twode. He took her wading in the warm, shallow waters of Lake Calidity, and bought her exotic fruits and fine cloth in the shadow city of the inscrutable Farwegians. From the traders of the Shifting Sands, the nomadic Houatauns, Ilerion purchased a fine mare for Arcinaë who immediately named her Zephyr—the west wind. They teased Nilus over his constant fussing, calling him "mother" when he was not listening, and made plans for a grand banquet to be held at Castle Baene as soon as it was ready.

They were returning from a long leisurely ride, Ilerion still giving instructions on the handling of the new mare. Arcinaë was reassuring Zephyr with soft touches and melodic words of enchantment when she caught the unlikely sight of Ilerion dozing in his saddle and laughed softly.

"You grow tired, Ilerion?"

"Nay, I grow happy, happier every day that you are with me."

"Then you shall grow very happy indeed, for I shall always be with you." She drew Zephyr closer to Caval so that she could take the hand Ilerion offered for their ride home together.

Nilus met them on the lawn, a frown etching his round face. "A woman has come. She waits for Arcinaë on the road."

Looking surprised, Arcinaë said, "I know no woman." Suddenly, her hands flew to her mouth and she grew very pale.

"What is it, Arcinaë?" Ilerion asked, immediately sheltering her in his arms.

"Cwen of Aaradan! In my joy, I had forgotten. I must go."

"Go? Go where?" Ilerion asked, stepping back and looking confused.

"Ilerion, I have pledged a quest. I promised Cwen of Aaradan to lead the wizard Lohgaen of Lochlaen into the mist of the Isle of Grave. He seeks the gryphonstone of his ancestors for it is said to lie there, somewhere on the isle."

"No, you cannot go. You are here, safe. You are my wife, Arcinaë." Ilerion's face clouded with disbelief and a hint of anger.

"And I will always be your wife. Ilerion, do not be angry. I made a pact. Cwen of Aaradan led me to the Sylph and, in return, I pledged my help to her quest once Grimmoirë was restored and I had been given wings. I was not your wife when I made this promise. We go into Grimmoirë. There will be no danger. Nesika will help me."

Reaching out she touched his heart and felt the pain of his hurt within her mind. "It was a pledge of honor, Ilerion. I cannot deny the quest. Have you not taught me that the price of responsibility is often high—that it demands us to do that which we do not wish to do when we are bound by honor? Send me away with your blessing, Ilerion. Do not send me away with your anger." Arcinaë's voice broke and a shuddering sob shook her. "I do not go because I wish it, but because I must. I pledged to her as the Sovereign of Grimmoirë. I have given my word."

A sad smile crossed Ilerion's face. "I have taught you far too well, Lady Arcinaë. You use my teachings against the desires of my heart. I will go with you to meet the woman."

Cwen waited at the side of the road, just beyond view from the castle. She wondered what she would do if Arcinaë simply refused to honor her word. She winced at the thought of telling the impatient Lohgaen if she returned without Arcinaë. Lohgaen had grown restless, almost anxious—behavior Cwen had never seen in him before. There was something beyond his desire to quest for the gryphonstone weighing on the wizard's mind, and Cwen intended to find out what it was. Lohgaen had been kind to her, saving her from capture when she had been charged with high treason. She owed him much.

Looking up at the sound of approaching voices, she saw Arcinaë and the man she had wed. Sighing, Cwen supposed this meant the Damselfly did not intend to accompany her on the quest. Preparing a less-than-honest smile, Cwen stepped forward to greet them.

"I forgot. In my happiness, I simply forgot your needs," Arcinaë admitted freely. "I am sorry."

Ilerion silently appraised the woman before him. She was not tall, but she was heavily armed and carried herself with strength and confidence. Her hair flared with red highlights and she had the golden eyes of a predator. While she did not openly offer threat, it lay just beneath her taut muscles and sharpened awareness.

"You are Cwen of Aaradan, niece of Yávië the Dragon Queen?" Ilerion finally spoke.

"Aye, and you are Lord Ilerion of Baene, savior of the Damselfly and Ælarggessæ." Cwen's voice was mellow, without hint of hurry or tension. "Arcinaë of Grimmoirë owes her service to the wizard Lohgaen. It was pledged while she acted as sovereign in exchange for my help locating the city of Keslbaen. The conditions of our agreement have been met, and I will assure her safety." Smiling at Arcinaë, Cwen added, "I know that you forgot. I watched you share your vows. I would have forgotten, too."

"You are not quite what I expected," Ilerion laughed. "Who else will assure my wife's safety?

Grinning at his implication, Cwen whistled and gestured over her shoulder toward the tall man who emerged from the trees carrying a heavy double-headed war axe. "Talin is always a good man to have around, though I am quite capable of defending both myself and Arcinaë."

Ilerion extended his grip to Talin, watching the young warrior's eyes as he accepted it—a good man, strong, and one who already protected a woman.

As Talin stepped back, the hiss of a bolt sounded and the short arrow went deep into the earth a thumb's width from the instep of his boot.

"He does not like me," Arcinaë stated. "And I do not like him, but he is good with the axe and can be trusted as long as he is in the company of Cwen."

Ilerion's eyebrows rose at Arcinaë's fierceness. "What is it you do not like about my wife?" he asked Talin.

"She is not strong and requires constant vigilance. She is a child to be cared for on a quest requiring the strength of warriors." Talin's words were blunt. "Though since I did not sense her threat until the bolt was already loosed upon me, perhaps she has become more accomplished," he added with a twitch of lips that could almost have passed for a smile.

"I taught her that." Cwen grinned proudly, winking at Arcinaë. "Do not mind Talin's surliness. He is still annoyed because Arcinaë drew his blood while sparring."

Again, Ilerion raised his eyebrows and looked at his wife. "Lady Arcinaë, it appears there is much you have not told me."

Arcinaë rose to her tiptoes and pulled Ilerion's face down to hers, kissing him deeply, and bringing a smile to Cwen's face but causing Talin to look away embarrassed. "They *are* married," Cwen said, elbowing him.

Drawing Ilerion away with her, Arcinaë held his face between her hands, kissing him again. "You are here," she touched her heart. "And here," she stoked the dragon's tear. "I shall be swift and return before you have time to miss me."

Ilerion pulled her to him and hugged her, crushing her wings against her back. "Already I miss you, and you have not gone." Releasing her, he stepped away, allowing her fingers to slowly fall from his.

"If harm comes to her, I will kill you both." His voice was without threat, but his eyes were not. With a last lingering touch, Ilerion turned and left Arcinaë to her quest.

Chapter 15: Quest for the Gryphonstone

"Arcinaë?" Nesika clicked with astonishment, staring at the humans who trailed behind the Damselfly. "Where is Ilerion? Are you harmed?" The Gryphon extended her neck and lifted the feathers along her back threateningly.

"Nay, Nesika, I am not harmed, nor in danger. Ilerion remains in Baene while I assist Cwen of Aaradan with a small quest." Arcinaë drew near and hugged the gryphon, allowing the comfort of Nesika's sheltering wing.

"It is not a 'small' quest, Arcinaë. If they have led you to believe it is, they have deceived you." Nesika glared at Cwen and Talin, asking suddenly, "Where is Lohgaen of Lochlaen? You cannot quest without him."

"He remains on Ædracmoræ, awaiting my return, Sovereign." Cwen bowed respectfully.

"But you intend to bring him here? To put Lady Arcinaë in jeopardy for the quest for the gryphonstone?" Nesika's voice was sharp and her clicks harsh.

"Nay, Sovereign, it is my intent to protect Arcinaë from injury as we seek the stone. Surely you must know that Lohgaen will not allow any to harm her."

Nesika gave a raucous laugh. "Lohgaen of Lochlaen sees only what suits him! He is brash and has been given more power than he can control, though it is obvious he has touched your heart."

"He has been good to me. He helped me when I needed help," Cwen agreed.

"You are a fool, young woman," Nesika said, shaking her head. "Arcinaë, if you insist on doing this, you will need Tovag. He will see you safe."

"And you?" the sovereign asked Talin.

"I return to Ædracmoræ to the House of Aaradan." Talin shrugged, as if he were uninterested in Cwen's quest.

"Lies," Nesika muttered, "but as yet you do not know it, so I shall forgive you."

Talin rolled his eyes at what he considered the madness of the enchanted.

"Go. Bring Lohgaen. I will counsel you when you return. Arcinaë will remain in Grimmoirë," Nesika snapped, her glare leaving no room for argument.

As Talin and Cwen turned to leave, Talin asked quietly, "Why is it gryphons are always so querulous?"

The rift was summoned by Brengven, and Cwen and Talin stepped through to be met by Lohgaen's glowering face and Synyon's seductive smile.

"Does she wait in Grimmoirë?" Lohgaen asked, scowling at Cwen.

"Aye, she is in Grimmoirë. Their sovereign insists on sending another along to protect her. One called Tovag. Apparently the new sovereign does not trust that your judgment will always favor the Damselfly's safety," Cwen said, looking over her shoulder and catching Synyon leading Talin off toward the trees.

"Talin!" she shouted.

He turned back and shrugged before wandering back toward her.

"We are leaving. Will you be at my father's when I return?"

He shrugged again and then laughed. "Cwen, I will find you when you return. You do not need to look after me."

"Someone does," Cwen hissed under her breath. "Synyon bewitches you, Talin. She has no honor and should not be trusted. I just do not want to see you hurt."

Talin grinned rather sheepishly. "I know that, Cwen, but I…like her. She is…I just like her." He looked back toward Synyon to see her leaning provocatively against a tree.

"Do not let the black wizard lead you astray, Cwen. He is no more trustworthy than you believe Synyon to be. Keep the wee Damselfly safe. I would not like to see her husband seriously angered," Talin admitted.

"Aye, I shall see her safe and Lohgaen's quest complete. Then we shall go to Bael for a bit of wagering or to Ælmondæ perhaps."

Talin nodded his agreement, his eyes wandering once again to the waiting Synyon.

"Go!" Cwen threw her hands in the air in exasperation as Talin, flashing a glance of irritation, went off to join Synyon.

For a moment, Cwen looked after Talin, shaking her head, and her eyes narrowed in anger at Synon, the beautiful and seductive thaumaturge.

Lohgaen laughed deeply. "She will do naught but break his heart in the end, and her pleasures are most likely worth his pain. He is far from a child needing a mother's care and most likely resents your interference. Come, Cwen, take me to the Damselfly."

With a final shake of her head and a deep sigh of exasperation, Cwen turned away, leaving Talin to his folly.

⁂

Synyon watched Lohgaen and Cwen step back through the rift before turning her dark liquid gaze on Talin.

"We have a problem," she stated. "Lohgaen has no intention of releasing Cwen, though he may still believe he does. You and I, my friend, need to locate Caen, for I do not intend to allow Lohgaen to hold Cwen with deceit. If she does not care for Caen, she may choose Lohgaen, but it should be her choice. Do you not agree?"

Talin's face grew dark and angry. "Cwen has already chosen Caen. Lohgaen was wrong to steal her memories, no matter what he may have believed. He is a threat. There is no goodness in his soul, though he pretends there is."

Synyon smiled at his fierce concern for Cwen. "I agree with your assessment, at least in this particular instance. Lohgaen is blinded by a desire he will not admit, and that makes him a danger to Cwen. The last word we had was that Caen could be found in Bael. Shall we see if it is true?"

"Aye," Talin replied curtly, stepping through the shimmering rift Synyon created into the port city of Bael.

⁂

In Grimmoirë Nesika sat back on her haunches, her long tufted tail switching with annoyance. "I have known you, Lohgaen, since you required help to change your woolens. You have grown strong and powerful but remain foolish. What you seek to do is far more perilous for you and Cwen than you believe. The Isle of Grave no longer lies within Grimmoirë but beyond the dark of the Mungandr's Vortex. 'Tis not only gryphons that rest there, Lohgaen, it is a home to many creatures far more formidable than gryphons. Yet you would risk the Damselfly without a thought in order to possess the gryphonstone. Your soul grows dark, Lohgaen, and you deceive that one," Nesika lifted her beak to point toward Cwen, "by holding the thief, Caen, from her mind."

"Only the Damselfly may take the stone. I will release Cwen's memories when I no longer require her focus. If I do not pronounce myself heir to the House of Lochlaen, Laoghaire will seek to claim it. Do you believe me and my quest to be a greater threat than Laoghaire, the black wizard?" Lohgaen asked.

"The one you call Father? Aye Lohgaen, Laoghaire is the greater threat, which is the only reason you are allowed to attempt this quest. Tovag, the Blue 'Taur, will accompany the Damselfly. Should he feel the danger is too great, your quest will cease. And Lohgaen, do not sacrifice the hearts of others to gain what you desire, and do not touch the Damselfly."

"I desire nothing but my birthright," Lohgaen said, averting his eyes from Nesika to glance covetously at Cwen.

"You must fool only yourself, Lohgaen," Nesika shook her head, "for you do not fool the dark thaumaturge or the man with the axe." With that she swung away, calling over her shoulder, "I shall send the Damselfly and the 'Taur."

208

Mungandr's Vortex

Lohgaen, Cwen, Arcinaë and Tovag stood uncertainly at the massive hole before them, its darkness increasing as it spiraled downward toward nothingness.

Arcinaë lifted from the ground and, with powerful pulsations of her wings, flew down into the vortex. Behind her, she heard Tovag utter an angry cry, then a hoarse shout and glanced over her shoulder to see the great Blue 'Taur spinning through the blackness. Cwen's call of surprise as she launched herself behind him was followed by the quiet flutter of Lohgaen's long cloak as the wizard jumped in after them.

Surging downward, Arcinaë's wings beat furiously as she tried to keep herself centered and avoid the swiftly spiraling edges of the spinning tunnel of space. Without warning, she found herself plummeting out of the vortex and on to the hard, stone-covered ground. Hearing Tovag's shout, she rolled away to avoid being crushed by his great blue body as he crashed to the ground behind her. Leaping to his feet, he grabbed Arcinaë and pulled her away just as Cwen cried out in pain at making an unceremonious landing on her buttocks. Lohgaen slipped from the vortex and landed lightly on his feet less than the length of a man from Cwen. He reached out a hand and pulled Cwen to her feet and she stood rubbing her bottom. Together the four stared into the mist-covered gloom of late twilight on the Isle of Grave.

"Stay close to me," Tovag commanded to Arcinaë. "I do not like the silence of this place."

Arcinaë nodded and moved a bit closer to the Blue 'Taur, a bit unnerved by his apparent unease. Gesturing in a wide graceful arc, she glared at Lohgaen. "Well, you are here. Find what it is you require so that I may return home."

For the first time since Cwen had introduced him, Lohgaen smiled. "It is not so simple, milady. I have no idea where to look. I had counted on the help of the gryphons, but Nesika was less than forthcoming with information about the stone."

"Are you telling me that, at your request, I have just leapt through a spinning tunnel to land in this dark, uninviting, fog-shrouded place—only for you now to say that you do not know whether what you seek is even here?" Arcinaë asked.

"Exactly," Lohgaen admitted. "What I do know is that I cannot claim the gryphonstone without you, and you have promised to assist me in its acquisition, so we may as well begin the search."

"Perhaps I should simply have Tovag cut off your head and return home."

Lohgaen grew quiet. He eyed Arcinaë and the giant blue bull-man she called Tovag. "It would not be wise to provoke me, Damselfly."

"Lohgaen!" Cwen warned. "Do not threaten her or anyone else. Let us simply get this done and return to Ædracmoræ as quickly as possible. It grows dark while we argue."

Tovag's axe now hung loosely in his hands, the cords of his neck bulged with fury and his dark eyes bored into Lohgaen's.

"We do not have time for this, beast," Lohgaen growled.

"We shall make time for it, human, if you threaten Lady Arcinaë again." Tovag gave a shake of his horns and blew steamy breath sharply from his nostrils.

Arcinaë placed a hand on the 'Taur's bulging arm, and said calmly, "Lohgaen intends me no harm, Tovag. He is merely embarrassed by his own ignorance and the futility of his quest. Come. Let us seek the stone so that I may return to Ilerion."

Cwen stepped between Lohgaen and the others. Placing her hand on his arm, she quietly reminded him, "I am pledged to see her safe, Lohgaen, and so are you. Do not forget it, for I would not like to be forced to be allied against you." She reached up to smooth the frown lines in his forehead. "And you are far more handsome when you are not snarling."

The wizard's eyes softened and he nodded. "You speak the truth. I apologize, Lady Arcinaë. You are partially correct. I am ignorant of the stone's location, but I cannot afford to fail in my quest to obtain it. This quest must not be futile, for Ædracmoræ's balance of power is at stake. If we are not successful, one far more evil than I will claim the third house and seek to overthrow the Dragon Queen. The result would be devastating to our world."

"I am sorry that I was rude," Arcinaë responded, offering her hand to Lohgaen only to have it snatched back by Tovag.

"He may not touch you," the 'Taur growled.

Lohgaen smiled sourly, "There are many rules surrounding you, Arcinaë of Grimmoirë."

"Baene," Arcinaë corrected, "I am Arcinaë of Baene."

"And the mother of the legendary halflings I have been told."

"I will not be the mother of any if I do not return to my husband," Arcinaë answered coldly, her fingers reaching to touch the dragon's tear resting at her heart.

"Lead," Tovag gestured ahead with his axe, "and we shall follow you."

Lohgaen pulled a torch from his pack, lit it and handed it to Cwen. He then lit a second, which he handed to Tovag. After lighting a third for himself, he led them off into the darkness of gathering storm clouds in search of a place to stay the night.

⊰≫⊱

The heavy rain intensified and Lohgaen led them off the stone path and into a dense stand of overgrown trees whose canopy offered some degree of protection from the storm.

Tovag dug an oval in the earth, carefully lining it with soft young leaves for Arcinaë. Cwen looked on in astonishment, and the Damselfly shared a soft, warm laugh.

"Tovag has watched over me from the time I was a child until I disappeared from Grimmoirë. He builds me a sleeping hollow as would be expected by my father. He will build you one if I ask it." Arcinaë looked expectantly at Cwen, who simply shook her head and responded, "Nay."

Shrugging, Arcinaë lay down in her custom-made bed, covered herself with her wings and, clutching the dragon's tear in her small fist, was soon asleep.

Tovag placed himself squarely before Arcinaë, his eyes glowing in the darkness as he watched Cwen and Lohgaen until he felt their sleep. Only then did he allow himself to close his eyes and rest.

Morning dawned clear and cold, sending the travelers scrambling for warm cloaks and hot tea. Lohgaen built a fire, boiled tea and heated the morning buns, slathering them with jam and passing them about.

Arcinaë sat with her hands cupped around the hot mug of tea, eyes still puffy with sleep, hair tangled and unkempt. She sat quietly, missing the morning routines she had come to share with Ilerion, her fingers constantly toying with the dragon's tear. In her mind, she could hear Ilerion's voice as he called to workmen and argued with Nilus. She choked back a small sob of loneliness. Taking a deep breath to keep from crying, she promised herself that if she were allowed to return to Baene, she would never again leave it.

Cwen sat down beside Arcinaë, observing the Damselfly's sadness. "You miss Baene?"

"I miss Ilerion. I miss Nilus. I miss my mare, Zephyr, and the stallion Caval and—yes, I even miss Baene. Do you miss no one, Cwen?"

Cwen felt an odd tug at her heart and recalled the voice in her dreams. "I miss a man I do not even know, a voice from my dreams. Perhaps one day I shall run across him in my travels. I do miss Talin, but I doubt that I am in his thoughts. He is wandering Ædracmoræ with Synyon, a companion of Lohgaen's. A tart." Cwen gave a short laugh before adding, "I should say a thaumaturge."

"And you are jealous?" Arcinaë asked.

Cwen laughed. "Nay, not jealous, concerned. Talin has never cared for a woman as I believe he cares for Synyon. I worry that she will hurt him. I have known Talin since we were very small. He is a friend."

Arcinaë tilted her head and gestured toward Lohgaen. "And he is also a friend?"

"Sometimes I believe he is and sometimes I do not know. Lohgaen is complex. I think he fears himself more than anything else." Cwen shrugged. "It is difficult to know Lohgaen."

"I do not believe I wish to know him. And I am sure that Tovag does not care for his company."

"And Tovag, he is your friend?" Cwen asked, staring across the fire at the enormous, bull-headed man. "I have never seen anyone with more strength, except perhaps a thralax."

"He is a caretaker—a friend would not bully me so!" Arcinaë laughed at her own joke. "He is fierce and set in the old ways of the enchanted. He nearly forbade my marriage to Ilerion. But none will harm me in his presence. It would be wise for Lohgaen to understand that."

Cwen sighed and glanced at Lohgaen, who glowered back over a mug of steaming tea. "Lohgaen is a very powerful wizard. He does not fear the 'Taur."

Arcinaë's laughter filled the camp, "He does not know?"

"Know what?" Cwen asked.

"That he has no power on the Isle of Grave. It is a sacred place, protected even beyond Révere and Grimmoirë. Neither of you has any gift for magick here—it was lost in the vortex. I am far more magickal than either of you."

"How is this so and why did Nesika not tell me?" Lohgaen spat.

"She no longer trusts you," Tovag rumbled. "It is why I was sent."

"And is either of you a healer?" Cwen asked.

"I was taught by your mother. Tovag knows the healing ways of the 'Taur, though I do not recommend them, for they generally require something to be cut off," Arcinaë stated in a matter-of-fact tone.

"It is my recommendation," Tovag said quite seriously, "that you not require healing until we return to Grimmoirë."

Beneath their feet the earth trembled, bringing a heavy scowl to the 'Taur's face. "It would be best if we broke camp and prepared to move on," he urged.

"What is it, Tovag?" Arcinaë whispered.

"The Dragons of Grave, war-like and imperious," he thrust out his chin toward Cwen and Lohgaen, "and not fond of humans."

Breaking camp, they hurried off. Tovag was in the lead and set a brisk pace. They climbed steadily upward, the Damselfly's hand clasped tightly in that of Tovag as she flew beside him. Cwen and Lohgaen clambered over the scattered rocks and fallen logs without aid. Behind them, the deep bellows of dragons filled the air, and in the stillness of the morning the crashing sounds of giant bodies colliding filtered up to the climbers. Pausing to look back, Cwen saw a tangle of talons, tails and long necks amid a rising dust cloud as battling dragons thrashed about in the clearing where they had spent the night. Shaking her head, she murmured to Lohgaen, "I will feel a great deal safer when we reach the summit."

As they climbed higher, the ground cover became sparser, the trees further apart and the boulders larger and less scattered. A number of sudden shrill cries rent the air, bringing a covey of harpies who surrounded the climbers with their threateningly outspread wings.

Recognition dawned and the harpy leader bowed her head, swinging to slap her sisters into submission until all finally knelt.

"Sovereign, I am Aendrith of Grave. These are my sisters. You honor us with your visit."

"I am—"

"The Sovereign accepts your homage," Tovag interrupted, glaring briefly at Arcinaë to silence her. "She has come for the gryphonstone. Can you direct us to its holder?"

A brief look of doubt crossed Aendrith's face as she glanced at the humans before nodding. "It is held in the eyrie of El'suun and Züryn on the face of K'nar Crag. Only Arcinaë, Sovereign of Grimmoirë, may approach the eyrie. You may accompany her to the summit, but they," Aendrith's gaze indicated Lohgaen and Cwen, "must remain below the first tel."

"Why have you brought humans to the Isle of Grave?" asked Aendrith, addressing Arcinaë directly.

"They are servants, sent to prepare my meals and carry my provisions," Arcinaë stated, looking back toward Cwen and Lohgaen and feigning disinterest. "They will comply and wait for me as it is ordered."

Cwen saw Lohgaen's lips move and elbowed him sharply, smiling when he turned to glare at her. Her silent words warned, *Do not interfere. Without the power to defend ourselves, the harpies would strip our flesh and cast our bones to the bastcats before Tovag decided whether we were worth protecting.*

You are not. Tovag's deep tones reverberated in Cwen's already unsettled mind.

"We shall announce your arrival in the eyrie," the harpy leader called, lifting into the air and calling out for her sisters to follow.

"How is it they do not know Nesika is sovereign?" Arcinaë asked Tovag.

"The Isle of Grave remains apart, undisclosed—fortunately for us," he replied, taking her hand as he began to climb the increasingly steep hillside.

"El'suun and Züryn will know. Züryn is Nesika's sister."

"El'suun and Züryn will not care. The gryphonstone is yours to claim, Arcinaë. It is so written in the law. 'Tis why the wizard sought to seal your pledge. Only you may take the stone."

"But, I do not understand. The stone is his. It belongs to the House of Lochlaen and serves to bind seven scarlet gryphons to his house. Why can he not take it?"

"He is not pure of blood. His mother took the wizard Laoghaire to her bed, resulting in the birth of Lohgaen. While he remains heir to the throne of Lochlaen, he is not sanctified to enter the eyrie of the gryphons and take the stone." Tovag shrugged. "Only you may take it from its resting place. You may then give it to Lohgaen if you choose."

When they reached the tel, its large standing stone bearing the mark of the scarlet gryphons, Tovag turned back to Cwen and Lohgaen. "Do not cross beyond this point. If you do, no healer can save you."

Cwen nodded, tugging Lohgaen back even further from the tel and pulling the wizard down to sit beside her. "We will wait, like good servants," she mocked, giving him a rueful smile to soften her words.

Tovag held out his huge hand and waited for Arcinaë to once again accept it before leading her onward among the giant standing stones. The path among the boulders was steep and serpentine, a seemingly endless series of blind switchbacks.

Without warning, the trail disappeared, bringing their progress to an abrupt halt and sending loose rocks and small stones clattering over the edge of the crag.

Lying on his belly, Tovag looked over the edge. Far below lay an emerald valley. Along the sheer vertical face of K'nar Crag, rested the eyries of the gryphons. Each was built on a narrow ledge large enough to hold only the woven-gold and chale-branch construction where the gryphon chicks were raised and the wealth of the adults was stored. Somewhere among the collection of valuables belonging to El'suun and Züryn was Lohgaen's coveted gryphonstone.

Tovag rose to his feet and placed his hands on Arcinaë's shoulders. "Fly swift and safe, milady. Züryn will expect you. Do not tarry and I shall have you back in Grimmoirë by nightfall."

With a wide smile, Arcinaë stepped off into space, broad strokes of her wings bringing her back to eye level with Tovag. "I shall indeed be as swift as possible. I want only to give the gryphonstone to Lohgaen and be rid of his company." Then she veered away, shooting down the cliff face in search of Züryn and El'suun's eyrie. Turning left, she paused before the first eyrie, her gaze met by inquisitive looks from a clutch of young gryphons who appeared to be unsupervised.

"Do you know the eyrie of Züryn?" Arcinaë whispered, so as not to frighten the chicks.

"On the west face," said a deep voice, punctuated with a series of clicks and clacks. The adult, a female scarlet gryphon of extraordinary beauty, landed heavily upon the nest, dropping fresh kill to her young. "The eyrie you seek is on the west face of the crag, near the top, but out of reach of hungry bastcats."

"I am Arcinaë—"

"Once of Grimmoirë but now of Baene," the gryphon finished.

"Aye," Arcinaë agreed with a shy smile. "And Grimmoirë rests in the hands of a strong and fearless sovereign who will lead the enchanted as they are meant to be led."

The gryphon tilted her head and examined Arcinaë closely. "Nesika finds you strong and wise as well. It is with great pride that the gryphons accept the new sovereign. Soon the scarlet gryphons will be summoned to the House of Lochlaen. It is good this day has finally come. We grow fat in the absence of the strife caused by humans." The throaty laugh of the gryphon followed Arcinaë as she flew off toward the west.

Rounding the west face of K'nar, Arcinaë saw the eyrie far above her. With her wings beating furiously, she shot upward, landing lightly on the edge of the great nest.

"Arcinaë of Grimmoirë," El'suun nodded, "you are expected." The great scarlet gryphon rose to reveal the shimmering gryphonstone among the golden threads deep within the woven chale branches. The stone pulsed as if it held a life of its own, the ceaselessly swirling multicolored hues imprisoned within it entwining and separating. Although not a large stone, it was clearly one of great power. Arcinaë stepped forward and knelt to lift the gryphonstone, slipping it carefully into the soft leather bag she carried draped across her chest.

"It is said that you have sealed Grimmoirë and returned its light by the sheer power of your will. It is also said that you have given up time in return for flight and married the human who will return law to Ælarggessæ. It is further said that you will bear a daughter—the halfling who will lift the enlightened world from the threat of darkness. These are great things, Arcinaë of Grimmoirë, great things indeed," El'suun stated with a nod of his large head.

"I do none of these alone. I was kept safe by humans and followed into battle by the enchanted. I am just a Damselfly," Arcinaë answered. "And I do not believe Ilerion wishes to be a leader."

"Perhaps not," the great gryphon acknowledged, "but it is not often the responsibility of the nobleman can be cast aside."

Arcinaë smiled. "We shall see. Now I must return to those who serve me if I wish to return to Grimmoirë before nightfall. I shall tell Nesika that we have spoken."

"Blessings, Arcinaë of Grimmoirë, on you and your human," El'suun called after her, as she lifted upward and back toward the summit of the crag.

Arcinaë landed next to Tovag, who sat waiting cross-legged atop the large flat stone on the tel.

"You have accomplished your task?" the 'Taur asked.

"Aye, I carry the gryphonstone. Let us go."

She lifted off again and preceded her guardian down the steep hillside, back toward Lohgaen and Cwen. Ahead, Arcinaë could see Lohgaen and Cwen sitting just as they had been earlier, silent and unmoving as an enormous dragon circled them, drawing a bit closer with each orbit. Arcinaë burst forward, wings fluttering noisily, and swept down in front of the dragon's face, causing it to draw back sharply and belch out a great steamy cloud of breath.

"What is it you do, Dragon?" Arcinaë shouted.

"I watch your servants, Sovereign, lest they attempt escape while you were away."

The pounding of Tovag's large bare feet against the stones became audible, as did his shouts of irritation at Arcinaë's foolishness.

"How can I keep you safe when you rush into danger without me?" he sputtered.

"There is no danger. It is only a dragon, Tovag. Not some wicked and untrustworthy human." Arcinaë shook her head.

Cwen looked up with a smile. "She fears men but not dragons, a true sign of noble enchantment. If only the Feie could be so brave."

Arcinaë landed lightly before Lohgaen, lifting the leather pouch holding the gryphonstone over her head and handing it to him. "My service to you is ended. If you do not believe it so, take it up with the 'Taur." Without a backward glance, Arcinaë headed toward the vortex that would return her to Grimmoirë and home again to Baene.

Chapter 16: Caen

While Cwen quested for Lohgaen's gryphonstone, Talin followed Synyon as she wended her way through the crowded streets of Bael. It had been long since Talin, Cwen and the nobleman Klæd had accompanied Caen, the thief, into this very city during their quest for the Wreken Wyrm shards that had brought a charge of treason against them. Now Talin and Synyon simply hoped to find the thief alive, alone and sober. Well—alive at least. Caen was not known for discretion where women and ale were concerned, though his loyalty to Cwen had once gone without question.

Talin still marveled at the respect bestowed on the beautiful dark thaumaturge. As Synyon passed amidst the detritus of Ædracmoræ, thieves, poachers and murderers looked away or stepped back as she made her way toward the noisy tavern. Talin smiled at a recollection of Synyon handling his heavy, double-headed war axe as if it were weightless—strength of the mind, she had explained, rather than strength of muscles. Talin loved her strength, as well as her self-assured manner and the power of her magick. Cwen was correct. He was more than a little bewitched by Synyon's charms.

At the entrance to the tavern, Synyon turned to Talin. "No matter what we find, we take him."

"Aye," Talin agreed, stepping through the door ahead of Synon, his hand on the dagger at his waist.

Raucous shouts and the odor of ale-fuelled vomit assaulted them as they entered. A half-hearted wrestling match over a bar wench was being waged by two poachers, the reek of their blood-soaked leathers pervading the tavern.

Talin paused to allow the poachers to crash past him, grimacing at the stench. Leave it to Caen to find such a superior drinking establishment in which to drown his sorrows. With a shake of his head, Talin moved further into the dimly lit tavern, scanning left and right for the man he sought. He heard Caen's voice before he saw him, but the angry snarl and utterance were so alien to the thief's nature that Talin's jaw dropped.

"No! Get away from me. I told you, I do not want your company!" Caen growled, pushing the heavy-breasted blonde wench so hard she fell to the floor.

Stepping quickly to the table, Talin held out his hand and pulled the woman to her feet. "Go—it appears he does not wish your comfort at this time," Talin murmured, sinking into the chair next to Caen.

Caen's eyes rose slowly, following his mug of ale as he drew it to his lips. "Axe-man," he said, lifting the mug in salute, "will you join me in a draught of ale?"

"Nay, you have had many draughts and stink of the streets and the filth of a tavern floor. Synyon and I have come to collect you. Cwen needs you." Talin stared hard at Caen, trying to elicit some focus from the thief.

Caen slammed his hand down on the table and roared with drunken laughter. "Cwen needs me? Nay, I do not believe she does. She made it quite clear when I left that she no longer wanted my company, and she has hidden well enough from sight that I could not find even a whisper of her, not even at Horsfal's Tavern."

"Caen," Synyon's voice was soft but urgent, "there is not much time. Lohgaen holds Cwen's mind. He allowed her to believe you dead and has now taken all thought of you from her. If you do not come, he will hold her through deceit and bind her to him with vows. Do you not wish to at least discover the truth of her feelings?"

Caen's wobbling gaze shifted to Synyon's face, and a foolish grin of recognition filled his eyes as he toppled from his chair and vomited on to the floor and across her boots.

With a look of utter disgust, Synon drew back, standing and wiping the toes of her boots against the fallen thief's filthy leathers. "I shall take that as an 'aye'. Bring him. I will pay for a room and a bath."

Talin grabbed Caen's limp body under the arms, pulling him up and tossing the drunken thief over his shoulder, only to have his back covered with a further expulsion of stinking vomit. "Cwen damn well better appreciate our efforts," he mumbled as he followed after Synyon.

Synyon stripped Caen as if he were a child, dragging the vomit-covered leathers from his legs and tossing them away like rubbish. Pausing, she examined the man's many scars before removing his woolens and adding them to the pile of filthy clothes.

"See that he is bathed while I purchase him some decent clothing," she said, giving Talin a wry smile. Synon pulled a small bag of coins from one of Caen's hidden pockets and weighed it in her hand. "He may be filthy and drunk beyond recollection, but he has obviously done well." Turning to leave, she added, "A cold bath will see him sober much more quickly!"

With a look of distaste, Talin lifted the unconscious Caen from the floor and dumped him headfirst into the cold bath, grinning widely at the thief's screams and sputtering as he surged up out of the water to stand, shivering and dripping in the tub.

Talin threw a wadded cloth and a bar of soap into the tub. "You have become even too foul to travel with poachers, Caen," Talin said with a shake of his head. "Wash and I will fetch a wench to add hot water for your rinse."

By the time Synyon returned with everything from socks and woolens to heavy winter leathers, Caen sat chilled but clean, and wrapped in a coverlet from the bed. She threw the pile of clean clothing onto the table.

"Dress," Synyon snapped. "We waste time we can ill afford. Lohgaen and Cwen return through the vortex with the gryphonstone. If we are not in Grimmoirë when they arrive, you may lose your chance to claim your woman, Caen."

⊰⊱

Speeding ahead of the others, Arcinaë flew up through the vortex into Grimmoirë. Without so much as a backward glance, she slipped through the shield that protected the sacred land of enchantment and into Ælarggessæ and the world of men, lifting swiftly to race toward Baene and Ilerion.

Behind, Lohgaen and Cwen trailed Tovag back toward the mirror that would return them to Réverē and Ædracmoræ. Suddenly, Lohgaen froze, a deep frown etching his fine features. Before him stood Synyon, and she was not alone. Talin and the one called Caen strode forward at her side.

"Cwen," Lohgaen reached out to take Cwen's arm.

"Nay, Lohgaen, do not hold her," Synyon said with a shake of her head. "I will ask you only once to release her. If you do not, I will." The thaumaturge Lohgaen had known so long was full of defiance as she gazed at him. "I warned you, Lohgaen."

With a sweep of her hands and a silent evocation, Synyon restored Cwen's memories, watching the woman's face change as truth flooded her mind. With a hand raised in warning against Lohgaen's interference, Synyon reached out and pushed Caen toward Cwen.

Caen stood, unmoving, his pale green eyes searching Cwen's face, waiting for her to acknowledge him. Talin and Synyon had told him that Cwen would not know him and, even now, it seemed they had been truthful.

Cwen's eyes welled with tears and she sank to the ground, her trembling legs unable to support her any longer. Her shaking hands covered quivering lips. "Caen?" she whispered disbelievingly. "Oh, Caen."

With an angry glance toward Lohgaen, Caen swept Cwen into his arms, murmuring soft words of comfort and understanding as she wept against him.

"I thought you were dead," Cwen's words poured out, "and then I did not think of you at all."

Looking up at Lohgaen, Caen spoke. "Your soul is black, Lohgaen. You promised that you would look after her until my return. What you have done is loathsome, more treacherous than a dagger to my heart, or hers."

Cwen pushed away from Caen, drawing her sword and storming toward Lohgaen. "How could you, Lohgaen? How could you betray my trust? You have stolen my life, taken what I held most dear without any thought for my feelings. Why?"

Lohgaen took a deep breath. "There was no time, Cwen. I could not afford to lose your focus."

"My focus?" she laughed sorrowfully. "You have lost far more than my focus." With a strangled cry of pain and rage, Cwen lunged forward, her long sword catching only the swirling blackness of Lohgaen's cloak as he vanished. She stared at the spot where he had stood, her sword dangling loosely in her hand. "I will make you pay for what you have taken, Lohgaen," she whispered to the emptiness, turning to hold Caen tightly when he touched her shoulder.

"You said that you would kill me if I returned," the thief reminded her.

Smiling through her tears, she corrected him, "I shall kill you if you leave me."

Looking from Talin to Synyon, Cwen whispered tearfully, "I am—"

With a shrug of her shoulders, Synyon interrupted Cwen's attempt at gratitude. "I could not allow Lohgaen to hold you through deceit. It was not in his best interest."

Ignoring Synyon, Cwen hugged Talin. *You know that I will kill her if she ever hurts you,* she whispered into his mind, earning a lopsided grin and a wink of acceptance.

Tovag stepped to Cwen's elbow and rumbled, "It is requested by the Sovereign that you and your companions return to Ædracmoræ. I will show you to the mirror."

With a nod to the glaring 'Taur, Cwen took Caen's hand and followed Synyon and Talin back through the mirror into Réveré.

Homecoming

Arcinaë landed before the castle entrance, calling out for Ilerion. The warm glow that should have spilled from the windows was absent, leaving her with a chill of foreboding.

"Ilerion?" she called more loudly as she raced under the raised portcullis, her fingers gripping the dragon's tear tightly. "Ilerion?" She had a sense of unease and there was an edge of panic taking hold. "Ilerion!" Arcinaë realized she no longer heard his voice within her mind, as she had during her absence when it had been there, always comforting—always there.

"Nilus!" Arcinaë screamed, panic now gripping her heart as she entered the Great Hall to find the fine new tapestries pulled from the walls and crumpled on the floor, tables overturned, the remains of a meal cast away. "Nilus!" Her voice strained with the attempt to reach the ears of those she loved. "Where are you?"

She raced up the wide staircase toward the rooms she shared with Ilerion, her hands clutching at her heart as she took in the destruction and the blood that covered the bedclothes and smeared the walls.

"No…" Visions of the rape of Grimmoirë flooded her mind. "Oh, no…please…no…" Determined to dispel the nightmarish images, Arcinaë flew back the way she had come, through the destruction of the Great Hall and down the steep steps leading to Nilus's workroom and the bedchambers. Splashes of blood covered the walls of the workroom, and the tears Arcinaë had blinked away suddenly flooded her eyes and poured down her cheeks, hot and salty. "*Nilus!*" she screamed again.

This time a soft moan reached her, but she could not tell from which direction it came. "Nilus?" she called, spinning about in the center of the room, eyes searching feverishly. Again she heard the barely audible cry. She whirled about and raced from the workroom, slamming open the door to Nilus's bedchamber.

"Nilus!"

Before her lay the evidence of a struggle she could never imagine. No piece of furniture remained upright. The bedclothes lay scattered and streaked with the black of drying blood.

The moans came again and she ran around the bed to kneel beside the broken body.

"Nilus," she whispered, placing her hands tenderly against his swollen face.

An attempt to open the least swollen eye caused the man to groan, but a tiny glint of recognition peeked out from beneath the drooping lid, and he lifted a hand slowly to grip her wrist. "They took Ilerion. Lazaro's men. I could not stop them. They came like thieves!" he spat. "In the night—like common thieves."

"Where? Where did they take Ilerion? Nilus, tell me, please tell me," Arcinaë begged, as she gathered rags to bind his injuries and murmured the healing spells that Cwen's sorceress mother had taught her. As the worst of Nilus's injuries were bound and his pain was lifted by the incantations, his grip strengthened on Arcinaë's arm.

"I do not know, Arcinaë. Lazaro's fortress is under heavy guard by Reduald's troops, as is the palace of the king. Lazaro's allies have denounced him and joined us against him. Only a few hunters remain at large and loyal to Lazaro. I do not know where they hide."

"I must find help, Nilus. Tell me what to do." Tears streamed down Arcinaë's face. "I cannot lose him, Nilus. I cannot."

"Find the wizard," Nilus murmured, as the healing sleep took hold. "Find Fenris the Feie. If he lives, he will help you."

"Fenris?" Arcinaë asked, but Nilus was deep within the healing sleep and could no longer respond. Arcinaë sank to the floor beside him and wept against his chest until exhaustion claimed her and she too succumbed to sleep.

❧❦

"Arcinaë." Fenris shook her gently, and her eyes instantly opened wide. He hushed and soothed her as she cried out in terror and looked around in confusion. They were no longer within the ruins of Nilus's room but in a small bothie bearing only a tiny bed, small table and a chair.

"Where is this?" Arcinaë sought the Feie's face, her vision blurred and her voice unsteady. "Where is Nilus?" Suddenly, she sat up, sagging with dizziness and the nausea of fear. "Ilerion? Where is Ilerion? Nilus said—"

"Shhhhh. Your fear will not help Ilerion. You must be strong. He needs you."

"You found him? Where is he? He lives? Is he dead?" Her words poured out incoherently, her mind caught in the terror of her loss and a frenzy of emotions.

"Nay, but I found you and I found Nilus. Now we will find Ilerion," Fenris assured her, brushing back the hair from her face and murmuring words that would soothe her and banish her fear. He watched her closely, nodding as he saw her draw a deep breath and straighten her back.

"Who will help me?" she asked, her bright eyes searching the Feie's face for an answer.

"Tovag and the one called Cwen," Fenris answered.

"Nay, they are too far." Arcinaë shook her head violently. "I must go now! They will soon kill him, if he is not dead already!"

"He is not dead," Fenris said positively.

"How can you know?" Arcinaë spat angrily, her face crumpling with pain. "How can you know?"

"The jewel glows with life," Fenris said, reaching out to touch the dragon's tear.

Staring at the pulsating crimson teardrop, Arcinaë looked into the Feie's eyes. "But, I cannot hear his thoughts."

"He sleeps."

"He does not sleep! At best, he is beaten unconscious like Nilus.

226

At worst he is dead and the tear has just not lost its glow!" Arcinaë screamed, leaping to her feet and grabbing her weapons from the table before suddenly realizing she wore a nightdress. "Where are my clothes?"

Fenris pointed to the hook beside the door, backing out of Arcinaë's way as she snatched them and began to dress, oblivious of his presence.

"Where is Nilus? I must speak to him before I go." Throwing open the door, she stared in disbelief. "You brought us to Grimmoirë? How long, Fenris? How long have I been here?" she pleaded, her voice filled with despair again.

Nesika, who had just arrived, answered for Fenris. "Two days, you have been with us for two days, Arcinaë." Compassion had softened her normally harsh-sounding voice. "Ilerion lives, Arcinaë. Nilus believes he may be held deep within the Tangled Chasm, in the abandoned fortress where Ilerion trained his army. It is a dark and hidden place, and one no one has thought to search."

"I will take Reduald's army," Arcinaë said, returning her sword to its scabbard and her dagger to the sheath at her waistband. "We will find the hunters and Reduald will rip out their throats."

"Arcinaë, you cannot take an army. If they see you coming, they will surely kill Lord Ilerion."

Arcinaë turned at the sound of Nilus's voice, and wept anew at the sight of his bandages and the walking stick that supported him. Seeing her tears, Nilus chuckled. "I shall heal, little Damselfly, just as you did."

She hugged him gently, wiping away her tears. "What will I do then, Nilus? Who will help me? You cannot travel, cannot fight. I am not strong enough to fight the hunters alone."

"Take the one called Cwen and the Blue 'Taur. They are strong warriors, and the woman is skilled in the ways of stealth. Fenris will give you the gift of shadow, allowing you to veil and hide your approach."

"Why should Cwen of Aaradan help me? I was nothing but rude to her when last I saw her, resentful at being forced to honor my pledge." Arcinaë looked at the ground, angry that she had ever allowed herself to be taken from Ilerion.

Sensing her thoughts, Nesika said softly, "If you had not gone to the Isle of Grave, you would be dead…or worse. At least you live to try and help Ilerion."

Arcinaë gave a small nod of understanding and swallowed back the vomit she felt rising. "They torture him. I know what they do. They are cruel. Their wickedness is beyond imagining. I have been touched by their evil and with every day that passes, Ilerion suffers at their hands. I will go to seek the help of Cwen of Aaradan but with or without it, I will find Ilerion and end his suffering."

A deep rumbling growl signaled the arrival of Tovag. "Come," he said. "While I did not wish your union to the human, it is done, and I will see him safe within your bed."

Arcinaë blushed, turning away to hide a bitter smile before looking up to accept the hand of the 'Taur. Together they followed Fenris into Révere to find Cwen.

Hunt for the Hunters

Cwen lay in the grass, looking up into the eyes of the man whom she had forgotten. A gentle smile played on her lips as she listened to his tale of loss and woe.

"What? No blonde wenches to comfort you?" Her eyes sparkled with mischief.

"Many offered, none were accepted. Besides, I was far too drunk to serve them well," Caen answered cheekily, pulling back to avoid Cwen's half-hearted slap.

"You are a thief and a scoundrel of the worst kind, and you had best not be having any heavy ale, lest I find you cannot please me."

Caen grew serious and kissed Cwen. "I no longer require ale, milady, for no longer do I sorrow. Always have I been made drunk merely by gazing upon your beauty."

"How could I have forgotten you?" Cwen asked, blinking away tears.

A sudden shimmer marked a rift, and Cwen and Caen leapt to their feet as Tovag stepped into Ædracmoræ, followed closely by Fenris the Feie and Arcinaë.

"I require your help, Cwen of Aaradan," Arcinaë said without preamble. "Ilerion is taken by those who slaughtered the Damselflies and brought Grimmoirë into darkness. If he is not found quickly, they will kill him." Her eyes shifted to the man who stood beside Cwen. Not Talin, but another not so tall or broad.

"Caen," Cwen introduced them, "this is Arcinaë, former Sovereign of Grimmoirë, now wed to Lord Ilerion of Baene."

"He is also a friend?" Arcinaë asked.

Touching Caen's face possessively, Cwen answered, "He is far more than just a friend."

Arcinaë nodded, searching Cwen's face. "And if he were taken, would you not seek help to find him?"

"Aye, I would. Indeed, I would. What is it you ask of me?"

"I must seek Ilerion without raising the suspicions of those who hold him. I am told that you understand stealth. I do not, nor does Tovag for he is not usually required to be subtle. Please, Cwen, help me. I will pledge anything you ask," Arcinaë pleaded.

"Even allowing Talin to join us?" Cwen asked, watching the shadow cross Arcinaë's face.

"Aye, if you believe he is necessary, I will accept him. I will accept anything if you will help me save Ilerion."

Cwen rolled her eyes skyward. "Even a dark and dangerous thaumaturge?"

A tiny flicker of recollection brought a flash of amusement to Arcinaë's tense features. "The tart?"

Cwen nodded, extending her hand to Arcinaë, "Aye—the tart. We shall gather our weapons and find Talin and Synyon. We will meet you in Grimmoirë," Cwen said, grabbing Caen's hand and pulling him away toward the Fortress of Aaradan.

"You called Synyon a tart?" he asked in disbelief.

"Well, not to her face," Cwen confessed. "Hurry, we must find Synyon and Talin and join Arcinaë in Grimmoirë for I fear her Lord Ilerion may already be near death."

The Tangled Chasm

Together in Grimmoirë the seven sat on the grass before Nilus: Arcinaë, Tovag, Fenris, Cwen, Caen, Talin and Synyon. They listened intently as Nilus instructed them on the features of the Tangled Chasm and the location of the abandoned fortress deep within its shadowed darkness. With the blackened end of a burnt twig, he drew a crude map and handed it to Arcinaë.

"Enter by darkness. Use the hidden southern entrance—even though it will take you longer to reach the fortress, you are less likely to be discovered. The fortress is deep, most of it lies beneath the canyon floor. There is a hidden entrance I have marked on the map. Many narrow stairways will lead nowhere or merely end in deep pits of sharpened chale spikes. It is a deadly place below ground level, but it is in the depths that you will most likely find Ilerion."

Nilus shook his head and sighed.

"You cannot take horses, for one call would echo through the canyons like a battle horn. Tovag, you may have to carry Ilerion to safety, for there is no doubt that he will be injured."

"Fenris can stop his pain and hold off death until we can reach safety," Arcinaë said, touching Nilus's hand as they shared their deep worry for their lord. "I will bring him home," Arcinaë promised. She got to her feet to ward off the darkness that threatened to claim her mind and make her useless. "I will bring him home," she repeated, closing her eyes against the memories of the threat of death she had felt near the city of the Sylph and visions of a blazing funeral pyre.

"We shall pass through the rift as soon as the sun falls below Ælarggessæ's horizon. The disturbance it will cause cannot be seen in the dark of night," Fenris advised. "Until then, it would be wise to rest, for there will not be another chance until Lord Ilerion is returned to Arcinaë."

Arcinaë stooped to hug the small Feie wizard who blustered in mock irritation as he tried to push her away.

⁘

Although pretending to rest, none slept and each was held captive to thoughts and visions until the Feie called them to pass through the rift into the darkness of the Tangled Chasm.

The silence of the night surrounded them like a heavy woolen cloak, for they could not risk the flicker of torchlight or the echo of a voice. Arcinaë carried a small Gaianite crystal. It provided only enough illumination to check the map—by peering as she held it a hand's breadth from her eyes—as they reached the end of each long stretch of rough rock wall. Throughout the long night, they crept along, inching their way in blindness, but creeping ever closer to the fortress where they hoped to find Ilerion.

As brilliant daylight reached Ælarggessæ beyond the canyon walls, the winding corridors of black stone merely became a lighter shade of smoky gray. The high walls were barely visible amidst the heavy shadows as they climbed skyward, ending five dragon lengths or more above. In order to avoid detection in the gloom of day, the seven slipped into a hidden canyon and settled down to wait for the deeper blackness of night.

Arcinaë sat alone, her heart heavy and aching, her fingers grasping the pale red glow of the dragon's tear in dwindling hope that Ilerion would live until she reached him. She glanced up to see Caen holding Cwen and answered his soft smile with a small half-one of her own. Arcinaë watched the thaumaturge as she whispered to Talin and hoped Cwen would be wrong about the hurt Synyon would cause him.

Tovag suddenly blocked her view, his eyes piercing under his heavy brows. "He will not die," he said, his voice a deep hiss as he attempted to whisper.

"He may," Arcinaë sighed with the admission, "but if he does I will still take him home. He is mine and I will have him, and none will keep him from me in life or death.

Arcinaë reached out and touched Tovag's muscular arm. "If he dies, Tovag, I cannot live." Her voice was calm and her eyes clear. "Will you see to my bier and bless my soul as it ascends?"

"He will not die, Arcinaë. I will not allow it." Tovag's brow puckered.

"I know you do not want to, but in case we fail, carry us home, Ilerion and me. Will you?"

The 'Taur's frown deepened and he nodded. "Rest."

Arcinaë closed her eyes, remembering her wedding, listening to Ilerion's voice as he spoke his vows. The words changed, his voice a hoarse, chafed whisper. *The Damselfly is dead, Lazaro, already dead. Why else would she not have been with me?*

Arcinaë's eyes opened wide and she grabbed Tovag's arm. "He tells them I am dead," she whispered urgently. "Still the hunters hunt me. Ilerion lives, but he is very weak. We must go now. We cannot wait for darkness."

"We must," Fenris whispered as he approached. "Even veiled, the shimmer of the shadows may be seen if any watch for us."

"Then I will go without you," Arcinaë said, rising to her feet and making her way along the wall toward the main canyon.

Cwen rose, as did Caen, followed by Talin and Synyon.

"If Arcinaë wishes to go, we will all go. Synyon can cast a deeper shadow spell to protect us, and we will move slowly to make sure our progress remains silent. It will be easier to make our way while we have even this small bit of limited vision."

Arcinaë looked back gratefully at Cwen before continuing to grope her way along in the heavy gloom. Behind her, the others joined the slow procession toward the fortress where Ilerion lay dying.

As the meager light finally waned, Arcinaë knelt to consult the map, holding the small glowing crystal above it and squinting to make out the details.

"Less than two leagues." She pointed forward and then left. "The ruins should lie there, amid a rock fall."

"Do not become too anxious and grow careless," Talin chided, only to receive a scathing look from Arcinaë.

"If it were your tart who lay dying, would you not hurry to her side?"

"Tart? What are you talking about?" Talin frowned.

"I believe she means me." Synyon smiled. "I wonder where she got the idea I was a tart?" The thaumaturge glanced fleetingly at Cwen, who shrugged and looked innocent.

"Remain here." Arcinaë's words were a command, drawing raised eyebrows from those around her. "I can travel more quickly if I fly."

"But you will also stir the air," Fenris reminded.

"It will not be noticed if I fly far enough above. I must hurry. I do not have time to argue. Follow if you wish, but I will no longer wait for you."

Tovag's great hand held her wrist, his eyes boring into hers as if he sought to read her mind. "You will travel with us. We will move more quickly." He looked to the dark thaumaturge. "Make our cloak denser and cast a spell of silence. I have seen others of your kind draw the darkness around them. Do it."

Synyon's eyes flared with anger at his demand, but Talin's hand on her arm brought her nod of agreement.

Quickly, Synyon summoned the shadows, watching closely as the gloom surged and deepened around the rocks and down the steep canyon walls, darker than the deepest blackness of the night. "No sound will escape the shadows," she said as she moved forward, ahead of the 'Taur's angry gaze.

Releasing Arcinaë, he watched her lift from the ground into a dense cloud of shadows. She moved swiftly and looked back at him only once before the sudden scream of an angry horse caused them to freeze as Arcinaë returned to the ground. They pressed themselves back against the wall and crouched down, holding their breath for fear of discovery.

"It is Caval," Arcinaë hissed. "They must hold him at the fortress."

Talin looked at Arcinaë with interest, "You can recognize the voice of a horse?"

She tilted her head and gave him a small smile. "I recognize the voice of that horse. He is Caval, Ilerion's warhorse, loyal, fierce and brave. I have heard him speak often. He sounds like no other."

Rising again, Arcinaë led them forward, finally pausing as she glimpsed the looming fortress towering within the face of the tumbled rock, blacker than the surrounding night.

Where lies the entrance? Tovag asked within Arcinaë's mind.

"The hidden entrance lies to the east, beneath the largest fall of rocks. Nilus does not believe it known to Lazaro or his hunters. If our good fortune holds, it will allow us entrance to the lower levels without being seen," she whispered.

Crawling among the great slabs of fallen rock, remnants of some long forgotten battle when the fortress was young, Cwen led the search for the hidden entrance that Nilus had indicated on the rudimentary map.

"Here," Talin hissed, standing at the yawning breach within the stones. Narrow slabs of glowing alabaster were faintly visible before disappearing into the depths of blackness.

Arcinaë pushed ahead, racing forward blindly. Her hand, wet with sweat and tension, gripped the dragon's tear tightly. Her mind searched for some glimmer of Ilerion's thoughts. Ahead, the stairs branched, one set continuing downward, the other veering sharply to the left before dropping out of sight in the gloom. Pausing, Arcinaë pointed ahead and then to Talin, Synyon and Fenris. Sensing rather than seeing their nods, she turned back to the others. "Someone must remain here to guard against hunters pursuing us if they should discover our presence." Her eyes locked on Tovag's.

"The thief will remain behind," the 'Taur said, exchanging glances with Caen.

Cwen reached out and touched Caen's heart, her fingers brushing softly against the leather of his shirt. "See that you do not die, Caen, for it would make me fiercely angry."

Caen leaned forward and murmured against her ear, "'Tis not in my plans, milady, to do anything to make you angry."

Cwen heard the soft sound of Caen's bolt being nocked behind her as she stepped away, heading down the steep staircase after the Damselfly and Tovag.

❧❦

As they approached a dimly lit corridor, Talin held out his hand to stop Synyon and Fenris. Reaching up, he pulled a torch from its wall sconce. Only the sounds of dripping water and scurrying rodents were heard as they edged silently forward, maintaining the heavy veil of shadow that kept them virtually invisible in the gloom.

A stench rose around them as they neared an intersecting passageway. "Death," swore Synyon, covering her nose and mouth. "Rotting flesh. Excrement."

Talin lifted his heavy axe over his shoulder and held it ready, leaning out to look forward and to the rear, drawing back swiftly at the sight of a sleeping guard leaning against the far wall to the right. Putting a finger to his lips and gesturing for Synyon and Fenris to remain where they were, Talin slipped around the corner and stepped quietly toward the heavy man resting with his back against the wall.

He swung the flat side of the axe against the guard's head and watched with satisfaction as the man fell forward and slid to the floor. Searching the guard, Talin lifted a set of keys and several coins from his pockets and relieved the man of his sword and dagger. He swiftly applied a gag and then bound the man's feet and hands before returning to Synyon and the Feie wizard, dangling the keys in front of them. "There is something worth locking up here—perhaps a lord?"

"I sense no life here, only death," Synyon whispered, looking at Fenris to see if he concurred.

"Perhaps the strong scent of death covers that of the living," the wizard shared his fading hope. Though he did not truly believe his own words, he could not speak aloud the thoughts that would tear Ilerion from Arcinaë.

"We must search. We cannot return to the Damselfly without being certain her lord is dead," Talin muttered, forging ahead and turning left, away from the guard.

At the end of the passageway, a further set of stairs led downward.

Twelve steps, a run to the left, twelve more steps and another turn to the left where the walls ahead were lined with the iron bars of captivity. A loud commotion behind him brought Talin's axe around to find Fenris flat on his back in a pool of slick, black blood.

Reaching down, he pulled the wizard to his feet. Talin scowled down at him. "Be more careful, your noise will tell any within earshot that we have arrived."

A soft, unidentifiable sound drifted back from the corridor ahead of them. Not quite human, it was an odd hissing noise as if air were escaping through a small hole. Creeping forward, they looked into the first cage on their right. Bones, tattered clothing and great lengths of chain littered the floor. There were no signs of life, and the sound they had heard was not repeated. The next cage was piled with bodies in different states of decay. None appeared to be recently dead, but the the stench from putrefying flesh was stomach-turning and quickly drove them away.

The soft hiss came again, ahead and to the left. Talin held the torch through the bars of a shallow cell, searching the darkness for the cause. Several bodies, still bearing the chains of their captors, rested on the stone. All were women, naked or nearly so. Talin felt his stomach lurch at the torture of the defenseless, and he glanced at Synyon to see fury burning in her eyes.

"They no longer suffer," Talin whispered, as if to comfort her.

"Pleeeeassse," a long shallow word—not much more than a breath—came clearly from within the cell before them. Talin pushed the torch further into the cage and swept it back and forth, looking for a sign or movement but saw nothing to indicate life.

"Unlock the door," Synyon urged. "Someone still lives among the dead."

Talin began to try the keys, one by one, cursing as each failed to unlock the ancient bolt. Finally, with a snarl of frustration, he struck it with his axe, breaking the rusted iron and flinging it away. He jerked open the barred door and stepped inside, pausing to listen. Again he heard the whisper of sound and knelt next to the first body, even though it had long been dead.

"Where are you?" Synyon asked, as she entered the cage behind Talin. "Speak so that we may find you."

A tiny sound came from the back of the cell, not a voice, not even a hiss, but a faint scratching, as if a small animal crossed the stone floor. Synyon stepped quickly toward the sound and knelt next to a huddled figure. Pulling off her cloak, she covered the shivering form and called Fenris to her.

"She is very near death. Do what you can to keep her life light here within her soul."

Fenris nodded, squatting next to the woman's body and swiftly incanting spells against pain. If the woman was going to die, she would do so without further suffering. Looking up at Talin, the wizard whispered, "Find water, even if it is not clean."

Within minutes, Talin was back with a pail half full of grimy, oil-slicked water and a clean cloth from his pack.

Fenris dipped the cloth into the sour water and dabbed at the woman's badly beaten face, holding the coolness of the cloth to the woman's parched and blood-caked lips. She finally moaned, a small sign of life, a glimmer of hope that she might be saved. Dipping the cloth again, Fenris swabbed away the blood and grit that coated the woman's face, leaning forward to squint at her in the dim light.

"Bring the torch," Fenris called, suddenly forgetting to whisper.

Talin held the torch nearer the injured woman, only to hear Fenris's gasp in horror. "It is Ananta the healer! We were told she was dead nearly two years ago. All this time she has been held by Lazaro! And yet she lives?" Cursing softly, Fenris pulled his bag to him, dragging out bottles and jars filled with healing herbs and oils. Swiftly he jerked away the cloak that covered Ananta's body and began to rub the oils into the worst of her wounds, murmuring words for her deep sleep.

As he completed his ministrations, he glared up at Talin. "Carry her. I will sweep those responsible for her torture into the bottomless abyss," the little Feie snapped, his small hands flashing as he released the chains that held Ananta to the floor.

❦

The glow of her dragon's tear seemed to be growing dimmer and Arcinaë's fear was becoming almost palpable. As if to contain the crystal's light and prevent it waning further, she kept the tear-like jewel clasped tightly within the closed palm of her hand.

"Do not die, Ilerion!" she said fiercely. "I am coming for you—*do not die!*"

Tovag shook his huge head, his heart growing heavy with sorrow as he watched Arcinaë become more and more desperate. Twice she had rushed into dark hallways that had resulted in dead ends, sending them backtracking and losing valuable time. Her words were becoming increasingly incoherent and, at times, no more than a constant high-pitched keen.

The most recent set of stairs was taking them back upward, away from the rows of empty barred cages and, in all likelihood, away from the place where Ilerion was held.

※

Once again Ilerion awoke to the agonizing burning sensations of broken bones and seared skin. Strangely he felt no fear, save for Arcinaë. He could only hope that Nilus had reached her safely.

A shuddering breath told him that this time ribs had been broken as the staff had crashed against them. He hung, suspended above a great barrel of water, wrists and ankles bound, stripped except for his tattered woolens. The rope holding him had been thrown over the wide support beam above, and his hands, arms and shoulder joints had at last become numb from the constant weight of supporting his hanging body.

A shadow passed before him. Lord Lazaro. The man's face was misshapen with bony protrusions where his untreated jaw had healed badly; one arm hung loosely at his side, a dislocation too long left untended. With a sneer, Lazaro brought the staff against Ilerion's side, causing him to bite his tongue rather than give his enemy the satisfaction of hearing his screams.

"If you tell me where she is, I will kill you and end it!" Lazaro shrieked, his spittle striking Ilerion's chest and slowly making its way toward the floor.

"I have told you she is dead, and all the beatings in the world will not make it any different," Ilerion hissed weakly through gritted teeth, consciousness fading again, the room slowly growing darker. A splash of freezing water caused him to gasp. He cried out involuntarily as the salt-filled streams ran into open wounds along his chest and ribs.

"She was seen," Lazaro spat, "seen entering your castle. She is not dead. Save yourself from the agony I will endlessly inflict on you, Ilerion. Tell me where the beast is!" He drew back the staff with two hands, striking Ilerion repeatedly as he bellowed the same question over and over.

"Dead," Ilerion murmured, as his beaten body finally succumbed to the release of unconsciousness. Beside himself with rage, Lazaro slammed the staff against the walls and furniture, screaming Ilerion's name and cursing his silence.

⋄⟐⋄

Arcinaë swung to face Tovag and Cwen. "He lives. Somewhere above us he still lives. I have felt his thoughts."

A sudden shout and the pounding of heavy boots brought a roar from Tovag as he swept Arcinaë and Cwen behind him. Cwen nocked a bolt in her crossbow and moved to the side in order to see around the 'Taur's massive body. She shouted back to Arcinaë, "Go! Fly above them. Find him." Lighting a small torch, she tossed it to Arcinaë.

Seeing the Damselfly lift from the ground and sweep away above them, Cwen turned back to face the hunters flooding into the passage, loosing her first arrow to strike a hunter high in the chest. She swiftly nocked another, far sighting her target as the men rushed toward them.

Tovag bellowed and charged forward, driving the hunters back and into the side corridor, as he swung his heavy axe before him. With a roar, he raced after them, the axe sinking repeatedly into the softness of human flesh.

Behind them Arcinaë flew upward toward the keep and Ilerion's fading thoughts, swearing to kill the evil men so that he would live. Tovag's silent message flooded her mind and lent her strength, *Do not hesitate to kill Lazaro, or you and Ilerion will surely die.*

As Arcinaë burst from the stairwell into the corridor leading to the keep, two hunters swung toward her from their station outside a massive oaken door. Arcinaë hovered before them, drawing her courage from Tovag's warning. She watched the disbelief settle on their faces as she drew her sword with one hand and her crossbow with the other.

Surging forward, she let loose the bolt into the first man and slashed swiftly across the second hunter's throat, dropping lightly to the ground before them as they fell. As always, the act of her own violence caused bile to rise within, leaving her palms sweaty and her legs trembling.

Covering her wings with her cloak, she took a deep breath and tried to still the pounding fury of her racing and fearful heart, for she could not save Ilerion if she could not kill Lazaro. She nocked a new bolt and rested the crossbow against her hip and then opened the door to the keep.

Ilerion hung in the center of the room, his face swollen and unrecognizable, his body covered with oozing sores and the multicolored bruises of many beatings. A man sat at the table, his head resting on crossed arms, his sword laid out before him and a staff leaning against the wall behind.

"Lazaro, I presume." Arcinaë's soft voice startled the man, bringing him to his feet, the sword in his hand.

Though Arcinaë inwardly cringed at the sight of him—his ugly contorted face, crooked jaw with mouth askew—she was outwardly cool and in control. "You are not what I expected."

"Who are you? A serving wench without ale? Some whore sent to pacify my anger until this piece of rotting flesh awakes?"

Arcinaë's eyes narrowed and she took one step closer to her enemy. "I will not allow you to take his life."

"And just how do you intend to stop me?" Lazaro demanded as he examined the small pale woman who stood before him, a frail woman obviously fearful and of little threat.

"I will kill you."

Lazaro threw back his head and roared with laughter, great gasping sobs of laughter that echoed off the walls of the keep. Arcinaë merely waited in silence, sword held loosely in her right hand.

As Lazaro became quiet, Arcinaë spoke softly in the language of her birth. "For my father, I will kill you. For the lives you have taken, I will kill you. For the loss of my innocence, I will kill you. For breaking all the laws of Men, I will kill you. And for what you have done to my husband, I will kill you."

"What babble is this?" Lazaro snarled, his eyes narrowing to slits.

"You speak the tongue of the hunter's beast-wife? What are you?"

With a slight shrug, Arcinaë allowed her cloak to slide from her shoulders, exposing her broad, iridescent wings slowly opening and closing. "I am Arcinaë of Grimmoirë, wife of Ilerion. I am a Damselfly." She circled her sword as Cwen had taught, drawing the hunter's eyes away from her left hand as it slipped down toward the crossbow.

Recognition flickered in Lazaro's eyes as he raised his sword to end the woman's life, but the bolt that struck his heart also dropped his sword arm. With a final exhalation he hissed "Beast!" through clenched teeth, his heart in seizure from its mortal wound.

"Nay, you are the beast," Arcinaë said, stepping past him to Ilerion.

Pulling the plug from the side of the barrel, she released a flood of water over the floor and across Lazaro's body, diluting his blood to a pale rose color. She placed her shoulder against the barrel and pushed it from beneath Ilerion's body, then dragged a chair beside him.

Standing on the chair, Arcinaë drew her dagger and cut Ilerion's bonds, dropping with him to the floor. She eased his head onto her lap and whispered, "I shall bring a healer," as she wiped a little of the blood from his face, and kissed his cracked and swollen lips.

He gasped at her touch, cringing at the pain of his own drawn breath. Tensing, his eyes searched for Lazaro's threat. Seeing the hunter's body, Ilerion sagged against his wife. "Arcinaë," he sighed, a tear slipping from the corner of his eye, "I can accept my death as long as you are safe."

"Nay, I cannot allow you to die, my lord."

"Why will you not let me die, Arcinaë?" Ilerion whispered.

"Because I want you to live," she answered. Stripping away his tattered woolens and placing warm healing hands on his ribs, she pulled the pain away as the sorceress Näeré had taught her.

From her pack, she brought a jar of healing salve and began to smooth it over his wounds and across his bruises.

"Fenris will heal your broken bones," she said, brushing the blood-encrusted hair away from his face.

"Fenris?" Ilerion murmured in confusion.

"Aye, we brought war to Lazaro. Fenris, Tovag, Cwen of Aaradan and her friends, and I have brought revenge, Ilerion. We brought revenge to Lazaro and his hunters."

The scrape of a boot brought Arcinaë's sword up, ready to defend Ilerion, but it dropped to the floor as she looked up at Cwen's golden eyes and Tovag's dark frown.

Seeing the bolt protruding from Lazaro's heart, Cwen gave Arcinaë a wink and said, "I taught her that."

"I need Fenris," Arcinaë said.

"He comes, as do Talin and the thaumaturge. They bring the woman healer," Tovag answered, looking back over his shoulder in the direction of the stairs. "It is time we returned to Grimmoirë and the light of day. I do not like this darkness, Lady Arcinaë."

With the sounds of pounding footsteps came a confusion of voices, all asking questions at the same time, until the crash of Tovag's axe across the table reclaimed silence.

Fenris worked feverishly, drawing the dangerous black blood from internal wounds and beginning the mending of Ilerion's broken bones.

"He will take time to heal, but he will not die," the Feie finally remarked, as he began to clean away the dried blood on the face of his patient. "Humans are such a conglomeration of intricate parts," he mumbled, "it just takes them longer to repair, even with magick as fine as mine."

Tears misting her eyes, Arcinaë knelt next to Ananta's litter, reaching out to softly stroke the healer's hand. "I thought you were dead. We all thought you were dead. If we had known, Ananta, we would have come for you."

Ananta attempted a smile but merely managed a grimace. "They did nothing to me they have not done to hundreds. I will survive because you did come. It is my reward to see you well."

A shout from the stairwell brought Caen. "I followed the trail of bodies"—he grinned—"after slaying the hunters I found around the stables. Now, let's go home."

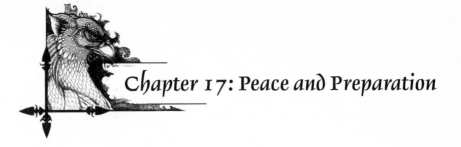

Chapter 17: Peace and Preparation

Within Grimmoirë, the injured healed under the constant watchfulness of Fenris the Feie. Bones knitted slowly and grew stronger until Fenris finally gave permission for Ilerion to leave the bothie to which he had been confined. Ananta remained on bed rest, for her body required purification daily until no seed of the hunters' wickedness remained within her womb. Meanwhile, Nilus grew fit and irritable over Fenris's continuous fussing, and insisted that he no longer needed a walking staff.

Ilerion's gait remained stiff and slow as he emerged from the bothie at Arcinaë's side. His bruises had faded to pale yellows and greens. The swelling had disappeared altogether, returning his ruggedly handsome face to normal though still with some faint discoloration. Nilus stood watching as they drifted unhurriedly toward him and smiled at Arcinaë's firm grip on Ilerion's arm, as if his lord could not stand without her support.

"I shall leave for Baene today and prepare for your return." Nilus offered Ilerion his walking staff and grinned when it was refused.

"Why would I use a staff when I have the arm of a beautiful woman?" Ilerion asked, reaching out to touch Arcinaë's face. "Dompet the farrier has collected the horses from the chasm?"

"Aye, Dompet has taken Caval and the others to his stables and will care for them until you require them. When will you return to

Baene, Ilerion? Has that evil healer gnome given his opinion on when you will be well enough?"

"Within a few days," Arcinaë answered. "Both Fenris and Ananta are returning with us. He has agreed to continue torturing Ilerion with his potions and spells at the castle. Fenris returned the blind cat to Ananta yesterday, insisting that the beast's presence will drive away any remnant of the hunters' evil. It seems that Cat is more resilient than any believed and slipped safely into Révere with some of the Kerleucans." Her eyes sparkled with humor at the disrespect shown by Nilus to Fenris—humans soon forgot their gratitude once they began to mend.

"If you will forgive us, Nilus, I require Lord Ilerion's undivided attention."

Ilerion looked down at his wife, eyebrows raised teasingly. "Have I committed some offense, milady? A secret so grave you cannot speak it before Nilus?"

Arcinaë blushed fetchingly. "Nay, I…"

"I shall leave you to your private conversations," Nilus said graciously, turning on his heel and setting off in search of the Feie to call a rift to Castle Baene.

"Why do you always tease me?" Arcinaë asked.

"To see you blush so becomingly, for though you are always fair, you are impossible to resist with the heat of roses upon your cheeks."

Without another word, she led Ilerion toward the glen where they were wed and, sitting beneath the arbor, she drew him down beside her. Taking his face between her hands she kissed him, feeling the instant heat of his response. She pulled back, whispering breathlessly, "I bear the halflings. I shall need to prepare for their arrival. I shall require a place for their cocoons, and the womb weavers must be summoned."

Seeing Ilerion's look of confusion, she explained gently, "Damselflies do not bear young as humans do. There will be no tiny babes. As the year falls to autumn's cool air, I shall release our daughters' eggs. They must be protected within cocoons, spun by the womb weavers. They will develop there throughout the winter. As spring brings new life, they will emerge fully formed, awaiting the calling of their souls by the speaking of their names, empty vessels to be filled by the gifts of the enchanted and molded by our teachings."

Ilerion's look had become one of concern, and Arcinaë bit her lip, suddenly feeling uncertain of his response to her tidings. "You do not wish our daughters?" she blinked, fearful of his answer.

"Arcinaë," Ilerion's voice was choked with emotion, his words halting and uncertain, "I wish this more than anything, but I do not know what to do or how to help you. Tell me what you need of me."

Her golden-brown eyes searched his face, and her words pierced his soul. "Teach them to be warriors so that they will never know the fears and weaknesses of a Damselfly. Tovag will come and serve as their protector, Fenris will teach them magick and you, my husband, must make them strong and fearless, for it is you above all others they will revere."

Ilerion pulled Arcinaë against him, cloaking her with his warmth, and promising her to give his daughters the fearlessness of warriors.

⚜

On the eve of their departure, the enchantress Davnë summoned Arcinaë to the Glen of Secrets. When Arcinaë arrived she was met by Sharaga the Sylph.

"The time of legend approaches, and it has been left to me to guide your hand. Daughters come to you, Arcinaë, and Ilerion." Sharaga rested her ethereal hand on the Damselfly's abdomen. "One gentle, fair and winged, a warrior armed only with words. And one fierce, dark and wingless, a restless spirit with the ability to leave the body and seek those lost to men. While one will not believe the mysteries of which you speak, it does not mean she loves you less.

"Do you know the tale of the Heteroclites, Arcinaë?"

Sharaga smiled at Arcinaë's discomfort and soothed her worried mind. "Too long your father waited to speak of the future, and too soon Lord Lazaro stole your kin. The tales are therefore mine to tell so that you may teach the halflings.

"Long ago the creators, the Spirit People, set us free to cross the Bridge of Light and walk the earth among men, but the Heteroclites denied the gift of light and chose to remain in the dark realm below.

They became aberrants with time, as did we. They are no longer able to bear the warm radiance of the daystar and we cannot exist without it. Now, a new ruler rises among the Heteroclites, a ruler who is envious of those of us who walk above. Already he has tested men and found them weak, a weapon to be used against us. It is said that by a wizard's bequest the Heteroclite ruler will gain the wisdom of creation's blood change, using it to steal our gift of light and take it for himself.

"Your choice to bind yourself to Ilerion has given us hope, for it is by the mingling of your blood with his within the veins of your daughters that there is promise for the future."

"I—"

With a soft swirl of her hand, Sharaga stopped Arcinaë's words. "By your acceptance of the gift of the Sylph your days are numbered. Count each one precious and share my words with your daughters as they grow within their cocoons."

"And Ilerion? Are his days numbered as well?"

"From this day never will you again be parted from Ilerion of Baene. This I promise you, Arcinaë of Grimmoirë." Sharaga drifted upward. "Go now, Arcinaë. Return to Baene, to your home."

❧❦

Home in Baene, Arcinaë sat at the dressing table and watched Ilerion with worried eyes. "Your wounds are not healed."

Ilerion slipped the shirt over his head, hiding a wince of discomfort from his wife. "They are healed sufficiently to attend a council meeting, Arcinaë. We merely meet to show our support for Reduald. Do you believe I will be forced to defend myself within Reduald's castle?"

"I do not know." Her frown deepened. "What if there is a challenge?"

Ilerion sank to his knees before Arcinaë and took her hands in his. "A challenge will be a formality, no more. A tournament devised to test the challenger against Reduald—all pomp, a mere show of skills. It will not happen on the morrow, but at first full moon following the demand."

She leaned forward and kissed him long and deep, before pushing him away and standing. "I shall go with you and assure your safety, my lord."

A slow smile captured Ilerion's mouth and made its way upward to crease the corners of his eyes. "Lady Reduald will be grateful for your company."

"And you, my lord? Will you not be grateful?"

"We shall see how much you nag me, wife."

He gathered her to him, breathing in the scent of freshly washed hair and warm skin. "You tempt me, woman, to return to the comfort of my bed."

She giggled and pushed away from him. "Dress. Nilus readies the horses. And Caval grows impatient—I can hear his grumbling and stamping from here!"

※

Good weather and good humor saw Ilerion and Arcinaë to Durover with Arcinaë filling Ilerion's head with tales of enchantment and the promise of his daughters.

The laughter they were sharing died on Ilerion's lips as he saw Lord Oeric of Wawne and Lord Saebar of Breden barring the way to the council chambers.

"You have no right to be here. You stand for Lazaro."

"Ilerion, we have every right. Reduald himself issued the invitation. And you should talk! A man who beds a beast!"

Arcinaë shrank away as Saebar reached for her wing.

The whisper of sword leaving scabbard and blade striking chain maille accompanied Ilerion's arm as it swept Arcinaë behind him. Saebar stood frozen with Ilerion's blade at his chest.

"If you ever try to touch my wife again," Ilerion warned, "I will not stay my hand." He sheathed his blade, eyes never leaving Saebar.

"I have come to challenge Reduald, Ilerion. Oeric and I stand for men and for Ælarggessæ. Your peace will not last. Men will not long tolerate the equality of beasts. When I am king, your wife and the rest of her kind will burn." Saebar turned on his heel and entered the council chambers followed by Oeric.

Ilerion felt Arcinaë shiver and hugged her to him. "Do not worry. Saebar stands no chance against Reduald. And he and Oeric are two against three." He kissed the top of her head and looked up at Lady Reduald's warm hail.

"Lord Ilerion, it is good that you have come. Arcinaë, will you take tea with me while the men decide our fate?"

"Lady Reduald," Ilerion acknowledged, "I shall leave my lovely wife in your care. I believe she could use a drop of tea and the counsel of a wise woman."

"Are you not afraid of Lord Saebar's challenge?" Arcinaë asked Lady Reduald.

"Afraid? No, my dear. Lord Reduald is championed by your Lord Ilerion. There could no greater gift for a man seeking to rule Ælarggessæ. Do you forget Ilerion's strength?"

"Nay, I do not. But I remember Lord Lazaro's wickedness as well, wickedness that is inflamed, if the Sylph are to be believed, by a Heteroclite's enchantment. And Lord Saebar and Lord Oeric stood at Lazaro's side, against us. I am afraid the darkness is not at an end."

"Is it not whispered that it was the kiss of the Damselfly that brought us victory thus far? Do not forget, your kiss is present even now as our lords seek to select a new king."

⁂

Around the council table sat the five remaining lords of Ælarggessæ. The chairs of Lord Iydaen and Lord Lazaro were conspicuously empty, sore reminders of loss and discontent.

"It is my right to request a challenge for the crown," Saebar sneered, "and I do demand that on the first full moon a tournament of challenge be set to test the skills of Reduald against the strength of my own arm."

Ilerion tensed, hand gripping the pommel of his sword, but he relaxed as Reduald accepted the challenge, naming Lord Ilerion as his second.

"My only regret is it will not be you I kill on the tourney field," Saebar hissed as he passed Ilerion in leaving.

"There will be no death, not even yours, Saebar, for as Reduald's second I am sworn to it," Ilerion said. "There is a scent of death about you though, and a darkness not your own. I will see the crown won fairly, without blood as the rules of the challenge demand, but I make no such promise for the days that follow."

❧❦❧

At first full moon, several thousand spectators camped in the woods beyond Reduald's castle. The central valley where the battle to save magick had taken place less than a year ago was now a tourney ground.

Three trials would determine the outcome of the challenge: trial by bow, trial by sword and the trial of the lance. Reduald, a formidable and experienced combatant, opposed by a younger, far less skilled opponent, was ready for the challenge of the crown.

"We must be alert for treachery," Ilerion cautioned. "It is unlikely that Saebar and Oeric will arrive without some scheme to tilt the trials in their favor. Any such plan will most likely take place during the joust, so I have appointed Nilus overseer of that challenge. All tack and weaponry will be checked after the two of you are mounted and Nilus will see that Saebar's second has returned to the gallery. Be alert, Reduald. Be alert."

Lady Reduald stepped forward to embrace her husband. "Indeed, my lord, use caution, for all this brutality is making Ilerion's fair wife extremely nervous." Kissing her husband soundly, Lady Reduald allowed Arcinaë to draw nearer.

"'Tis not mere nervousness, but a deep feeling of foreboding, or perhaps I wish so desperately to see the White Laws of Equality enforced and enchanted and man reunited that even a whisper of threat tends to grip my heart darkly." Arcinaë drew a small amulet from the bodice of her gown and lifted its shimmering chain over Reduald's head, tucking the precious spell bag inside his chain maille. "Strength and protection for our future king."

She stood on her tiptoes to kiss Reduald's cheek. "For Ælarggessæ and Grimmoirë, my lord. May your arm be strong and your arrow straight. I know the steed you ride is sound."

"Aye, Arcinaë. Lord Ilerion said you calmed the beast yourself."

"Caval will serve you well, Lord Reduald. He told me so himself." Arcinaë's smile was brief, but the hand she offered was strong and certain.

A light breeze lifted the banners, sending ripples across the raven's widespread wings—the wisdom of the raven, symbol of the House of Lord Reduald. The banners of Saebar were emblazoned with crossed swords, an icon of strength.

The combatants drew lots, and Reduald drew the smaller stone, allowing him to choose his position. Wisely he chose to exhibit second, which permitted him the prize of seeing Saebar's marksmanship before revealing his own.

The crowd roared its approval as Saebar's archery skills proved insufficient to match Reduald's three out of three centers.

Saebar fared better in the trial by sword, scoring best as his blade unerringly struck each dye mark on the effigy against Reduald's two out of three.

As the warriors mounted and settled for the trial by lance, each attended by his second, Nilus stood scowling near Saebar's stallion.

"I would see your lance."

"One would think you suspected me of some treachery, fat man." Saebar's lips thinned in an ugly smile.

"I merely distrust the word of a dishonest soldier with an insincere second. The lance," Nilus demanded.

Saebar shifted the lance, lifting it into position for a throw before slipping it forward into Nilus' waiting hands.

"It is as blunt as a mother-in-law's tongue and weighted according to tourney rules," Oeric said. "You will find no treachery on this end of the field, Nilus of Baene."

Nilus slipped his hand along the length of the lance, searching for the false head he believed it held. He found nothing and looked up again to see Saebar's satisfied smile.

"If you will permit me my lance, I will ride forward to claim my crown."

Nilus tossed Saebar the lance and stepped back to Ilerion's side. "I found no falseness, but they are up to something. Saebar is far too confident."

Ilerion gave a sharp nod and headed back to Reduald's end of the field, leaving Nilus to call the challenge of the lance.

"Seconds to the gallery!" Nilus shouted.

"Combatants, places on the field!"

Saebar and Reduald took their places and lowered their helmet shields, each watching the other across the rail through the narrow slit of the face plate. Their warhorses, held in tight reign, were stamping in eagerness for the charge.

At center field Nilus held the flag aloft, the scarlet silk flying in the midmorning breeze and bringing whinnies of anticipation from experienced mounts. Nilus dropped his arm, dragging the blood-red cloth to his side and freeing the challengers to spur the eager warhorses into action.

At the touch of Reduald's spurs, Caval grabbed the bit in his teeth. With a body leap, he threw himself forward toward his charging opponent.

Turning to duck beneath the rail, Nilus caught the gleam of a steely light near Saebar's inside stirrup as he drew his leg to spur his horse.

Screaming, Nilus waved his arms in Ilerion's direction. "A dagger! There is a dagger beneath Saebar's inside stirrup leather!"

Ilerion leapt to a standing mount and raced onto the field, charging headlong toward Saebar on the same side of the rail. He watched Saebar's left hand dip and the dagger rise in readiness to throw.

"Pull up!" Ilerion bellowed at Reduald and watched an angry Caval fight the bit as his rider dragged him about, away from the rail and the oncoming challenge. Caval reared up, head shaking vehemently against the demands and bellowing his fury. Ilerion swept past on the far side of the rail, and the great warhorse leapt to strike out as Reduald sought to control him.

Without armor or lance, Ilerion swung low in the saddle, away from the enemy's dagger and slammed his mount into Saebar's battle-armored warhorse. The collision sent the warhorse staggering and Ilerion's smaller, unprotected mount screaming as it crashed through the rail in a splintering of bone and wood. Ilerion pushed off from the falling horse to land heavily on his shoulder as he rolled away from the thrashing hooves.

Dazed, he heard Arcinaë's cries before she had completed her race across the tourney field, wings lifting her from the ground as she surged toward him ahead of Nilus and Lady Reduald.

"Beast!" Saebar's furious cry caused Ilerion to look around to see Reduald's lance plow deep into the weakness between Saebar's breastplate and tassets, a slender dagger dropping from his fingers as he was driven to the ground,

Arcinaë struck Ilerion hard enough to knock him flat on his back.

Her arms were in a stranglehold around his neck, her hair a velvet veil as she leaned her forehead against his. He kissed her and struggled to his feet, lifting then setting Arcinaë before him, and smiling as her hands flew over him, searching for injury.

"I am sound, Arcinaë."

Arcinaë glared.

"You cannot do this to me, Ilerion! I will not tolerate it!"

"How did you become so fierce and demanding Arcinaë of Grimmoirë? What happened to my docile Damselfly?"

She tried valiantly to retain her scowl, but finally collapsed with relieved laughter within his embrace.

The spectators roared as Nilus lifted Reduald's arm in triumph and proclaimed him King of Ælarggessæ through victory of challenge. As Arcinaë and Ilerion approached him, Reduald placed his hand on Ilerion's shoulder.

"I will need your strength, Ilerion. As Ælarggessæ's Oversoul you will counsel me and lead us along the path of equality. With Lady Arcinaë at your side, there is no better man for the job. Is this acceptable to you, Lady Arcinaë?"

"Oh, Lord Reduald!" Arcinaë hugged him tight. "By your decree you set my heart to dancing!"

"Then come, and let us celebrate a kingdom of peace."

The Halflings

The cool cellar where Arcinaë had once spent long hours reliving, in terrifying nightmares, her defilement at the hands of Lazaro's hunters was being transformed. The womb weavers had taken over, their abdomens swollen with fragile silk, and were spinning their magick.

Soothed and prepared by the enchantresses, Arcinaë released the sparkling spheres that contained new life. No larger than perfect pearls, the precious eggs were bound within their silken cocoons by the womb weavers. The Damselfly halflings-to-be would spend the long, cold winter months in the nurturing protection of the cocoons as their bodies took form through the enchantment of transformation. In the warmth and renewal of the spring, the promised daughters would emerge.

Throughout the dark season of dormancy, Arcinaë and Ilerion tended the braziers and filled the wall moats with sacred waters to keep the womb room warm and moist as required for the metamorphosis of a Damselfly.

Day after day Arcinaë, the last Damselfly, sat alone in the dimly lit room and shared Sharaga's wisdom with the unbound spirits of her daughters.

"You are the best of both our worlds, your father's and mine. You are destined to a greatness I neither know nor understand but believe in with all my heart."

❧❦❧

Arcinaë watched the flutterings of her daughters inside the pale silk, their internal struggle becoming increasingly evident as the silken threads surged and subsided with the exertions of the burgeoning life within. At the first sight of long slender fingers breaking through a small rent in the first cocoon, Arcinaë approached and spoke the name of her eldest daughter to summon the soul that would occupy the new body.

"A'Janae, first-emerged daughter of Arcinaë and Ilerion, come forth. Cast the light of your gaze upon Ælarggessæ."

A tiny gasp came from A'Janae's lips as her gentle soul entered its body and looked out through bright new eyes on her world. Continued struggles finally gave full release from the silken womb, her efforts leaving her damp and weakened. Blood coursed through her wings, strengthening and straightening. Pale as starlight, veined with sparkling golden fire and covered with silky soft scales, the wings of A'Janae unfurled.

Alongside the first-born emerged the second halfling, the dark twin of A'Janae. As her mother whispered her name, the soul of J'yorie, filled with the fire of discontent, the desire for wings she did not bear and the flame of human passion, settled within her body.

Gazing out beyond her mother and sister, J'yorie's midnight eyes sought those of her father, Ilerion. With her soft, newly discovered voice promising loyalty and love, she looked at him and said, "I am your daughter, Father."

PART II

THE TIME OF LEGEND

Chapter 18: Trials to Come

Nurtured by the gentle wisdom of enchantment and the stubborn strength of man within their parents, A'Janae and J'yorie jealously warred with one another and learned the ways of men and magick. As Ilerion watched J'yorie storming off across the training field, he felt Arcinaë's gentle touch. "She is her father's daughter. I worry that J'yorie does not feel the calling of her destiny though I wish A'Janae was fiercer."

"A'Janae is strong, Arcinaë. She wields the power of words with the skill it will take to counsel Reduald. He has asked that she sit on Ælarggessæ's council. It will suit her well. J'yorie is a fine seeker and warrior—I have never seen a stronger woman. I could place her in charge of a regimen, and men would follow her into battle. When the day comes, she will meet her challenge. They will come to terms with one another, Arcinaë. They will."

"Mother! J'yorie does not listen to your words. She does not believe in the legends that unfold. To her everything is a battle to be won by strength of arm."

"A'Janae, the strength of your sister J'yorie balances your quiet wisdom and acceptance of the trials to come," Arcinaë said, soothing her winged daughter. "It is only the uniting of your strength that will see you through the days ahead. When the day comes, J'yorie will understand the message."

"J'yorie will kill the messenger before his voice is even heard. I swear she will, Mother!"

"Father! A'Janae weeps over the death of a sparrow. How can she fight if she cannot bear to see a soul separated from its body?"

"J'yorie, strength does not always lie in the sword arm. Diplomacy and compassion are also great weapons."

"I would like to see compassion and diplomacy save her from death at the tip of a blade," J'yorie snapped, drawing a reproving look from her father. "Well, I would! I will not always shadow her and keep her safe. One day she will be called to defend herself. If she has no more than words to wield, it will be her own soul she mourns."

⊰⊱

J'yorie slammed a stone into the pool, watching the ripples race outward and slowly die. "Fool!" she hissed under her breath.

"Your father or your sister?"

J'yorie turned to find E'teihl the Wyndwryn leaning nonchalantly against a tree.

"All of them," J'yorie said with a sigh. "My father does not see the danger my sister puts us in with her weakness and A'Janae does not care. Before and since our emergence my mother has filled our heads with tales of curse stones, Heteroclites, aberrant knights and the fulfillment of legends, and A'Janae believes them all. She believes we do not control our own destinies and it leaves her weak."

"But you and I are strong," E'teihl said, his eyes flashing with amusement.

"We are, and because we are we must care for everyone else. I tire of watching over the weak."

Reaching out, E'teihl lifted a dark strand of J'yorie's hair, bringing it to his lips. "We could run away together," he murmured.

J'yorie slammed into him, knocking him to the ground, her forearm across his throat. "Is that all you ever think about!" she yelled in mock exasperation before jumping up, offering her hand and pulling the grinning Wyndwryn to his feet.

"Well, it is what I am best at. Fighting is my second finest skill."

"I wish I could run away, but I cannot leave my father," J'yorie sighed heavily. "I could never leave my father."

❧❧❧

A'Janae tossed within the sweat-dampened sheets as black dreams brought a low moan of anguish. A searing scream shattered her fitful sleep, and her eyes opened wide, searching wildly in the dark.

Silent, pain-filled words forced their way into A'Janae's sleep-fogged mind,

Run! A'Janae, run!

Ignoring the night's heavy chill, A'Janae leapt from her bed and raced along the corridor toward her parents' bedchamber. She struck the heavy doors at a run, the impact of her shoulder swinging them open.

Filled with foreboding, A'Janae's eyes scanned the room. A high wailing, terror-filled scream was wrenched from her throat. On the floor near the doors leading to the terrace was the broken body of her father. The still form of her mother lay lifeless across the bed.

The sound of her sister's terrified screams jerked J'yorie from deep slumber. She leapt from her bed and charged across the bedchamber to pull her dagger from its scabbard, small sparkles of magickal light trailing the sweep of its blade as she raced up the hall.

"A'Janae?" J'yorie called as she entered her parents' room, her eyes instantly drawn to the body on the floor. Her father's crumpled form. Eyes filled with disbelief, her gaze moved to the bed. Arcinaë's head hung over the edge at an odd angle, her wondrous veil of hair sweeping the floor.

Desperately trying to comprehend the scene that confronted her, a sense of movement drew J'yorie toward the terrace where a tangle of deeply shadowed forms was speeding away across the lawn beneath. She grabbed A'Janae's hand and jerked her around. Dragging her weeping, hysterical sister behind her, J'yorie raced back down the dark corridor and out of the castle, calling for E'teihl, her voice shrill with horror and dread.

A sudden shifting of the wind brought a gathering of heavy clouds. Lightning split the darkening sky, blinding J'yorie and A'Janae before deafening them with the resounding crack of thunder that followed. As J'yorie's vision cleared, she saw a deeper shadow detach itself from the gloom. A fiery energy crackled along its emerging form, and swept toward them with alarming speed.

"Come! And be swift about it!"

A'Janae's eyes widened at the sight of the dazzling beast. J'yorie forced her sister to take cover behind her while extending her blade toward the threat. In front of them pranced the lightsteed of her mother's legends, Raer, guardian of the Bridge of Light.

"You are legend, called to stop the Heteroclite's threat and bound to both worlds by your halfling blood. Come! We must not tarry here. War calls the minds of men. They will destroy you if you remain. Already the Heteroclite plants the seeds of fear and fallacy and distorts the legends of your power and your blood," the beast called.

"Reduald leads the race of men along the path of light. His heart is pure. My father chose him out of all men!" J'yorie argued.

"Reduald is dead—murdered in his bed, as were your parents. Even now your resistance draws the evil, feeds its power, as it crawls from the black pit pulling despair and wretchedness behind it. The pall of death will suffocate Ælarggessæ before the daystar rises. The minds of men fill with madness and the desire to dominate. The enchanted flee toward Grimmoirë and to the worlds beyond."

"We must go with him," whispered A'Janae to a startled J'yorie. "We must fulfill the legend as Mother taught."

J'yorie stared at their mother's dragon's tear necklace dripping from A'Janae's fingers.

"You should have listened, J'yorie, should have believed Mother. We have to go with the lightsteed. We have to go with him now."

"We cannot go without releasing the souls of our parents. And I cannot go without E'teihl!" J'yorie snapped.

"There is no time! The Wyndwryn's path is not yours! You must seek the man beyond the wild woods within the mountains of Æselvanæ." The beast pranced impatiently.

Ignoring the agitated lightsteed and with the weeping A'Janae in tow, J'yorie raced back toward the fortress. She continued to scream for E'teihl, but her calls were drowned by the crash of thunder and the roar of the winds.

The castle walls loomed black against the sooty shadows of the roiling clouds. Raer, the lightsteed, swept past them, skidding to a halt and blocking their headlong flight. A sudden rumbling bubbled up from the earth's core, the violent shaking sending the great stone walls tumbling. With a great heave, the earth erupted before them, flinging the massive stone blocks of the fortress into the sky and then crashing them to the ground around them.

"E'teihl!" J'yorie's frantic cry was once again lost amid the chaos.

They darted around Raer, stumbling and thrown to the ground by another upheaval and the tremors that accompanied it.

A flash of blinding light scorched the air in front of the sisters, leaving a glowing being standing there. Extending a hand, the golden man allowed a small smile to touch the corners of his mouth.

"Come." His silken voice was as a caress, the seductive power within his single utterance drawing A'Janae to her feet to accept his offer.

"No!" J'yorie shouted as she clutched at A'Janae's gown and desperately tried to drag her back.

"Master! The Heteroclite Goibniu approaches." The lightsteed's warning drew J'yorie's eyes back toward the castle—now nothing but a pile of burning rubble. The shadows deepened and shifted to allow the silhouette of the man called Goibniu to be revealed against the murky drifts of darkness.

"Your death comes, Daughters of the Damselfly. If you remain here, both of you will die."

Lifting A'Janae to the lightsteed's back, the glowing being offered his hand to J'yorie once again. "Come with me."

"No. Go—take my sister to the safety of Grimmoirë. I will fight for the right to bury my father, and then I will look for her there."

Flashing eyes bored into J'yorie's. Leaping up behind A'Janae, the golden man swung the lightsteed around and, sending a surge of brilliant light ahead, charged toward the approaching blackness. Goibniu roared in fury as the fiery ball of light struck him, flinging him away into the clouds and back into the black city that was his realm.

"Bury your father, but do it quickly. The harbinger and the knights that serve him will swifly return and hunt you all the nights of your life."

"J'yorie! Do not leave me! Please, come with us!" A'Janae's shrill voice begged, as the flaming horse sped away.

"I cannot." But J'yorie's voice fell on emptiness. The lightsteed and those he carried were already gone. With heavy heart and dragging footsteps, she returned to search the ruined fortress for the bodies of their parents.

Farewell and Commitment

J'yorie stood alone before the twin funeral biers, a lighted torch held loosely in her left hand. Each bier held the tightly wrapped body of her parents, Lord Ilerion and Lady Arcinaë of Baene, a human and a Damselfly, by whose union she and her twin sister A'Janae had been created. King Reduald had once called A'Janae a magnificent creature as he had eyed her luminous wings. While there was no such outward sign of her own heritage—nor did she feel magnificent—J'yorie knew that she was as much a Damselfly as her winged sister, for there were no others like them. "Half-flies" was how men referred to them, a new species that had once been foretold in the black legends of men.

J'yorie moved to stand before her mother's shrouded form. Her steps were slow and heavy, her voice tremulous with shock and grief. "I have sent A'Janae to safety in Grimmoirë, a place where words will be weapons enough. I did not know what else to do. I will miss your wisdom, Mother, your soft voice and gentle touch, and the sheltering cloak of your wings. Who will speak of enchantment now that you no longer walk the meadows of Ælarggessæ?"

Leaning forward, J'yorie lit the dry brush at the base of the bier and watched the fire flicker and take hold—the fire that would free her mother's eternal soul to rise on the ash-filled air. She waited quietly until the blaze consumed itself and sent oily black smoke into the dying twilight.

As she faced her father's bier, J'yorie found herself without words, her thoughts jumbled and her soul adrift with sorrow at her loss. She tried to separate her father from the greatness of his thoughts and actions, and the esteem in which he had been held.

"Father, why is it that you are now gone? What enemy remains that you failed to slay? What wickedness comes to claim the minds of men? Am I to believe in the legends of the Damselflies? I do not know what I will do or where I will go, but know this, my father—I will carry your strength and your sword with me. I am your daughter, Father. I will avenge your death."

She touched the torch to the dry branches, instantly wishing she could retract the action as if in some way the flame was a final admission—the fire a confirmation of her loss.

"Many should be here honoring them." E'teihl's silken voice caressed her.

"It is rude to attend a funeral when you are not invited." J'yorie spoke without turning to look at her friend, the handsome Wyndwryn.

"We must go, J'yorie. An army masses against you."

"Where will we go? There is no safe haven."

"Grimmoirë. We should look for A'Janae. Tovag and Fenris will help us, tell us what to do. You could take work as a seeker, perhaps within the borders of Ærathbearnæ or Æselvanæ," E'teihl reminded her, his deep voice unintentionally soothing J'yorie's shattered nerves, a simple gift of the Wyndwryn's tones. "I will stay with you," he swore, reaching out to stroke her hair.

J'yorie gazed back over her shoulder at E'teihl, aware that his usual exuberance had been subdued by the depth of her pain. Sighing, she turned back toward the fires, watching the embers drift skyward.

"We will go to Grimmoirë for A'Janae and then on to Æselvanæ where we should be safe." Her soft voice floated back to E'teihl.

"I will wait for you in the woods," E'teihl said as he offered a second comforting touch.

While not seeing him leave, she felt the coolness of his absence. Long into the night, as the ash of the fires cooled, J'yorie gathered the still warm bones of her parents and buried them together beneath an ancient braid tree.

E'teihl's hoarse cry shattered the silence of J'yorie's reverie. "We must go. Now! The shadows gather in the west."

Swinging to face the west, J'yorie saw the dense, suffocating darkness that indicated the promised death was on its way. Giving a shrill whistle to summon the warhorse Caval, she raced to meet him as he charged across the field toward her. Leaping lightly to his broad back, she grabbed E'teihl's arm to pull him up behind her as they raced past.

"Grimmoirë! Head for Grimmoirë! The aberrants cannot pass through its shield!"

A brief nod showed J'yorie's agreement, and she crouched over Caval's withers, urging him forward as he pounded the earth at a furious gallop.

Sweeping across the long central valley of Baene, they raced over the border into Halhmor, slowing long enough only to refresh Caval with water and a handful of grain. They sped onward with even more determination as the clamorous voices of the howling Heteroclite knights reached them. When the great horse tired, E'teihl flew beside him, lightening the load and soothing Caval with dulcet-toned words while urging him on.

At last the shimmering shield of Grimmoirë became visible. Caval leapt forward with a final surge of strength, stumbling to his knees and onto his great heaving side, hurling J'yorie away as exhaustion finally claimed his great heart. Behind them, the frustrated howls of the deviant enchanted preceded their own terrified screams as Grimmoirë's shield flashed, the scorching flames leaving the aberrant knights writhing in the agonizing throes of fiery death.

Within Grimmoirë the enchanted stood open-mouthed as the great warhorse slipped through the glistening rift and collapsed at their feet, flinging the rider end over end across the scarlet field. They watched in horror as evil burned in the protective shield.

E'teihl fluttered weakly to where J'yorie lay, too fatigued and sorrow-burdened to rise.

"Bring a healer!" the sovereign Nesika clicked in her harsh gryphon's tones, scattering the enchanted as they sought Fenris the Feie.

※

J'yorie awoke beneath the warmth of silken coverlets to find E'teihl's bright but worried eyes watching her. Pushing the damp cloth from her forehead, she attempted to rise but fell back, exhausted. No strength remained after enduring the grief of her loss and the arduous journey. Fenris mopped the cold sweat of wicked dreams from J'yorie's brow and murmured words of healing for her pain-filled soul.

"Has E'teihl told you?" J'yorie asked when next she woke, almost choking as she took a sip of the soothing cool tea from the Feie.

"Aye, now that Ilerion and Arcinaë are gone, A'Janae has been sent into the safety of Æselvanæ."

"Not gone—murdered!" J'yorie swept the cup from Fenris's hand. "Dead. Murdered." She wept until the deep sleep of Fenris's compassionate spell claimed her once again.

Tovag was standing beside the bed when J'yorie opened her eyes again.

"You are in grave danger, J'yorie. Allow me to protect you."

"No! I will not endanger another. My parents are dead because of A'Janae and me. Everyone in castle Baene is dead, crushed beneath the stones because wickedness seeks to destroy the halflings of men's legends. A'Janae will need you, Tovag. Protect her."

"She has gone, fled to the safety of Æselvanæ. Like you, she rejected my offer of protection, forbade me to follow her."

She reached out to touch the giant, blue, bull-headed man who had kept them safe during their childhood and early adolescence. He had taught J'yorie the skills of weaponless fighting and listened to her angry tirades against the weakness of her fair, winged sister. "I must go alone Tovag. I can no longer be the daughter of the Damselfly. I must disappear, become nothing, no one. If you wish to serve, find my sister and keep her safe. She is in far more danger than I—fairness and wings mark her as a Damselfly."

"Next time we meet, I shall act as if I do not know you," Tovag said, a deep sigh revealing his sorrow at her words.

A bitter laugh escaped J'yorie as she realized that the lack of what she most desired would allow her to walk among men in relative safety—just another displaced woman, recognized as part enchanted only by her ability to seek, an ordinary halfling with no tie to the legends of Damselflies.

She watched Tovag leave the bothie, certain that her refusal would weigh on him and cause fresh marks of new sorrow to be carved into his flesh. Calling to E'teihl and gathering her belongings, J'yorie made ready to become lost in the world of humans.

Chapter 19: Encounters

J'yorie's eyes opened instantly, her fiery dagger drawn and ready to ward off her attackers, but once again no one threatened, no one was present—at least not within the visibility afforded by the firelight's fading glow. She allowed the blade to fall to her side and moaned as she heard the furious pounding of her blood. J'yorie tried to slow her panicked breathing and calm herself. Regardless of her choice of sleeping place, the visions found her every night. In a bed at an inn, a nest in the bough of a tree, or the cold hard ground—it made no difference, the evil came for her. Though she had not seen them, she knew they were the Heteroclite knights, those aberrant arcane assassins who had pursued her most recently in Æselvanæ's wild woods. Their eerie howls and cries prevented her from peaceful, dreamless sleep and left her exhausted and stunned by the mind-created images of their passing. They pursued her just as the golden man had warned.

A small wry laugh escaped her parched throat and she rose to drink deeply from her flask. Here on Ærathbearnæ the Heteroclites were only night terrors, nothing more. J'yorie had not passed back into Æselvanæ since the knights had pursued her there. As for Ælarggessæ, she had not returned since the murder of her parents, Arcinaë and Ilerion, more than five summers ago.

Sliding her dagger back into its sheath, J'yorie drank again, recalling another voice. "Work for me," Daegn had said. He had made it sound so easy, as if it were nothing more than selling bread at market. After another unsuccessful search for A'Janae, she had arrived in Daegn's camp a few days late—too late—and had not found his body until two weeks later. Now he too was gone, fallen victim to those who hunted her. His flesh was eaten away by filthy reptilian bloodrens as the empty vessel of his body fell to decay.

Another long swallow of heavy ale in her flask left her eyelids heavy. The effort required to keep them open was too much. As the flask slid from her fingers she fell back to the ground. Let the dark knights come, let them take her, she no longer cared. She had not cared since the death of her father.

The sound of a slight rustle just beyond the dying light of the fire brought instant awareness and sobriety. Seeking some evidence for the disturbance, J'yorie slowly scanned the distant tree line. It would not be the damned Heteroclite knights, for they never came quietly. Some night beast perhaps, a grass cat or a downy flier—harmless creatures compared to the shifting shadows of her nightmares. A small gleam of light caught her attention, just a glimmer of firelight catching the shine of moist eyes: eyes too high for cats, too large for fliers, but not too large or tall for a crouching man. J'yorie blinked, trying to focus on the spot to separate the tiny light from the natural shadows and reflections within the woods.

Hands grabbed her roughly, one pulling her left wrist up between her shoulder blades, the other gripping her around the waist. With a scream of rage she drove her free elbow into the offender's belly and lifted her feet off the ground, throwing them upward and back over her captor's shoulder, using her weight to break his grip. As she landed, her foot shot out slamming the man in the small of the back, throwing him face-first into the smoldering embers of her fire where he rolled away howling. A second man stood before her. His hands were outstretched, palms up and weaponless. He was far too tall for the remnants of the fire to illuminate, and his face remained in deep shadow.

J'yorie crouched, dagger in hand, eyes flashing a warning, voice low and threatening. "I will kill you if you do not go."

The man who had touched her now stood on the far side of the fire, rubbing the side of his face and speaking quietly to the silhouetted man still facing J'yorie.

"Killing will not be necessary this time. You worked for Daegn, as a seeker." There was something achingly familiar in the deep tones of the voice.

It was not quite a question, yet J'yorie saw no reason to deny the truth. "Daegn is dead. I work for no one."

"Which is why you stay in such fine accommodations," her attacker said, his voice spitting with disdain.

"At least I have not been beaten and thrown in the fire by a drunken woman," J'yorie tossed back, earning a low laugh from the one who knew of her deal with Daegn.

"She has a point, Marig," the tall man said, using his thumb to flip something toward her. "I have come on business."

Reaching out, she caught it—a coin. Though she could not see it in the dim light, it was large and covered with raised markings. A hiss brought a sudden flare as the stranger struck a match and stepped nearer to illuminate the token. But, it was not the coin that drew J'yorie's gaze. It was the man's face. The face of Daegn.

"What evil magick do you weave?" she hissed, backing away, dagger extended before her. "I saw you dead, smelled the stench of your rotting flesh. I mourned you as the funeral fire took your soul."

"Not me, but my brother. You mourned Daegn." The match flickered and died. "I am Roh'nan," spoke the voice that resembled Daegn's so well.

"How is it you are so like Daegn?"

"We shared our mother's womb, were born in the same hour. It does not often happen, but when it does the two who are so born can seem as one," Roh'nan explained. "Marig, build up the fire so that we might see one another while we bargain with the seeker."

The fire flared as the soft-bellied man added kindling and fanned the flame with a leafy branch to brighten the light.

"If you are the brother of Daegn why is it you travel with an emissary of Ærathbearnæ's crown?" J'yorie asked Roh'nan, maintaining a wide and comfortable space between them.

"What makes you think I am—"

"I felt your softness when my elbow sank into your belly and I saw the mark on your ear as I swept over your head, Councilor," J'yorie interrupted, watching the crown's councilor reach up and touch the small scar on his ear. "I am, after all a seeker, trained to be observant."

"But not trained to be on time." Roh'nan's voice was filled with insinuation.

"Just what do you believe you know about your brother's death? Do you seek my arrest? Is that why you bring the crown? My delay was not intentional. There were circumstances that kept me away, made me late. I could not have saved Daegn even if I had been there. I barely escaped Æselvanæ with my own life."

"The crown and I share a common interest, the discovery and destruction of those responsible for Daegn's death."

J'yorie laughed. "Then both you and your crown are fools. They were Heteroclites—enchanted aberrant knights, nearly impossible to catch and hold, let alone bring to trial, or put to death. What is it you really seek?"

Roh'nan glanced toward Councilor Marig, who shook his head.

Ignoring the warning, Roh'nan answered, "We seek the place of their origin. Fyrki, the void said to lie beyond Æselvanæ. The dark Heteroclite knights come and go more and more freely. They have already taken many lives on Æselvanæ, and it is feared these knights will soon determine how to enter Ærathbearnæ. It is worth a great deal of coin to the crown if this can be stopped. I was told that the token in your hand would add credence to my request."

"If you return to Æselvanæ, your only payment will be death," J'yorie said, glancing down at the coin in her hand, the clear image of a Wyndwryn leaping out at her. "Where did you get this? Where is E'teihl? He would never have given this to you freely."

"Well, he did. He is unharmed and waits for us at the fortress of Aendrith."

With a short laugh, J'yorie gave utterance to her dark thoughts, "E'teihl must be held by the crown, or you would have brought him to insure my agreement instead of this Councilor."

"J'yorie…"

Roh'nan's voice was soft and insistent, his eyes holding hers in the same way that his brother had done so effectively.

J'yorie leapt to her feet. "No, do not use my name! I will not be drawn into your trap. What you want is impossible. I have business of my own. I do not intend to be added to the crown's victims and placed in some oubliette where I am forever forgotten."

"That is exactly what will happen if you fail to accept our offer." Councilor Marig's voice was heavy with the sweet success of power as he lifted his hand and beckoned to someone beyond the circle of trees.

Crashing sounds from the thick undergrowth brought forth soldiers, weapons drawn in anticipation of the seeker's fury.

"And you believe I cannot kill you both before your henchmen can take me?" J'yorie's eyes burned with indignation.

Roh'nan rose to face her. "We know that you can. I merely hope that you will not. There is no need of this. E'teihl is not held against his will. He knows that what we seek must be found, that the Heteroclite knights must be driven from Æselvanæ. We cannot accomplish this without you, J'yorie. Daegn swore that you were the finest seeker he had ever met and that your birth blood gives you gifts that no others bear. E'teihl has promised his allegiance if I can convince you to do this. Please, do not die here today, for there is no reason. If you are so willing to die, then at least make it meaningful. Help me, J'yorie."

Spinning toward the closest soldier, J'yorie flung a stone from the fire ring to crash against his helmet, dropping him to the ground.

As the tall elegant halfling stepped in front of Councilor Merig, Roh'nan raised his hand to stop the forward movement of the other soldiers. "Do not ever doubt what your fate would have been should I have chosen to fight," she said.

"You will come?"

J'yorie looked at Roh'nan. "I will accompany you as far as Straeth. There I will give you an amulet that will bring E'teihl to me. See that you do not have a councilor in your company when you arrive with my Wyndwryn, for if you do I shall simply be gone. Do you understand me?"

"Aye, perfectly. Councilor Merig, you should return to the fortress in the company of your guards," Roh'nan said.

"You cannot order me away," Merig protested as he rose, gulping as J'yorie took a step toward him.

"It is for your own safety. I shall escort the seeker to Straeth before I return to the fortress. Tell E'teihl that she has agreed to accompany me as far as Straeth and I shall bring a talisman to show the promise of her intent."

"An amulet," J'yorie corrected him. "You will bring E'teihl an amulet."

"Aye." Roh'nan picked up J'yorie's pack and held it out. "Shall we leave for Straeth?"

Without a word, J'yorie grabbed the pack and headed off into the darkness.

Straeth

"**E**xactly how is it you are tied to the crown? 'Tis obvious you are no wizard, since you cannot tell the difference between an amulet and a talisman," J'yorie called back to Roh'nan.

"If you will slow down, I shall tell you who I am." Roh'nan stopped in the center of the road, waiting for J'yorie to walk back to him. "Why is it you must run everywhere you go?"

"Had I not been fleet of foot on Æselvanæ, I would be dead. It would be best if you were stronger."

"You think me weak?" Roh'nan's voice rose in surprise.

J'yorie shrugged. "I have not yet tested you, but your complaint does make it seem so. Come, we should reach Straeth before dusk if we are swift."

"Daegn told me you were difficult," Roh'nan said as the halfling strode off ahead of him, "though he did not say you were impossible."

"What else did Daegn tell you?" J'yorie called back with a glance over her shoulder.

"Nothing personal. Well, nothing terribly personal. He did tell me that you were a halfling. That your father was human, but he did not know the identity of your mother."

"The circumstances of my birth seem quite personal to me. Some say my mother was a demon, others believe she was a 'Taur. I prefer to think she was something more exotic."

Roh'nan chuckled, a low pleasant sound. "More exotic than a 'Taur?"

"I suppose that would depend on which 'Taur." J'yorie allowed herself a small sad smile and thought of the blue-skinned bull of a man who had helped to raise her.

They walked on for a while in silence, Roh'nan lengthening his stride to stay abreast of the seeker.

Suddenly J'yorie prompted, "Are you not going to ask?"

"Ask what?"

"If there is a Tell, something to indicate which beast was my mother."

Roh'nan grinned. "Now that would indeed be very personal. If you wish me to know, I am certain you will tell me. Did Daegn ask this of you?"

J'yorie's eyes glittered with mischief. "Nay, though I am sure he always wondered. Now, what is it you do for the crown?"

"I do not serve Ærathbearnæ's crown. I am the Oversoul for the Æselvanæ council. A woman of some significance has been taken, a halfling, A'Janae of Baene. We believe she is held beyond Æselvanæ, somewhere in the lands of Fyrki."

J'yorie's fist shot out, striking Roh'nan in the jaw hard enough to drive him back several steps. "A'Janae is not just any halfling. She is a Damselfly halfling, a legendary creature of great importance. Just what game is it you play?"

"It is not a game," Roh'nan answered, flexing his aching jaw and careful to maintain the distance between them. "A'Janae came to Æselvanæ after the death of her parents. She said she sought a place of safety from the inequality imposed by the new leadership of the Council of Men on Ælarggessæ. She wanted only privacy and peace. We granted it."

"As Oversoul was it not your place to protect her?" J'yorie snapped, fists clinched, nails biting into her palms.

Roh'nan pointed to J'yorie's angry fists. "Do not strike me again, or I will be forced to defend myself. It will not end well for either of us. I did not become Oversoul by being weak, J'yorie."

Closing the distance between them, J'yorie slammed the flat of her hands against Roh'nan's chest, knocking him to the ground. "Do you believe yourself my equal?" The question went unanswered as Roh'nan leapt to his feet and tackled J'yorie, driving her backward into the dust of the road. She let out a howl and flung herself away, tossing him up and over her head where he landed hard behind her. J'yorie rolled to her feet, only to find herself facing Roh'nan's sword.

"I told you not to strike me." His voice was gentle, contrasting sharply with the cold threat of the sword's blade.

J'yorie held out her hand to call the sword.

"Your magick will not work against me, Seeker, no more than it would work against Daegn. It is a waste of time for us to fight with one another."

"I will decide what wastes my time." J'yorie charged forward, striking out with both feet, kicking the sword from Roh'nan's hands as he brought its flat side toward her. Snatching her from a midair lunge, he pulled her to the ground and rose to straddle her, his hands locked on her wrists. "Why must we do this?" He felt her relax and tightened his grip on her arms. "Do not do it J'yorie."

She bucked beneath him, and flipped him over her head, then spun her body to land hard on top of him, breaking his grip. Leaning forward, she whispered into his ear, "We shall continue this later. We draw an audience." Rolling away, she stood to face those who had been drawn by the rising cloud of dust from their scuffle, casually nodding her acknowledgment to the startled onlookers before walking off toward the city gates.

Roh'nan rose to his feet, brushing away the dirt and dust as his eyes followed J'yorie. "Perhaps your mother *was* a demon," he muttered, gathering his sword and returning it to its sheath.

Roh'nan located J'yorie in the Maraen-owned tavern called Leifitë's. Aware of her critically appraising gaze, he sank into the chair next to the halfling.

"You are strong but not strong enough."

"Woman, you talk in riddles. You are contrary and obstinate, and in spite of your beauty I find your company less than pleasurable." He pulled a mug forward and filled it from J'yorie's pitcher. Taking a swallow, he coughed. "And you have very bad taste in poisons."

"Darkness approaches, and therefore I must find a companion to keep me awake or a potion to put me to sleep. I prefer a strong Maraen brew to the company of most men."

Sudden warmth announced the arrival of the tavern's owner. Leifitë was tall and slender, with skin of deep indigo and eyes alight from the heat within. She rested a hot hand on Roh'nan's shoulder, her deep laughter causing a rattling of the the scales that ran from the top of her head to the base of her spine. "What brings you here, Roh'nan? Æselvanæ's magick no longer satisfies?"

Roh'nan tilted his head back to meet the Maraen's eyes. "J'yorie brings me here, and now I am both bruised and burned." He glanced meaningfully at the Maraen's hand on his shoulder.

"Perhaps it is the company you keep." The clatter of scales brought the burst of heat that always accompanied the excitement of humor in a Maraen. "Did no one warn you that this seeker bites?"

Looking at J'yorie's grim expression, Roh'nan chuckled. "I believe her mother may have been a serpent."

Roh'nan caught J'yorie's hand just before it struck his face, bringing a new burst of laughter and waves of heat from Leifitë. "J'yorie is magnificent, Roh'nan. Why is it you fight with her?"

"I do not wish to fight with her, only to employ her skills," he said, looking at J'yorie and releasing her hand as he added, "I want only to employ your skills as a seeker."

"You are not strong enough to make war on Fyrki or to save A'Janae if she has truly been taken there. I have heard the howls of the aberrants, felt their pull on my mind. You are not strong enough to fight them, Roh'nan."

He smiled at her use of his name. "Not alone, but with your help and that of the Wyndwryn—perhaps. You can find her. I know that you can. Daegn said you need only a person's name to locate them."

J'yorie pushed back her chair and stood looking down on Daegn's double. "Take this"—she pulled a small spider cloth bag from around her neck—"and give it to E'teihl. If you do not return within two days, I will be gone. If you are in the company of anyone other than E'teihl, I will be gone. Do not attempt a trap, Roh'nan, for I would be forced to kill you."

Roh'nan reached out, taking the hand that held the amulet between his own. "I shall return by this time tomorrow with the Wyndwryn and no other. I give you my word as Æselvanæ's Oversoul."

Withdrawing her hand, J'yorie left him holding the amulet and made her way unsteadily toward the bar.

"What will she do?" Roh'nan asked Leifitë, his gaze following J'yorie.

The Maraen grimaced, showing sharp white teeth. "She will drink herself into a stupor, and one of my men will put her to bed. We have an agreement, she and I. In return for her services as seeker, I make sure she is not bothered in my establishment."

"And her mother? What do you know of her?"

"I am surprised at you, Roh'nan. Your curiosity may get you killed. Can you not see she has the heart of a dragon?" Leifitë threw back her head and laughed.

Reaching out, Roh'nan grabbed Leifitë's wrist, earning a sharp warning glance as he quickly withdrew his burning hand. "What is it she wishes to escape?"

"Besides the loss of your brother? Only her own history. I like you Roh'nan, I really do, and so I warn you: J'yorie is dangerous, perhaps as dangerous as the Maraen in her own way. Beware."

"Tell me Leifitë, what was she to my brother?"

"Nothing. An employee. He did not make demands, and you would be wise to follow his course. Go, and bring the Wyndwryn E'teihl. Go. You waste time with questions for which there are no answers."

With a last glance toward the bar and J'yorie, Roh'nan rose and set off to collect the seeker's Wyndwryn.

⊰❦⊱

"Let him out," Councilor Marig ordered, indicating the Wyndwryn in the cell and backing away as the soldier unlocked the barred door and swung it open.

The Wyndwryn shot out of the cell, slamming into the councilor and knocking him to the ground before flying up to hover near the vaulted ceiling.

"Enough!" Roh'nan's voice was a sharp command. The Wyndwryn's eyes focused on the Oversoul who was helping the hated Marig to get to his feet. "J'yorie waits in Straeth, in the care of the Maraen—Leifitë. She sent this," he tossed the amulet up to the Wyndwryn, "and said it would bring you to her."

"You told her the truth? That you seek A'Janae?" E'teihl asked, catching the amulet and tucking it into his leathers without a second glance.

"Most of it, and I bear the bruises to prove it." Roh'nan touched his jaw where it bore a faded purple discoloration. "She is tough, your mistress."

"Aye, and I imagine you suffered other damage as well. 'Neath your shirt and leathers, perchance?" E'teihl grinned, his black eyes sparkling with the joyous thought of Roh'nan's battering at the hands of the halfling seeker. "Did she believe me held captive? Of course she did. She knew I would not part with that coin unless it was wrested from my hands by brute force."

Roh'nan ignored the Wyndwryn's goading. "If you are quite finished, we should go. She will wait no more than two days. I promised I would deliver you by dusk. You are free to go. Just how good is your word, E'teihl? Do you intend to help me find A'Janae?"

"Of course I do. I said I would help you convince J'yorie. Why did you not just take me with you? You would have saved the councilor's handsome face and the soldier's rattled brain."

"You were a prisoner of the crown, and I did not trust you," Roh'nan admitted, staring up at the winged man with the burnished bronze skin. "I am regretful I did not insist on taking you, but Marig thought you would simply…fly away. How do you know J'yorie sent that amulet if you do not even look at it?"

"I saw the glow of the aura she left on it. Just because you cannot see something does not mean others cannot. You are an inferior being in spite of your physical strength, Roh'nan, and you would be wise to remember it. You will take less knocks if you do," E'teihl cautioned as he drifted to the floor, wrinkling his nose at catching a whiff of Councilor Marig's body odor. "Where is my sword, you sorry scop?"

"It is in the guard room. We will collect it on our way out,"

Roh'nan advised, urging the Wyndwryn away from the councilor before he could inflict further damage. "It would not hurt you to treat Marig with a bit of respect. We may need his help."

"He is a simple bully who takes pokes at those whose weapons he has stolen," E'teihl sniffed. "What possible help could he give?"

"He has the power to petition the crown on our behalf. What if we should need an army or a wagonload of gold?"

"Ah, he could get a wagonload of gold?" the Wyndwryn asked, eyes filled with undisguised greed.

"Aye, or an army, or a pardon for a thieving Wyndwryn, so it would be wise not bait Councilor Marig any further," Roh'nan suggested.

"Am I pardoned?"

"Nay, but you will be when our task is done."

"Did you tell J'yorie? That I was caught?" E'teihl had the decency to look embarrassed, earning a gruff laugh from Roh'nan.

"Nay, for some reason I did not."

Pausing before a heavy door, Roh'nan banged on it with his fist until the cover on the rectangular peephole was pulled back and the soldier acknowledged him.

"I come for the Wyndwryn's weapons," Roh'nan stated, relieved to hear the heavy bolt drawn and the door opening. "Wait," he held out his hand to stop the anxious E'teihl, "unless you wish to be gutted by some fearful guard. This is not Æselvanæ, and you are not accepted as an equal here. Remember that."

Accepting the slender sword and pulsing crystal-bladed dagger, Roh'nan returned them to E'teihl, watching as the Wyndwryn drew the sword from its scabbard and examined it before buckling it in place across his back, beneath his right wing. He slipped the dagger into a hidden sheath on the side of his leathers and then looked up at Roh'nan. "Well? What are you waiting for? Let us find J'yorie and the Damselfly A'Janae."

Chapter 20: The Heteroclite's Captive

A'Janae woke to the pain of a cramped wing and the clinging pungency of the spell-casting herbs used to sedate her. Her captors had come silently, waiting until the Oversoul Roh'nan had left her and she had been lost in bitter dreams. She recalled the deep, soothing whisper that had calmed her when she had stiffened in fear. "I wish you no harm milady, but I cannot allow you to remain free."

Attempting to rise, A'Janae discovered herself bound. Instead of the coarse ropes of thieves and poachers, her bonds were the slender silken threads of a wizard. She tried to adjust her position and relieve the weight on her uncomfortably folded wing. Her failure left her fretful, tears of frustration welling along with a stifled sob.

"I would prefer to offer you the comforts of a guest rather than the ignominy and pain of a prisoner. There is nowhere to go. All possible exits are heavily guarded." The gentle voice seemed to be emanating from the gloom of a distant corner.

"My wing aches. It is folded beneath my shoulder, and I cannot seem to free it. If you do not wish me harm, why do you hold me here in darkness? I will die if you do not release me."

The man stepped forward from the shadows, his features unclear in the torchlight's soft flicker. The turn of his hand brought a brighter flame, sending the shadows fleeing from his face.

"I am Goibniu, milady, ruler of the Heteroclites. You are here only to draw your sister to me. J'yorie believes you are destined to fulfill a prophecy. She believes you will rise to lead an army against the Heteroclites." His eyes glittered with sudden amusement. "Your sister is a fool, A'Janae."

A'Janae cowered as Goibniu's hand shot forward, but he merely swept away her bindings, freeing her to lift her weight from the throbbing wing.

"Thank you." A'Janae sat up, iridescent glass-like wings stirring the air and sending the torch flames flickering as she flexed her cramped shoulder muscles,

"You are beautiful."

"So I have been told by many."

The soft rustle of silk preceded the arrival of an elegant woman, one of dark sculptured beauty and regal presence.

"Taerys, my queen, will see to your needs." Goibniu swung and strode from the room.

"Your fairness fascinates his lordship. He has never before encountered a woman of the light. Come, I shall find you more suitable clothing and show you his kingdom. Perhaps you will then understand his desire to steal yours."

A'Janae touched the neckline of her gossamer nightdress, heat rising to claim her pale cheeks as she recalled Goibniu's gaze.

"Ours is a marriage of power, not passion. If he desires you, he will have you. It does not mean we cannot be friends."

"I will fight him."

"Then you will die."

"He does not seem as evil as the—"

"Golden One warned? You have offered no resistance, Damselfly. You have not watched the black heat of his fury rise to consume him when he is defied. He rules this realm as inflexibly as an iron rod. He is as improbable a being as you will ever encounter. Living in darkness for so long has changed us. While we remain powerfully enchanted, each of us is no more than an aberrant reminder of what we once were." Goibniu's queen sighed before adding, "It will sadden me to see him break you."

As they approached the end of the corridor, a servant hurried to throw open the door to allow their entry to the queen's rooms. Inside chambermaids curtsied, eyes averted, as they offered a selection of soft gowns.

"Choose whichever suits you."

A'Janae reached out to touch the delicate cloth of a deep scarlet gown, closing her eyes with pleasure at its silken finish.

"This."

"You must wish death to come quickly," Taerys said.

"Already my life-light dims and I grow weak. As I am sure you are aware, the fair enchanted cannot be held in darkness. The warmth of the daystar is needed for our wing-blood to flow. If Goibniu plans to force my acceptance, he had best be swift. He does not have the luxury of time, and my sister will kill him when she comes."

"How is it your sister need not fear the darkness?"

A'Janae smiled weakly, as if it took great effort. "J'yorie will come with the power of the crown, and she does not wear the wings of the Damselfly."

Shaking her head in doubt, Taerys pointed to the scarlet gown. "Dress, and I will take you to him."

Sliding the nightdress from her shoulders, A'Janae heard Taerys' gasp of disbelief. A'Janae's skin was so fair the shadow of her heart was visible as it beat beneath her breast. The handmaiden helped A'Janae into the dark red gown, adjusting the laces below her wings, drawing them tightly to hug the Damselfly's slender waist.

"You are beautiful, milady," the servant whispered.

"So it has been said."

Another maid stepped forward to brush A'Janae's pale silver hair and offer soft slippers for her delicate feet.

With a flutter of wings, A'Janae went to stand before the polished brass mirror, the fading light of enchantment gradually slowing the pulsation within the veins of her shimmering wings.

Glancing at Taerys, she murmured, "Let us go to seal my fate."

Taerys opened the door and led the way toward Goibniu's chambers.

"This labyrinth of darkness is the home we were given by the Spirit People—separated from light for all time, now forgotten by the creators and left to fester with the agony of loss. You have been here less than a full cycle of your shadow clock and already you fail.

Imagine the pain we suffered and the fury we feel." Taerys' terse words slapped A'Janae.

"I can bring you into light."

The distant walls resounded with echos of the queen's cool laughter, spilling on to the small bridge they were crossing and into the pit below. "We are as fragile in the light as you are in the darkness. No Heteroclite but the aberrant knights wearing the shield of their protective armor may pass across the Bridge of Light. The warmth of the daystar that you crave is as hot as the fires of the forge upon our skins. Death is what light now brings to us. It will only be after Goibniu has brought the blood-change to our people that we may emerge."

"It cannot be done. No man has the power to change an entire race. Not even the Wizard-Elect has such power. Only the Curse Stone could wield…" A'Janae faltered, a sudden weakness dropping her to her knees. Taerys' grip saved her from slipping off the narrow bridge and into the depths of the void. "He cannot have the power of the Curse Stone. It is heavily guarded within the House of Hexus…" A'Janae's words begged an answer—one that she did not wish to hear.

"But, he will. It was the bequest of your great wizard DaeAer. Goibniu merely waits on the gifts your sister brings, which will allow him access to the Chamber of the Stone and the knowledge to wield its power. Then he will free us to walk your worlds."

"He will not do that. Every enlightened enchanted on the surface of the worlds will die. To grant the blood-change requires a similar race with whom to exchange the blood. Only the fair enchanted…he would not be so cruel."

"You will soon see just how cruel he can be. Look around you! Do you truly believe we care what happens to the fair enchanted? They cared naught for what became of us."

"The Spirit People will stop him." A'Janae watched Taerys shake her head.

"They abandoned both races long ago. They no longer lead. If the Spirit People are the well from which your hope springs, you will die in the darkness of disappointment."

"If this is true, J'yorie will know and she will not come." Scalding tears burned A'Janae's cheeks.

"She will know nothing. She travels in the company of Goibniu's—"

"Taerys!" Goibniu sprang from behind, grabbed his wife and flung her aside. A'Janae screamed, sinking to the ground in horror at his cruelty.

"Hush! Screaming will not save you. You can come with me, or you can join Taerys." Goibniu offered his hand. "Live or die, I do not care, for your sister will come to me regardless of your condition."

"You care nothing for me?" A'Janae responded, allowing her chin to rise and her eyes to affect a sultry gaze as she searched the madman's face.

Goibniu laughed. "You are nothing but bait within a trap."

Taking his hand, A'Janae slowly stood up. She brushed the dust from her gown. She noticed that her movements attracted Goibniu's gaze as he studied her sensuous form, lingering on the curve of her breasts and hips. "I am the warm glow that lights your dreams, the warmth your chilled body craves. Tell me it is not so, and I will throw myself into the chasm."

His hand rose as if to touch her before falling back to his side. "Even as you slowly grow cold, you risk what little life is left in the hope that my desires outweigh my wickedness. Come, I will take you to the wall of light where you can warm yourself and restore your vitality."

"You have light? If you have light, why did you not use it to save yourself from the damage of the darkness?"

"It was a gift given in an attempt to save the Heteroclites. It was given by a foolish wizard who sought to restore our ability to bear the light, but it was far too little and offered far too late. Now it is used to torture and burn those whose service displeases me."

"Why is every word you speak intended to shock and frighten me?"

"Because, daughter of the Damselfly, you should be frightened. There is no mercy here." Goibniu again presented his hand, frowning as A'Janae hesitated before accepting it.

"You tremble with chill and weakness. Why did you not tell me how badly you needed the light?"

"I thought you knew." Her warm breath caressed him as she collapsed against his chest.

With a snarl of rage, Goibniu shouted for a knight. He handed A'Janae to a suitably shielded warrior and urged him toward the room that housed the wizard DaeAer's wall of light.

From beyond the shadows of his ebony crystal shelter, Goibniu watched as the great mirrored wall brought the warmth of its surface light to A'Janae's body. Standing behind him, Taerys folded her great leathery wings and hid them beneath her cape.

"You are wise, husband. Your trick will make her fear your anger, and the wall warms her for your pleasure."

Goibniu gave a deep throaty chuckle. "She is braver than you believe. A warrior of words, willing to risk what little life she believed she had left. She fearlessly chanced to play upon my passion in the belief that she would soon die in our cold darkness and be free of me. Imagine her surprise to find the gift of light here." Turning sharply, he urgently pulled his wife to him, crushing her frigid lips beneath his and growling with frustration as she struggled against him. Abruptly pushing her away, Goibniu wiped away the tart, unpleasant taste of her mouth. "I will enjoy stealing the Damselfly's sweet heat."

"Just be careful Goibniu, that she does not break that brittle shard of ice you call a heart. Is it true you dream of her?"

Holding Taerys' arm in a painful grasp, Goibniu snapped, "I dream of warmth that does not blister my skin, and light that does not sear my eyes. What form it takes is unimportant. Can you tell me that you do not eagerly await the return of the walker? And did the heat of his passion not bring you the greatest pleasure of your cold, dark life?"

Angrily shaking off Goibniu's hand, Taerys stabbed his chest with a long, sharply pointed fingernail. "Just know that what I want is freedom. Freedom from you and freedom from the chill of this black pit we have too long called home. The walker is mine. You promised him to me once his task is completed."

"He is yours to keep. I have no further use of him once they have gathered the gifts that will unlock the Curse Stone's magick, and J'yorie is led to me. Be sure that you do not mingle your thoughts with his while he travels with her. If you do, she will find them and all of our plans will be for nothing."

"Will you keep her?" Taerys asked as she watched the winged woman rise on the far side of the ebony crystal wall.

Showing fine white teeth, Goibniu admitted, "Perhaps I will keep them both."

A Pact

"J'yorie?" The name penetrated J'yorie's fog-filled mind, and she lifted her head from her arms. She wiped her eyes with one hand and the trail of spittle from the corner of her mouth with the other. As the face before her finally came into focus, she gave a slow smile and reached out to stroke the Wyndwryn's cheek.

"E'teihl, they have freed you." Suddenly J'yorie jerked upright and spun around, seeking Roh'nan. "You came alone? With none other than E'teihl?"

"Aye, though I could have come with an army and carried you away, you would not have even noticed." Roh'nan shook his head with disgust. "Why must you—"

J'yorie's open palm struck his face. "Do not tell me how to be, or what to do. Already I tire of your company. E'teihl, were you harmed? Why did the crown hold you?"

E'teihl sat down, crushing his wings against the back of the chair and resting his bare feet, ankles crossed, upon the table beside J'yorie. "I was caught stealing the jewels of Councilor Marig's daughter. I believe she would have given them to me had I asked, but she was asleep. I served her well J'yorie. You know how grateful women are for my service."

Choking back her laughter, J'yorie poured a mug of ale in the hope of composing herself only to have Roh'nan yank it from her grasp, the deep purple brew splashing over his hand and across the table.

"Nay, Seeker, you will be sober and ready to travel within the hour. We cannot wait while you drown your sorrows. You need a bath and some willow bark tea."

J'yorie snapped back, "I do not suggest you try giving me either!"

Without a word, Roh'nan snatched J'yorie and threw her up over his shoulder. Ignoring her howls and screeches, he held her in a vise-like grip and stormed up the stairs. Slamming open the door to the first room, he dropped J'yorie unceremoniously in a heap on the floor. "Undress or I will do it for you."

Looking over Roh'nan's shoulder, J'yorie saw E'teihl hovering outside the door, the enormous grin on his face telling just how much he was enjoying her torment. Pulling off her boot, J'yorie threw it at him only to see it sail past, over the banister and down into the tavern. She glared up at Roh'nan defiantly. "I will cut out your heart if you touch me again."

Crouching before her, Roh'nan grabbed her other boot and pulled it off, dragging her across the floor. "Water!" Roh'nan snarled at the startled wench standing next to the tub, "Fill the tub with water, preferably very cold." He swung back to J'yorie to find her crawling away toward the door. "You smell like the floor of a tavern, and your reflexes are slower than tree sap."

J'yorie's foot swept out, catching him behind the knee and knocking him to the floor next to her. "I would say my reflexes are just fine!" She kicked him again, this time connecting solidly with his backside, squealing as he reached behind him and clasped her ankle pulling her around toward him.

"Bastard!" she screamed, clawing at the floorboards in search of some purchase, a leverage—anything to aid her resistance.

"Exactly what is it the two of you are doing?" Leifitë's eyes were wide with curiosity, waves of heat distorting the air around her as she stood watching from the doorway. "If this is some sexual ritual engaged in by half-humans just say so, and I shall close the door and leave you to it."

"It is!" Roh'nan said, causing J'yorie to erupt into a fresh fit of howling and thrashing.

"Then I shall send up the water." Leifitë gave a low throaty laugh as she backed out of the room and pulled the door closed behind her.

"Get your hand off my leg," J'yorie said, kicking away Roh'nan's hand.

A soft tap on the door brought a succession of servants, each with a bucket of water for the bath. A small meek woman curtsied and explained, "We have the water my lord, but 'tis not cold. Mistress Leifitë insisted we bring warm because the cold would shrivel your manhood." She glanced away, cringing as if she expected Roh'nan to strike her.

J'yorie's caustic laughter echoed off the stone walls. "If he touches me again I intend to remove it regardless of its size and form." She looked around for Roh'nan and found him leaning against the wall next to the open door, arms crossed, a doubtful expression etched across his handsome features. "You do not believe me?" J'yorie asked haughtily.

"I believe that in your current condition, you are not nearly as fearsome as you think yourself. Warm water is fine, though I do not intend to join you. You do not strike my fancy J'yorie, and I believe your braying alone would drive away a legion of deadly knights."

Roh'nan kicked the door closed behind the last of the retreating servants. "Now get in the bath. Where do you keep your clean clothing? I will send E'teihl for it while you bathe."

"You fetch it. 'Tis in my bag behind the bar, just ask Leifitë. Allow E'teihl to remain with me while I bathe. I give my word I will not attempt to flee."

"Suddenly docile and agreeable, J'yorie? I am an Oversoul. I will not fall for your trickery. Your magick is wasted on me, and you are not sufficiently skilled in the art of persuasion to convince me of your righteous intent."

"Why is it you wish to see me naked?"

"J'yorie, I have no desire to see you naked. I shall order a screen to assure your privacy if you like, but I will not leave you alone in this room. The crown has freed the Wyndwryn into my custody and agreed not to seek you for dereliction of duty in the instance of my brother's death as long as you agree to assist me in the search for A'Janae. I can see your thoughts. You believe you can find her and save her alone, but you cannot. Even together we stand only a slim chance."

"What are you, Roh'nan?" J'yorie's thoughts suddenly rushed backward and latched onto Leifitë's remark, the bath and nudity forgotten—sexual ritual engaged in by half humans, the Maraen had said. "Why does Leifitë call you half-human?"

"Because I am. Do you wish to see my tail?"

J'yorie's eyes widened with disbelief. "You have a tail?"

"No, I do not. Like yours, my Tell is within, not visible to others."

"What makes you believe I do not simply hide the Tell beneath my clothing?" J'yorie tried to look mysterious, but managed only mild puzzlement.

"I believe I would have felt it with all the groping you have forced me to do. Now, into the bath!"

J'yorie began to unlace her shirt, watching Roh'nan's eyes for a change in expression. His gaze remained focused on her face, even when she drew the shirt off and tossed it at his feet. Abruptly he turned away, opening the door and shouting at the wench waiting in the hall, "I need a privacy screen—now!" He remained blocking the door until the girl returned. Snatching the leather screen, he slammed the door closed and removed the key.

Without looking at J'yorie, Roh'nan placed the screen around the tub. "You should hurry, before the water grows cold. I will send E'teihl for your clothes."

Behind the screen, J'yorie removed her undershirt and carefully unwound the cloth bindings that flattened her breasts to keep them from the gaze of men. Slipping out of her leathers and woolens, she stepped into the water, sinking beneath its surface and allowing the warmth to soothe her aches. Her thoughts drifted to the Ælarggessæ of her childhood. Fearless among both men and beasts, bred of the magick of enchantment and the cunning of a human father, she had grown up hunting the fierce bane boars with the Wyndwryn E'teihl. Always she had shielded the fearful A'Janae, protected by their father's enforcement of the White Laws of Equality—laws no longer enforced since the deaths of Ilerion and King Reduald. She damned Roh'nan for not protecting A'Janae on Æselvanæ. She damned herself for not going with A'Janae when she had asked, and for not being on time to meet Daegn, for not saving him. She damned Daegn for dying and leaving her to Roh'nan's unwavering intent to return to Æselvanæ and death. Daegn's brother and A'Janae—a deep sigh escaped J'yorie as she realized she was eternally bound to both. Forcing away the dark thoughts, J'yorie soaped and rinsed her hair and body, hating to admit that it did make her feel more human to be clean. In Æselvanæ the condition of being human no longer mattered, for their united councils had long upheld the White Laws. The threat in that place came from beyond its borders, the void beyond the Bridge of Light. J'yorie suddenly wondered just how much Roh'nan knew—she would have to be careful with her thoughts lest he see too much, too soon.

As she dressed in the clothes that had been hung over the screen, J'yorie took great care to bind her breasts tightly so they would not be at risk during the "groping" scuffles she knew she would be forced to share with Roh'nan until he conceded that she was the stronger. The thought brought a smile that she quickly hid before stepping from behind the privacy screen.

Roh'nan held out a cup of steaming willow bark tea whose odor caused J'yorie to gag.

"Drink it," Roh'nan insisted, pushing it into J'yorie's hands.

"It will make me sick," she said, looking at the still bubbling sludge with distaste.

"Nay, it will settle your stomach and clear the foggy remnants of ale-induced calm from your mind. Make you sharp. Set your reflexes humming like a tautly drawn thread. Drink it. It is good for you."

"Where is E'teihl?" J'yorie asked, shuddering as she sipped the hot tea.

"He provisions us. We will leave for Grimmoirë at daybreak."

"Grimmoirë? Why do you wish to go there? You said A'Janae is believed to be held somewhere within the void of Fyrki." J'yorie emptied the cup and placed it on the table, running her fingers through her thick damp hair in an attempt to remove tangles.

"Will you sit?" Roh'nan asked, pulling a chair from the table.

J'yorie eyed the chair as if it held some form of trap but finally sat after pushing it a bit further away from Roh'nan.

"We need the help of a Blue 'Taur. His village is within Grimmoirë's stronghold.

"Tovag? You seek Tovag? He will not help you. He obeys only A'Janae, and without her token you stand no chance of obtaining his help. By the Ancients, you are a fool, Roh'nan!"

Roh'nan held out his hand. In it rested the crimson dragon's tear crystal bound to a braided gold and silver chain. J'yorie's eyes widened in recognition. "How did you get that? It once belonged to A'Janae's mother, given by her father on their wedding day. A'Janae held it more dear than her very life."

"It was found in her room. The clasp is broken—I believe it was broken when they captured her. It will serve as a token to the 'Taur. We need him, for his strength is formidable, and he will do anything to protect the daughter of the Damselfly."

"You have given all of this a great deal of thought, haven't you? Who else is on your list of 'must haves' for a successful rescue? A wizard? A sorceress? Dragons and gryphons? Just whose army will you lead into Fyrki?"

"There is a small wizard on Æselvanæ who might be helpful, but I am primarily depending on you, J'yorie, and your skill as seeker." He searched her face, meeting only a glare of stony resistance. "What is it? Why do you fight me, J'yorie?"

Her chin lifted insolently. "I fight everyone. Do not think yourself special."

"But why? Why must you fight? I do not wish to control you. I only seek your help. Do you not see the difference? Did you fight like this with Daegn? "

"No, but I should have. Look where my succumbing to persuasion got your brother. It got him dead. Roh'nan, I am a seeker. Daegn did not train me. Seeking is a gift from the blood of my mother. I will seek you right into an early death, Roh'nan, just as I did your brother. I do not want that burden. Look at me! I cannot even bear the burdens I already carry. I drink to avoid thinking—and seeking. They are one and the same to me. My life is spent between the bombardment of the consciousness of others and the exhausting power it takes to suppress it."

J'yorie tensed as Roh'nan suddenly stood up. To her surprise, he moved to her side and knelt next to her chair. In a voice no more than a whisper he asked, "What were you seeking for my brother, J'yorie? What drew death to my brother, Daegn?"

Unable to keep a single tear from slipping beneath her lashes, J'yorie closed her eyes against the great sorrow that a sobered mind could no longer contain. "I was to seek Rygeian's Rift. Your brother sought something he called Rygeian's treasure—he had a key, a crystal key, slender and cylindrical. I do not know what killed Daegn. I came into the camp and he was gone, just gone. I sought him, but the path made no sense. It backtracked into Ærathbearnæ and returned to the camp. I finally found him near Whytahl's Woods, leagues from his original camp. He left no mind trail. It was as if he just suddenly lost all thought." Opening her eyes she looked at Roh'nan, tears now flowing freely. "I should have been there sooner, touched the key and sought the rift."

Roh'nan reached out and gently touched J'yorie's hand. "Yet Daegn hired no protector. I offered my service and he refused it. You are not a protector, J'yorie. You are a seeker. If you will help me find A'Janae, I will protect you from whatever lies in Æselvanæ. I can evoke a spell of aversion that will keep even the demons of the dark abyss from stepping within the boundaries of its casting. This is my gift, J'yorie. Let me protect you, and together we will find your friend, the Damselfly halfling, and bring her home."

J'yorie stared at Roh'nan's fingers where they rested lightly on the back of her hand. Looking up, her cool dark eyes filled with unshed sorrow, she asked, "Who is your father Roh'nan? Who gave you such a power?"

"Not my father, but my mother, J'yorie. My mother is Eshwyn, an enchantress. She lives with my father, Lord Théroe, in the city of Kyrenia on Æselvanæ. My father is a councilor there. My mother is an artisan and the keeper of the Holy Flame. So you see, there is nothing special about me." He smiled and shrugged. "No tail."

Sighing, J'yorie lifted Roh'nan's hand and turned it over, examining his palm, her eyes growing soft and distant as she sought his truths. "I do not see your death, nor do I feel deviousness within your conscious thoughts. You truly believe that you can keep those who travel with you safe from harm. You love a woman, the one who broke your heart. You detest Councilor Marig though you act as if you respect him. You hold dear a secret place that you have shared with no other, and you carry a great deal of gold upon your person." She paused, staring into his eyes. "And you really did want to see me naked."

Roh'nan emitted a soft laugh, his eyes gleaming with amusement. "I shall have to be more careful with my thoughts—and my gold! I am relieved you do not see my death, for I have much to accomplish before I go willingly. Will you come with me to Æselvanæ, J'yorie?"

The door opened revealing E'teihl. "You called me?"

"Aye, we leave for Grimmoirë. Collect our belongings from Leifitë and find the boot I lost over the stair rail." J'yorie wiggled her bootless foot at the Wyndwryn. "Roh'nan grows anxious to be off."

As E'teihl flew off to do J'yorie's bidding, she leaned toward Roh'nan, her eyes hard as stone. "Do not lie to me again." She raised her hand against his protest. "E'teihl was held against his will, but you told me he was not. Failing to disclose that you once shared A'Janae's bed, while not a lie, feels like one." Again she held up her hand to stop his words. "You are the one who wanted me sober, for with my sobriety comes my power to seek. I do not care about your relationships with others, including A'Janae. Just do not lie to me."

Catching the boot E'teihl tossed from the door, J'yorie slipped her foot into it and stood, shouldering the pack the Wyndwryn dropped beside her chair.

"Shall I call the rift to Grimmoirë, or will you?"

Without a word, Roh'nan drew the symbols that created the shimmering passage into Ælarggessæ's land of enchantment.

Hunting the 'Taur

"**E**'teihl!" The small Feie wizard called from his position next to Nesika. Bowing respectfully to his sovereign, the fiery-haired man hurried toward the newcomers as fast as his short legs and stout body would allow. "J'yorie? What brings you to Grimmoirë? Who is this human?" Fenris the Feie pointed to indicate Roh'nan.

"I am Roh'nan, Oversoul of Æselvanæ, halfling son of Eshwyn the enchantress and Councilor Théroe," Roh'nan introduced himself, receiving a scowl in response from the Feie.

"Filled with pompous bullram scat, isn't he?" Fenris sniffed. "So you are a visiting dignitary? That is what you are trying to express?"

J'yorie suddenly sank to the ground, hugging the short man with the flaming whiskers and foul disposition and whispering a hurried warning against revealing her identity to the Oversoul, "Do not give me away old friend." Then, in a voice loud enough for all to hear, she continued, "Roh'nan seeks our help in locating A'Janae. She has gone missing from her home on Æselvanæ and it is feared she may have been taken against her will."

"How is this possible? On Æselvanæ of all worlds! And you, mister Oversoul, you did nothing to protect her?" Fenris puffed irritably.

"A'Janae was very private, and she did not confide—"

"They were lovers, and for some reason she lost faith in him and got herself 'napped in a snit of broken-heartedness while he was off somewhere...," E'teihl offered helpfully, earning withering stares from both Roh'nan and J'yorie. "What? I heard you say he shared her bed, J'yorie. Makes sense that what I say is true," the Wyndwryn defended.

Fenris stared at them in disbelief. "A'Janae captured! By whom?"

"We are not certain," J'yorie said, glaring at the loquacious E'teihl, daring him to share any other ideas he might have on the subject.

With a derisive snort, the handsome Wyndwryn spread his wings and rose from the ground. "I am off to visit my cousins. Call me when you have found the 'Taur." Sweeping away, he left Fenris scowling at J'yorie and Roh'nan.

"What does he mean 'found the 'Taur'?"

"Roh'nan would like to ask Tovag for his help," J'yorie answered, cringing at the cross look she received.

"Just who do you think you are? Coming into Grimmoirë and stirring up things that ought not to be stirred," Fenris snapped, glaring at Roh'nan.

"I think that I am the Oversoul of Æselvanæ, and I have come to request the help of one Grimmoirën citizen in finding another Grimmoirën citizen. Just exactly how is that so unreasonable?" Roh'nan said, glaring back at the Feie.

J'yorie sighed, reaching out to touch the small wizard. *Roh'nan does not know, Fenris. I did not tell him. He believes that A'Janae entered Æselvanæ seeking some peace and privacy after the death of her parents, nothing more. It is what she told their council.* Silently she again warned him against telling Roh'nan who she was. *Roh'nan does not know I am A'Janae's sister.*

Fenris plopped to the ground, cross-legged, patting the grass beside him. "A'Janae's father was Lord Ilerion of Baene, well-loved and respected. He enforced the White Laws of Equality and kept the peace. When he and A'Janae's mother were murdered, A'Janae fled ahead of the assassins. That is how she ended up in Æselvanæ."

"Why did she not ask my help?" Roh'nan seemed truly mystified.

"You got too close," J'yorie whispered, "and she felt she could not risk your life."

"But I could have protected her."

"Aye, perhaps, though it does not matter now. Fenris, we really need Tovag's help, his strength and dedication to A'Janae. I know he was angry at not being allowed to protect her, but surely he will want to help us find her and bring her home."

"Maybe, if you had a token. Without one, he will not even speak to you," Fenris said.

"Show him," J'yorie said, gesturing with a flourish of her long slender fingers.

As Roh'nan pulled the dragon's tear from his pocket. The sight of it brought a gasp and soft sobs from Fenris.

"I created it for Ilerion to give to Arcinaë on the day of their wedding. He did not have a gift to offer the Damselfly, and Tovag insisted upon it. It kept Ilerion close to Arcinaë. His thoughts were always with her. And now they are gone, the dragon's tear is dark and A'Janae may be lost as well." A tear dripped from the end of the Feie's bulbous nose, and he drew a handkerchief, blowing hard and sniffing back his sobs. "Take it and show it to Tovag. He camps beyond the Lake of Death. Tell him I said if he does not help you, I shall curse him with a serious case of the boils."

J'yorie gave Fenris a hug and allowed Roh'nan to pull her to her feet.

"I am sure that will be more than enough to gain Tovag's support, Fenris. Will you tell E'teihl that we have gone to fetch the 'Taur, and he had better be finished visiting his cousins by the time I return?"

"Aye," Fenris said with a snort of disgust.

※※※

J'yorie and Roh'nan slipped through the rift on to the sandy shore of the Lake of Death. Silent white sands stretched along the deep green water's edge, water that killed those who unwittingly drank it and left weeping sores wherever it touched the skin. Although the Formidable River that fed it carried the pure water of the mountain melt, the lake forever remained lethal, poisoned by the deadly sludge that oozed upwards from its basin's deep center six hundred dragon lengths below.

Drawing nearer, large and deep impressions upon the dark alluvial silt that fanned out across the pale sand gave evidence of a lone 'Taur having passed by. The sharp crack of a sapling ahead confirmed his presence.

"He builds a temporary shelter for the night. Let me go first," J'yorie cautioned, as she began to move off in the direction of the falling trees. "He will recognize me, and even if I am not welcome, he will not harm me."

Tovag reached out and grabbed the three-year-old sapling, snapping it off at the base as if it were no more than a twig. As he reached for another, the rustle of shifting grasses brought his head around and his hand to his axe. "Hold there!" his voice rumbled toward the approaching woman.

J'yorie paused, reaching to release her hair from the leather binding, allowing it to flow freely about her face as the light breeze lifted it. The Blue 'Taur took a stiff step forward, sniffing and staring. "J'yorie? It is not safe for you here. Why is it you wander near the Lake of Death?"

"I seek you, Tovag. I have great need of your help. No one must know who I am, not even the one who travels with me."

Cautiously, the 'Taur slowly stepped closer and revealed the new scars of self-mutilation that scored his bulging thighs. The loss of the halflings under his care had burned him deeply.

Roh'nan shifted position slightly to better see the giant, pale blue, bull-headed man, rippling with iron-like muscles, receiving an angry, steaming snort for his trouble. The tattooed symbols that covered the 'Taur's arms and chest were meaningless to the Oversoul, and the raised red scars across both thighs looked new and still painful. This was definitely a man built to protect, and just the man they needed on their search for A'Janae.

Tovag shook his head and snorted again at the stranger who stood close behind J'yorie, eyeing the human from head to foot and dismissing him as no threat. "Who is this?" the 'Taur asked sullenly.

"He is—"

"I am—"

"I do not speak to you human, but to the halfling seeker."

"He is Roh'nan, Oversoul of Æselvanæ. He assists me in my quest," J'yorie finished, casting a warning glance at Roh'nan.

"You are a seeker, J'yorie. Why would you require my help?" Tovag shook the coarse black hair that covered his head and back. "I am bound by sorrow and cannot accept a quest."

"Tovag, we seek A'Janae. She has been taken by beings we do not know or understand. I need your strength and protection. I cannot continue without it." J'yorie accepted the dragon's tear from Roh'nan and held it out to Tovag. "She dropped this. It is her request for our help."

A heavy frown creased the 'Taur's brow. "Who was her protector?"

"I was," Roh'nan admitted.

The 'Taur's backhand blow lifted the Oversoul from the ground and tossed him a good half dragon length, leaving him stunned and breathless.

"We will not need his help," Tovag snarled, striding to stand over Roh'nan.

Tovag, he did not fail her. A'Janae did not allow his help. She was afraid. She told no one, let no one get close enough to discover the peril that shadowed her. Please, Tovag, help us. She took comfort from the Oversoul, Tovag, and 'tis why she did not risk his life. The soft tones of her confession flooded Tovag's mind. *The same reason I did not wish to risk yours. I did not reject your protection, I simply feared for your life.*

Ignoring J'yorie's silent declaration, Tovag reached down, grabbing Roh'nan's shirt and lifting him to his feet. "You do not smell of human? What is your birthblood?"

"I am a halfling, like J'yorie." Roh'nan shook off Tovag's hold and brushed the earth from his clothes. "I was told you would do anything necessary to protect A'Janae. Was that a lie?"

Tovag scraped his horns against the tree, leaving great white gouges where rich dark bark had grown. "Do not doubt my bond to the blood of the halfling Damselfly, Oversoul. I was commissioned to serve her by her mother." His gaze shifted briefly to J'yorie with a silent promise, *I serve all who carry the blood of the Damselfly,* before returning to warn Roh'nan, "But you, Oversoul, hold no say in what is done. Your death would be inconsequential."

The 'Taur strode back to his partially built shelter, quickly shouldering his pack and returning to tower over J'yorie. "I will serve you, Seeker, but first, I require the counsel of the wizard DaeAer. He is known for his knowledge of the laws of light and the unenlightened. It is said he once crossed the Bridge of Light and spoke with the lightsteed, Raer. If in truth A'Janae is held in the void beyond the bridge, his counsel may keep us alive long enough to save her."

"Where can we find this wizard, Tovag?" Roh'nan asked, receiving a cold stare from the 'Taur.

"For an Oversoul you do not seem to know much. DaeAer serves as Wizard-Elect within the House of Hexus. On Ærathbearnæ."

"The House of Hexus was closed and sealed by the Council of Men more than seven years ago. So perhaps I do know a bit more than you believe, 'Taur," Roh'nan spat at Tovag.

"You are both correct," J'yorie said smugly. "The House of Hexus was indeed closed and sealed by Ærathbearnæ's Council of Men, but the order was ignored by Ærathbearnæ's enchanted. They merely enter through the underground passages below the sacred mountain and continue their studies as they did before the sealing. It is said they know more history of the universe than any others, and their Wizard-Elect is privy to all their knowledge. What he does not know, he can search out for us—a very good recommendation, Tovag."

Roh'nan frowned in irritation, muttering to J'yorie under his breath, "Why is it you side with the 'Taur."

"Because it was his idea and he is right. Now, let us go collect E'teihl."

Tovag scowled. "The Wyndwryn still travels with you? He is useless."

"He is my friend, Tovag. And he can be useful. His powers of persuasion are amazing."

"Only when he is persuading some poor woman out of her clothing and into his nest!"

Roh'nan coughed to suppress a laugh. "While we may not like one another 'Taur, I must agree with your assessment of the Wyndwryn."

J'yorie's eyes teased. "Oh, and this from a man who hardly knows me, yet wishes to see me naked? I will control the Wyndwryn—just see that the two of you control yourselves." With a flourish, she extended her hand and called the rift prior to stepping into the main village of Grimmoirë.

Tovag stared after J'yorie with a pensive expression. "Why is it that you halflings have so much interest in mating?"

"Perhaps it is the company we keep," Roh'nan responded, remembering the words of Leifitë the Maraen as he followed J'yorie, hard on the heels of the 'Taur through the rift.

Chapter 21: DaeAer and the Scrolls

E'teihl was not waiting for J'yorie when she arrived back in Grim-moirë but had to be rousted from the nest of one of his conquests. A lovely young Wyndwryn—dewy-eyed with lips swollen from E'teihl's passion, she laughed shyly and flew to the highest branches of the braid tree to avoid Roh'nan's stares and Tovag's grumbles.

Grabbing E'teihl by the nape of the neck, Tovag held him out and shook him as a child might shake a grass doll. "You waste my time Wyndwryn. Curb your carnal nature or I will curb it for you." With a final shake, Tovag let him drop only to have E'teihl flutter about the 'Taur's head, sword drawn, promising to cut off his hairy ears. Swatting at E'teihl, Tovag let out a roar of annoyance and shouted at J'yorie, "I thought you said you would control him! Is this your idea of a man in control? He is nothing but a—"

"Wyndwryn," J'yorie finished, beckoning E'teihl to her. "I have promised that you will be on your best behavior. Do not disappoint me or make me wish I had not gotten you released from Ærathbearnæ's prison by demanding your presence."

"J'yorie," E'teihl purred in his most seductive tone, "I cannot help what I am. Wyndwryns are meant to serve. It is our lot in life." He glared at Tovag and Roh'nan over J'yorie's shoulder as he massaged her neck. "If you would remove your shirt I could do your shoulders too. You are really quite tense."

"E'teihl!" J'yorie snapped. "It is you who are making me tense! I am not in need of a massage. Now stop it!"

Roh'nan and Tovag stared at E'teihl's unabashed behavior, Roh'nan's mouth open slightly as if he wanted to remark but dared not.

E'teihl managed to look wounded at J'yorie's dismissal. Nonetheless, he still contrived to shoot a self-satisfied glance at the two males—drawing their attention to his warm brown hand resting possessively on J'yorie's shoulder, insinuating his claim without her awareness.

As the rift to Ærathbearnæ glimmered before them, Roh'nan whispered his question to Tovag, "Just what is their relationship?" earning a push forward and a derisive snort from the great blue man.

"He is a Wyndwryn. She is a woman. That is their relationship."

Innermost Sanctuary

Pale rose-colored snow covered the sacred mountains. There was no evidence of life, and their pristine splendour was without burrow or fallen leaf. As the daystar sank toward the horizon, the pale rose deepened to crimson, giving the illusion of blood when viewing the mountains from afar.

As J'yorie stepped forward the snow fell away, sinking into the earth and leaving open the approach down into the temple.

"It does not seem a very secure entrance," Roh'nan remarked, drawing dismissive looks from the other three. "What? It simply opens when you step upon the snow. Does that seem secure to you?"

"It opens only to believers and those in their company. Had you arrived alone, a much less pleasant experience would have awaited you." J'yorie rolled her eyes and shook her head. "Tovag is right. You know very little for an Oversoul."

"I am the Oversoul of Æselvanæ. I have been to Ærathbearnæ a total of four times, including this one. I am not a wizard with knowledge of the whole universe!"

"Obviously," E'teihl sniffed, receiving a scathing look in return.

"You are right, Roh'nan. I charged you with ignorance unfairly," J'yorie conceded as she led them downward to find the wizard DaeAer, taking the stairs two at a time.

J'yorie rushed through the long corridor, obviously familiar with the twists and turns between the surface and the temple's innermost sanctuaries. Beyond their torchlight, rooms became visible, though none but Roh'nan slowed to glance at the opulent tapestries and golden altars. It was clear that he was the only stranger to the House of Hexus.

As they approached the next room, a veiled and scarlet-robed prophetess stepped out on to the stone walkway, blocking J'yorie's headlong rush.

"Prophetess," J'yorie said, stopping abruptly to avoid knocking the woman over and bowing respectfully—covertly elbowing Roh'nan to do the same. E'teihl and Tovag required no prompting and both knelt, one knee to the ground, heads bowed.

"J'yorie," the woman acknowledged in a voice so mellifluous it flowed across them like a warm bath, the result of training at the Cloister of Belasis on Ædracmoræ. That training included thaumaturgy, offensive fighting and mind control, as well as heightening any pre-existing powers in their students. Few qualified to be called prophetess, for it was seldom that a woman had the inclination and ability to complete the thirteen years of structured study and seclusion that were required before the taking of vows. Xamë had taken the vows two summers earlier and been assigned to the hidden House of Hexus. As a scryer, her sudden appearance was far from accidental, for her knowledge of scrying was exceptional.

Reaching out from beneath her scarlet cloak, the prophetess placed a burn-scarred hand on Roh'nan's arm. "You search for the dark ruler, Goibniu. To reach him you will be forced to face the obscurity of Fyrki. Between this world and that rests the soul of one man. The seeker will guide you. The Wyndwryn persuades, the 'Taur protects. DaeAer expects you."

She removed her hand from Roh'nan's arm. He was pale, and sweat glistened on his forehead. From beneath her veil, the prophetess nodded and backed into the room from which she had come, murmuring a blessing as she did so and covering them with her strength.

Roh'nan looked at his trembling hands and then into J'yorie's wide eyes. "What does she mean?"

"That we need to find DaeAer and have him unravel her message," J'yorie answered, grabbing Roh'nan's hand and heading down a set of previously unseen stairs, followed closely by a subdued E'teihl and a reverent Tovag.

They entered a workroom. It was clearly that of a practicing wizard. Floor-to-ceiling shelves lined three walls, each covered with potions and philtres, their powerful knowledge simmered down into useable liquids and powders. Herbs and strange and noxious substances littered the lower shelves. Three hairs from the head of a bastard child lay across an open tome next to several dragon scales and the bones of a bloodren—all waiting to be ground and cast into the bubbling brew in the cauldron that hung within the great stone fireplace. An assortment of wands and weapons graced a table, awaiting the wizard's magick. Highly polished lamps, lanterns, holders and bells were stuffed into every corner of the room. Within these arcane displays, the sheen of burnished surfaces and flickering candle flames created an inspired interplay of shadowy actors—a perfect cast for an eerie game of tag. Deep in a dimly lit corner was a second door of heavy willow planks. Reinforced with iron, it held no knob or handle and bore no evidence of a keyhole.

Within a circular stone stand hung an unimpressive, tubular bronze-cast bell, its stone striker attached by a long golden chain.

Without hesitation, J'yorie lifted the striker and struck the bell a single blow. A surprisingly sonorous chime reverberated through the workroom and out into the adjacent quarters. A moment later, the door in the corner swung inward to reveal a tall, stoop-backed, gaunt figure cloaked in the fine cobalt and sacred scarlet of the Hexus Wizard-Elect.

A pale aura surrounded him, as if a servant followed with a flickering torch scattering multi-hued ribands of light across his path, walls and floor, but leaving the wizard's face in darkness. As he stepped forward into the light his great age became apparent in the heavily wrinkled skin around his eyes and mouth and across the backs of his folded hands. His once blonde hair was a faded yellow, now growing white, but his watery gray eyes still burned with the wisdom held within. Silently he bade them sit and, after taking several parchment scrolls from a nearby shelf, joined them at the table.

"I am DaeAer. Xamë sends you. She says you need a bit of history, and magick. What is it you believe you seek?" The wizard's damp eyes bored into J'yorie's before shifting to the 'Taur.

"Tovag, it is good to see you. While one halfling is lost from your care, another cries out for your help." Tovag glanced at J'yorie, his heavy brow raised in question. "E'teihl, the verification of your health is in your loins, the glow remains even now." E'teihl puffed out his chest with pride. "Roh'nan, you seek the woman lost to you." A look of curious confusion softened Roh'nan's strong features, making him seem less secure, inexperienced and almost boyish.

"J'yorie, J'yorie. Turmoil boils within your soul." J'yorie's gaze remained on her hands, twisting them in her lap, knowing the wizard saw her deceit and praying he would not betray her lie in front of Roh'nan.

"I...Roh'nan asks my services as seeker. A'Janae the Damselfly halfling from Baene is said to be lost, perhaps taken by aberrant knights to the city of Fyrki beyond Æselvanæ."

"A'Janae is indeed gone," DaeAer replied, his voice soft and sure. "Already the light of legend fails. And what," the old wizard asked, "of the second Damselfly halfling?" He probed J'yorie's thoughts to determine the reason for her deception and found only fear.

"Dead. The second daughter of Arcinaë and Ilerion is dead. She was killed along with her parents in the fall of Ilerion's fortress. A'Janae barely escaped with her life, carried away by the beast that is said to guard the Bridge of Light. E'teihl was there. It is he who sent the souls skyward," J'yorie lied adeptly, years of practice allowing the fluid recitation of this untruth.

Who can you trust, if those with whom you travel you deceive? DaeAer's voice resonated within J'yorie's mind, bringing a flush of shame to her cheeks.

Turning to Roh'nan the wizard asked, "You also seek to find those responsible for the death of your double?" A knowing smile shifted the creases around DaeAer's mouth. "If this is true, you would be forced to hunt for his very soul, for it is Daegn alone who is responsible for Daegn's death. Greed and the search for that which was not his to find brought him to his dreadful end."

Untying the leather binding on the first of the three scrolls, the wizard unfurled it, resting a candleholder on its far corner. "In the days of old, when the race of Man was still new, the fair truth enchanted—the Enlightened—emerged from the city of Fyrki to live among men while the dark truth enchanted—those you call Heteroclites—remained behind. Until recently there had been no true conflict. Oh, there had been the occasional seizing of men's minds by a solitary aberrant who filtered through and stirred up a bit of war, but the goodness of strong men who believed in the power of the Enlightened's magick curbed those with weaker minds. The worst was the near loss of Grimmoirë and all magick on Ælarggessæ. There, men and enchanted fought together against the rage of darkness that occurred within a few wicked minds.

"In recent years, the race of Man has been left to create its own laws. Some keep the White Laws of Equality, others do not. On some worlds, magick and men are stirred and melded, while elsewhere they remain separate, or manage an uneasy alliance. But now it seems that Goibniu, the new ruler of Fyrki, is no longer happy to remain in the shadows. His leadership is rooted in the heavy magick of the dark truth, the magick of the Heteroclites. It is his wish to rule both realms. He sends his shielded knights to test the strength of the Enlightened and finds it wanting. Eventually he will feel courageous enough to lead an army out of Fyrki in the hope of claiming the power of the Curse Stone for himself. The battle to control the minds of men will be fervently renewed. Men are weak and many will fall. Without the power of the Damselfly halfling, the fair enchanted will be overcome and lost, burned away in the blood change while the minds of men will remain forever bound by the Heteroclite's dark magick."

"Why do the creators not stop the Heteroclites?" Roh'nan asked, his companions nodding to indicate their interest in DaeAer's answer.

"They do. The Spirit People call you as their army. They call on you to protect the Curse Stone that now lies beneath the House of Hexus," DaeAer said as he untied the leather binding of the second scroll. "If Goibniu controls the Stone, he will control the realms of Man and enchanted."

"We—"

"How—"

"Impossible—"

"Who—"

They all began at once, then stopped, staring at each other.

Finally, Roh'nan spoke. "An army? There are four of us. A 'Taur, who is certainly fit for any battle, a lustful Wyndwryn who appears to be useless, and a female seeker who spends both days and nights so drunk she cannot raise her head—"

"And you?" J'yorie snapped angrily. "What are you, Roh'nan?"

"An Oversoul, whose only power rests within the Council of Æselvanæ. We are no army."

"You will seek a man, Roh'nan. It is this common man who will help you find what you need to lead a handful of faithful against Goibniu."

"And just who is the man? What is his name? Where will we find him?" J'yorie asked, shaking with anger. "I cannot seek one whose name I do not know."

"The name is not written in the scrolls of wisdom. Seek this man in the mountains beyond the Wandering Woods. Here." The wizard pointed to the scroll. There, within its center, rested a group of seven faded symbols, arranged to form a cross.

"What are they?" Roh'nan stared at the unrecognizable markings.

J'yorie rose to lean forward over the parchment, squinting at the faint scratches of fading ink. "Pictures?" she asked, looking up into DaeAer's face. "Just drawings, not even words." She sat down and rested her head on her crossed arms, wishing she were in Leifitë's tavern with a pitcher of dark Maraen ale. "Most are so faded they cannot be seen," she murmured, raising her head to stare at her companions. "It is futile. We do not even like one another and cannot travel half a league without arguing."

DaeAer loosened the final scroll. On it rested more ancient symbols. A circle containing the drawing of a willow, a three-sided fence holding a group of silver runes and the figure of a seated man enclosed within a square.

"More meaningless drawings—of what help are these?" E'teihl asked, trying to look as if he had some interest in the discussion, though in reality he was thinking about finding someone to warm him through the coming night. The longer he waited, the more difficult the task.

"No, these are not meaningless," Tovag's deep voice rumbled. "These are seals of sanction. Three of the nine are seals of the creators, the Spirit People. Held by the Spirit Whisperer, or so an old Feie tale tells."

"Perhaps not meaningless, but certainly as useless as our friend the Wyndwryn," Roh'nan said with disgust.

"The gift of authority?" J'yorie once again attempted to gain the agreement of DaeAer, but he merely smiled and shrugged.

"My task is done. Begin with the man. That is all I can tell you," the wizard said, getting to his feet, preparing to leave the chamber.

"Stop! The Bridge of Light that leads into the city of Fyrki. It is rumored that you once crossed it, entered into the realm of the Heteroclites and returned safely. Is this true?" J'yorie asked of the wizard's back. "And what of A'Janae? You say the light of legend fails? Is she dead?"

Without turning to look at her, DaeAer answered, "It is true. I am the reason you are needed. It is I who showed the dystopian harbinger the way into the light. A'Janae's life light is held in darkness. It grows dimmer with every passing mark of the shadow clock, but surely *you* can feel this, Seeker. I can help you no more than I have." With a small bow, he made his exit.

J'yorie leapt to her feet and raced towards the now closed door, attempting to find some way of opening it. She clawed at it until her fingernails broke deep enough to bleed, then pounded at it and screamed her fury until Tovag lifted her away, setting her on her feet beside the table. "There is no use. He will not return."

With a strangled snarl, she snatched the striker and began to beat the bell. The door did not open. The wizard did not appear.

"Why have they done this? Placed this burden on us and given us no hope of bearing it? Why?" Her eyes shifted from Roh'nan to Tovag and back, ignoring E'teihl who had curled up before the hearth and fallen asleep.

"You are hopeless? And yet, you have not begun." A small voice came from high on a shelf.

"Beasts of the abyss! Now we are to be hounded by sprites?" J'yorie cursed, sweeping the parchments from the table and sending the candleholders rolling off the far side.

"Nay, merely a downy flier," the small creature called, leaping from the top shelf to glide gently onto the table, looking very much like a small furred carpet with a head and bushy tail. Sitting up on its hind legs, the flier began to groom itself, pulling out the baggy skin that ran from foreleg to hind and licking it furiously. Pulling its long tail around, it repeated the grooming procedure using a tiny grooming claw. Lastly, it sneezed a bit of moisture into its tiny paws and rubbed them thoroughly over its face and ears. Finally satisfied that it was clean of shelf dust, it gazed up into J'yorie's startled eyes. "Why is it that the larger one is, the less useful they are?" the downy flier queried, looking from J'yorie to Roh'nan.

With a short laugh, Roh'nan said, "I hardly think we are useless, though we may verge on madness since we are sitting in a wizard's workroom talking to a small woodland beast."

The downy flier shrugged his tiny shoulders and fluffed his tail. "You are indeed useless if you do nothing. Have you not been chosen to protect the Curse Stone?"

"And just what would you have us do, squirrel?" J'yorie snapped in frustration.

"'Tis a cup," the flier stated, "and do not call me squirrel, for I am no more a squirrel than that one is a bird." He pointed off toward E'teihl, earning a snort from J'yorie and an actual laugh from Roh'nan.

Tovag stood watching with arms crossed and brow deeply furrowed. "Where is there a cup?" he asked.

"The drawing on the parchment, the one on the bottom is a cup. See if I am wrong." The flier scratched above one eye, scampered to the edge of the table and looked down at the parchment. "There, a cup."

Tovag stooped and recovered the parchment, laying it flat before J'yorie. "Well, is it a cup?" the large blue man asked.

J'yorie rolled her eyes and shook her head, at last leaning forward to peer closely at the image drawn in the center of the cross of symbols. "What do you think?" she asked, glancing at Roh'nan.

Roh'nan stared at the drawing, pulling it nearer for a better look. "I think our furry friend may be correct. It could be a cup."

The downy flier stood on his hind legs, placing his right paw on J'yorie's arm. "A cup. Do you have any bannock? Or bread and jam?" His bright black eyes pleaded. "DaeAer will not return, and I shall get no supper."

Lifting her pack from the floor, J'yorie dug deep, pulling out a bit of bannock, dry and hard, but edible, and handed it to the small mammalian. The flier accepted it gratefully and began to nibble. "I am Nicholas, and who would you be?"

"It appears we are an army," Roh'nan answered with a scowl, "an army in search of a cup. Would you care to join us? You could be no more ill-prepared."

Nicholas paused in his nibbling, as if he were indeed pondering the wisdom of joining such an unlikely group of heroes. Hopping onto J'yorie's shoulder, he kissed her cheek with his furry gray lips and asked, "Might I sleep within your bodice?"

With a purse of her lips to stay a giggle, J'yorie asked solemnly, "Just what is it about a woman's bodice that fascinates every male of every species?"

"It is the softness and the warmth," the flier answered, flipping his tail and slipping inside J'yorie's shirt.

"I suppose we might as well return to Æselvanæ," Roh'nan said. "We can visit the Feie wizard I mentioned before and see if he has any ideas about our 'cup' or the other symbols and seals."

"There is an ancient mirror here within the temple that will allow us passage into Kyrenia. From there we can seek your wizard," Tovag suggested.

Careful not to disturb her furry passenger, J'yorie rose and shouldered her pack. "Somebody, kick E'teihl," she said, heading out the door and up the long stairway, smiling at the commotion behind her as E'teihl was rudely awakened.

Xamë the Prophetess waited for them beside the Dragon of Fire that guarded the great brass mirror. Again she rested her scarred hand on Roh'nan's arm and spoke.

"You have been given great wisdom in ancient images and a small voice. Now begins the gathering. Rest assured your steps are guided by the Spirit People."

She slid a key into the palm of his hand, bowing her head and backing away as she had before.

"To open the cage," the prophetess whispered as she stepped beyond the doorway.

"Cryptic!" J'yorie muttered. "Why is nothing straightforward?"

"Come, Seeker, and let us find Aodh the Feie," Roh'nan laughed, pushing J'yorie ahead through the polished brass of the ancient mirror as the seeker's mind snatched the name and prepared to seek the Feie called Aodh.

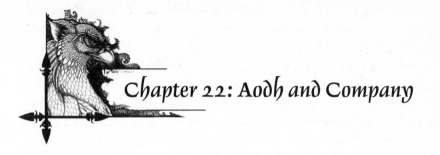

Chapter 22: Aodh and Company

In a sprawling meadow just beyond the city of Kyrenia, J'yorie stopped beneath a great tree and pulled a heavy cloak from her knapsack. Wrapping it around her body, she sank to the ground, her back against a cranny in the huge, gnarled trunk.

"I will require a protector for my body while it lies empty." She looked up at Tovag. "It would be best if it were you." The frown that crossed Roh'nan's face was brief, but not unnoticed. J'yorie addressed him, "Your wizard snores loudly and should not be difficult to locate. You may cast a spell of aversion over this place if you wish. It may keep the curious from noticing that we seek someone."

With a curt nod, Roh'nan stepped away from the others to evoke the spell of aversion, his voice deep and low.

"I shall be off to visit—"

"You will lie at J'yorie's feet and guard her as if your life depended on it, Wyndwryn, while I keep watch on the road," Tovag ordered, eyes ablaze with irritation at the smaller winged man.

Drawing his sword, E'teihl rose from the ground glaring with offense. "You will stop snarling and ordering me about. I am not in your service and have not sworn my allegiance or given you my pledge. Until I do, do not speak to me."

"E'teihl," J'yorie sighed, "I need you here. I trust you and you know what to do if I do not return. The others do not."

E'teihl dropped to the ground and sheathed his sword. "I shall remain with you J'yorie and watch over your body while you travel as if it were my own."

With a wink at Tovag, J'yorie said, "If he touches me. Cut off his hands for I have no need of his nurturing."

The 'Taur snorted appreciatively, shaking his massive head and scraping his horns across the bark of the tree as he eyed the look of false hurt on E'teihl's handsome face.

"You defame me J'yorie," E'teihl muttered. "I have no need to take advantage, and an empty body would not provide much diversion."

Roh'nan returned from his spell casting, assuring J'yorie and the others that none would venture within the circle of aversion he had invoked. "It will keep even the most curious well beyond view of this meadow. What is it you will do J'yorie? I have never seen a seeker leave the body."

"My consciousness will lift from the shelter of my body. I shall follow the thought images and sounds of your wizard. I can already sense him. He is not far. My body is defenseless during my absence and must be protected. Should it be destroyed or stolen by another, well...let us just say that I am at great risk whenever I leave its safety. The body can only be left alone for short periods of time. If for any reason I do not return—and before my body begins to show signs from the stress of emptiness—E'teihl will cast the spell to draw me back." Seeing Roh'nan's brow furrow with concern, J'yorie added, "I have never been late returning in all the years I have been a seeker. Having someone remain with the body who knows the words of recall is merely a precaution. E'teihl has done this many times—waited and watched. He will not fail me."

Roh'nan's look of doubt brought a small unintelligible mutter from E'teihl. The Wyndwryn reached out to stroke J'yorie's hair, only to have her brush his hand away.

J'yorie settled down against the tree, cushioning her face with her hands. "I shall return shortly," she whispered, closing her eyes and allowing her mind to free itself from the confines of the body. Roh'nan watched with amazement as a shimmering image of J'yorie rose and stepped away from the resting body.

Glancing back at the physical J'yorie, he saw that she no longer breathed and her skin had grown very pale. Not so much as an eyelash fluttered. In fact, she looked quite dead. Looking back to her spirit he discovered it gone.

Roh'nan glanced at E'teihl, but the Wyndwryn merely shrugged and settled near the feet of his mistress. Squatting on his haunches and drawing his cloak around his shoulders, the Wyndwryn prepared his mind for J'yorie's calling should she become troubled.

❦

High above, free from the encumbrance of her physical body, J'yorie followed the pale light trail left by the consciousness of Aodh the Feie and the stranger who had traveled with him. The wizard's light was brilliant with glittering sparks of enchantment. By comparison, the light of the other was dim and clearly that of a veiled human or a beast.

A commotion within the dense dark woods below caught J'yorie's attention. A group of poachers had captured several Equus, the enchanted horse-like creatures who made their home within the misty meadows surrounding Kyrenia. With a flare of anger, J'yorie descended near the first of the Equus, sending her silent words into the mind of the hobbled mare. *I have come to free you.*

Seeker, the Equus responded, echoing the understanding within J'yorie's consciousness.

Aye, J'yorie acknowledged before moving off toward the laughing men. Although the White Laws were strictly enforced on Æselvanæ, the black market for the Equus cloaks that allowed a human the ability to veil were highly sought, drawing the wickedness of poaching like marsh flies to a rotting carcass.

No better than assassins! J'yorie snarled inwardly.

Gathering the energy of her mind, J'yorie prepared to smite the three laughing men who were making ready to butcher the frightened Equus. It was energy she could ill afford to expend, but she could not see any other way. Summoning E'teihl would take far too long—the Equus would be slaughtered before he and the others arrived. With a silent sigh, J'yorie released a charge of mental energy and a long string of angry oaths that sent the poachers somersaulting backward into the surrounding trees. The sounds of their heavy thuds, cracking bones and startled, painful wails were as the chorus of the Siren's song to J'yorie's ears. Sweeping back, she manipulated the release of the hobbles that held the four Equus captive. "Go!" she urged the freed creatures, watching as they spun around and galloped away, their glistening white manes and tails flying in the wind.

J'yorie again focused on her task. She relocated the wizard's trail in the growing darkness and followed it until it ended, not far from a drab cottage sequestered deep within the woodlands. She circled the small dwelling once before slipping in through an open window. The house was filled with the clutter of Feie wizardry: crystals and stones, candles and wands. A surprisingly long staff, nearly twice the height of an average Feie, had been placed against the wall near the front door.

The sound of snoring drew J'yorie into the bed chamber. When she saw the Feie, she could not stifle a soft giggle. His loud snoring was interspersed with mumbled phrases from spells and snatches of conversation from his dreams. He rested on his stomach, arms crossed beneath a tangled mass of fiery whiskers. Long crinkly hair poked out at odd angles. The little Feie's knees were drawn up tight against his chest, his plump rounded buttocks—barely covered by his nightshirt—sticking up in the air.

The pull from the thoughts of another drew J'yorie into the cozy sitting room where a fire blazed in the fireplace. A stranger lounged in an ornately carved chair, its high back and deep cushions mostly hiding him from view. Only the booted feet of long, leather-covered legs extending beyond the chair, crossed and resting on the hearth, were visible.

As J'yorie's mind projected around the chair she focused on the face illuminated by the fire. The man slept. His muscles were relaxed, softening the fine lines and giving the face a youthful look that belied his nearly thirty summers. A thin, raised scar, white with age, began just below the corner of his right eyebrow and disappeared beneath the coppery hair that had fallen forward to cover it. J'yorie had a sudden, intense desire to brush the hair away and trace the path of the scar with her lips.

As if receiving her thought, the stranger's eyes opened. Mercurial and intense, they scanned the area around him as far as possible without moving his head, his hand slipping slowly and silently to the dagger at his waist.

J'yorie stilled her mind, her invisible presence hanging before him. *He senses me,* she thought. *He senses a presence though he knows not what it is.*

Although certain something unbidden lurked within the room, it was clear the man felt no danger. He stood, stretching knotted muscles, twisting at the waist to loosen the tension in his lower back.

With the swiftness of a striking serpent, his blade swept through the air, scattering particles of J'yorie's consciousness to regroup near the apex of the high ceiling, out of harm's way.

I know you are here, traveler. The man's thoughts collided with J'yorie's as he turned in search of the intruder. *I can feel you. Show yourself, or go. I have no time for games.*

Unable to resist the challenge, J'yorie drifted around behind him and permitted silken tendrils of warm thought to brush the warrior's neck.

Her quarry froze, eyes crinkling at the corners. "A woman! You are a woman. It has been long since I have gazed on the rounded softness of a woman. Show yourself and grant me this pleasure—if you have the power." His voice hummed with the humor of the taunt.

Gathering a burst of energy within her mind, J'yorie sent the tall stranger headfirst into the chair where he had been sleeping. With a smile, she turned and began retracing the astral pathway to her companions and waiting body.

⊰❧⊱

J'yorie's eyes opened wide, catching E'teihl by surprise. "Brute!" she snarled, staring at a startled Roh'nan. "I have seen Aodh the Feie. The wizard shares a cottage with a human, in the north, within the great woods." Her voice was a feral hiss. "A loutish male human. One who has the ability to mind speak."

E'teihl gave a low chuckle. "It is amazing that you can be offended even without the burden of a woman's body."

Spinning around, J'yorie pinched the Wyndwryn hard, causing

him to shout and jump about as if in great pain. "You would be wise to keep your opinions to yourself," J'yorie snapped, turning to send a warning glare at Roh'nan and Tovag should they have also thought of offering unwanted comments.

"Perhaps it would be best if we went to meet this foul human ourselves," Roh'nan suggested, turning away to hide a chuckle.

"Indeed," Tovag agreed, pulling his heavy pack to his shoulder and covering himself with a cloak against the sudden rain.

The others grabbed satchels and bedrolls, draping cloaks over themselves to keep as dry as possible. Together they made their way northward toward the sleeping wizard and the stranger who so disturbed J'yorie.

❦

As daylight cast its pale orange glow across the eastern sky, J'yorie, Roh'nan and Tovag stepped into the clearing that held the Feie's cottage. E'teihl had stopped along the way, seeking the warmth of a female in the cold dampness of the night, assuring J'yorie that he would catch up by midday.

The aroma of hot bread and sugar root tea filled the glen, bringing stomach rumbles to the travelers.

"H'lo the house!" Roh'nan shouted, "Aodh!"

The door was thrown open and the small, fiery haired Feie rushed out, a wide grin creasing his face and almost eclipsing his eyes within plump wrinkles. "Roh'nan my lad, it has been far too long! Where have you been? And your parents, they are well? Who is the lass? I heard you had married. And the 'Taur? Come! Come in, have tea and tell me tales of your adventures since last we met."

Shaking his head at the Feie's chatter, Roh'nan clamped his hand over the small man's mouth and looked him in the eye. "If you will wait until the tea is served, I shall be happy to answer all of your questions. It would be wise not to call the woman 'lass,' for she has an aversion to all things feminine, and we are definitely not married."

Clapping his hands, Aodh turned on his heel and led them into the cottage and through to the sitting room where J'yorie had seen the sleeping human. There was no evidence of him, and the long staff that had leaned against the wall was gone.

"Sit, sit," the Feie encouraged, pulling cups from a hook near the hearth and pouring tea for his guests. He pushed a plate of warm bread, slathered with prickleberry jam, toward the 'Taur, remarking that such an immense man must require a great deal of food. Then, turning to J'yorie the Feie wizard asked bluntly, "Why do you not like to be a woman?"

"I—"

"For you are striking—even flattened and less than clean, you are quite a beauty. Is she not?" Aodh asked, staring at Roh'nan, who coughed out his tea, eyeing J'yorie warily as he weighed several possible answers.

"J'yorie is a fine seeker," Tovag responded, saving Roh'nan the hazard of such a perilous question. "I am Tovag, and I have known her since before she could speak."

A sudden tingling of disquiet crept along the hairs at the nape of J'yorie's neck. She turned and looked toward the doorway. Standing silhouetted against the pale morning light was the stranger from the chair, the long staff in his left hand and a brace of hares in his right.

"Traveler," he acknowledged her, tossing the hares into a basket near the door. "So you were not just the dream of a lonely man."

Roh'nan bristled and Tovag stood up, both staring at the tall, well-muscled human now entering the room.

"Fahlcaen," Aodh introduced before introducing in turn each of his guests. "Roh'nan, Oversoul of Æselvanæ, and his seeker, J'yorie. The 'Taur is called Tovag."

Fahlcaen exchanged grips with Tovag and Roh'nan before turning back to stare at J'yorie. Extending his hand he whispered, "Although brief, I enjoyed our previous meeting."

Speechless, J'yorie stared back, unable to look away from the scar above his eye. Withdrawing his ignored hand, Fahlcaen reached up and touched the scar. "An aberrant's claw," he said in answer to her unspoken question before taking a seat in the chair where he had spent the previous night.

Giving herself a mental shake, J'yorie returned to the chair on the opposite side of the hearth and stared at her hands in a deliberate attempt not to look at Fahlcaen. She jerked her head up suddenly, staring at him as she felt his thoughts probe her mind. *I have seen them, J'yorie. I have seen the ones you seek.*

"How is it that you have the ability to mind speak, human?" she asked, pushing his thoughts away and hiding her own.

Fahlcaen pointed to Aodh. "Just a gift," he replied as he poured his tea and took a sip, his eyes never leaving J'yorie's face.

"And what other 'gifts' has the wizard given?"

"I have been training Fahlcaen for several summers, whenever his work allows him the freedom to rest awhile," Aodh answered, watching the uncomfortable exchange taking place between his student and the seeker. "He is an apt pupil—for a human. Caught on quite quickly to the ways of mind speak, beast speak and the use of simple spells of enhancement. Does a fair job of healing minor wounds as well."

"What is your work Fahlcaen?" Roh'nan asked, his voice holding a cool edge.

"He is an assassin," J'yorie answered, her voice a whisper no louder than a falling leaf striking a spider's web, her eyes dark with displeasure.

"Aye," Fahlcaen admitted without embellishment.

Rising, Fahlcaen went to J'yorie and knelt beside her chair. "Death begets death," he said quietly. "It has always been so." Without another word he made his exit from the cottage, leaving behind a rather leaden silence.

"More tea?" Aodh asked. Receiving no response, he proffered information instead. "He is a good man. He offers his services for a token to those who might otherwise receive no justice."

J'yorie shuddered. "His heart is black with it."

"Aye, and that is why he seeks a wizard's counsel," Aodh said, warming J'yorie's tea and handing her the cup. "He is burdened by the wickedness of those whose lives he ends and the pain of those he serves. It is a heavy yoke he wears. Do not judge him so harshly, Seeker."

"He is a murderer, nothing more. No better than those who would poach the Equus, or trap the fire sprites for their light." J'yorie looked to Tovag for agreement.

"J'yorie, he is a requiter, an avenger for those who have suffered harm and have no recourse but to hire an assassin. It is the way of humans, and 'Taur alike. There is no dishonor in such service." Tovag's words held the weight of his conviction.

"It is not the revenge I see dishonor in, it is the fact that he is paid to kill. It is naught but sport to such men." To Roh'nan, J'yorie excused herself, "I shall leave you to discuss our task with your wizard. I will find E'teihl and return before dusk."

As the three men watched her leave, Aodh declared, "She wanted to find only goodness in Fahlcaen. There is no such man as one who carries no grain of sin."

⚜

J'yorie sprinted away from the house in the glen, not pausing until she was deep within the sheltering canopy of the forest. She leaned her forehead against the rough bark of a tree, her breathing heavy, her hand against her pounding heart. Neither the panting nor the panicked pulsations were caused by the exertion of her run, but from the inexplicable desire that Fahlcaen had aroused. The mere thought of his name brought warmth. His voice had burned and his gaze had seared. An assassin. She shook her head—she wanted an assassin!

Tears blurred J'yorie's vision, and her throat and chest succumbed to a feeling of tightness. Covering her mouth with her hands, she reminded herself that she did not need the encumbrance that accompanied a man—especially a human assassin. Lost in her thoughts, she attempted to logically assess her desire. Was he handsome? Yes, in a rather rough sort of way. Strong? Obviously. Intelligent? It would seem sufficiently so to remain alive even though he pursued murderers.

Murderers! Already her traitorous mind was creating excuses for the assassin.

Turning from the tree J'yorie sprang back, astonished to find herself facing Fahlcaen and his inquisitive stare. She had not even heard him approach—clearly Fahlcaen was a very dangerous man.

"I am sorry you are disappointed," his said though his voice offered no hint of regret. "But many would call me a saint, a paragon of justice, a paladin. I do not believe you truly feel what I do is as frightening as the fact," he said, stepping closer, "that you want to touch me."

"I do not!" J'yorie protested, her denial sounding false even to her own ears. She reached up and swept an errant, drifting strand of hair behind her ear.

With a sense of time itself being suspended, J'yorie watched as Fahlcaen lifted his hand toward her. Fahlcaen saw her throat move as she swallowed. Her eyes grew wide and lost focus. His hand touched her hair, slowly drawing the leather tie away and releasing its silken softness. His hand slipped around the back of her neck. He felt her shiver.

"Yes, you do," Fahlcaen whispered, burying his face against the side of J'yorie's neck and causing the small downy flier within her bodice to leap away to the safety of the tree.

Against the urgent warnings of her mind, J'yorie's arms rose to draw Fahlcaen closer. Her last coherent thought was that perhaps her mother had been a wayward Wyndwryn, not a delicate Damselfly.

※

In the Feie's cottage Roh'nan rummaged for the scrolls. "There are two parchments," Roh'nan said, pulling them from his pack and handing them to Aodh. "Both contain symbols or signs. Tovag believes one to have seals of authorization. The other is difficult to make out, but the center one may be a cup?" Roh'nan pointed to the symbol, deciding to omit the fact that a downy flier had already given them this information.

The Feie wizard stood on his chair and leaned forward over the table. He placed a small circular glass over the parchment, mumbling unintelligibly and squinting with concentration.

"And what did the prophetess say?" he asked without looking up.

"She said we would be looking for a man. The wizard DaeAer said the same thing and something about wisdom in the images and small voices. Said we would fail without the Damselfly halfling. Oh, and the prophetess gave me a key, to open a cage." Roh'nan drew the key from his pocket and placed it on the table next to the parchment. "The wizard said he was the reason we were needed— called us an army."

Aodh suddenly looked up. "The army of the Spirit People?"

"Aye."

"Great goddess!" the Feie shouted. "You have been called to gather the gifts of the creators and fulfill the legend of the Damselfly's daughter! To bring death to the dark Heteroclites and protect the

Curse Stone! It is legend! You are legend! And I know you! I know one of the chosen!" Aodh jumped up and down on the seat of his chair until it tilted at an angle sufficiently dangerous to curtail his excitement to that of merely clapping and shouting. "Are you asking me to join you?"

"Aodh—" Roh'nan began.

"Of course I would have to ask Fahlcaen to accompany us because it would be rude to exclude him. He is a highly skilled warrior and would be of great value to your little army. I wonder where he's gotten to. It is not like him to leave the hares un-cleaned." Aodh looked up expectantly. "You are taking us with you aren't you? It is a great honor to be included with those called by the creators."

A pounding on the door brought forth E'teihl wearing a very smug expression on his handsome face.

"Who is the man in the woods with J'yorie?" he asked, winking at Roh'nan and chuckling at their looks of disbelief.

❦

"I...we...this cannot happen again." J'yorie looked around searching for her shirt among their hastily discarded clothing and feeling Fahlcaen's eyes watching her.

"Are you absolutely certain?"

"It was foolish and...it was foolish." She glanced back to see him holding up the strips of cloth she used to bind her breasts and reached out to take them from him. He grabbed her wrist and pulled her down beside him kissing her neck and shoulder. "Are you absolutely certain it cannot happen again?"

"Fahlcaen," she said breathlessly.

"Yes J'yorie?" he murmured against her skin.

"Please." Her voice grew softer as her fingers rose unbidden to trace the scar above his eye.

"Are you not pleased, J'yorie?" Fahlcaen asked, taking her hand and kissing its palm.

"You...I..."

"Yes, you and I...?" he repeated, tracing the curve of her jaw.

"I cannot think if you do not stop," J'yorie said, laughing at her own confusion.

"Then do not think," Fahlcaen said, pulling her closer and lifting a leaf from her hair. "Perhaps you think too much, J'yorie."

"Perhaps I do not think enough, or I just do not listen to my own thoughts." Her eyes searched his face as if she sought to memorize it. "We must go, before they come looking for us. It is growing dark and I must find E'teihl."

"The Wyndwryn?" Fahlcaen asked, pulling J'yorie's shirt from beneath him and handing it to her.

"Aye, do you know E'teihl?" J'yorie asked with surprise.

"Nay, but I saw his shadow flutter past."

J'yorie paled, clutching the shirt against her. "He saw us?"

"We were not hidden, J'yorie."

"He will tell them. Tell Roh'nan." J'yorie closed her eyes.

"Are you bound to Roh'nan?" Fahlcaen asked, covering her with his cloak against the chill of the sudden breeze.

"Nay, but still…" J'yorie stood, flinging off the cloak and pulling her shirt on over her head, the breast bindings forgotten. She grabbed her woolens, catching Fahlcaen's appreciative look as she dragged them up over her long legs and narrow hips, following them with her leathers. Sitting, she pulled on her boots and went back to take the binding cloths from Fahlcaen's extended hand, stuffing them quickly into her pack. Looking back at him, J'yorie paused to watch him dress, her eyes resting on the scar an arrow had left high on his right shoulder.

He caught her glance and grinned. "It was not some woman's husband."

J'yorie sighed. "I know nothing about you, except you are a murderer of murderers. Why is it I can no longer read your thoughts? They were clear to me earlier."

"You are blinded by your passion. It will fade quickly enough, and you will be privy to my every passing notion, so it is a good thing I am not a liar."

"Fahlcaen," J'yorie's voice was soft with regret, "I do not wish to be tempted by you, but I am, and I was from the moment I saw you asleep in the wizard's chair. It has been a great while since I felt the longing to hold a man, and my desire could not have come at a worse time, for you threaten my heart and cloud my judgment. This desire will hinder my search for those I have been asked to locate. I am not bound to Roh'nan, but I have given him my word that I will serve him as seeker. But even misplaced jealousy would eat away the fragile trust that I have with him. Do you understand?"

Fahlcaen picked up his pack and shouldered it before meeting J'yorie's eyes. "Just your presence soothes me. Nay, more than that, just the presence of your mind before I knew your body, blessed me with a feeling I have not known before. Peace, J'yorie. You have given peace to a soul at war with itself, something the Feie wizard could not do." His hand reached up to lift the tousled hair away from her eyes. "I will ask no more than that, and because you wish it, I will give the Oversoul no cause for jealously." He added, though too softly to be heard, "But I will watch him carefully, for he is not what he seems."

As J'yorie moved off ahead of him, Fahlcaen's eyes followed her. With a pensive expression on his handsome face, he projected a thought that caused her stride to falter and her heart to beat more quickly.

You will not always be duty-bound to the Oversoul by the promise of your word. I will wait. I am your destiny.

Chapter 23: Wee Wisdom

All eyes turned to J'yorie as she re-entered the home of Aodh the Feie. Ignoring them, she picked up the parchment containing the cross of symbols.

"A lyre and a shield," she said, handing the sheet of symbols to Roh'nan. "The one to the left top of the cup is a lyre. The one to the right is a shield."

"How do you know?" Roh'nan studied the images in an attempt to recognize a shield and a lyre, but the images remained illusive, a few wandering lines upon the page.

"The squir—"

"I am not a squirrel!" Nicholas the downy flier barked, jumping from J'yorie's pack and onto Roh'nan's shoulder. "Any more than you are part Wyndwryn."

J'yorie blushed at the memory of her final thoughts as she had succumbed to the mesmerizing temptation in the woods. "It seems our furry stowaway was once a close friend of the one we seek. The little fur ball saw fit to disclose that tidbit of information as I returned from my interrogation of Fahlcaen," J'yorie said.

"And what did you learn from this interrogation of the assassin?" Roh'nan asked, ignoring Tovag's warning look.

Without hesitation, J'yorie replied, "I learned that he is considered a paragon of justice by many. And he is not a liar."

Roh'nan glanced from Fahlcaen—who had returned and was belatedly cleaning the hares at the chopping block—to E'teihl, wondering just what the Wyndwryn had seen.

Aodh was leaning forward, his chin resting on folded hands as he stared intently at the downy flier who now sat in the center of the second parchment.

"What is it, Aodh? Is this wee beast truly capable of having the knowledge we require?"

"Aye, Roh'nan. Nicholas is indeed the possessor of a great deal of information. He was the man's companion."

"So the flier knows the name of the one we search for?"

"Nay, I do not." With a final flip of his bushy tail, Nicholas interrupted his bathing to answer. "I simply called him Master. The Chalice of Change, Æselvanæ's Sacred Shield and the Liar's Lyre are the tokens that you seek. I am surprised to recall them, for it has been many years since I dwelled within that master's chambers."

"What else do you know? What else that might help us locate your master?"

"The master was last seen in the Wandering Woods, which is of little value since they wander," Nicholas offered.

"The Wandering Woods?" Tovag questioned, "DaeAer said to seek the man in the mountains beyond the Wandering Woods. Do such woods truly exist?"

"Aye, 'tis a highly enchanted bit of forest that moves randomly over Æselvanæ's surface and takes with it all within its boundaries. It is a favorite haunt of those attempting to elude assassins and a hiding place for the shyest of the enchanted folk—nervous nymphs and secluded sirens," Fahlcaen answered, wiping the blood of the hares from his hands and coming to join the others around the table. "Legend says that there is a fortress there."

"Aye," the downy flier bobbed his wee head, "'twas in the fortress that I lived with the master. He fed me butterpillars and kept the history of Men. Then one day my master disappeared. Left with nothing but his staff and never returned. Another came to claim the master's house, Vuaia the Spirit Whisperer. She said she waits for the master." With a shrug of his tiny shoulders the flier added, "But I do not really know. I left the Woods with DaeAer when he passed by and was with him until I joined you at the House of Hexus."

"Perhaps this fortress would be a good place to begin our search, provided we can locate the Wandering Woods," Roh'nan suggested, looking up at J'yorie for confirmation.

"Tales of the Feie. It is said the Feie are drawn there? Is that true Aodh?" the seeker asked.

"Aye, 'tis not hard to find the Woods, but there is no way to know where we will exit, for there is neither rhyme nor reason to their shifting. They travel across the world as a cloud above the sea, appearing one moment and winking out the next. We might enter near Kyrenia and find ourselves across the ocean in Daplesfar when we leave."

"Then let us go and try to find some word of the man we seek." J'yorie held out her pack, allowing the wee flier to slip inside before following the Feie wizard from the small house in the glen.

❧❧

Wind, rain and deep bone-chilling cold were the companions of Roh'nan's unlikely army as they followed the lead of Aodh the Feie toward the Wandering Woods. Bedraggled and miserable, they sought the shelter of a seemingly small cavern amid the fallen stones of Korpusl, an abandoned quarry once worked by a hundred trolls under the control of their wizard master. The trolls had gone to ground with the death of the master and none had been seen on Æselvanæ in more than one human lifetime. No babes or women had been stolen from the surrounding villages, and half-eaten remains were no longer found along the roads. It was not known where the trolls had gone or what sustained them.

Roh'nan, Tovag and Fahlcaen gathered wood to build a fire, allowing Aodh to cast a spell to dry it sufficiently to keep it alight until the kindling flared and caught the larger pieces. The travelers shed their rain-damp cloaks, laying them out among the tumbled boulders nearest the fire in hopes of dry and warm coverings for the night ahead. As the men settled down around the fire, J'yorie stepped to the rear of the cavern to change into dry clothes behind a large rock outcrop.

She called out to her companions as she returned to the fireside. "There is an opening at the rear of the cave. Not large, but big enough for any but Tovag to pass. Shall we explore?" she asked, lighting a torch and waiting expectantly for the adventurous to join her.

"Since the opening is too small for my bulk, I shall see if I can locate a stag to volunteer for our supper," Tovag answered, gathering his axe and wet cloak.

"I must remain alert for the shifting of the Woods," Aodh dismissed.

"I am going to remain near the fire—I am nearly frozen!" E'teihl replied, frowning as he looked up at J'yorie.

"Roh'nan? Fahlcaen?" J'yorie looked at them hopefully. "Surely one of you is brave enough to accompany me."

"I shall go," Fahlcaen answered, standing up and lighting a torch of his own.

"Oh, all right," Roh'nan said, rising to join them, "though I cannot imagine what you expect to find in a place so long abandoned. There is not so much as a sliver of bone within this cave to indicate any other has ever been here."

"Perhaps the evidence lies deeper," J'yorie said, leading off and sliding through the narrow opening at the back of the cavern.

The next chamber was large and its chill even deeper. Pools of water had been created by the dripping rivulets that ran along the cracks within the ceiling. There was no sign of occupancy, and the dust-covered floor held no prints other than their own.

As they searched the walls for an exit, J'yorie whispered into Fahlcaen's mind, *I had hoped to talk to you alone.*

As he passed her, and making certain that Roh'nan did not see, Fahlcaen allowed his fingers to trail along her shoulder. In her mind J'yorie smiled at his response. *Talk? I thought we agreed it could not happen again?*

Roh'nan's voice close by startled her and caused him to look at her peculiarly before repeating his words. "A low passage exists there," he said, pointing, "but I do not believe it large enough that we can pass."

"I can," J'yorie said, squatting near the low overhang and holding out her torch to light the interior. "It appears to be an old magma tube. I will slip in and see what lies beyond while the two of you look for another entrance."

Stretching out on her belly, J'yorie snaked her way forward, pushing her torch ahead and listening for any sound of threat. Several body lengths beyond, the tube emptied out onto a ledge below which lay an enormous chamber filled with the bones of trolls. Back-pedaling, J'yorie gasped as Roh'nan's hands gripped her ankles and pulled her backward and out of the narrow passage.

"The bones of the trolls lie beyond. What could have killed so many trolls?"

"We have no time to investigate the death of trolls," he admonished. "Their death should be considered a blessing regardless of the circumstances."

"The death of that many trolls should terrify us!" J'yorie cried. "Only a thralax could kill trolls like that. Only a thralax would feed on trolls as if they were no more than hares, and a thralax would not hesitate to feed on the likes of us. We are certainly easier prey than trolls!"

Fahlcaen's hand landed softly on J'yorie's shoulder, drawing looks from the others. E'teihl grinned, anticipating J'yorie's reaction.

In her mind J'yorie heard Fahlcaen's secret words, *Strike me, for it will end their suspicions and make me look a fool.*

Aloud he murmured, "Arguing gains us nothing, J'yorie."

Glaring at the hand on her shoulder, the pupils of J'yorie's eyes dilated, and she whirled on Fahlcaen, kicking his legs out from under him and knocking him to the ground. With her dagger at his throat she whispered, just loudly enough for all to hear, "Do not ever touch me assassin, for if you do it again I shall be forced to kill you."

Standing, J'yorie stared at Roh'nan. "It is more than just the death of trolls. I sense another—one who is not a troll—in great fear and suffering. His image is not clear but changes as if there were more than one creature sharing a single body. We must help him, for I believe he is of great importance. I have learned to trust such feelings, Roh'nan. When a being comes to me unbidden, and I do not even know his name, it is wise to find out why."

Slamming her hands into Roh'nan's chest to clear her path, she snapped at E'teihl, "Watch over me while I locate the foreigner."

The Strangeling

"**S**trangeling!" The loud gravely voice and a sharp pain in his side brought the one so named into full consciousness. His eyes opened, and the fog of sleep—or death—faded from his mind as the giant man-beast before him came into focus. Drawing away in disgust and fear, the Strangeling discovered he could go no further since his back had collided with iron bars. He was in a cylindrical cage, filthy with the waste of its previous captives and so narrow he was unable to fully extend his arms.

"Strangeling." The giant poked at him again.

"Strangeling?" the trapped man repeated in confusion, rubbing his side to relieve the sharp sting from the sharpened staff. "What is this word?"

"You are the Strangeling, given to me by these poachers in an attempt to save their pathetic lives." The giant gestured, indicating a mass of hair and bones, the remains of last night's foul meal. "It is said you have the ability to shift, to change your appearance. If you can do as they said, you may just save your own miserable life. If you cannot I shall just eat you along with the others."

"Others?" The one called Strangeling raised his head to look beyond the confines of his own cage. He was not alone in the cave, others were held captive as well. Trolls—their large misshapen heads, massive chests and heavy arms recognizable even in the low light— woodland creatures, stags, rams and boars had all been detained in suspended cages.

"Well?" the giant asked. "Can you shift your image, or was it truly no more than the lies of desperate humans?"

The Strangeling sat silent, lost and confused, without memory of himself or his past predicament with the poachers. A sudden jab of the sharp stick caused him to cry out again, cringing away from the great beast's cruelty.

"Stop. I do not know what you ask!"

Again the beast pricked the Strangeling, laughing at the apparent duplicity of the dead poachers. "Lies, the lies of frantic men who for a moment believed words could save them from the jaws of a thralax."

Pulling a key from his belt, the thralax unlocked the cage door and dragged the Strangeling forth, tossing him to the cavern floor, kicking him, spitting viscous yellow phlegm and roaring his displeasure. Drawing his dagger, the thralax grabbed the Strangeling's hair, pulling his head up and back to expose his throat, ready to slaughter the disappointing creature for the next meal.

A hoarse gurgling cry came from the pale hairless Strangeling as the surface of his skin began to ripple with the change taking place beneath. His scalp grew dark as black hairs sprouted, quickly growing long and coarse. His skin darkened, taking on the bronze tones of a healthy human.

The thralax jumped back with a joyous bellow. "You are truly a shape-shifter! I shall be rich after all!" Pulling the still heaving Strangeling from the ground, the thralax threw him back into the cage and slammed the door, muttering all the while, "A shifter, a shifter!"

The Strangeling looked down at his trembling hands, watching in horror and pain as his fingers lengthened and the nails rounded from their original claw-like daggers. "What am I?" he lamented. "What am I?"

※

Fahlcaen watched J'yorie's spirit leave her body, noting the momentary hesitation before she swept away through the wall at the back of the cavern.

"How long Wyndwryn, before her body stresses at the loss of its mistress?"

"One half revolution of the shadow clock, but she is never

gone anywhere near that long." E'teihl stared at Fahlcaen with open curiosity. "What is it she finds in you that she does not find in other men, assassin?"

Glancing around to make sure that Roh'nan was out of earshot, Fahlcaen lowered his voice conspiratorially. "Do you believe in predestination, Wyndwryn?"

With a cock of his head and a roll of his eyes, E'teihl snorted, "Nay, I believe each man makes his own way without the interference of the creators. Of course, I do believe a man or a woman can be led by the spell casting of the enchanted. J'yorie's path will lead her far beyond the yoke of a common man's bond."

"Because her mother was a Damselfly?"

E'teihl leapt to his feet. His sharp tones penetrated Fahlcaen's mind as his dagger drew blood at Fahlcaen's throat. *Do not ever speak that aloud again, not even in a whisper—do not even think it without first shielding your thoughts! How is it you know this?*

Gripping E'teihl's forearm, Fahlcaen pushed the blade from his flesh, wiping the blood away with the back of his hand.

"I dreamed it. Whose betrayal does she fear? Is it Roh'nan? Surely it is not the Feie wizard or the 'Taur. Or you."

"She fears everyone." E'teihl shrugged, turning his back on Fahlcaen. Over his shoulder he mumbled, "I did not tell them what I saw."

❧❦❧

J'yorie's spirit entered the cave of the thralax and shimmered with a sharp shudder of revulsion. As much as she detested trolls, their butchery at the hands of this giant disgusted her. Sweeping the cavern, she followed the pull of fear and uncertainty, and the loud sobs coming from one of the many hanging cages. Using a great deal of precious life force, and shortening the allowable time outside her body by more than half, J'yorie slipped inside one of the enclosures. She focused her consciousness to project her luminous image to the Strangeling.

"Look at me quickly, foreigner, for I cannot hold this image long."

With a sharp cry the Strangeling looked up. At the sight of the mirage-like shimmering woman, he cowered against the bars to the back of his cage. "What are you?"

Raising a finger to her lips in warning, J'yorie calmed him. "Shhhhh… do not fear me. I have come to help you. I heard your call.

"I am just a woman, a seeker. Somehow your image reached my mind unbidden, and so I have come to set you free. Be quiet while I manipulate the lock."

She allowed her image to fade, and slipped outside the cage to examine the heavy lock. It was far too complicated to be manipulated by her mere consciousness and she looked up to tell the captive being.

The Strangeling's hands covered his mouth, and his eyes were wide with fear. He was focused on something over J'yorie's left shoulder. As she spun around to look, a myst net dropped over her, trapping her spirit within its dense magickal folds.

E'teihl! J'yorie sent her silent scream.

"J'yorie?" E'teihl's head snapped up, and he reached out to touch her foot and grab her cool hand. His ancient words poured over her still form, calling her spirit back to its rightful place.

"Narou eg matan, shevan mord casatdl. Fe mord nen!"

"What is it, Wyndwryn?" Tovag asked, poking E'teihl's shoulder and knocking him off of his feet.

"She does not return. Something holds her consciousness."

Jumping to his feet, E'teihl rose from the ground, wings beating frantically in his unexpected helplessness.

"Find her! Find the one who holds her with his magick! If you do not, her body will die and her spirit will no longer have a home! Go! What are you waiting for?" E'teihl grabbed Tovag's ear, pulling and twisting.

"How long does she have?" Fahlcaen's voice came from the back of the cavern.

"Less than seven shadows! Go now!"

Tossing E'teihl aside with a sweep of his arm, Tovag jerked his axe from over his shoulder and struck the wall beside Fahlcaen, widening the narrow opening to allow for their passage. They raced forward through the empty chamber to the lava tube that led to the cavern filled with troll bones.

Roh'nan and Fahlcaen searched the walls for evidence of a larger passage leading onward as Aodh muttered an incantation to call a vision of J'yorie's location. A cloud of mist rose before the Feie wizard. He saw the image of the thralax and its lair—hanging cages filled with beasts waiting for their slaughter, piles of hair and bones, treasures stacked by kind—and, in the center, the one they sought.

A thralax equaling Tovag's height and bulk stood holding the myst net containing J'yorie's consciousness. The beast's lips were drawn back in a grimace of pleasure at the acquisition of the seeker's spirit.

"Where?" Tovag snarled, glaring at the Feie.

With a roll of his wrist Aodh scattered the image and swung about to face the south wall. "Through there!"

Tovag slammed into the wall with the force of a small dragon, sending rock and silt cascading around him as he pushed his way forward toward the Damselfly's daughter. Bursting through into the lair, he gave a deep roar and charged at the enemy.

Whirling around, the startled thralax flung the net containing J'yorie's life-force aside and drew the great curved dagger resting at its waist. With a bellow, it charged at Tovag, slashing viciously across the 'Taur's chest.

Tovag grabbed the thralax and slammed his knee upward into its flat muzzle, snarling and swinging his great horns to slice across the beast's muscular shoulder. Lifting the thralax from the ground, Tovag threw its body to the hard-packed earth, leaping on top and driving the blade of his axe into its back.

The thralax bawled, rolling away from the 'Taur and leaping to its feet, sharp clawed hands whistling through the air as Tovag ducked and weaved. A bolt of fiery energy cracked against the side of its head as the Feie added his magick to the 'Taur's attack. Stunned, the thralax tried to shake off the temporary blindness caused by the wizard's bolt.

Roaring with rage, Tovag lowered his immense head and charged at the crouching thralax, burying his horns into its belly at the rib junction. Shaking his head furiously, the 'Taur ripped the thralax open, spilling stomach and intestines onto the ground. The thralax collapsed to its knees, clutching the mortal wound, blood-red eyes dimming fast and locked on the 'Taur. With a powerful backhand, Tovag knocked the creature to its death, emitting a final triumphant roar before searching for J'yorie.

A low rumble alerted Roh'nan to the 'Taur's approach. He lifted the filmy myst net to allow Tovag to claim J'yorie's fading consciousness.

Tovag took one look and called E'teihl, snarling and glaring as the winged man settled to the ground beside him.

"Do what must be done," Tovag growled, eyes piercing the Wyndwryn's.

E'teihl shook his head. "It is too late. She is not strong enough to return alone. Bring her in the net." Without waiting, E'teihl swept back toward the cavern that held J'yorie's cooling body.

Tovag knelt beside the body of J'yorie and released the magick silvery mesh to free J'yorie's spirit. Only the faintest pulse of light was visible against the enchanted threads.

"Place her consciousness upon her chest. Perhaps it will be strong enough to enter."

"Perhaps?" Tovag raged, "If it does not I will kill you all!"

With immense tenderness and care, Tovag allowed the spirit of J'yorie to slip from the mesh to rest upon her unmoving chest.

E'teihl closed his eyes, clutched J'yorie's cold hand and whispered again the words of binding. "Narou eg matan, shevan mord casatdl. Fe mord nen!"

"Again!" came Aodh's sharp command as he added his Feie voice to that of the Wyndwryn.

"Narou eg matan, shevan mord casatdl. Fe mord nen!"

Unbidden, the others added their voices to the chant that had become a plea.

"Narou eg matan, shevan mord casatdl. *Fe mord nen!*"

Aodh lifted his hand for silence at the tiny flutter over J'yorie's breast. The faintest glow began to flicker through J'yorie's weakened life-force as it settled into her pale, cold body.

Dragging the cloak from his shoulders, Roh'nan covered J'yorie, drawing her against his chest. "She does not breathe."

"Bring her to the fireside. Her body has grown too cold from the long absence of its spirit," Aodh urged, spreading his cloak on the ground near the glowing coals.

Fahlcaen tossed what wood remained into the stone-encircled fire pit, fanning the embers, drawing them to flame. With the quick, efficient movements of one used to camping alone, he filled the pot and tossed in a handful of willow bark and a scattering of fire fern for a medicinal tea.

E'teihl sat limp-winged, looking across the fire at J'yorie's lifeless form.

You have been her friend since her emergence. Fahlcaen's words pierced the Wyndwryn's sorrowful thoughts.

Glancing up, E'teihl gave a slight nod in Tovag's direction. "The 'Taur will truly kill us all if she does not live."

Tovag sat next to J'yorie, the steam of his heavy breath visible in the gloom of the cave. A low purring rumble came from deep within the 'Taur's chest, and Fahlcaen was certain the great bull-headed man spoke his thoughts to J'yorie's silent form.

Feeling Fahlcaen's gaze, Tovag looked up, a heavy frown creasing his broad forehead. His rumbling thoughts crashed into Fahlcaen's mind. *What have you become to her?*

Shaking his head in response, Fahlcaen slowly got to his feet. With the 'Taur's suspicious gaze following him, he walked out into the light rain of the evening.

Tovag rose and approached Roh'nan.

"We must return to the lair of the beast and collect the one J'yorie calls the foreigner. This being is held within one of the cages in the lair."

"She has recovered?" Roh'nan asked, stepping away toward J'yorie's bundled form.

"Nay, it will take some days." Tovag's iron grip dragged Roh'nan back. "I merely recall the reason for her risk."

Pushing Roh'nan ahead of him, Tovag made his way back through the bone-filled cavern and into the creature's lair. Sniffing and blowing at the stench of death, Tovag searched for some sign of the one J'yorie had sought.

Near the center of the room a pair of terrified eyes peered out between the white-knuckled fingers that gripped the bars of a narrow cage.

"You! Are you the one the seeker came for?" Tovag snarled, striding toward the shrinking man.

"Do not kill me! Or at least if you must kill me, do it swiftly," the caged man blubbered.

Tovag drew back, pushing Roh'nan ahead. "Tell him we will not kill him. I will free the woodland creatures. We will leave the trolls to rot."

Roh'nan paused outside the cage, examining the man within for signs of injury. "Are you harmed beyond the bruises and scrapes I can see?"

"I do not know. I was different when I arrived. My body changed without cause. I do not recall who or what I am, or where I was before this cage." The man gave a great shuddering breath.

"What do you mean 'changed'?" Roh'nan asked.

"I was pale and hairless, with clawed hands, then an attack of great pain struck me and I am what you now see."

"It appears you are a man, a bit misshapen but still a man." Roh'nan drew his sword to strike the heavy lock, but paused recalling the words of the prophetess: "A key to open the cage." Pulling the key from his pocket, he slipped it into the keyhole, springing the lock open to release the door and allow the man to crawl from the cage and drop to the ground.

"Come. We will find you something to wear and warm you by our fire. Perhaps together we can figure out who, and what, you may be."

"Where is the glowing woman? The one the giant captured?" The Strangeling wiped tears from his face, recalling his failure to warn his savior of the beast's approach.

"She continues to rest in our camp," Tovag called, gesturing ahead through the opening in the wall.

Aodh stared at the new arrival. His eyes squinted so that they were barely visible amidst his wrinkles. "What were you before?"

"I do not know. My hands were clawed. My skin was pale and hairless."

Nodding, Aodh leaned nearer the newcomer. "And the thralax called you Strangeling?"

"Aye, he said the poachers brought me to him, or tried to trade me for their lives. I really don't recall the beast's words. I was terrified."

The Strangeling glanced about the camp, eyes darting nervously from one being to another. A high wail escaped him when his gaze fell upon J'yorie's cloak-wrapped form. "She is dead?" he asked Aodh.

"No, but the breath of life has not yet returned with her spirit."

In the tottering gait of one still not used to his legs, the Strangeling went to sit next to J'yorie, drawing instinctive distrust from Tovag,

Roh'nan and Fahlcaen. E'teihl watched from his seat on the other side of J'yorie.

"She was kind to me. Said she came to set me free. Who is she?"

"She is my friend, a seeker from the world of Ælarggessæ. She thought you to be a being of some importance and felt it necessary to rescue you," E'teihl said. "Her name is J'yorie. Her spirit was too long away from its body. I am not certain it will ever bring life to her again. We are waiting. The 'Taur will kill us all if she dies."

The Strangeling glanced briefly at Tovag, averting his eyes at the 'Taur's steely gaze.

"J'yorie," the Strangeling whispered, reaching out to stroke the unconscious woman's hand, "you were kind. I would like to have known you."

With a deep, shuddering gasp, J'yorie drew her first breath, gasping as the life force replenished her starving body. A rush of color flooded her pale cheeks.

"J'yorie wakes!" E'teihl jumped up grabbing Tovag's face and kissing the 'Taur on the end of his nose, leaving the great blue bull-man spluttering and swatting at the Wyndwryn.

Aodh the Feie muttered shrewdly and slapped Roh'nan on the back. "I knew it! The Strangeling is cursed! He is some sort of being bewitched!"

J'yorie's lashes fluttered and her eyes opened to meet those of Fahlcaen's. "You gave us a scare, milady. E'teihl had already prepared us to die at the hands of the 'Taur."

"Quiet," she murmured through a soft smile. "You talk too much. Leave me to rest."

Chapter 24: Warnings

During the days and long nights of J'yorie's recovery, the behavior of the Strangeling grew even more mystifying. In one of his violent nightmares he had shifted yet again, his new form resembling something between a raven and a bastcat. His head and torso were bird-like and included a set of sleek wings covered with dense black feathers, while his hindquarters sported the soft paws and retractable claws of a cat.

After promising to meet again at "the master's house" Nicholas the downy flier left them. J'yorie, meanwhile continued to toss in restless slumber sheltered by Tovag's imposing bulk. He had not permitted either Roh'nan or Fahlcaen to approach the Damselfly since her close call in the lair. Though her shrill cries of "Beware the walker!" brought the men to their feet, Tovag's low growls of warning kept them at a distance.

At last J'yorie sat up and yawned broadly. She tossed the cloak from her shoulders and attempted to stand, but her legs were as unsteady as a newborn colt. Wobbling, she rested one hand upon Tovag's shoulder and leaned heavily upon him as he helped her to recover her balance and thus her strength.

"I was concerned," Tovag grumbled, turning his shaggy head to examine his charge.

"Would you truly have killed them all if I had died?"

His great shoulders shrugged, and the 'Taur stared across the camp at the men waiting to speak to J'yorie. "What is a walker?"

J'yorie tilted her head and met Tovag's gaze. "I do not know. Where did you hear that word?"

"You spoke it, J'yorie. In your dreams—'Beware the walker'—those were your words. What is a walker?"

"I do not recall it, Tovag. Just a dream—it could have been about anything. I have had strange dreams since returning to my body. Perhaps it is something I remembered from the thoughts of the thralax."

Tovag snorted, "It is unlikely the beast had thoughts!"

"Tovag, the thralax are as capable of thoughts and as magickal as we are. They are simply less civilized." Seeing Fahlcaen get to his feet, J'yorie called to him, "Come, take my arm and walk with me."

As Fahlcaen approached, Tovag rose to tower over him. "Do not walk far," he warned.

"Tovag," J'yorie chided, "I walk where I wish, and now I wish to walk and sit closer to the warmth of the fire."

I do not trust him. The 'Taur's deep tones rumbled in J'yorie's mind sending a touch of laughter bubbling up as she called back, "You trust no one."

"I will keep her safe, Tovag," Fahlcaen said in response to the 'Taur's disbelieving frown.

"So you say," Tovag snapped back. "Why should I not believe you have come in your professional capacity?"

"You think I am here to kill J'yorie?"

"Convince me otherwise."

"Stop!" J'yorie's demanded. "I am too cold and tired to listen to your nonsense. I want to sit nearer the fire and warm myself with a cup of tea. If neither of you can help me get there, I will ask another. Tovag, I need to talk to Fahlcaen—privately. Will you distract Roh'nan?"

Tovag's frown deepened. "I do not trust—"

"I know. You will just have to trust me," J'yorie pleaded, the sudden tremor in her voice bringing Tovag's nod.

"Oversoul! We should seek meat for tonight's meal." Tovag picked up his axe and went to meet Roh'nan at the edge of the camp.

"What is it, J'yorie? You are trembling." Fahlcaen steadied J'yorie and eased her to the ground beside the fire, pouring a cup of tea and handing it to her. A glance and a nod at Aodh brought the little Feie to his feet, urging the Strangeling to assist him in gathering more wood.

"What is it?" Fahlcaen asked again, dropping down to sit next to J'yorie.

Taking a great shuddering breath, J'yorie leaned against Fahlcaen. "Something is wrong. I do not grow stronger, and I dream terrifying dreams of you and the others, dreams of betrayal and death. It has been nearly two weeks since I was captured by the thralax. I should be well. I fear something in my dreams or the Strangeling's touch has caused me some harm."

"J'yorie it was the Strangeling's touch that brought the breath of life back to your body. Before he touched you…"

"I know. I do not think it is anything he did intentionally but rather some side affect of whatever curse he carries. Will you ask Aodh? Ask him what he thinks? Is it possible I could be touched by the wickedness in my dreams?"

"Why do you not ask him yourself, J'yorie?"

"He does not like me because I am a woman."

Fahlcaen laughed out loud. "J'yorie, he is a Feie wizard. He believes women to be inferior, merely ornamental. He likes you. He just does not understand you or your warrior-like behavior."

Seeing her crestfallen expression, Fahlcaen took her hands, rubbing them to warm away the chill. "J'yorie, I am sorry," he said as tears welled in her eyes.

"Fahlcaen, I am so weak that I fear if Tovag knows the truth he will kill you all before he stops to reason why."

Nodding, Fahlcaen called to the Feie.

Aodh squatted before J'yorie, scowling at her tears and muttering about her still being too cold and spitting out snatches of healing spells. "Your body cannot heal without heat. I am going to give you a bit of broth laced with heavy ale. Do not tell the Oversoul. He seems to believe you have a problem with ale, but it will serve to warm you."

"Aodh, what are walkers?" J'yorie asked, her eyes fastened on those of the small wizard.

"Walkers? Who spoke to you of walkers?"

"No one. I think I dream of them." Her glance shifted quickly to Fahlcaen and back again.

"It is said that walkers are humans or halflings trained to move between Fyrki and the worlds above without need of shielding armor. Rumors say that Lord Goibniu uses such beings to manipulate the minds of men. Most likely walkers do not exist, but there have been tales."

"Why would I dream of them? Unless I touched the mind of such a man. You? Is it you, Fahlcaen?"

"J'yorie, Fahlcaen has been with me for years," Aodh said. "Do you not think I would have sensed it if he were in some way bound to the Heteroclites?"

"Is it you?" J'yorie's hand rose to stroke the scar above Fahlcaen's eyebrow. "Is it? You said a Heteroclite knight gave you this scar. Was there more he gave you? Tell me."

"No J'yorie, I do not serve the Heteroclites. I hunted a man, one rumored to be a walker. A knight was with him when I found him."

"And you killed this knight?" From the little distance that separated them, Roh'nan's voice called, echoing through the cavern, as he and Tovag returned. "Did you? Are we to believe that you killed a Heteroclite knight?" They stared at Fahlcaen with mounting distrust.

"Aye," Fahlcaen said as he stood, meeting the deepening suspicion in their eyes. "I killed both the knight and the man. I am an assassin."

Picking up his pack, he knelt before J'yorie. "Stay close to Tovag and be wary of the Oversoul." With a last look around, Fahlcaen disappeared into the gathering shadows of Æselvanæ's approaching night.

"Fahlcaen!"

Roh'nan glared at J'yorie. "What is he to you?"

"Nothing, Roh'nan. Fahlcaen is nothing to me. He is just another man. A man who warmed me in a moment of drunken carelessness."

From a branch overhead, E'teihl heard the hidden heartbreak in J'yorie's voice and headed off in search of the assassin.

"Do not leave her." The Wyndwryn dropped to the ground in front of Fahlcaen.

"I do not leave her unattended. She is safer with you and Tovag than with any others."

"Aye, except you. She has needed no one for so long, and now she needs you. Do not leave her." E'teihl leaned back against a tree.

"Our passion was nothing, E'teihl. What you saw was just a moment's foolish indiscretion. Surely, as a Wyndwryn you can understand that. And as I recall, you do not believe our destinies are entwined. Did you not tell me J'yorie's path will lead her far beyond the yoke of a common man's bond? I cannot travel with her as long as I am the focus of distrust. It is not safe. What must be done will require great faith among you if you are to succeed."

"How is it you seem to know so much about our task? You were not with us when the Wizard-Elect DaeAer spoke of our journey."

"I am just a common man who has heard her thoughts. She will be better off without me."

"A man. The wizard DaeAer did speak of a man. Is it you?"

"Nay, Eteihl, I am not the savior you seek, nor the walker you fear. I am merely an assassin."

Tovag's throaty grumble preceded his arrival through the trees. "You leave far too easily, Assassin."

Fahlcaen stiffened. "I leave her with you, under your protection. Is that not your profession, 'Taur? Are you not the protector of the daughters of the Damselfly?"

"How is it you know who she is?"

"He has lain with her," E'teihl provoked. "I saw them."

"What do you hope to accomplish by this, E'teihl? I told you it is best that I go. That it is safer for J'yorie. What can be more important than her safety? Why do you attempt to anger Tovag?"

"I would see if you can kill a 'Taur as easily as you say you killed a Heteroclite knight."

"No. There will be no bloodshed to satisfy your curiosity. Tovag knows that I am his match. Don't you Tovag?"

E'teihl watched with disbelief as the great blue protector of the Damselflies nodded his massive bull-head.

"It is so."

"How is that possible? You are three times his weight! I just watched you kill a thralax!"

"The little wizard assisted with the killing of the beast. Fahlcaen is an Absinthian, a wormwood warrior—far more than just an assassin."

Fahlcaen extended his hand, grinning as Tovag accepted his forearm, testing the assassin's strength. "I must go. Keep our lady safe." He nodded his farewell to the open-mouthed Wyndwryn and disappeared on silent footfalls.

"What does that mean? What is a wormwood warrior? An Absinthian?"

"Hush, J'yorie comes."

"Tovag? Where is Fahlcaen?" J'yorie demanded.

"He has gone."

J'yorie stared into the woods, the desire to follow stealing her breath and crippling her judgment.

"No J'yorie." Tovag's hand gripped her shoulder. "He is not what you believe. He is a danger to you."

"Why do you say this?" Her eyes filled with tears. "I just want…"

Tovag pulled her to his chest allowing her to weep. He cast a warning glare toward the Wyndwryn—mouth still open—a clear indication to keep it closed. The 'Taur lifted J'yorie and carried her to the fireside. A stag was roasting, and Roh'nan waited with a questioning look on his face.

"The assassin is gone. J'yorie is tired and needs food, warmth and rest before we enter the Woods. See to it."

Turning on Aodh and the crouching Strangeling, Tovag asked, "Is it the Strangeling's curse or the pull of the wormwood that weakens J'yorie?"

"The wormwood?"

"Do not feign ignorance, wizard. It would take little aggravation to make me crush your bones."

"If it is the pull of the wormwood, and if he has gone, then she will be strong by sunrise." The wizard paused for a moment and then asked, "How is it you know he carries the taint of wormwood?"

"When he did not fear me, I knew," Tovag snarled, slamming his fist into the palm of his hand. "How could you allow her to encounter him? You know what she is!"

"Just what is she?" the Strangeling asked, looking across at the silent J'yorie.

"The other daughter of the Damselfly and the only hope of our salvation—and this foolish wizard exposed her to the wormwood!"

"What is wormwood? What are you talking about? Aodh, what is he talking about?" Roh'nan asked.

"Fahlcaen is an Absinthian, an assassin whose blood has been magickally enhanced by the sap of the wormwood. It strengthens him, but exposure over time can be deadly to a Damselfly. I did not know it would harm a halfling. If I had, I would never have endangered her, nor would he. He is not the threat, but something"—the wizard's eyes shifted briefly to the huddled Strangeling—"or someone endangers us all."

"So you are saying it is actually possible that the assassin killed a Heteroclite knight?"

"No, I am saying he did. If he told you he killed an aberrant, then it is the truth. Have you ever seen an Absinthian assassin kill? Nay, I did not think so. They carry only a staff because they need nothing more."

Lost in their thoughts for a moment, they were startled at the sound of J'yorie's soft voice and turned to her as she asked, "So now that you know who I am, which of you is here to kill me? It is not the assassin, for he has gone in order to keep me safe."

"You cannot seek her, can you?" Roh'nan's words were edged with sharpness.

"No." J'yorie drew the flask from her bag and held it out to the wizard. "Ale, heavy ale, Maraen ale if you have it.

"I have not felt A'Janae since we parted at the death of our parents. But I know where she is. She is held within the city of Fyrki across the Bridge of Light. We all know that, and we shall travel through the Wandering Woods and find the man we seek—the downy flier's master—within the mountains beyond. He will know how to find the bridge. I will avenge my father's death, and we will find A'Janae and bring her home." Snatching the flask from the wizard she drank deeply, pausing only for breath until the flask was dry. She flung out her hand, tossing the flask back to Aodh. "More."

"But J'yorie," E'teihl soothed, "we must protect the Curse Stone. We are chosen."

"No. Roh'nan must protect the Curse Stone—Roh'nan's little army. Remember? His and his wizard's. It is not mine, not Tovag's and not yours. We will find my sister, and I will avenge my parents' murder. This is my legend—this Damselfly halfling's legend. Nothing more. The Curse Stone lies safe beneath the House of Hexus. If it is threatened, DaeAer and the prophetess of Belasis will protect it. If Roh'nan needs to be a part of that, then he should go there. I want no part of it, and you are nothing but a Wyndwryn." She tilted the freshly filled flask and allowed the dark Maraen ale to slip down her throat, burning her belly, deadening the ache within her heart and silencing her screaming thoughts. Reaching out and stroking the velvet softness of the Wyndwryn's wing, her voice slurred, "Build a nest and comfort me. It is, after all, what you do best."

E'teihl drew back but caught Tovag's frown and kept the angry retort to himself.

"Aye, J'yorie it is what I do best. Come, drink your ale and forget him."

"Aye." J'yorie stood and stumbled after the fluttering Wyndwryn.

⁂

E'teihl woke to J'yorie's screams and an elbow to his ribs.

"Get off me! You filthy fallowass! How dare you!"

A misjudged roll sent J'yorie over the side of the large nesting place, crashing through the tangled branches to land with a resounding thud and the panting of forced exhalation. She struggled to her feet, grimacing at the rapidly swelling bruise on her hip and pointing up at the grinning Wyndwryn. "If you touched me…! If I find any remnant of your passion, I will cut off your most valuable appendage and feed it to the first boar that crosses my path!"

"J'yorie, you asked me to!"

"I was drunk!"

"Is that not your usual state?" Roh'nan snapped from behind her.

She spun around, catching his thigh with a well executed kick that knocked him to the ground, pouncing on him with all the fury of a wild cat protecting kits.

Tovag waded in, lifted J'yorie off and shouted at E'teihl, "Tell her you slept in the cavern, Wyndwryn!"

Slipping from the nest, E'teihl drifted to the ground, chortling with delight over J'yorie's unfounded annoyance.

"Aye! I built the nesting place for you, and then left you alone, J'yorie. I did not fancy spending an entire night listening to your drunken snoring and breathing the constant stench of belched ale. I only came to warm you in the chill of early morning. Truly, J'yorie, there was no…"

"The Woods!" The urgency of Aodh's shrill voice silenced the Wyndwryn and sent them racing to gather packs and bedrolls before following the little wizard and his exhortations to hurry into the silver mist of the Wandering Woods.

Chapter 25: The Wandering Woods

"I need you sober." Roh'nan snatched the flask from J'yorie's lips and tossed it to Tovag.

"You bastard!"

"Aye, and worse, but I will not allow A'Janae to die because her sister is a drunken strumpet."

J'yorie's hands curled into claws as she swung around, but too slowly. Roh'nan caught her wrists and dragged her to the ground, straddling her and forcing her arms to her sides.

"I did not simply bed your sister in a moment of recklessness, J'yorie. She is my wife."

J'yorie went limp. "That cannot be. I would have known."

"Three years ago, winter solstice, the cathedral of Telfair, in a ceremony officiated by my father and witnessed by no less than a hundred guests. You did not know because you were drunk and could not feel her cry for you."

"Then how could you let them take her? Why was she alone?"

"I could not sleep. I left our bed to get a breath of air. When I returned she was gone, and only her dragon's tear necklace remained. And I searched for you, hoping you would care enough…"

J'yorie pushed against Roh'nan, rising as he rolled away, and stood next to a confused E'teihl and a disbelieving Tovag.

Aodh shook his head and mumbled, "I told you. I heard you had married."

"And you have known who I was all along? This is why you sought my services as seeker? Why didn't you tell me? Why did I not see it when I searched your palm?"

"I hid it, J'yorie. There is much I did not let you see. It is easy to hide thoughts from a drunk."

"Do you love her?"

"Yes, and I feel the trembling of her soul each time…," Roh'nan drew a ragged breath, "each time Goibniu steals her warmth. She will die in darkness and sorrow if we do not reach her soon."

J'yorie stood silent, eyes closed as she recalled the last pleading words she had heard her sister say: "J'yorie! Do not leave me! Please, come with us!"

"It is you Goibniu wants. He merely holds A'Janae to assure you will come to him."

"How is it you know this, and why do you tell me now?"

"Because *I* am the walker you so fear. Because the Lord of Fyrki knows I will do anything to be with the woman I love. I care nothing for the Curse Stone or Goibniu's plans to rule. I care only for my woman and if you must die that she may live…"

Tovag's snarl set the forest echoing with his rage.

Roh'nan pulled J'yorie against him and faced the others, his dagger pricking her pale throat and sending a rivulet of blood out of sight beneath her shirt.

"Don't be foolish. While I cannot kill J'yorie, I am sure Goibniu will not mind if she suffers on her journey to his home. Go! Take the Wyndwryn and go. Aodh, you must help me find those things needed to free and use the power of the Curse Stone. Once we have them you may go."

"Roh'nan? There must be another way."

Roh'nan shook his head, lips curled in bitterness. "No, Aodh. I cannot risk A'Janae's life. Goibniu will know if I do not follow his instructions. His knights track us. J'yorie is like a beacon to them."

"The dark woman in my dreams, are you not a beacon to her? Were you not drawn from your bed by her murmured promises?" J'yorie whispered.

"Aye, she is Taerys. Goibniu's queen. I was spellbound by her, but I would never willingly betray A'Janae."

"She will never set you free, just as the Heteroclite ruler will never free A'Janae."

"They have sworn it to me."

"I do not believe they will honor their oath, but I will go with you. Together we will free A'Janae. Tovag, go, take E'teihl and return to Grimmoirë." J'yorie smiled at Tovag's deep frown. "I must free A'Janae for it is I who failed her with my scorn and my discontent. I should never have left her."

"No, J'yorie, I will not leave you. Roh'nan, I cannot allow you to take the daughter of the Damselfly," Tovag drew his axe and stepped forward, "and you say your master told you she must live. I will kill you where you stand if you do not let her go."

A sound like the buzz of angry insects accompanied the furious ball of fur that launched itself at Roh'nan, latching onto his dagger hand with tiny razor-sharp teeth and stinging claws. Roh'nan dropped the blade and clutched his bleeding hand as the wee flier, barking fiercely, jumped onto J'yorie's shoulder.

"You are all fools!" Nicholas chattered. "Each one of you thinking only of yourself. What good will it do to save A'Janae if what the Heteroclite plans will only end her life? None of you can do a thing without the others. Where is the Strangeling?"

Startled, they looked about only to realize the Strangeling had disappeared.

Wrapping his tail around him, Nicholas sat up off his haunches and pointed to the center of the Woods. "The master's fortress lies there, but it has fallen to ruin, and there is no sign of Vuaia the Spirit Whisperer. I did, however, find the cup you seek. Come, I will show you."

He scampered several paces before looking back and giving a warning bark, "And no more foolishness!"

J'yorie dug in her bag and dragged out a length of cloth. She stepped forward and took Roh'nan's bleeding hand, wrapping it tightly.

"We need not threaten one another. Together we will find and free my sister, regardless of the cost. The downy flier is right. It will take all of us to accomplish it."

One by one they followed the flier toward the entrance of the Woods and his master's fallen fortress.

J'yorie knelt and lifted the heavy chalice. "I expected gold or at the very least, silver."

The cup was black with age, undecorated and unimpressive, just a heavy tavern goblet, dented and worn. J'yorie tossed it to Tovag and watched as he examined it and placed it in his satchel.

"What purpose do you suppose it serves?"

J'yorie shrugged and looked at Roh'nan. "You seem to know more than the rest of us. What do you think it does?"

Roh'nan scowled, rubbing the burning bites beneath the bandages on his hand. "I don't know, and I don't care. Goibniu and Taerys want it, and we will give it to them in exchange for your sister's freedom."

"Every step of the way you have lied. Why should we believe you now?"

"*I* have lied! J'yorie, you have not spoken the truth once!"

"Stop," Tovag grumbled, "or you shall have more than the bite of a downy flier to bind."

E'teihl plunged in from overhead. "The wizard calls you. The mountains lie beyond the border of the Woods and we must go."

Nicholas bounded from the ruins and scrambled up J'yorie's arm to disappear within her bodice. With a tickle of his whiskers he reappeared. "We must find the Strangeling."

"Aye, I hear his cries as well, but we cannot linger here. The call of the man within the mountains rings unrelentingly. We will seek the Strangeling once A'Janae is found."

A Common Man

A glimmer of silver in the glowing twilight swept away the Wandering Woods and left the travelers standing on a narrow path that wound out of sight through the shadows cast by pink-flowering mountain laurels.

Barking with excitement, Nicholas leapt from J'yorie's shirt. "The Master is here. There—above us!" He raced away without waiting to see if they would follow.

Shadows deepened, but still there was no answer to their calls. The flier had disappeared into the mountains, and the gathering gloom made it impossible to find his tracks among the branching trails.

"Camp. It is all we can do." Tovag broke off a small sapling, looking over his shoulder at J'yorie. "Shall I build you a shelter against the rain, or will you sleep in the Wyndwryn's nesting place?"

"What rain?" Roh'nan muttered.

Aodh chuckled and gave a wave of his hand, calling a small opening in the earth and scrambling into it as the rain began to pelt them.

"It seems sensing nature's changes is not among the Oversoul's skills."

"The Oversoul seems to be missing many skills," E'teihl spat in disgust and flew to the sheltering branches of a nearby tree to begin constructing his nest.

Tovag pulled his great cloak from his pack and draped it around

J'yorie's shoulders, pulling up the hood and pushing her into a hollow within a dead tree. "I will call when the shelter is done."

Roh'nan stood, drenched and alone. Finally he crouched beneath the minimal protection offered by a thicket of waffle root.

Once she was dry and warm, Tovag questioned J'yorie.

"Shall I kill Roh'nan in his sleep?"

"Tovag! He says he is my sister's husband."

"It would not be difficult. He would not hear me approach beneath the pounding of the rain. He is a worthless fool who, at the very least, allowed A'Janae to be taken from his own bed."

"He says he loves her."

"Does he? How can we know that? He is a liar."

"So am I, but it does not mean I cannot love."

Tovag's low laugh sounded like a purr. "Aye."

"We cannot kill him until we stand before A'Janae and she tells us she does not love him."

The great Blue 'Taur drew the cloak closer around J'yorie. "And do you love?"

J'yorie's bit her lower lip. "I could love him. There was more than just physical desire shared between us. There was a kinship. A warmth that had nothing to do with passion's heat. How could that be, Tovag? How could a man of such violence cloak me in such peace?"

Tovag snorted, filling the small shelter with moist warmth. "What he does and what he is are two very different things. But it does not matter. He carries the wormwood in his blood and…"

"Is there no way?" J'yorie's closed her eyes to avoid seeing the truth in the deep brown of Tovag's.

He reached out and brushed the hair from her forehead, allowing his great hand to linger there. "If there is, we will find it."

Morning found Roh'nan sullen, Aodh cranky and E'teihl muttering about being so long alone. J'yorie was solemn and Tovag starving. As they sat around the fire, Aodh's fiery tea washing down dried berries and molding remnants of damp bread, a deep male voice hailed from beyond the camp.

"Greetings! The wee flier says you are in dire need of help." A man in warrior's leathers leant heavily on a crooked staff as he limped into sight, his sharp green eyes searching each face.

"I am Ellicott," he extended his grip to Roh'nan, "and you would be the 'fool Oversoul' I assume. Nicholas has bent my ear throughout the night with unbelievable tales of traveling with a 'clan of simpletons' and a 'fine figure of a woman.'" Ellicott knelt before J'yorie and offered his hand, accepting hers and lifting it to his lips. "And I must say, I do agree with Nicholas. He has always been an excellent judge of the feminine form.

"Tovag, E'teihl and Aodh, it is good to make your acquaintance. Any friend of Nicholas and so on…"

"What is it you do that makes you, Ellicott, so important to the wizard DaeAer?" Roh'nan asked, staring at the newcomer with open suspicion.

"DaeAer. It is many years since I have been plagued by visitors bearing that name. Long ago I did serve the Wizard-Elect, though I am no longer in his hire."

"He said you could help us. Help us locate a cup, a lyre and a shield. Tools needed to cross the Bridge of Light."

Ellicott's laughter was curt and his voice lost its tone of smooth civility. "You seek the tools of destruction? The tools to free the power of the Curse Stone? It is not likely you are sent by DaeAer. Who really sent you here?"

"It is true." J'yorie dug in her bag for the parchments the wizard had given. "DaeAer did tell us to seek the man in the mountains beyond the Wandering Woods. He gave us a scroll and told us we would need to gather the tokens drawn on it. He did!"

"Aye," E'teihl added, "he called us an army and said we would protect the Curse Stone from the ruler of Fyrki."

"What do you know of the Curse Stone?"

"That it lies beneath the House of Hexus, protected by the Wizard-Elect and the Prophetess of Belasis. That it was left behind by the Spirit People."

"That legend says it has the power to allow the Heteroclites to leave the darkness of Fyrki and walk within our sunlight," Tovag added.

Ellicott shook his head. "It is an instrument of both creation and destruction. It can lift the aberrant taint from the blood of the Heteroclites allowing them to live freely in the light of the surface, but to do so, the Heteroclites must find a sister race to receive the taint. Such a change would leave every fair enchanted being burning in the light of day and Goibniu will rise to power over Man and earth. Or the Stone can be used by the power of the Damselfly to create the illumination that will destroy the Heteroclites. Which power do you serve?"

Rising to tower above the seated Ellicott, Tovag proclaimed: "We all serve the daughters of the Damselfly." The 'ayes' of his companions echoed the 'Taur's commitment.

"Then you serve the power of illumination," Ellicott said with a smile, "and I shall show you how to use it."

Turning to J'yorie, Ellicott asked, "Why did you not simply tell me you were a daughter of the Damselfly?"

"I have hidden so long in the lies of fear that I can no longer speak the truth. My sister, A'Janae, is held by Goibniu."

"So the light of legend already fails with the loss of one Damselfly. Let me see your parchments, and together we shall set in motion the feats to thwart the Heteroclites and see if we can save your sister." He spread the parchments out on the earth before them, squinting to see the faded lines. "You will need the seals of sanction. Here on this second parchment, see them? You can claim them from Vuaia by presenting her with this decree. See? It has DaeAer's mark."

"Vuaia the Spirit Whisperer? She was not at your fortress in the Woods. The fortress was in ruins, and we found only the cup among the fallen stones," Roh'nan said.

"Aye, she is here with me. It was no longer safe within the Woods. Goibniu's aberrants search for all who hold the keys to the Curse Stone. We have hidden here within the mountains for several seasons.

"Feie wizard, you and the Wyndwryn will go with Nicholas to claim the seals of sanction while we reclaim the lyre and shield from the witch in Sheering's Crossing."

Ellicott rose and lifted the sleepy Nicholas from his pocket. "Off you go my wee friend. Be swift, for we will meet you at the Bridge of Light before darkfall on the morrow. Good journey."

J'yorie beckoned E'teihl to her side, handing him the scroll of seals. "Do not leave the wizard. There is no time to waste with women. I know you will not fail me, E'teihl. A'Janae's life depends on us." She pulled him to her, kissing him quickly and feeling his flutter of pleasure.

"It truly is a shame you love another, J'yorie. I will remain with Aodh and gather the seals. We will meet you at the Bridge. Bright blessings on your journey."

Ellicott lifted J'yorie's pack to her shoulder, nodded to Tovag and Roh'nan, and led them off toward Sheering's Crossing, a half day's journey to the south. Behind them Nicholas guided the others deeper into the mountains.

Seals and a Scryer

"Walk!" Aodh fussed. His wrinkled round face was covered in sweat, slick as a cherry, from the effort of keeping up with his companions. He stopped, leaned forward with his hands on his knees, inhaling great gulps of air in an attempt to catch his breath. E'teihl dropped to the ground beside him, calling out to the rapidly disappearing Nicholas.

"Flier! The Feie tires. We must let him rest."

Nicholas hopped back a few steps before flopping onto his belly, legs fully extended to allow his little body to take full advantage of the cooling grass.

"How…much…further?" Aodh wheezed.

"Not far, less than a league. Ellicott's home is hidden within a fall of standing stones beyond the creek. The winds whip and scatter the scent to keep the aberrants from finding it."

The little flier jumped up and scampered back to sit beside Aodh the Feie. "I shall ride on your shoulder and you may set the pace."

"Aye, a far better plan than racing forward at break-neck speed." Aodh took a deep gulp from his flask, wiped his mouth with the back of his sleeve and patted his shoulder in invitation to the furry flier.

"Let us be about it. I do not want the foul temper of the young woman fixing on me because we arrive late at the Bridge."

They laughed, hurrying forward as quickly as the wizard's short, fat legs would permit.

❧❧

Vuaia looked up from the row of prickleberries she was hoeing. A sound, but not of the wind, had touched her ear. She lifted the hoe, resting its blade on her shoulder, and stepped beyond the fence onto the dusty road. In the distance she could make out the silhouettes of two beings. Both were short. One winged and the other stout with a fly-away mop of fiery hair. A Wyndwryn and a Feie wizard.

"Vuaia!" Hearing her name called in the shrill squeak of the wee beast's voice brought a smile to her face.

"Nicholas! You return. Where is Ellicott?"

"He guides others to Sheering's Crossing to claim the tools they require. I bring these two to you on another matter. They bear an order from the Wizard-Elect DaeAer."

E'teihl held out the parchment. "I am E'teihl, this is Aodh the Feie."

A tinkle of laughter bubbled up from deep within the Spirit Whisperer. "I could see that from three dragon lengths. Come inside where the wind will not whip us to shreds. I hate the wind, but it has been effective in keeping our scent from the aberrants."

Once inside, Vuaia unrolled the scroll and frowned at DaeAer's mark. "DaeAer grows old and weak, his hand trembles. Three seals he grants you—sufficient to allow five to cross the Bridge of Light, a man and a 'Taur, a female halfling and two enchanted. Who travels with you?"

"Æselvanæ's Oversoul, Tovag the Blue 'Taur and J'yorie, a halfling Damselfly."

"Indeed? The legend of the Damselfly at last comes to pass. So, Ellicott has gone in search of the shield and the lyre? I left the cup at the fortress within the Wandering Woods in the hope that when the day came, it would be found."

"Aye, we have it. Nicholas led us right to it." Aodh nodded, eyeing a loaf cooling on the kitchen bench.

"Forgive me, I forget my manners. We have had so little company since we came here. In fact Nicholas was the first." Vuaia gathered bread and cheese, a shoulder of broiled stag and a pitcher of sweet berry cider. "Eat. And I shall prepare the seals."

While Aodh gorged on the fatty meat, E'teihl slipped from his chair to stand behind the Spirit Whisperer.

"It is said you can speak to the divinities."

"Aye, it is so. They have given me the gift of godspeak and permitted me to feel the wrong in people. It does not always feel like a gift. Sometimes it is more of an encumbrance when I see a wrong that causes much sorrow to another and know I can do nothing."

"Do the creators plan the lives of some from birth?"

"Are some predestined to greatness or obscurity? There are always choices, E'teihl."

The Wyndwryn's brow furrowed with his uncertainty and he sighed. "What of love?"

Vuaia searched the winged man's face, reaching out to touch his shoulder. "Aye, sometimes there is only one."

"But what if that one is not possible?"

"Some are meant to live alone, but if the promise of love has been made, then there will be a way."

Within her hands the small disk-like seals glowed white-hot. Her whispered words brought forth the symbols of the Spirit People on each seal—first a man, then the rune stones and lastly, the weeping willow. Vuaia drew a silken bag from a pigeonhole and dropped the three coins inside, pulling the drawstring tight and knotting it. She handed the bag to E'teihl and rested a reassuring hand on his shoulder with a promise. "He will find a way to be with her."

"Now, both of you should rest. In the morn I will have Nicholas guide you to the Bridge."

❧❦

Ellicott lifted a hand, signaling them to stop. A shadowy group flowed over them, a flock of giggling young Wyndwryn. J'yorie added her infectious laughter, earning a grin from Ellicott and frowns from Roh'nan and Tovag.

"What? They are delightful. Probably the only ones left who truly enjoy every moment of their existence. The rest of us war and worry, drown ourselves in ale, or kill ourselves with work."

"They have no sense of responsibility," Tovag snorted.

"We had best hope that J'yorie's Wyndwryn takes his task seriously and does not lose the seals of sanction before he reaches the Bridge," Roh'nan added, looking as if he had swallowed a bitter bug.

"He won't. He promised me he would stay with Aodh."

"Until he sees one of those lasses—nothing could keep him from a night spent nurturing one of them!"

"Let us not argue about the Wyndwryn. We have a witch to see." Ellicott headed off down the left fork and its winding way through the tattered village that was Sheering's Crossing.

Ellicott banged on the door of a dilapidated cottage. The dirt-encrusted door creaked open the width of an eye, allowing its cataract-clouded lens to peer through matted strands of graying hair.

"Whut do ye wunt?" rasped a voice as dry as a waterless well.

"I bring the Damselfly halfling, old woman," Ellicott offered, resulting in a wider crack and a two-eyed glare.

"Show 'er."

Ellicott stepped back, forcing J'yorie forward. The old woman was startlingly swift. Her age-worn and crippled claw gripped J'yorie's wrist and jerked her inside. Releasing her grip, the crone used her ample backside to slam the door closed.

"Sit," the old woman ordered and pointed to a wooden stool covered with dust.

"I have come—"

"No talk, sit."

J'yorie brushed away the worst of the dust from the stool and, as her eyes adjusted to the candlelight, looked about the cluttered room. Apart from a narrow walkway amid the piles of scrolls and tablets, there were no bare surfaces. Benches and tables were covered with stones and bones, and a massive scrying crystal sat in the center of the room.

The scryer moved to the far side of the immense stone and beckoned for J'yorie to place her hands on its sides. Light bloomed—slowly, like a rose releasing one petal at a time—and filled the room with images from J'yorie's life. She saw her parents holding hands and wandering along the path within the garden. A'Janae weeping as J'yorie chastised her for her poor form in weaponless combat. E'teihl,

Tovag and J'yorie hunting stag within her father's woods. The image of a stranger came, tall and dark with his face hidden behind a light-reflective mask, leaping from the terrace off the room where her parents lay dead. And the bodies of her parents on their biers, enshrouded in flames and oily smoke.

A deep, wrenching sob forced itself through J'yorie's lips. Her hands lifted from the crystal, leaving the room dark once more.

"Hands." The witch beckoned again.

Sniffling and wiping tears away with the back of her hands, J'yorie touched the scrying stone again. Once more the room filled with images. J'yorie asleep, drunk and drooling on a tavern table, a quick coupling with a stranger, Roh'nan's angry voice as he took her flask, bodies entwined and the soft, sweet sounds of J'yorie and Fahlcaen's lovemaking. The sharp scent of sweat and desire quickening J'yorie's heart, leaving her lost in the joy of the moment now past. Fahlcaen's voice soft and low within J'yorie's mind: *You will not always be duty-bound to the Oversoul by the promise of your word. I will wait. I am your destiny.*

J'yorie pulled her hands away, nails biting into palms, and she forced them between her knees.

"Please," she moaned, "don't make me look anymore. Why do you do this to me, old woman?"

A lopsided smile showed caverns among a few remaining teeth. "Ye do it, not I. It is your life, innit? Are ye proud of it? Do ye wunna change it?"

"I cannot change my life. It is past."

"But t'morrow will come new, and ye can change yer life. Whut do ye wunt lass? Touch the stone."

"I cannot." J'yorie clutched her diaphragm as though punched, rocking herself as she murmured over and over. "I cannot."

"Ye must."

Tears streamed down her cheeks, blinding J'yorie to the new images being revealed as her trembling fingers made contact with the crystal. She closed her eyes, squeezing them tight against more hurt, but the soft rustle of leaves and her sister's golden laughter forced her to look.

A'Janae with Roh'nan! J'yorie gasped for air as she alternated between choking coughs and convulsive sobs.

"A'Janae," she whispered, "I am so sorry."

"Not sorry, not sad, but happy, 'im and 'er. Kill 'im, kill the Heteroclite. Kindle the orbs. Take 'is blood and burn 'im with 'is own trick. Take the happiness."

"I don't understand you." J'yorie leaned forward resting her head against the stone. "I don't."

"See t'morrow," the old woman cackled with jubilance. "Look girl, see it!"

J'yorie lifted her eyes. The image was of her, but she was not alone. Fahlcaen smiled before her, his left hand bound to hers, and she heard the hushed words of the handfasting promise, "To join with J'yorie whom I love."

"Fahlcaen?" she reached out, then drew her hand back. "No, it is just a ruse! A picture summoned by your wicked desire to torment me."

"Girl, the future will be in yer hands. I shall place it there." The witch stood and waddled to a long, low bench. She lifted a cover, filling the air with the grit and cobwebs of long abandon. Picking up a small, delicate lyre, she brushed the dust of disuse away and sent the strings vibrating. "When the lyre sings, the way will be opened." She handed it to J'yorie, grinning as the girl hugged it against her breast. "Ye believe me now?"

"I believe you can tell me how to save my sister."

The scryer's smile widened to reveal rotting teeth, and the foul odor of her breath washed across the room as she hooted, "That, my girl and much more. I will tell ye how to live. Live in the t'morrows."

"And the shield?" J'yorie asked.

"Aye, I'm fetchin' it as fast as I can," the old woman gurgled as she leaned into the cold fireplace. "Up the chimney, 'tis safe from the howlin' aberrants whut came for it."

She lifted to her tiptoes, disappearing into the cavity of the flue, her words hollow as she continued her instructions, "Don't be too quick. Wait. Let the Heteroclite free the stone. Leave 'im think 'ee's won. Follow the lyre's song. When the blood is in the cup and 'ee speaks the words of the blood change, spill the blood before the final sound."

The witch ducked from the chimney and carried a long slender shield to J'yorie.

"'Tis as long as a man, light as a feather and old as a dragon's tooth. Shield ye'selves and speak the lovers' names afore the last drop and the final sound. Free us all."

"I don't understand. Whose blood will he spill? What final sound shall I hear? Whose names shall I speak?"

"Yes," the scryer nodded, "go now. Save us. Ye have everything ye need."

"But I don't—"

The old woman opened the door, calling sharply to Ellicott, "Take 'er. I am done with 'er."

"Please, I don't understand." J'yorie dropped the shield and lyre and fell to her knees, clutching the woman's skirt. "I just don't understand what I am to do."

"Ye will. When the time comes, ye will." The witch patted J'yorie's cheek, freed herself from the girl's grip and backed into the darkness of her home.

Roh'nan and Tovag circled J'yorie, their questions a cacophony of brutal sounds that caused her to duck away and cover her face.

"Leave her be. Don't crowd her. You act like anxious fathers on a daughter's wedding night. She has seen the portal to our future and been given the keys."

"How could you do this?" J'yorie looked up at Ellicott. "That witch may have held the lyre and shield safe, but she is crazy and told me nothing that will help us. Look? The lyre does not even have a song." She grabbed it up and drew her fingers across the strings, which vibrated without a single note. "And the shield? Have you looked at it? It is made of skin so thin it would not guard against a sword of silk."

"We should go. It is a healthy distance to the Bridge of Light." Ellicott picked up the shield and held it out to J'yorie. "We do not always see the colors of a rainbow in the hour before dawn."

She snatched the shield away, swinging it over her shoulder and adjusting its strap across her chest. "You are as crazy as she is!" she shouted after him.

Roh'nan scowled. "I should have questioned the scryer. Had I done so, we might know what we are to do. I was wrong to believe there was any hope to be found with you and your lazy, lurking Wyndwryn. All I have done is bring death closer to A'Janae with every—"

Tovag's hand slammed in to Roh'nan's chest and sent him

staggering backward, scrambling to maintain his balance as the 'Taur shouted, his large finger punctuating the air, "I would have killed you in your sleep, but J'yorie would not allow it. She is the only reason you live. I do not believe her sister chose such a weak man, a man who did nothing to protect his own wife. You are the reason A'Janae is lost, for she was solely in your care."

The 'Taur spun around, grabbed J'yorie's wrist and pulled her down the road, leaving Roh'nan glaring after them.

"You should have let me kill him. He is no leader, and his indecisiveness leaves us weak."

J'yorie jerked her wrist from the 'Taur's grip, rubbing away the redness. "We cannot kill him. Not yet. I must know if A'Janae loves him. The witch showed me their future happiness. If it is true I cannot take that from my sister."

A glance over her shoulder showed the Oversoul jogging to catch up.

Now we must meet E'teihl and Aodh and cross into Fyrki. J'yorie's silent tones filled the 'Taur's mind.

⁂

Muffled giggles awoke E'teihl in the darkness of Vuaia's house.

"Wyndwryn, do you sleep alone?" whispered the sweet, silken voice of a girl. He lifted himself up on one elbow and searched the shadows. There on the windowsill sat a female, her form backlit by the pale moonlight, wings swaying in the gentle night breeze.

"Aye, I quest for the Damselfly's daughter and cannot leave my charge."

"You need not leave. I am here." The young female dropped to the floor and drew closer. "Would you not like some company?"

"Aye." E'teihl reached out and pulled her to him, covering her face with kisses, luxuriating in the satin softness of her wings, stroking her smooth, firm, unfettered flesh.

Her coos of delight encouraged him. Her passion left him weak, and with her arms wrapped around him, he succumbed to sleep.

"Wyndwryn!" the wizard's hoarse voice crashed in on sultry dreams. E'teihl opened one eye to stare at the flustered Feie.

"Come, E'teihl, the hour grows late, and we must hurry if we are to meet J'yorie at the Bridge."

The Wyndwryn rose, pulled on his leathers, patting the pockets in search of the bag of coins, but it was not there. He snatched the covers off the bed, shaking them in search of the silk pouch. He dropped to his knees and sighed with relief as he discovered the prize beneath the cot.

"For a moment I thought that I had lost them," he mumbled, pulling the drawstring open to look inside. Two coins, not three. The seal with the willow was missing.

He looked up to find Aodh staring at him. With a shrug and a laugh he said, "What can it matter? Two or three?"

Chapter 26: Into Fyrki

The reflected brilliance of the Bridge of Light could be seen silhouetted against the background of gathering storm clouds.

"We shall go no farther," Ellicott said, holding Nicholas beneath his chin. He gave him a tickle at the base of his tail, making the flier chirp with pleasure. "Your legend ends in Fyrki, beyond the Bridge. Tomorrow we will awake to a new beginning, illuminated by the purity of the Damselfly or shadowed by the rule of the Heteroclites. The decision is yours J'yorie."

The eyes of the Damselfly halfling glittered with unshed tears, and her throat closed with the fear of failure.

"I do not know."

"You will," Ellicott reassured.

Offering his grip to each of them, he bade them good journey before turning away.

Roh'nan watched Ellicott until he disappeared from sight and then swung on Aodh and E'teihl. "Do you have the seals of sanction?"

"We do," Aodh answered. "The Wyndwryn carries them."

E'teihl pulled the pouch from his pocket and tossed it to the Oversoul. "Your seals my lord."

J'yorie grabbed the bag from Roh'nan and opened it, dumping the glowing contents into the palm of her hand. "Two? There are only two? There were three symbols on the parchment, were there not?"

"Aye, but I will not be crossing with you. You do not need the third."

"What do you mean you won't be crossing with us? You were there—DaeAer said your purpose was to persuade!" Roh'nan said, glaring at the Wyndwryn.

"What have you done, E'teihl?" J'yorie searched the handsome face of her friend. She watched his eyes slide away, unable to face her.

"What have you done?"

"The third was stolen in the night." E'teihl's head dropped and he stared at the earth before J'yorie's feet. "A female took it."

J'yorie stepped back. "You promised me, E'teihl. Promised you would not betray me. How could you do this? How? It is my sister's life. A'Janae may die because you could not refuse a single night's pleasure."

E'teihl felt the heat rise to his face. His heart hammered as if it might burst within his chest. He looked up at their angry faces, at J'yorie's hurt and disbelief. He swung away, racing forward to fling himself into the air and fly from their disapproval and despair.

J'yorie looked down at the coins in her hand. "Sanction for three men and a single key to the rune stones. I am the key. And you are the men. I do not know how E'teihl's actions may harm our quest, but we cannot merely walk away." She dropped the seals into the pouch, drawing the string and lifting it over her head. "Come."

Unspoken fears hung in the air as three men and a young woman floundered toward their fate.

The Bridge of Light

The beauty of the Bridge of Light stunned them. They stood motionless, transfixed, staring in speechless wonder. Suspended within every dimension of time and space, it transcended all, separating the kingdoms of light from the cavernous stronghold of Fyrki. Aflame with the power of creation, it was a sacred testament to the supremacy of the Spirit People and a guardian against the spread of dark magick into the realm of light. A sharp crackle announced the arrival of the lightsteed, legs disappearing into the blaze below and fiery mane and tail trailing in the shimmering haze of the hot winds.

"So you live!" The golden man slid down from the flaming steed. "In spite of it all, you live. You bear the strength of legend, and now you seek to stop Goibniu's upward surge, to pull your sister from the shadowy grave. But, if you falter, if you hesitate, then you will fail. There are no second chances, J'yorie. This is the day of your reckoning, the day of metamorphosis on which legend emerges in illumination or dies in darkness."

"Who are you?"

"I am the pulse, the power of the Damselfly's golden blood, the guiding light of futures past and the tomorrows of yesterday. If you carry the seals of sanction, I am the gatekeeper."

J'yorie lifted the pouch from over her head, opened it and spilled the coins into the hands of the golden being. His blazing eyes bored into hers.

"The Enchantment seal is missing."

"It was lost."

"Two men and the Damselfly halfling are given sanction, the Feie must remain behind."

"But Aodh is a male. Surely he may pass under the seal of Man."

"Three seals were gifted to your quest, one for Man, one for the magic key of the Damselfly, and one for enchantment. You bear only those of Man and magick. The enchanted wizard may not cross."

"Without the enchantment of the Feie wizard we will be unprotected against Goibniu's dark magick. Aodh must be allowed to pass or we are doomed to fail. Damn your Wyndwryn!" Roh'nan snarled.

"And what of Man enchanted?" the voice of an unseen one asked from behind.

It was the Strangeling. His skin was blistered and bubbling with the boils of change and beside him sat the downy flier, Nicholas.

"Master Ellicott said this was the Strangeling's place," Nicholas shrugged, "and so I brought him to you."

J'yorie turned her gaze back to the golden man. "And what of Man enchanted?" repeating the Strangeling's question.

"Man is Man."

The glowing being leapt to the back of the lightsteed, and together they raced toward the Bridge of Light. As they neared its fiery threshold, the golden man flung out his hand, sending the seals of sanction into the blaze.

The flames lowered, flickered and died.

"Run! Make your passage swift for the fire of the creation waits for neither Man nor Damselfly."

Tovag, Roh'nan and J'yorie raced across the smoldering bridge, followed by the staggering sounds of the Strangeling's awkward gait as he hurried to keep up. Behind them lightning flashed and the flames reclaimed the bridge as Aodh stared helplessly after them.

Ahead the open maw of Fyrki loomed, black and menacing.

❧✦❧

Roh'nan and J'yorie lifted torches from the wall. J'yorie held hers out to Tovag, but he merely shook his head and raised his axe in a two-handed grip.

"There are no guards. Why are there no guards?"

The Strangeling moaned and squatted down, hugging himself.

"Strangeling?" J'yorie knelt beside him. "Are you in pain?"

"No, it is the pain of another, somewhere ahead." His words were followed by a woman's screams of refusal, screams that echoed around the cavern.

"Your sister," Roh'nan whispered, leading the way into the velvet darkness.

J'yorie patted the Strangeling's hand. "We will return for you."

He nodded and struggled to rise and make his way along the wall after her disappearing shadow.

❧❦

The halfling fought fiercely, nails raking Goibniu's face and neck, gouging at his eyes. A'Janae's refusal to surrender only fanned the flames of his desire. She became exhausted quickly, unable to offer any real threat or resistance. The screams against her violation turned to sobs, then to whimpers and pleas for her freedom but inevitably ended with numb, glassy-eyed resignation.

Goibniu never allowed her sufficient strength to fly away. She was permitted just enough light and warmth to keep her alive, but still earthbound and easy prey. Again and again he had promised her freedom, promised a day when she would be reunited with her sister. Each time she clung foolishly to that thread of hope until he next came for her.

Goibniu lay on his side next to A'Janae, his fingers tracing a golden vein along one pale wing. His touch became more intimate. He heard her moan and felt her shiver of revulsion as she tried to draw away. At the touch of his lips, her hands rose feebly as she made an attempt to cover herself. Aroused by her cries, he forced her hands away, squeezing the softness of her warm flesh as the passion of his kisses increased and his touch became more demanding.

"Open your eyes and look at me."

A'Janae swallowed the bitterness that threatened to gag her and opened her eyes to face her tormentor.

"Your sister comes for you. She will be here soon. Would you like to go home, A'Janae?"

He lowered his mouth to hers, stealing the hot sweetness of her lips and tongue. She tried to pull away only to have his hand grasp her head and bring her nearer.

"Why do you always fight me? What I ask is nothing that you have not already given Roh'nan." He rolled away, angry, and stood beside the bed looking down on the pale beauty of the Damselfly's daughter.

"Dress."

She clutched the ebony sheet, covering herself and waited for him to look away so that she could put on her gown without his gaze.

"I grow weaker."

He looked back at her. "It will not matter much longer. Your sister is coming, and I will no long require you."

"Will you let me go? Let me go home?"

Goibniu swung on her and gripped her shoulders. "Is that what you want? To go home to the charred remains of Castle Baene? Or home to your husband, or Grimmoirë? It does not matter, since you will all be dead before another sunrise."

"Goibniu, please do not do this. Do not take the lives of the innocent."

"Innocent? There is no innocence, A'Janae. Everyone is guilty of some sin. The world will be cleansed of the fair and ruled by the Heteroclites. It is my turn to shape the minds of Men. They are cruel and merciless, their hearts filled with iniquitous desire. All I will ask of them is that they follow their true nature as I know they yearn to do. I will give them freedom at last, freedom from their false morality."

"There are good men. My father…"

"Your father! He would not even save himself. I offered him freedom, told him he could even keep your mother if he would only grant me the blood of his daughters, but he declined. Then he died." Goibniu smiled and slid his hands down A'Janae's arms. "Take off your dress. I find our talk of men and death quite stimulating."

Her eyes widened and her hands clutched the bodice of her gown.

The sound of the first scream had propelled Roh'nan forward, the second sent him slamming into the room where Goibniu held A'Janae.

Roh'nan cursed. "Act wounded. J'yorie comes along with the 'Taur."

Goibniu lifted his hands from the sobbing Damselfly, allowing her to roll away and cover herself.

"A'Janae?" Roh'nan said with a laugh. "I bring you J'yorie."

A'Janae cowered, refusing to look at the false Oversoul or the Heteroclite ruler.

"Your husband speaks to you, A'Janae. Can you not even greet him? And your sister? Do you not want to see your sister?"

With the sound of approaching footsteps, Goibniu allowed himself to tumble to the floor, smiling up at the Oversoul.

J'yorie burst into the room, crashing into Roh'nan and knocking him forward, imbedding his sword in the tangled of sheets. Goibniu jumped to his feet and jerked J'yorie forward, spinning her around and wrapping his forearm beneath her throat, his dagger piercing just below her left breast.

"Draw your dagger and drop it. Slowly and carefully. I would not like to cut you again."

J'yorie eased her dagger from its scabbard and let it fall at her feet.

Tovag entered the room, freezing at the sight of Goibniu's dagger at her heart. His eyes widened and he gripped his chest. "J'yorie?" he gasped, opening his mouth as if to speak. His teeth and tongue were covered with blood. "J'yorie?" he repeated with a gurgling sound, choking on the blood rising within. His huge body slumped forward, the hilt of Taerys's enchanted sword protruding from his back.

Goibniu shouted to his queen above J'yorie's screams, "Taerys, you are such a good wife, so predictable. Have you come for the walker? He waits for you. Nightfall nears, and I must prepare for the journey to the House of Hexus."

Roh'nan rose from the bed, pulling Taerys to him and kissing her deeply before pushing her ahead of him past the fallen 'Taur. He swung back and hissed in J'yorie's ear, "I told you I was the walker you feared."

Goibniu laughed and pushed J'yorie onto the bed, pulling the shield from her back and grabbing Roh'nan's sword away as she reached for it. "Shame on you! Shouldn't you be comforting your pale, weeping sister?" He laughed again as J'yorie rolled away from him, swung her legs over the far side of the bed, and crawled to Tovag's side.

"I am sorry I cannot introduce you to my passion, but I have no time to waste. Where are the cup and the lyre?"

J'yorie shook her head. "Why do you do this?"

Goibniu snarled and backhanded J'yorie, then jerked her up by the hair. "I asked you—where are the lyre and cup?"

"I don't know. Roh'nan had them," she spat at him, holding her fast-swelling cheek.

"Liar." Goibniu smiled as he pushed her away and lifted Tovag's pack to rummage through the contents. "Look, the cup! Now, where is the lyre? In your bag? Of course it is! You wouldn't trust another, certainly not the Oversoul. He gave her to me, you know. And she has been sweet, your sister."

He squatted before J'yorie and beckoned for her bag. She slipped it from her shoulder and held it out, her chin rising defiantly, eyes glittering with hatred. He accepted the satchel with his left hand, his right snaking out to drag her forward.

"These are your last hours. They can be spent here with your sister, or in torture at the hands of the aberrants who wait below. The choice is yours." He crushed her lips beneath his, bruising her flesh against her teeth, then flung her away. Her head struck the wall with the soft, wet sound of splitting flesh and she collapsed.

"A'Janae, you should care for your sister. It seems she is not as strong as I had been led to believe! If she lives, bathe her and dress her in something more becoming."

Goibniu gathered the artifacts and slammed out the door, dropping the heavy bolt into place.

A'Janae rose on trembling legs.

"J'yorie? Do you live?"

Chapter 27: Intervention

"In the wizard's chambers of the House of Hexus, Fahlcaen stared at his old friend with disbelief.

"I could kill you, old man." The assassin stood before the Wizard-Elect with his staff poised to strike.

"Perhaps you could, Fahlcaen, but it would not solve your problems. What is it you want me to do? I gave them the required sanctions; if they have been careless it cannot be undone."

"Look at the Wyndwryn! You must have known he would fail, that they would be sent into Fyrki without the Feie's magick. Is that not why you sent E'teihl?"

DaeAer turned to look at what remained of E'teihl, a hollow shell of hopelessness and regret, wings limp and waterlogged, bright eyes dimmed by his own betrayal of a lifelong friend—a desperate man attempting to drown himself, saved by the assassin.

"Some must be sacrificed."

"Sacrificed!" Fahlcaen slammed his staff across a shelf, wiping it clean, sending its contents flying. "You will be the next sacrifice if you do not help me!"

DaeAer gripped the edge of the table, steadying himself in the face of Fahlcaen's anger. "I should never have chosen you, never have given you the power of the wormwood."

"Then take it back!"

DaeAer threw back his head and laughed. "Do you not believe I would if it were possible? You were like a son to me. The very thing the halfling does is the only thing that can relieve you of the wormwood's curse—a change of blood. But who will volunteer to take your curse, Fahlcaen? What other man would willingly accept such a fate? And you do not have the heartlessness to demand it. It is your own goodness that keeps you what you are."

"I had nothing to lose when I asked for the spellbinding. Now I want my freedom, and I want hers."

"Oh, Fahlcaen, you still have nothing to lose. J'yorie does not know it, but a halfling must give her own life to save the others."

"Then I shall give my life to save hers. As you say, I was once like a son to you, DaeAer. Help me."

DaeAer sank into a chair, resting his face in his hands. "I can give you the orb of light, but without a miracle it will kill one of them when it is kindled. Can you truly kill one daughter of the Damselfly?"

"I am an assassin. Give me the orb and tell me what to do."

E'teihl sat in the fading sunlight with his wings open wide to receive its lingering warmth.

"Are they dry?" Fahlcaen asked from the edge of the crystal filled fracture.

E'teihl remained silent, hands hanging between his knees, downcast eyes fixed on his dangling, tearstained fingers.

Fahlcaen knelt before the Wyndwryn. "I know that you feel her smile will never again be for you, that she will never forgive what you have done, but you must help me. If you don't, she will die."

"Will you really kill A'Janae?" Fresh tears spilled from E'teihl's pain filled eyes and streamed down his cheeks, over his fingers and into the earth.

"I do not intend to kill anyone. But once it begins to grow light we will have no choice but to kindle the orb. We cannot let the aberrants escape Fyrki."

"I may drop you. You are heavy."

"And you are strong." Fahlcaen reached out and drew the winged man to his feet. "I trust you, E'teihl."

Fahlcaen eased himself over the lip of the fissure and braced his feet on a crystal outcrop. E'teihl took a deep breath and grasped the assassin's forearm as he hovered above him. Fahlcaen winked, smiling as he let his feet slip from the stone. Supported only by the Wyndwryn's determined strength, Fahlcaen hung suspended in the opening to DaeAer's wall of light.

With hands locked in an iron grip on the assassin's wrist, shoulder joints aching, bicep and pectoral muscles bulging, wings beating furiously, E'teihl lowered Fahlcaen down the shaft.

"I cannot hold you!" E'teihl's palms were greasy with the sweat born of fear.

"Then let go. I will fall to my death, igniting the orb and killing everyone below."

"I mean it! I cannot hold you! You are slipping."

"Then find a ledge where we can rest."

E'teihl slammed into the wall, dropping Fahlcaen and crashing to his side on a narrow ledge of crystal.

"Graceful," Fahlcaen muttered, rubbing the blood from his elbow and leaning over to look below. "We are almost there. The ground is within view and there are many stones offering hand and foot holds. I will climb down from here. You go and get Aodh. Come back here for the Damselflies."

E'teihl stood and offered his hand. Fahlcaen gripped his forearm and pulled him forward, hugging the winged man to his chest.

"Go my friend. We may need the Feie's magick."

The Wyndwryn watched the assassin disappear over the ledge before flying upward to find the little wizard.

⟡

Without warning, the door swung open and sent A'Janae scuttling back against the wall, moaning and keening. The stranger raised a finger to his lips and softly closed the door behind him.

"Shhh, your cries may bring our enemies. Where is J'yorie?"

A'Janae looked towards her sister's still form. Fahlcaen first knelt next to Tovag's body, feeling for life signs and finding none. He then moved quickly to J'yorie.

"She lives," A'Janae whispered. "Who are you?"

"Fahlcaen. I am here to help you. You are J'yorie's sister?"

"Aye, I am A'Janae. You know my sister? Take her to safety. Goibniu intends to kill her."

A slow smile spread across Fahlcaen's face, and he reached out to gently smooth A'Janae's hair. "I will take you both to safety," he said, and then asked, "Where is the Heteroclite? Does he have what he needs to free the Curse Stone?"

"I do not know where he has gone, but he took Tovag's cup and J'yorie's shield and lyre. The Oversoul is with Taerys, Goibniu's wife."

Fahlcaen moved to J'yorie, his fingers probing her scalp as he looked for the source of blood. On examining it, he mumbled to himself.

"It is only a flesh wound, but she will sleep for some time. Come, I will take you to safety and return for J'yorie."

"I am too weak to fly."

"Then I will carry you." He knelt beside her, wrapped her in his cloak and lifted her to his chest. He eased the door open and looked into the dim passageway, then slipped out, silent as a shadow, down the hall and back into the room that housed the wall of light. Binding A'Janae into a sling on his back, Fahlcaen climbed to the ledge where E'teihl had left him.

"E'teihl and Aodh the Feie will be here shortly and take you to Grimmoirë. There you can heal under the protection of the enchanted."

As Fahlcaen turned away, A'Janae grabbed his arm. "He did not come to save me. It is his fault I am here. There is something not right about him. Do not trust Roh'nan."

"I never have. You are safe here until E'teihl comes for you. Rest."

"Have you found my husband?"

"Yes."

For a moment, as she watched Fahlcaen disappear, A'Janae pondered the tremor of his doubt, and then fluttered to the ground on weakened wings, re-entered the darkened corridor and slipped along to follow Fahlcaen.

❖

J'yorie was gone. Fahlcaen slammed his staff against the wall, cursing his own stupidity.

"Who are you?"

The assassin spun around sharply, his staff immediately whistling through the air and snapping the speaker's neck. The woman crumpled in a whisper of silk and lace, her cloak falling away to expose leathery wings.

"Taerys!" Roh'nan gasped, dropping beside the fallen queen.

Fahlcaen stabbed Roh'nan with the staff, driving him from his knees onto his back and into the wall.

"You gave her to them. Gave them A'Janae and then gave them J'yorie. What was their promise? What could they possibly have offered you that would buy the last blood of the Damselflies?"

Sneering, Roh'nan rose. "You would never understand. Life, they offered a full, freedom-filled life. You are an assassin. Life holds no value to you."

"I hold some life precious—just not yours! I do not know who you really are, but you are not Roh'nan, Oversoul of Æselvanæ."

Fahlcaen drove the left end of his staff into Roh'nan's diaphragm, jerking back only to snap forward with the right end and break his nose. Letting the staff slide through his fingers, Fahlcaen withdrew a little and smashed it against the center of the Oversoul's back, crushing his spine and crippling him as the man spun away.

The assassin pulled his dagger and made a deep cut across the palm of the fallen man's useless hand, collecting his blood in a small vial before turning to the Heteroclite queen and doing the same. He did not see A'Janae as she shrank back into the shadows at the far end of the long hallway, nor did any see the Strangeling peeking from behind a fall of rock.

Fahlcaen returned to Roh'nan and, bending down, slipped his fingers into the man's vest pocket and drew out the golden coin, a seal of sanction with the raised symbol of the willow tree, replacing it with the grape-sized pulsing orb of light, now marked with the blood from the vials.

"Did you really believe one Wyndwryn would let another bear the blame? You really are a fool, Roh'nan, and about life...I will leave you what remains of yours. You have until the hour before daybreak."

Fahlcaen raced away, the music of Roh'nan's hoarse howls in his ears. He burst from the mouth of Fyrki shouting for the lightsteed and its golden rider.

They swept toward him across the Bridge of Light. The golden man leapt upward and caught the seal of sanction as it sailed from Fahlcaen's fingers into the blazing footpath, dampening the flames as the warrior dashed over the Bridge and came to a halt.

"I need to borrow the horse."

❦

A'Janae left her hiding place and crept forward along the dimly lit corridor. Ahead lay the crumpled body of a man and over him crouched a shadowed being. The sound of a footfall scraping on stone alerted the strange creature to A'Janae's presence, and it drew away in fear.

"I did not kill this man. It wasn't me, it was another did it. I did not harm him. I mean…he is not even dead."

"What are you?" A'Janae stared at the being's heaving flesh and pus-filled boils.

"I do not know. They call me Strangeling. I have been told that perhaps I am spellbound by some wizard's curse, but I do not recall my past."

"Your eyes…I know your eyes…" A'Janae reached out to touch the suffering man. "Can you bear the light?"

"Yes, I came from above, across the Bridge with the woman J'yorie and her companions."

"Come with me. I know a safe place."

"A'Janae? Is that you?" the Oversoul's head lolled to the side. "Help me!" he croaked as he tried to raise his upper body. "Help me?"

The Strangeling rose and accepted the hand A'Janae held out. "What of him?"

A'Janae looked down on the man who had professed to be her husband.

"There can be no help for such wickedness," she said, then looked up at the Strangeling and smiled, "but there is hope for us—if we hurry!"

Hand in hand, they sped back toward the ledge in the room that held DaeAer's wall of light.

388

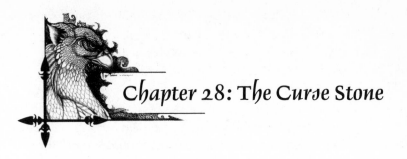

Chapter 28: The Curje Stone

"Good fortune." The golden man gripped Fahlcaen's forearm as he slipped from the back of the lightsteed.

"Destiny is all that remains," Fahlcaen called back as he leapt across the backs of the heretical aberrants who, in their attempt to enter the sacred House of Hexus, had fallen to the poison of the surrounding snow.

The assassin ducked into the doorway and knelt beside a scarlet-robed body. A Prophetess of Belasis lay dead in a pool of rapidly coagulating blood.

"DaeAer!" Fahlcaen shouted as he raced toward the Wizard-Elect's workroom.

The door stood ajar and he pushed it open, expecting another death, but the wizard sat at his table, eyes closed, lips moving wordlessly.

"DaeAer," the assassin said, reaching out to grip the old man's shoulder. "I bring the blood of one willing to take my curse. Where are Goibniu and J'yorie?"

DaeAer looked up and raised his hand to Fahlcaen's cheek. "I should never have chosen you," the ancient wizard whispered, falling sideways into Fahlcaen's arms to reveal his blood-soaked robes. The assassin eased him to the ground, repeating his question, "Where has Goibniu taken J'yorie?"

The wizard lifted his hand over his head to point to the corner door. "To the Curse Stone, but you are too late. You must not kill him, Fahlcaen. She must speak the lovers' names before the last drop and the final sound, if any of us is to be saved."

"I cannot be too late." Fahlcaen palmed the wizard's dagger. He leapt through the doorway and bounded down the stone steps that spiraled toward J'yorie and the Heteroclite who held her captive.

The sound of a voice mingled with a whistling of wind halted Fahlcaen's headlong rush. Pressing himself against the wall, he listened to the unintelligible utterances. He silently lowered himself to the floor and crawled forward to peer into the room beyond.

Just out of reach rested an odd shaped shield. The assassin stretched forward and placed it behind him on the stairs.

The great room was guarded by shielded aberrant knights, those who had crossed into Hexus on the bodies of their comrades. Each faced the same direction as Goibniu and waited for the ruler's command.

Goibniu, the Heteroclite ruler, lay prostrate before the altar of the Curse Stone with his feet pointing towards the stairs, wings fully extended. His arms were outstretched above his head, and he held a delicate lyre. On the sacred table, locked by six stone arms, lay the Curse Stone, its high, thin whistling call audible above the turbulence of the Heteroclite's words.

To the left of Goibniu sat a carved stone trough in the shape of a man. Behind, and to his right, J'yorie sat bound to a chair in a growing pool of blood. Blood had filled the cup beneath her bleeding wrist and ran in rivulets over the side with each new droplet that fell.

Gritting his teeth in order to silence the curse rising in his throat, Fahlcaen slowly and stealthily got to his feet. He remained poised to throw the wizard's dagger into the madman's back, but DaeAer's feeble words filled his mind and stayed his arm.

You must not kill him, Fahlcaen. She must speak the lovers' names before the last drop and the final sound, if any of us is to be saved.

Fahlcaen closed his eyes and clenched his jaws, squeezing them until they pained him. He slowly loosed his grip on the dagger, flipping it over in his hand as he began to creep, inch by inch, toward the chair.

A movement by Goibniu stopped Fahlcaen in his tracks. He held his breath and waited for the man to see him but the Heteroclite ruler merely rose to a kneeling position and held up the lyre, a new string of incantations flowing over the Curse Stone. The thin, reedy sound emitted by the Stone grew louder, and Fahlcaen resumed his forward motion.

He edged to the side of the chair away from the Heteroclite and looked up into J'yorie's pale face. Her eyes were closed, and unconsciousness left her features loose. Lifting the dagger, Fahlcaen sliced the rope binding her hands and tied a length of it just above her bleeding wrist, slowing the flow of blood. The assassin looked up at a change of inflection in the sound of Goibniu's voice, but the words to free the Stone had required only a slight modulation for the new, final cadence. His dagger sliced through the rope holding J'yorie's ankles. With another glance at the Heteroclite, Fahlcaen leaned into J'yorie and lifted her over his shoulder, grabbing the tilting chair just in time to return it to its four-legged position. One arm wrapped around J'yorie, Fahlcaen tipped the cup beneath the chair, pouring the Damselfly's blood into the existing puddle. Slipping the vials from his pocket, he replaced J'yorie's spilled blood with that of the Heteroclite queen and the Oversoul. Then he backed away toward the steps and the shield.

As Fahlcaen reached the steps, Goibniu strummed the strings of the lyre and sent a golden-toned vibrato echoing around the chamber that freed two of the stone locks. Turning left, he strummed the lyre again, and the second two locks sprung open. He then turned outward to face the stairs, the aberrant knights turning around at the same time.

Face to face, both men froze. Fahlcaen with the unconscious J'yorie over his shoulder and one foot already behind on the first of the steps, Goibniu with the lyre poised to strike again. Neither man moved. J'yorie moaned. The Heteroclite responded with a bellow of laughter. In hollow simulation, a roar issued forth from the knights as they awaited their master's further direction, the silence being restored immediately as Goibniu raised his hand.

"Whoever you are, take her! It no longer matters. I have the blood, the sacred blood of the Damselfly, blood that will free the

Heteroclites who wait in the depths of Fyrki to walk in sunlight at its very zenith—freeing me to rule the land of Men, freeing my knights of the dark and cold. Every enchanted one who sat in the warmth of today's light will die in tomorrow's sunrise!"

Again Goibniu struck the lyre, its third sweet tone calling forth the freedom of the Curse Stone. A grinding sound accompanied the opening of the two final locks. The stone rose from its resting place to hang suspended in the air above the head section of the man-shaped trough, its high-pitched, whistling-wind tones strengthening. The Heteroclite Goibniu glanced at the intruder again and then lifted the cup from beneath the chair.

"Blood of the Damselfly," he cried above the voice of the Stone, the aberrants following with their howls. "The Blood of Change!"

Fahlcaen backed up the stairs, out of sight of the madness, and lifted J'yorie down from his shoulder. He rested her across his lap as he examined the wound in her wrist. The bleeding had slowed to a seep. He loosened the rope tourniquet slightly to allow her blood to flow more freely. From his pack he took soft bandages, padding and wrapping the wound before removing the tourniquet completely. He dampened a cloth with water from his flask and dribbled it over J'yorie's cracked lips.

"J'yorie," he hissed into her ear, wiping her face with the cool cloth, "the Heteroclite has freed the Stone and the lyre sings. DaeAer says only you can do what must be done to stop him. Do you hear me, J'yorie?"

She moaned again, lifting a hand to push away the wet cloth. Her eyes fluttered open and then closed again. Below, Goibniu was calling on the ancient creators to honor the power of the Curse Stone.

"J'yorie?" Fahlcaen shook her gently. "Look at me. It is Fahlcaen, I need you."

She twisted in his lap and he murmured, "Ah J'yorie," leaning over to cover her mouth with his, drawing her nearer and sheltering her with his embrace. He felt her stir, felt her lips soften as she accepted the kiss. He drew back and whispered, "This is a very bad time."

He saw himself in her eyes, shook his head and smiled. "I shall not mind death as long as I am allowed to share it with you."

"Goibniu has the lyre, the cup and the shield. All he needs is the blood of the Damselfly to free the Curse Stone and…," J'yorie whispered.

"J'yorie, he took your blood, but I took it back. I gave him the blood of another. You need not die."

She looked confused and he lifted her bandaged wrist. "See, he has taken the blood of the Damselfly, but it is spilled upon the ground."

"I cannot stop him. Not without the shield."

He grabbed the shield and held it up before her. "I have the shield. Do what you need to do, J'yorie."

"I don't know what to do." She turned away, consumed by visions of betrayal and failure, death and burning.

Fahlcaen stood and lifted J'yorie to her feet, supporting her with one arm around her waist, the shield held in the other. "Look at Goibniu. He has called forth the lyre's song and freed the Stone. It floats above the altar. He has called on the creators for the power of the Stone. He holds the cup of blood. Look at him and do what you must do."

J'yorie focused her eyes on the Heteroclite as he poured the blood into the opened Stone. She watched as the blood dripped into the body-shaped trough at the base of the holy table. She heard his words, listening intently as he promised the blood of the Damselfly in exchange for the freedom to rule the earth and the race of Men. She saw him wrap his wings about his body and lie down with the bath of blood allowing it to caress his forehead drop by drop as it fell from the stone. The Damselfly saw him raise the lyre and heard its sweet call as one by one his fingers freed the notes to fill the sacred chamber.

A drop of blood formed at the base of the stone. It grew round and full, heavy with life. J'yorie stared as it hung above Goibniu's head. Stolen blood. Stolen life.

'Tis long as a man, light as a feather and old as a dragon's tooth. Shield yourselves and speak the lovers' names afore the last drop and the final sound. Free us all.

The witch's words.

J'yorie pulled the shield from Fahlcaen's grip and fell back into his waiting arms, covering them with its flimsy shelter as "long as a man, light as a feather and as old as a dragon's tooth."

Goibniu plucked the last string, freeing the lyre's closing note. The final drop of blood grew so heavy the call of the earth forced its release.

"The lovers' names…the lovers' names…Ilerion and Arcinaë," J'yorie whispered. Beneath the fragile, vitreous shield, she watched the final drop of life strike Goibniu's bloodied forehead.

It began as a sudden stillness that preceded a subtle shift in the quality of the air, an aridness that sent hairs rising along arms, legs and napes of necks. It quenched the flaming torches with a gentle breath that was followed by a crackling sound, no louder than a dry leaf underfoot. The blood on the floor began to roil and stir the stench of death. Goibniu's triumphant laughter filled the room as within his veins his own life's liquid grew warm, but his rejoicing quickly turned to screams of agony as his blood boiled within and about him. White light flared as the fire of creation consumed the room, and the crescendo of thunderous roaring reached its climax. The screams of the aberrant knights were drowned as their flesh was seared and burst, soaking the walls with gore, sacrifices to the blood of the Oversoul walker and the Heteroclite queen.

The powerful pulsation of light moved outward, channeled up the narrow stairway and thence throughout the House of Hexus. Above and around J'yorie and Fahlcaen, it flowed as they clung together in a terrified embrace, deaf and blind beneath the infrangibility of their shield. With a final sonorous boom, the cleansing light returned and siphoned itself into the Curse Stone, accompanied by a thin, shrill, whistle-like sound that ended in the silence and crypt-like darkness of a tomb.

In the city of Fyrki the orb of light fractured, releasing its purifying brilliance and devouring the Heteroclite queen, while filling her wailing walker with the strength and power of the wormwood. It flashed through the maze of passages in search of others with a like-tasting liquid of life and found hundreds of them awaiting the blood change.

※

Safe on a ledge in a fissure within the wall of light, A'Janae held the Strangeling in her arms and watched him take his true form, the destruction of the Heteroclite ruler having freed him of Goibniu's curse.

Chapter 29: Wormwood Redeemed

Clinging to one another, Fahlcaen and J'yorie stumbled upward, out of the House of Hexus into a cloudless, golden sunrise. The snow and the bodies that had obscured it were gone. Only glistening blades of grass covered the meadow before the House of Hexus.

"I am cold." J'yorie shivered as Fahlcaen eased her to the ground.

"You have lost a bit of blood and suffered quite a knock to the head. Rest here and I will start a fire and brew a tea of herbs to ease your pain and restore your strength."

"I have no pain, and I am strong enough. Hold me and give me your warmth. I may die from the wormwood you carry in your blood, but I do not care. I have suffered so much loss, Fahlcaen. I cannot watch you walk away again."

He lay down beside her, warming her and whispering against her hair, "I no longer bear the taint of the wormwood, J'yorie. It has been given to another. I must take you to Grimmoirë. I promised A'Janae."

Seeing that she slept, he eased away and stood looking down on her. "You are beautiful, J'yorie, daughter of the Damselfly."

As he filled his flask at the creek, the sudden shimmer of an opening rift caught his eye. Dropping the water, he drew his staff and suddenly became aware that he no longer bore the strength of an Absinthe assassin.

"J'yorie!" he shouted as he raced back toward the sleeping woman.

There, between him and a rising J'yorie, stood Roh'nan, eyebrows raised and sword drawn.

"I must thank you for your kindness, Fahlcaen. Whatever you did with my blood has healed me and given me great strength. I have come to claim your Damselfly. You owe me since you murdered Taerys and took the new life she promised me."

He drove forward slamming his sword against Fahlcaen's upraised staff, splintering it and leaving the assassin unarmed.

Fahlcaen rolled away, taking with him a blazing branch from the fire, and then leapt forward to drive Roh'nan back.

The Oversoul backhanded the flaming torch with the flat of his sword and sent a scattering of burning cinders across the back of Fahlcaen's hand and arm. Again, Fahlcaen jabbed at Roh'nan with the torch and set his sleeve afire.

Rolling away, Roh'nan suffocated the flames beneath his body and lashed out at Fahlcaen's approaching leg, slicing across the man's thigh. The assassin's leg gave way, dropping him to the ground as Roh'nan surged toward him, sword held above his head in a two-handed grip.

The sword plunged blade-first into the earth at Fahlcaen's knees as the Oversoul gripped the glowing hilt of the wizard's dagger buried in his chest. He fell and sprawled onto his back, looking up into the eyes of his killer.

"J'yorie?"

The seeker dropped to her knees and without a word, closed her hands over Roh'nan's and drove the dagger deep into his heart.

"I should have let Tovag kill you in your sleep. Then he might still be alive."

She crawled to Fahlcaen's side and unlaced his trousers, dragging them down over his legs.

"J'yorie, this is a very bad time."

Her head dropped forward, dark, shimmering hair hiding her smile as she searched for a clean bit of sleeve and tore it free.

"J'yorie? Roh'nan is not the husband of A'Janae."

Ignoring him, she wadded the cloth and covered the wound in his leg, binding it in place with a second strip of torn sleeve.

"He is probably not even the Oversoul of Æselvanæ."

J'yorie lifted her head and met his eyes. "You talk too much, Fahlcaen. What will you do without your staff?"

"My staff is fine."

"I will need a man of action."

"You need tea and a healer," he murmured against her lips as he drew her close and his arms tightened around her. Neither of them noticed the shadow of the Wyndwryn as it drifted overhead.

"I found them!" E'teihl shouted excitedly as he landed near Aodh. "They are outside the House of Hexus, and there is a dead man on the lawn. He looks like your husband." He indicated the man standing next to A'Janae, a new wrinkle of confusion marred the Wyndwryn's handsome features. "Just who are you again?"

"I am Roh'nan, Oversoul of—"

"Æselvanæ," E'teihl finished. "Then who is the dead man at the House of Hexus?"

"I don't think we shall ever know—just a walker who took my face when Goibniu cast the spell of the Strangeling over me. But I assure you, E'teihl, I am the real Roh'nan."

"Aye, I would know your eyes anywhere." A'Janae stood on tiptoe to kiss the corner of her husband's smiling mouth. "Now let us go and collect my sister. Too long have we been apart and in sorrow."

Epilogue

From the apex of the monument's towering pillars, the figures of Ilerion and Arcinaë soared into the skies. Below, in a chamber dug by hand under the cloak of many nights, lay the Curse Stone sealed within a stone coffer. A'Janae and J'yorie, sisters so different yet so united in their shared birthright, stood hand in hand before the glistening monument to their parents. J'yorie glanced over her shoulder at the assembled troops. "They feared and hated us for what they did not understand. They were convinced we were a curse against the race of Man."

"Goibniu believed men are inherently cruel and merciless, but they are not. They are merely self-serving and easily led. The world is not a safe place. It is filled with those who would lead them into the darkness of fear and fallacy. J'yorie, it is our destiny to guide them as they grow, to sow the seeds of enchantment in their children."

Eyes crinkling with delight, J'yorie reached out to touch her sister's swollen belly. "You sow seeds and guide them gently with your smile. I will simply seek out the wickedness and kill it where it stands."

"They come," A'Janae said, returning her sister's smile.

They watched the two mounted men break away from the others and ride toward them at a leisurely trot.

Roh'nan slid from his mount and handed J'yorie the reins. "Your horse is filled with bone-rattling vigor." He gave the stallion Caval a slap on the neck and received an energetic head butt in return.

Gathering the reins, J'yorie leapt to the saddle and leaned forward, eyes sparkling with mischief. "Take care of that winged woman, Roh'nan, for if you do not, then I have an entire army at my disposal to put you in your place."

"Just be back in time to wash off any entrails before our coronation, Lady J'yorie—and consider that an order from your king!"

"I shall see that she is," Fahlcaen promised, reaching out to squeeze J'yorie's thigh.

J'yorie winked and whirled her mount around, charging forward toward her soldiers and shouting back at Fahlcaen in hot pursuit.

"You will have to catch me, my Captain!"

❦

Dragon Queen

ISBN-10: 1-933538-46-5
ISBN-13: 978-1-933538-46-4

Imagine being summoned from the slumber of death, awaking in a shattered world you do not recall, betrayed by sibling, parent and lover…imagine your search for the truth. *Dragon Queen* is a legend of magic, adventure and courage set in the mythical world of Ædracmoræ; a tale that explores strength and weakness, hope and fear, and what it means to be a guardian in a world where peace hangs by a fine, golden thread.

Without knowledge of the past, Yávië and her guardians stumble on a quest more filled with peril than any that have come before, a quest that will test the depths of their loyalties and which paths they will choose. Together they embark on a journey to discover the truth of Yávië's birthright and a world they no longer remember.

With the discovery that she was born of the Dragon Queen, Yávië is given knowledge of the powerful artifacts that will reunite the shattered kingdoms into a single world. However, with the rebirth of Ædracmoræ will come the opening of portals that bring chaos and shadow to the new world—an evil that may be far worse than the original destruction of the realm of the Dragon Queen. It is within this darkness that the guardians and their young queen struggle to gain control of what they have unleashed upon the kingdoms.

The Wrekening

ISBN-10: 1-933538-30-9
ISBN-13: 978-1-933538-30-3

When a great stone army of shadow warriors is discovered within a cavern beneath the enchanted isle of Révere, Yávie the Dragon Queen and her Guardians must prevent this evil from spreading. They enlist the aid of a young woman and her companions to covertly gather the Wreken Wyrm shards that will activate the ancient threat.

As Cwen, the estranged daughter of the Guardian Nall, and her fellow travelers begin the quest to recover the magickal shards, they discover there is far more at risk than war with a demonic army.

In this epic tale, enemies and allies abound; the true test is in telling one from the other.

Ancient Mirrors Glossary

A

Absinthian [AB sinth ee an] – a man enhanced by the power of the Wormwood

Acolyte [AK oh lite] – an assistant or follower

Aendrith [AIN drith] – a city in Ærathbearnæ named after a harpy

Aendrith of Grave [AIN drith uv grav] – a harpy living on the Isle of Grave

Aewicaen [ay WIK an] – mother of Arcinaë

A'Janae [ah JAW nay] – winged daughter of Lord Ilerion and Arcinaë

Algor [AL gore] – frozen region in the north of Farwegia

Algorian [AL gore ee an] – race living in the frozen north

Ananta [uh NON tuh] – a healer

Aodh [od] – a Feie wizard

Arcaedya [ar KAY dee uh] – an ancient city that fell to a war of the enchanted

Arcinaë [ar see NAY uh] – the last Damselfly, rightful Sovereign of Grimmoirë

Astomi [AZ toe mee] – a Damselfly surname, father of Trew

Azaeria [AZ air ree uh] – matriarch of the Suunflyte Dragons

Azrea [AZ ree uh] – matriarch of the Emeraldflyte Dragons

Æ

Ædracmoræ [DRAK mor] – realm of the Dragon Queen
Ælarggessæ [lar GAY suh] – a country
Ælmondæ [LA mond] – a country
Ærathbearnæ [RATH baren] – a country
Æselvanæ [SELL van] – a country

B

Bael [bale] – a port city in Ælmondæ
Baene [bane] – a kingdom in Ælarggessæ
Baeob [BAY ob] – a scarlet gryphon
Bailey [BAY lee] – outer wall of a castle
Bastcat [BAST kat] – demon cat person
Blue 'Taur [blu tar] – a blue skinned, bull-headed race of enchanted beings
Bothie [BAW thee] – a small cottage constructed of chale wood and longgrass
Breden [BRAY den] – a kingdom in Ælarggessæ
Brengven [BRENG ven] – a Feie wizard
Bridge of Light [brij uv lite] – barrier between the surface world and Fyrki

C

Caen [kane] – a thief, Cwen's lover
Caval [ka VAL] – Ilerion's warhorse
Cesta [ZEZ tuh] – matriarch of the Wood Sprites
Cethe [seth] – a Hunter in the service of Lord Lazaro
Cheneis [SHUN ace] – a kingdom in Ælarggessæ
Cloister of Belasis [CLOY stur uv bay LASS us] – a training center on Ædracmoræ for thaumaturgy and other magick
Colne [COL nee] – a Hunter in the service of Lord Lazaro
Curse Stone [kers stone] – relic with the magickal power to exchange the blood between two races
Cwen [kwin] – daughter of the Guardian Nall and the Sorceress Näeré
Cylacia [sigh LAS ee uh] – a Damselfy, deceased wife of Lord Ilerion of Baene

D

DaeAer [DAY air] – Wizard-Elect for the House of Hexus
Daegn [DAY gan] – deceased brother of the Oversoul Roh'nan
Damselfly [DAMZ ul fly] – a winged, enchanted race
Danfor [DAN for] – Captain of Lord Tondhere's soldiers
Daplesfar [DAP elz far] – A region across the ocean from Kyrenia
Davnë [DAV nee] – an enchantress
Dryads [DRI adz] – spirits of the woods
Dompet [DAWM pet] – a farrier in the service of Lord Lazaro, but loyal to Lord Ilerion
Durover [doo RO ver] – a kingdom in Ælarggessæ
Dystopian [dis TOE pee an] – of an imaginary place where everything is unpleasant or bad, the opposite of Utopian

E

Edric [ED rick] – a soldier serving Lord Ilerion of Baene
Elduuf [ELL duff] – lord of Twode
Ellicott [EL ee cut] – man with knowledge of the lyre and shield needed to command
Equus [EK wus] – enchanted horse-like creatures
Eshwyn ESH win] – an enchantress
E'teihl [EH teel] – a Wyndwryn, companion to J'yorie
Eun and Euné [AY oon and AY oo na] – twin moons of Ædracmoræ
Eunean [YOON yun] – an ancient race; Nall is the last Eunean
Evalio [eh VAL ee oh] – a Hunter in the service of Lord Lazaro
Eyrie [I ree] – nesting home of gryphons
Eyrie of El'suun and Züryn [AYE ree uv EL sun and zurn] – on the face of K'nar crag—home of the gryphonstone

F

Fáedre [FAY druh] – matriarch of the Deathstoneflyte Dragons
Faera [FAIR uh] – matriarch of the Kilstoneflyte Dragons
Fahlcaen [FAL kan] – an absinthe assassin, J'yorie's lover
Farwegia [FAR wee gee uh] – shadow city of the inscrutable Farwegians
Feie [fay] – a race of short, stout, fiery-haired, enchanted wizards

Felldan's Fen [FEL danz fen] – a marshy, flood-prone area outside Baene

Fenris [fen RIS] – a Feie wizard

Fyrki [FIRE kee] – home of the Heteroclites

G

Garrell [GAR el] – warder of Baene, father of Twica and Ydeta

Gaztin [GAS tin] – a Hunter in the service of Lord Lazaro

Getter [GEH tur] – archer for Lord Tondhere

Ghyvol [GUY vul] – an elder of the Feie

Glen of Wisdom [glen uv wiz dum] – meeting place of Grimmoirë's Council

Goibniu [GOYB new] – ruler of the Heteroclites and lord of Fyrki

Golden Man [GOLD en man] – protector of the power of the Damselfly, gatekeeper of the Bridge of Light

Grimmoirë [GRIM or uh] – a kingdom of enchantment within Ælarggessæ

Grumbleton [GRUM bul tun] – one of a group of ancient wizards created by the Tree of Creation and Keeper of all Knowledge

Grundl [GRUN dal] – a gryphon, mate to Nesika

Gryphon [GRIF un] – enchanted, winged being with an eagle-like head and body of a lion

H

Hahlmor [HAL mor] – a kingdom in Ælarggessæ

Halfling [HAF leeng] – those born of union between Damselfly and Man

Harpy [HAR pee] – enchanted beings with the head and torso of a woman and the tail, wings, and talons of a bird

Heteroclite [HET er oh clite] – dark enchanted race of Fyrki

Horsfal's Tavern [HORZ falz TA vern] – a drinking establishment frequented by Cwen and her friends

Houatauns [HOE tunz] – traders from the Shifting Sands

House of Hexus [howz uv HEX iss] – hiding place of the Curse Stone

I
Ilerion [eh LAIR ee un] – a Hunter, rightful lord of Baene
Ilvaria [EE var ee uh] – matriarch of the Ice Dragons
Indoli [EN doh lee] – poison strong enough to kill a Guardian or dragon
Isle of Grave [IL uv grav] – hidden home of exiled gryphons
Iydaen [EE day in] – lord of Cheneis

J
J'yorie [JOR ee] – daughter of Lord Ilerion and Arcinaë

K
Kasia [ka SEE uh] – matriarch of the Stone Sprites
Keep [keep] – the strongest or central tower of a castle or final refuge
Kerleucan [kur LOO can] – small, fox-like enchanted race
Keslbaen [KES uhl bane] – city of the Sylph
Kintol [KIN tul] – a Kerleucan from Grimmoirë
Klaed [clayd] – a nobleman, friend of Talin and Cwen
K'nar Crag [nar krag] – home of the gryphonstone and gryphon eyries
Koiy [KOH ee] – mother of Tresa
Korpusl [KOR pus el] – An abandoned quarry on Æselvanæ
Kyrenia [kigh REN ee uh] – a city on Æselvanæ

L
Lake Calidity [lak KUH lid it tee] – a warm, shallow lake in the kingdom of Baene
Lake of Rhymes [lak uv rimez] – sacred lake of Grimmoirë
Lamaas [LUH moss] – a kingdom in Ælarggessæ
Laoghaire [LEER ee] – black wizard seeking to be heir to the house of Lochlaen
Lazaro [LUH zar oh] – lord of Lamaas
League [leeg] – about three miles (nearly five kilometers)
Leifitë [lef EE tuh] – a Maraen tavern owner
Leuc [lewk] – a Hunter in the service of Lord Lazaro

Lightsteed [LITE steed] – a fiery horse, guardian of the Bridge of Light

Litter [LIT ur] – framework for transporting the sick and wounded

Lohgaen [LOW gan] – a dark wizard, rightful heir to the House of Lochlaen

Lule and Laud [lool and lawd] – golden coins of the Feie

Lymaen [ly MON] – a Hunter in the service of Lord Lazaro

Lyrë [LI ruh] – the Enchantress, former Sovereign of Arcaedya (since fallen), now Sovereign of Révere

M

Maelau [muh LOW] – coastal city in the kingdom of Baene

Magyr [MAY gur] – a Hunter in the service of Lord Lazaro

Mangonel [MAN ga nel] – catapult constructed on the site of a siege

Maraen [MAR ain] – an enchanted race with the ability to use the heat of their bodies as a weapon

Marig [MARE ig] – a councilor of Ærathbearnæ

Mungandr's Vortex [MUN gan durz VOR tex] – link between Grimmoirë and the Isle of Grave

Myst net [mist net] – magickal netting used to capture souls

N

Näeré [nair UH] – a Guardian and sorceress of Ædracmoræ, mother of Cwen

Nall [nahl] – a Guardian of Ædracmoræ, father of Cwen

Nesika [neh SEE ka] – a gryphon, mate to Grundl, Sovereign of Grimmoirë

Nicholas [NIK oh lus] – an enchanted downy flier

Nilus [NI lus] – a Hunter and thief, servant of Lord Ilerion of Baene

Norgeau [NOR go] – a Hunter in the service of Lord Lazaro

O

Obour [OH bur] – a Hunter in the service of Lord Lazaro

Oeric [OH rick] – lord of Wawne

Olcus [Ol cuss] – a scarlet gryphon

Oubliette [OO blee et] – a secret dungeon with access only through a trapdoor in its ceiling

P
Paeric [PAY rik] – a Wyndwryn, dark cousin of Arcinaë
Parapet [PAR uh pet] – a low protecting wall along the edge of a roof or balcony
Philter [FILL tur] – a love potion, a drink to excite
Portcullis [PORT kul es] – a heavy grating that can be raised or lowered on either side of a gateway
Postern [POS turn] – side or back entrance

R
Raer [RI air] – lightsteed, guardian of the Bridge of Light.
Reduald [RED wald] – lord of Durover
Réverē [REV ur ee] – a protected realm of the enchanted on Ædracmoræ
Roh'nan [ROW nun] – Oversoul of Æselvanæ
Rygeian's Rift [RI gee unz rift] – place of legendary treasure

S
Saebar [SAY bar] – lord of Breden
Scop [skop] – a bard or a poet, a storyteller
Scryer [SKRY ur] – one with the ability to see the future and past using a crystal
Seeker [SEE kur] – one with the ability to leave the body and seek those lost to men
Sharaga [shar AH ga] – one of the seven Sylph sisters
Sheering's Crossing [SHAR unz Kros eeng] – a village in Æselvanæ
Sisters of the Seven Winds [SIS turz uv thuh SEV in windz] – the Sylph of Keslbaen
So-elle [SO el] – a harpy
Sojourner [SO jur nur] – mystickal travelers of an unknown origin
Spirit People [SPEER it PEE pul] – creators of long ago
Spirit Whisperer [SPEER it Wisp ur ur] – one who communicates with the Spirit People

Straeth [strayth] – a city in Ærathbearnæ
Strangeling [STRANJ leeng] – a man under a wizard's curse of shape shifting
Sylph [silf] – powerful, female air elementals
Synyon [SIN yun] – a thaumaturge, companion of Lohgaen

T
Taerys [TAIR iss] – Goibniu's wife, Queen of the Heteroclites
Talin [TAL in] – companion to Cwen
Tassets [TASS ets] – One of two pieces of armour plate hanging from the fauld (fold) to protect the upper thighs or chest
Tel [tel] – An earthen mound or standing stone indicating an ancient habitat or burial site
Telfair [TEL fare] – a city in Æselvanæ
Tell [tell] – evidence of Halfling status that can be revealed through a skill or gift, or externally such as tail, wings or scales.
Thaumaturge [THOM a turj] – scholars of the arcane, users of dark offensive magick
Thralax [THRAY lax] – a sentient, fur-covered, man-shaped, and flesh eating giant who collects treasures from those it kills and eats
Tondhere [TAWN deer] – lord of Hahlmor
Torpa [TOR puh] – leader of the Wyndwryn
Tovag [TOE vawg] – a Blue 'Taur (bull-man), protector of the Damselflies
Tresa [TRAY suh] – wife of Yce
Trew [tru] – a male Damselfly, son of Astomi
Troll [trol] – a supernatural creature of giant proportion, which lives in caves and works the Gaianite mines for wizard masters
Twica [TWICK uh] and **Ydeta** [YUH det uh] – sisters in the employ of Lord Lazaro
Twode [twod] – a kingdom in Ælarggessæ

U
Úlanovë [OO lah no vuh] – King of Ælarggessæ

V
Vuaia [VOO aye uh] – a woman with the ability to talk to the Spirit People, a Spirit Whisperer

W
Wad [wahd] – a Kerleucan from Grimmoirë
Walker [WAHK ur] – a human or halfling capable of moving between the surface of the world and Fyrki
Wandering Woods [WAHN dur eeng wudz] – enchanted woods that move randomly over the worlds
Wawne [wahn] – a kingdom in Ælarggessæ
Wehta [WET uh] – matriarch of the field sprites
Willowort [WIL oh wort] – one of a group of ancient wizards created by the Tree of Creation and responsible for all law and prophecy
Whytahl's Woods [WHIT alz woodz] – wooded area in Ærathbearnæ
Wombe [WOM bay] – small, furred bird, hunted by the Algorians
Wormwood [WURM wud] – a magickal sap used to enhance the strength of a man
Wreken Wyrm [REK en wirm] – ancient legless, wingless dragons controlled by the symbiotic, ethereal race of Wreken
Wyndwryn [WIN dren] – a winged race of enchanted with the ability to persuade and soothe
Wysdym [WIZ dem] – leader of the seven Sylph sisters

X
Xamë [zah MAY] – a Prophetess of Belasis

Y
Yávië [YAH vee uh] – Queen of Ædracmoræ, a Dragon Queen and Guardian
Yce [YAH say] – ruler of the Algorians
Ydeta [YUH det uh] and **Twica** [TWICK uh] – sisters in the employ of Lord Lazaro

Z
Zephyr [ZEF ur] – mare purchased by Ilerion for Arcinaë from the desert nomads, the Houatauns

About the Author

Jayel Gibson is the author of the Ancient Mirrors fantasy series. From the tip of her Marto of Spain sword to the hem of her fifteenth-century reproduction Italian gown, her effervescent enthusiasm encourages a belief in enchantment. A student of Celtic history, folklore and faith, she weaves the magic of timeless adventure throughout her tapestry of tales.

Ms. Gibson lives on Oregon's southern coast with her husband, Ken. They share their home with a Molluccan cockatoo and five sugar gliders.

She is currently at work on her next novel.

(Footnotes)

♥ Adapted from the 21 Spells of Domesius © Communi-Clear 2000
♣ Adapted from the 21 Spells of Domesius © Communi-Clear 2000